APOLLO'S OUTCASTS

OTHER BOOKS
BY ALLEN STEELE

NOVELS

Near-Space Series

Orbital Decay
Clarke County, Space
Lunar Descent
Labyrinth of Night
A King of Infinite Space

The Jericho Iteration
The Tranquillity Alternative
Oceanspace
Chronospace

Coyote Trilogy

Coyote
Coyote Rising
Coyote Frontier

Coyote Chronicles

Coyote Horizon
Coyote Destiny

Coyote Universe

Spindrift
Galaxy Blues
Hex

NOVELLAS

The Weight
The River Horses
Angel of Europa

COLLECTIONS

Rude Astronauts
All-American Alien Boy
Sex and Violence in Zero-G
American Beauty
The Last Science Fiction
  Writer

NON-FICTION

Primary Ignition

ALLEN STEELE

APOLLO'S OUTCASTS

an imprint of **Prometheus Books**
Amherst, NY

Published 2012 by Pyr®, an imprint of Prometheus Books

Cover illustration © Paul Young
Cover design by Nicole Sommer-Lecht
Frontispiece illustration © Rob Caswell and Allen Steele

Inquiries should be addressed to

Pyr
59 John Glenn Drive
Amherst, New York 14228–2119
VOICE: 716–691–0133
FAX: 716–691–0137
WWW.PYRSF.COM

16 15 14 13 12   5 4 3 2 1

Library of Congress Cataloging-in-Publication Data

Steele, Allen M.
    Apollo's outcasts / by Allen Steele.
        p. cm.
    ISBN 978–1–61614–686–3 (cloth)
    ISBN 978–1–61614–687–0 (ebook)
    1. Children with disabilities—Fiction. 2. Coups d'état—Fiction.
3. Regression (Civilization)—Fiction. 4. Space colonies. 5. United
States—Fiction. I. Title.
PS3569.T338425A66 2012
813'.54—dc23

                                                        2012023582

Printed in the United States of America

for Florence, Aaron, Jack, Nicholas, Susan, Krystal, and Kristin—
my nieces and nephews

CONTENTS

FIRST PHASE: ESCAPE VELOCITY

SECOND PHASE: CITY ON THE MOON

THIRD PHASE: ONE SMALL STEP

FOURTH PHASE: INVADERS FROM EARTH

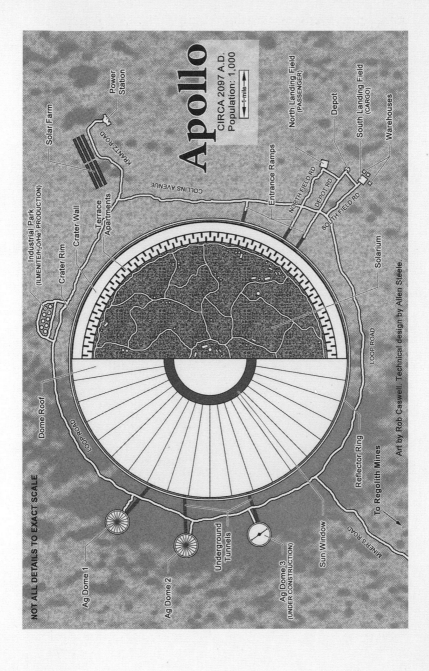

Apollo

CIRCA 2097 A.D.
Population: 1,000

◄——►1 mile

NOT ALL DETAILS TO EXACT SCALE

Art by Rob Caswell. Technical design by Allen Steele.

Power Station

Solar Farm

KRANTZ ROAD

COLLINS AVENUE

Industrial Park
(ILMENITE/H₃ohe³ PRODUCTION)

Crater Rim

Crater Wall

Terrace Apartments

Entrance Ramps

North Landing Field
(PASSENGER)

Depot

South Landing Field
(CARGO)

Warehouses

NORTH FIELD RD.

DEPOT RD.

SOUTH FIELD RD.

Solarium

Dome Roof

LOOP ROAD

LOOP ROAD

Reflector Ring

To Regolith Mines

MINER'S ROAD

Ag Dome 1

Ag Dome 2

Underground Tunnels

Ag Dome 3
(UNDER CONSTRUCTION)

Sun Window

FIRST PHASE

ESCAPE VELOCITY

1.
MIDNIGHT JOURNEY

On my sixteenth birthday, I went to the Moon.

"Jamey, wake up." My father's voice was soft and persistent in the darkness of my bedroom. His hand was on my shoulder, gently prodding me out of sleep. "C'mon, son . . . you need to get up."

"Huh? What?" It took a few seconds for me to realize I wasn't dreaming; he really was there, and he really did want me to get up. I pried open my eyes to see him sitting on the edge of my bed, silhouetted against a sliver of light seeping in through the half-open bedroom door. It wasn't morning yet; there was no reason for me to get up so early. "Lemme 'lone," I mumbled, rolling over. "Wanna sleep."

"I'm sorry, but you have to get up." Dad shook me again, and when I didn't budge he let out a sigh. "Lights on," he said.

My bedside reading lamp and the ceiling light came on at once. "What are you doing?" I groaned, wincing against the unwelcome glare. I pulled a pillow over my face. "It's too early . . ."

"I know it is, but you have to get out of bed." Dad took the pillow away from me. "And you need to hurry. I want you dressed and in your mobil in five minutes." His voice gained a no-nonsense edge as he stood up. "I mean it, Jamey. Up and at it . . . now."

He left the room before I could negotiate with him, or even ask why he was doing this. I gave myself a few seconds to rub the sand from my eyes and take a deep breath, then I told the bed to elevate to sitting position. My crutches were leaning against the wall where I always left them when I went to bed. Swinging my legs over the side, I took hold of the crutches and used them to help me stand up.

On the way to the bathroom, I noticed the calendar on my desk terminal: 12:07 AM AUG. 22 2097. *What the . . . ?* I thought. *It's mid-*

night! Sure, it was my birthday, but there was no reason for him to wake me up this early.

Across the hall, I heard Melissa yell something nasty. At first I thought she was saying it to Dad, but then I heard Jan's voice and realized that Dad had given my oldest sister the task of waking up my next-oldest sister. Smart guy, my father. Melissa might be able to argue with him, but there was no way she could win a fight with Jan. But why did my sisters also have to get up, too?

Too tired to think, I put everything on automatic. A quick trip to the toilet, then I hobbled back into the bedroom and told the closet to give me something to wear. I realized that it must be unseasonably cool outside when it extended to me a pair of jeans and a sweatshirt. Yesterday had been pretty hot, though, and I figured that I'd probably be switching to shorts and a T-shirt by lunch time. For now, though, I'd take the home comp's advice and dress warm. I continued to lean on my crutches until I shoved my feet into a pair of mocs, then made my way over to my mobil and carefully lowered myself into it.

The mobil woke up as soon as its padded seat registered my weight. "Good morning, Jamey," it said. "You're up early."

"Tell me 'bout it."

"I'm not sure what I can tell you. If you'd be a little more specific . . ."

"Never mind." I yawned and shook my head, and a sharp beep from the mobil's biosensors warned me that this small motion put a slight but noticeable strain on my upper spine. I ignored the warning as I folded my crutches and leaned over to lock them in place on the mobil's left side. "Living room," I said.

"Certainly." It started to roll forward on its two fat tires before it abruptly came to a halt. "I've just received instructions from your father. He's told me to tell you that you're to pack an overnight bag with a toilet kit and a change of clothes. And you're to hurry, too."

Okay, this was too much. "Dad!" I called out. "Why do you want me to pack a bag?"

No answer. From Melissa's room, I could hear her bickering with Jan; apparently she was even more cranky about all this than I was. I spotted my prong where I'd left it on my bedside table, and went manual to swing the mobil around so that I could pick it up. Fitting the prong into my right ear, I said, "Dad? Why do you want me to bring an overnight bag?"

"*We're making a little trip, son,*" he replied. "*You'll need to take along a few things.*"

"Where are we . . . ?"

"*I'll tell you and your sister later.*" His voice became stern. "*Please don't argue with me. Just do it.*"

When my father spoke like that, I knew better than to quarrel with him. So I muted the prong and turned toward the closet, where I used the mobil's manipulator arms to pull out a nylon bag and stuff it with clothes. Figuring we weren't going far, I chose cargo shorts, a light shirt, and sandals; as an afterthought, I threw my trunks and swim fins into the bag, too. Maybe this was a surprise birthday trip to Virginia Beach or somewhere else where I might be able to get in the water. Swimming was my sport, and I knew Dad wouldn't take me anywhere that I'd have to completely depend upon my mobil to get around.

I was only half-right, but I didn't know it then.

I unplugged my pad from its solar charger and stuck it in my pocket. Another visit to the bathroom for my toothbrush and my medicine box, which I tossed into the bag before I zipped it shut, then the mobil carried me out of my room. Melissa's door was half-open; she'd put on a fashionably short skirt and a halter top that showed off as much of her breasts as she dared. Looking good for the boys was a big deal to her, but her uncombed dark hair resembled a rat's nest. She glanced up from putting on her sneakers to give me a scowl that was pure hatred. Apparently she figured that her little brother was to blame for being hustled out of bed at such an ungodly hour. I ignored her as the mobil rolled past her room.

Jan's door was shut, but I could hear her moving around. I recalled what my father had said to me: *I'll tell you and your sister later.* Sister, not sisters; singular instead of plural. So Jan already knew what was going on. Which made sense, if you knew my family. Although she was only two years older than Melissa and four years older than me—make that about three-and-a-half, counting today's birthday—Jan was almost as much of a surrogate mother as an eldest sister. Dad never remarried after my mother died, which happened so long ago that I had no memory of her, and lately he'd come to depend on his first-born daughter to shepherd his two younger children.

Jan must have heard my mobil, because she opened the door as I rolled past her room. She wore slacks and a sleeveless T-shirt, and was tying back her long blond hair. Before she graduated from high school last year, some of her classmates used to ask me whether she was available. *If you have to ask,* I'd tell them, *then you haven't got a chance with her* . . . which was both a good dodge and also the truth. Jan was as serious-minded as she was beautiful; she was going to the local community college when she should have been at MIT or Stanford simply because it allowed her to continue living at home and help Dad take care of Melissa and me. Mainly me; Melissa wasn't the one who'd be good as dead if she fell out of her chair when no one else was around. So getting and keeping a boyfriend was the farthest thing from Jan's mind.

"You've got your —?" she started to say, then she spotted the bag in my lap and nodded. "Oh, okay . . . good. Dad's waiting for you."

"Yeah, I know." I stopped the mobil. "What's going on?" I asked, dropping my voice to a whisper. "Where are we going?"

Jan didn't say anything, but instead regarded me with a solemn gaze with which I was familiar. A long time ago, we'd reached an agreement: *ask me no questions and I'll tell you no lies.* I knew at once that this was one of those times. "You need to hurry," she finished, turning away from me. "I'll be there in a minute." And then she glanced back and smiled. "Oh, and by the way . . . happy birthday."

"Thanks," I said, even as a chill went down my back. I knew that Jan hadn't answered my question because Dad had told her to lie to me if I asked. And because she wasn't going to do that, this meant that whatever was happening here was serious. Really serious.

The living room was dark save for the reading lamp above Dad's lounger, and I noticed that the curtains had been drawn. The kitchen lights were on, though, and I saw that the back door was open. I took me a second to put all this together. Although the mobil could climb down the back steps if necessary, the front door had a ramp for my convenience. So if the living room lights were off and Dad had propped open the kitchen door, that meant that he didn't want any of our neighbors to see that we were about to leave.

Nonetheless, I was more curious than apprehensive as I rolled through the kitchen to the back door. The night was colder than I expected, the first chill of approaching autumn setting upon our sub-urban Maryland neighborhood of two-century wood-frame houses. Our van was parked in the driveway, its side-hatch already open and its ramp extended. In the luminescence cast by the dome light, I spotted the top of my father's grey-haired head. He appeared to be kneeling beside the open driver's side door, working on something beneath the dashboard.

Dr. Stanley Barlowe was a scientist, but he'd never been much of a mechanic; what was he doing down there? Dad raised his head to peer over the front seats as my mobil lowered its auxiliary climbing wheels and began to slowly descend the back steps. "Jamey . . . good! You have your bag? Excellent." He pointed the screwdriver in his hand toward the van's rear compartment. "Get on in. I'll find your sisters as soon as I'm done here."

"Dad, why are we . . . ?"

"Not now." His head disappeared again; the quiet snap of a service panel being shut, then he stood up and walked around the back of the van, the household tool kit in his left hand. "Climb on in. I'll be back in a sec."

I'd maneuvered the mobil into the van and had just finished clamping its wheels within the floor chocks when Jan appeared. She was carrying a small bag of her own, and she gave me a nervous smile that was meant to be reassuring—and wasn't—before she opened the back gate and tossed the bag into the back. "You okay there?" she asked as she strode past the side hatch on her way to the front passenger door. "Want me to put your bag back with mine?"

"No, that's okay." I liked having the bag in my lap; it gave me some small comfort. A quick glance at the kitchen door; neither Dad nor Melissa were in sight. "Jan, please . . . will you tell me what . . . ?"

"*No!*" Melissa yelled. "I *don't* want to go on some *stupid trip!* It's the *middle of the night* and I just want to *sleep!*"

She appeared in the kitchen door, hauling a sequined pink overnight bag as if it was loaded with bricks, complaining every step of the way. Dad must have made her change; the teenage-slut outfit was gone, replaced by jeans and a hooded pullover. But her hair was still a mess, and it must have irritated her to no end that she was being forced to leave the house before she had a chance to spend an hour primping at her mirror just in case she happened to meet the boy of her dreams.

Dad was right behind her. "You're going, MeeMee—" our family nickname for her, which she detested, "and that's final." He planted a hand against her shoulder, not exactly shoving her down the steps but not giving her any choice in the matter either. "Now get in the van with your brother and sister."

"But I haven't even *showered* . . . !"

"Melissa." Jan jerked a thumb toward the back seat next to where I'd parked my mobil. "Get in. Now."

That shut her up. Melissa might give Dad trouble, and she seldom listened to me, but when Jan put a certain tone in her voice, she knew better than to argue. Seventeen years of futile resistance had taught Melissa a few lessons she'd never forgotten; Jan wasn't a bully, but she didn't back down either. A final, melodramatic sigh, then

Melissa marched around behind the van, taking a second to hurl her pink bag into the back before yanking open the rear passenger door and climbing in to sit beside me. A cold glare in my direction—*say anything and I'll murder you*—was meant to keep me meek and quiet, but I couldn't help myself.

"Nice bag," I said.

"Drop dead." She pulled out her pad and started to tap something into it. No doubt she was about to text her friends—all 78,906 of them—and tell them her tale of woe.

Dad saw this. "Melissa . . . no, you can't do that." Before she could object, he reached forward and took the pad from her. "I'm sorry, but this is something you can't talk about."

She squawked about this, but he wasn't listening to her. He took the pad into the house and returned a moment later without it. Melissa could always buy another one from the next vending machine she saw, of course, but as my father closed the back door and used his remote to lock it, I realized again that secrecy was something he was taking very seriously.

Dad slammed shut the van's side hatch and rear gate, then climbed into the driver's seat. He thumbed the ignition; the engine beeped twice, but he didn't switch on the headlights. Instead, he placed his hands on the wheel and slowly pulled forward, moving down our short driveway to the street so unobtrusively that even the neighbor's cat couldn't have been awakened.

But when he turned right and drove past our house, I noticed that he'd left the bedroom lights on. That wasn't like him . . . unless he was deliberately trying to give the impression that we were still home. And it wasn't until we were away from the house that he finally switched on the headlights.

"Okay," Melissa said, "I've had it. I've *really* had it. I want to know . . ."

"Be quiet, MeeMee, and listen to me." Dad glanced back in my direction. "You, too, Jamey. This is important, and I only want to say it once." He paused, taking a deep breath as he slowly drove through our darkened neighborhood. "I know this is unexpected, and I know you'd rather still be in bed. If there was any other way . . ."

He stopped himself, then went on. "Something has come up, and you've got to leave. Not tomorrow, but now . . . right now. So I can't have any arguments or disagreements from anyone. I just need for you to do what I say, with no ifs or buts about it. Understand?"

Jan nodded, even through his words weren't meant for her. Melissa opened her mouth to protest, but then she caught Dad staring at her through the rear-view mirror. Apparently she realized that this was a bad time to be hard-to-please MeeMee, because she sulkily folded her arms across her chest and nodded.

"I understand," I said, "but . . . why won't you tell us what's going on?"

My father didn't respond, but Jan did. "Trust me, *mon petit frère* . . . the less you know, the safer you'll be."

That's when I began to get scared.

* * *

Burtonsville, the town where we lived, is just north of Washington, DC, about a quarter of the way to Baltimore. Dad got on I-95 just outside of town and headed south. This was the route he normally commuted to his job at the International Space Consortium's American headquarters in DC. He went to hover mode and retracted the wheels, but he didn't switch to auto. Instead, he kept his hands on the steering wheel, carefully watching the dashboard display so that he kept within the 80 mph speed limit. That wasn't legal; cars on the interstate were required to be navigated by the local traffic control system unless there was an emergency.

Melissa noticed this, too. "You're going to get pulled over," she said, smug in her knowledge that our father was breaking the law.

"No, I'm not," Dad replied, not looking back at her. "I removed the GPS and traffic control chips before we left and put in ringers instead. So far as anyone is concerned, we're still parked in the driveway." He pointed to the traffic scanners we passed every hundred yards. "When they tag us, the phony chips identify us as another car and tell the system we're on auto. So long as I maintain a constant speed and don't make any strange moves . . ."

"It'll think we're someone else and won't be able to track us," I finished. "But why . . . ?"

Jan gave me one of her looks—*no questions, Jamey*—and I shut up. At least I knew what my father had been doing when I caught him beneath the dashboard. And I had little doubt as to where he'd been able to lay his hands on outlaw tech like this; ISC was full of guys who could make ringers in their basement workshops. But Dad had always been the law-abiding type. Why would he do something like this?

From behind us, the warble of a siren. Turning my head, I looked back through the rear window to see flashing blue lights. A Maryland state trooper, approaching fast.

"Dad . . ." Jan had spotted it, too. "Do you think . . . ?"

"No. Take it easy." Without reducing speed, my father moved quickly and easily from the center lane to the right, just as cars under traffic control would do. But he seemed to be holding his breath as the police cruiser came up on us. For a moment, I thought my father was wrong and that we were about to be pulled over. But then the cop flashed by . . .

And right behind it, the two hovertanks and three troop carriers the state trooper was escorting. We hadn't seen them earlier because the vehicles were in camouflage mode, darkened pitch-black so as to blend in with the night. Probably coming from the Navy base in Aberdeen.

Why would they be out on the highway at this time of night with a state police escort? I was about to ask this when Dad let out his breath. He glanced at Jan, and she slowly nodded.

"You were right," she said, looking straight ahead. "It's started."

"*What's going on here?*" Melissa yelled.

"MeeMee . . ." Dad began.

"Don't MeeMee me!" she snapped, which should have been funny but wasn't. She slapped the back of Dad's seat so hard that he jerked; the van swerved for an instant, and I found myself praying that the traffic control system wouldn't notice the slight deviation. "I want to know what . . . what this is all about!"

"Melissa . . ." My father started to reply, then shook his head. "Just shut up, okay." Melissa stared at him; he'd never spoken to her that way before. "Radio on," he said after a moment of stunned silence. "Scan news channels."

The radio skipped through the channels, pausing every few seconds so that we could listen to one news station or another. Baseball and soccer scores, a local weather forecast, a couple of late-night talk shows. "Nothing," Jan said after a few minutes.

"Didn't think so," Dad replied. "They're not going to make any sort of announcement until they've got the Capitol locked down." He gripped the yoke a little harder as he stared straight ahead. "They'll be closing the Beltway soon. I just hope we're not too late."

I-95 had just merged with the I-495 Beltway leading around Washington, DC; we were headed southeast, following the signs to the Maryland coast. I noticed that there was little traffic, unusual for the Beltway even in the early hours of a Wednesday morning. It wasn't hard to imagine armed soldiers taking up positions at the interstate ramps, forming roadblocks to prevent any vehicles from getting on the Beltway. But why . . . ?

"The president is dead," my father said.

For a second or two, neither Melissa nor I knew what to say. Then I found my voice. "What . . . what did you say? How do you . . . ?"

"I got a call from . . . from a friend . . . just before I woke you up. He told me that President Wilford died a few hours ago."

Dad spoke as matter-of-factly as if he was discussing the mineralogical contents of main-belt asteroids, his usual line of work, but he couldn't have shocked us more. "The president's *dead?*" Melissa shrieked. "What . . . how . . . ?"

"I don't know that yet, but . . . well, something is going on." Dad shook his head. "It's too much to explain now, but . . ."

His voice trailed off, but it wasn't hard for me to guess the rest. "It's about the vice president, isn't it?" I asked.

"Uh-huh. Lina Shapar will be sworn in as president, if she hasn't already. And according to people I know, she's going to declare a national emergency."

"Which they haven't done yet," Jan added, "only because they're still getting everything in place. But it's coming, and when that happens . . ." She looked back at me again. "Dad will be in danger. We'll all be in danger."

"But *why?*" Melissa demanded. "I don't get it? What's this got to do with us?"

I closed my eyes and shook my head. Melissa lived in her own world of clothes and boys and sock bands, and rarely paid much attention to anything else, even when it was happening inside her own house. "This has something to do with the ISC petition you signed, doesn't it, Dad?"

My father didn't reply at once. In the soft blue light of the dashboard, his face was grim. "Yes, it does," he said after a few moments. "Shapar didn't like the position we took. From what I've heard, she considers everyone who signed it to be a political foe . . . and she's not the sort of person who tolerates opposition. If things happen the way I think they will . . ."

"They're going to be coming after him." Jan twisted around in her seat to look back at me. "Shapar is going to order Dad to be put under arrest, along with anyone else she considers to be an enemy." She paused. "And they may come after us, too. As collateral, to make sure that he cooperates."

"But they can't *do* that!" Melisa protested. "It's against the law!"

"You're right, MeeMee . . . sorry, Melissa, I mean. Not under the

Constitution, at least. But Lina Shapar has never been a big fan of constitutional law and neither are her cronies, so there's no reason to believe that she's going to let a small matter like the Bill of Rights get in their way."

I was gazing out the window as Jan and Melissa spoke. In the far distance, beyond the rooftops of Washington's northeast neighborhoods, I could make out the spotlight-illuminated dome of the Capitol, the Washington Monument rising behind it like a tiny white pencil. The sight was familiar to me, and its serenity made it hard to believe that a crisis was unfolding within a stone's throw of these historic buildings.

The radio was still on, turned to a late-night sports talk show. A couple of guys were discussing the Orioles when a new voice broke in: *"We interrupt this broadcast for a special news report from . . ."*

"Turn up the volume," my father said.

The radio obeyed, and another voice came on. *"We have received official word from the White House that President George F. Wilford is dead. Repeat . . . George F. Wilford, the president of the United States, died tonight in Washington, DC. White House Press Secretary Andreas Sullivan confirmed the initial Secret Service reports, and has stated that the president appears to be a victim of assassination carried out by a lone gunman who managed to penetrate White House security. . . ."*

"Oh my God!" Melissa's eyes were wide. "He was shot!"

"I don't think so." Dad's voice was very quiet, almost lost beneath the radio. "That's what they're saying, but that's not what my friend told me."

I stared at him. "How do you know? I mean, how could *they* know? The White House . . ."

"Quiet, Jamey." Jan reached over to turn up the volume.

". . . Reports that Vice President Lina Shapar was summoned to the White House from her official residence at the Naval Observatory, where she was sworn in as the new president by Supreme Court Chief Justice Marco Gonzales. In response to the crisis, President Shapar has declared a national

emergency, and issued an executive order placing the District of Columbia and its environs under military curfew. She has requested that the FBI and federal marshals immediately detain any individuals who may have played a role in President Wilford's death . . ."

"I'm on the list." My father's voice was little more than a whisper. "You can count on that."

"But you're not involved." I stared at the back of his head.

"You *couldn't* be involved," Melissa insisted, almost as if to reassure herself. "You're not, are you?"

"No, Melissa, I'm not . . . but neither was Wilford assassinated." He let out his breath. "Look, I can't tell you anything else. At least not while there's still a chance that we may be arrested. Right now, the main thing is to get you kids to a place where you'll be safe."

"Where's that?" I asked.

A tense smile. "The last place they'd ever think of looking for you."

2.
WALLOPS ISLAND

T he fifteen minutes it took for us to get the rest of the way out of Washington were tense. Just before we left the Beltway, we spotted another military convoy, this one in the northbound lanes of I-495. My father continued driving as steadily as he could, maintaining the pretense that our van was under local traffic control, and the vehicles swept past us without incident. We left the Beltway at the New Carrolton exit and continued east on Route 50, and when we didn't see any more convoys we were able to breathe a little easier . . . but not much.

We listened to the radio, occasionally changing channels in an effort to get more info. By then all the stations had interrupted their normal routine to carry news about President Wilford's death. A lot of reporters must have been woken out of bed for this, but none of them seemed to have learned much more than what had been reported in the first few minutes. In the meantime, the White House imposed a press blackout until 10 a.m. local time, when President Shapar was scheduled to address the nation from the Oval Office.

I wanted to go online and see if I could learn anything from sites I regularly visited, but Dad stopped me. That would mean I'd have to uplink my pad through the van's satphone; like the GPS and traffic control systems, this could allow someone who might be searching for us to track our location. So we had to rely on normal radio stations for what little information we had.

We passed through Annapolis on our way toward the Chesapeake Bay. When we approached the long causeway that would take us to the other side of the bay, Dad headed for the cash-only tollbooth even though our van had all-state plates with toll stickers. The guy sitting in the booth was only half-awake; he didn't appear to notice that my father had stopped to hand him a few dollars when we could have driven straight through.

"Why did you do that?" Melissa asked after we moved through the tolls and entered the causeway. "We have stickers."

"Because the scanner would have recorded our plates," I said before Dad or Jan could reply.

Dad nodded. Jan gazed pensively at the dark waters of the Chesapeake Bay below us. Once again, Melissa asked where we were going, but neither of them would answer her.

On the other side of the causeway, Dad turned south on Route 50. As before, he continued to driving on manual, not switching to traffic control even though we were on a four-lane highway. There were only a few other cars on the road this time of morning, and there wasn't much to see except mile markers and motels. Now and then I'd catch sight of one the bay's many inlets and rivers; they glowed beneath the light of the full moon, an omen whose portent I'd only later appreciate.

After awhile I cranked back the mobil's seat and shut my eyes. I don't know how long I slept, but I was awakened by the soft jar of the van's wheels being lowered. Dad had taken the van out of hover mode; that meant that we must be on a road that didn't have a traffic control system. Sure enough, when I looked out the window, I spotted a sign stating we were now on Route 13. And a moment later, another one: WELCOME TO VIRGINIA.

"Where are we?" I asked, elevating my seat back to sitting position. Melissa had gone to sleep as well, but she didn't wake up when I did.

"The Outer Banks." Jan had pulled up a map of the Virginia coast on the van's dashboard screen. As I peered over her shoulder, she pointed to a long, narrow cape that separated the southern end of the Chesapeake Bay from the Atlantic Ocean. "We'll be there soon," she said. "If you look out MeeMee's window, you'll see where we're going."

I turned my head to the left. Through the windows on Melissa's side of the van, I could just make the dark expanse of the ocean. It was just a little after 3 a.m., so the sun hadn't come up yet, but I could see the tiny lights of ships heading to and from the Atlantic Sea Wall locks just south of us. If Dad was heading for Virginia Beach, where our family occasionally went for vacations, he'd picked an odd way to get there; a little shorter, maybe, but not as quick as if we'd stayed on the interstate.

Then I spotted something: a long string of lights, low upon the horizon, which extended straight out toward the ocean. Flashing red and green against the night sky, they resembled those you'd see on an airport runway, only the single row they formed was much longer. I'd just realized what they were when the van slowed to make a left turn. As Dad pulled onto a side road, I caught sight of a sign:

WALLOPS ISLAND SPACE LAUNCH CENTER
INTERNATIONAL SPACE CONSORTIUM
RESTRICTED AREA – AUTHORIZED VEHICLES ONLY

"That's the magcat!" I exclaimed.

That woke up Melissa. "Whu . . . where?" she said sleepily. "Are we there yet?"

"Yes, we are," Dad said. "And you're right, Jamey . . . that's the magcat. There's where you and your sisters are going."

Because my father was a planetary geologist who worked for the ISC—along with other reasons—I knew a little more about space than the average guy. Perhaps not quite as much as Jan, who actually aspired to go out there, but I'd picked up a few things over the years, not only from dinner table conversations but also from books and vids I'd downloaded into my pad.

One of the things I'd learned was a good working knowledge of ISC launch facilities. There were three in the United States: the primary one at Cape Canaveral, Florida; a slightly smaller one on

Matagorda Island in the Gulf of Mexico off the Texas coast; and the smallest, located on Wallops Island, Virginia.

A long time ago, this place had been operated by the National Aeronautics and Space Administration as a launch site for experimental rockets. After NASA was dissolved, ISC took over Wallops and expanded it to become the major East Coast launch spaceport. Rising ocean levels had damaged many of the launch pads at the old Kennedy Space Center before the Florida stretch of the Atlantic Sea Wall was finished, but Wallops had been protected by the mid-Atlantic part of the wall, and for awhile it and Matagorda Island had served as the two biggest US launch sites.

And the magcat was the principal means of sending people and cargo into space.

Something occurred to me just then. A thought that nearly stopped my heart.

"Dad," I asked, "why are you taking us to the magcat?"

He didn't reply, but instead stared straight ahead.

"Dad, are you putting us on the magcat?"

"Oh, no . . . no way." Melissa was fully awake by then. "There's no way I'm going to . . ."

"Hush, Melissa." Jan opened her armrest compartment and pulled out a laminated card. She placed it on the dashboard below the windshield. "Whatever you do, just be quiet."

The van was approaching another causeway, this one above a river. It was blocked by a security gate. A uniformed guard stepped out of a booth beside the gate and held up his hand. Dad came to stop beside him; rolling down his window, he held up his ID badge. The guard briefly inspected it, gave the dashboard card a quick glance, then nodded and walked back into the booth. The gate opened and Dad drove through.

Jan let out her breath. "We're in. So much for the hard part."

"No . . . that's just the beginning." Dad looked back at me. "All right, Jamey . . . now you and Melissa can hear the rest. Yes, I'm putting all three of you on the magcat. There's a cargo shuttle scheduled for takeoff at 5 a.m., just about—" he checked the windshield display "—an hour and a half from now. All three of you are going to be on it."

My fingers involuntarily curled around my mobil's armrests. "Dad . . . you know I can't ride that thing. It'll kill me."

One of the reasons why I was interested in space was because I was born on the Moon. However, I'd always figured that vids and books would be the closest I'd ever get to going there. Because I'd spent my infancy in low gravity, my bones were weaker than normal. Lunar Birth Deficiency Syndrome was why I'd spent almost my entire life in a mobil. I couldn't walk without crutches, and it was only in the neutral-buoyancy environment of a swimming pool that I was able to move about without assistance.

Sure, I could have been fitted with an exoskeleton, but they were incredibly expensive, and besides, I didn't want to go through life looking like a robot. So I'd tried to build up my muscles over the years, and swimming laps had put me in pretty good shape. There wasn't much anyone could do about my bones, though. Even with calcium supplements and other medicines I routinely took for LBDS, I'd break my legs if I tried to run, and a hearty bear hug could crush my ribs.

Mom made a major mistake when she decided to go to the Moon with Dad, but it wasn't her fault; neither of them realized she was pregnant. I was beginning to suspect that Dad was about to make a similar mistake, but this time consciously.

"Relax," he said. "We've taken that into account. There's a way of sending you up that won't hurt you. Trust me . . . you'll see."

We were on the causeway by then, and I could see the magcat more clearly. No longer simply a row of lights, it was now an elevated monorail nearly two and a half miles long that extended straight out toward the Sea Wall. Until then, I'd regarded it much the way just as about anything else I'd read about. A nice bit of engineering, but nothing I'd ever thought I'd have to experience myself.

Suddenly, that changed. Now the magcat was utterly terrifying.

I didn't reply to what my father said. I just hoped that he was right.

* * *

We reached the other side of the causeway and drove past marshland and saltwater ponds; Dad had left his window half-open, and a cool sea breeze drifted in. After a mile or so we turned left onto another road, this one running parallel to the beach. A chain-link fence barred our way, but the scanner mounted above its gate read our dashboard card and opened the gate for us.

A half-mile down the road, we entered the launch center. We drove past administration buildings, the containment dome of the fusion reactor that powered the magcat, and three giant spacecraft hangars—the doors of two were shut, and the third was open and empty—until we reached a semicircular building with a control tower rising from its domed roof. TERMINAL, its sign read.

Dad entered the parking lot, but he didn't head for the front entrance. Instead, he drove around back to the employee lot. Two cars were parked next to a rear door; a small group of people stood near them, apparently waiting for us. Dad brought the van to a halt beside them; as he got out and walked over to them, Jan opened the side hatch and lowered the ramp for me. Melissa reluctantly removed our bags from the back; her uncustomary silence told me that she was just as frightened as I was.

I hadn't yet received my last surprise this morning. The next one came when I told my mobil to take me toward the people waiting for us. The group included three kids, and among them was someone I knew well.

"Logan?" I asked. "What are you doing here?"

Logan grinned at me. "Same thing as you, I think."

Logan Marguiles was my best friend. We'd known each other for as long as I could remember; his father was another ISC senior administrator, and our families were close. We were classmates at school. I'd seen little of him since the summer trimester had ended last month, but that wasn't unusual; his family traveled more than mine did. I expected that we'd be on the swim team again when the fall trimester began next month.

It was looking like it would be awhile before either of us swam relay again.

Dr. Marguiles was talking to my father. Logan's mother was with them, and she was wiping tears from her face. Another pair of grownups was nearby, kneeling beside the other two kids. The boy was about two or three years younger than Logan and me, and his sister couldn't have been any older than eight or nine; I'd never seen either of them before.

Logan nodded to Jan and Melissa. Jan smiled back at him while Melissa pointedly looked away; it was obvious which of my sisters liked my friend and which didn't. Stepping closer to me, he squatted beside my mobil.

"Guess your dad signed the same petition as mine did," he said quietly.

"Looks like it," I whispered back. Logan and I didn't often talk about what our fathers did; for us, ISC was just the place where they went to work every day. But we knew about the petition, and Logan must have learned that it made his father just as much a marked man as mine was. "I'm getting the feeling they worked this out ahead of time, just in case."

Logan raised an eyebrow. "He didn't tell you?"

I shook my head. "Only Jan knew. I'm just the little brother, remember?" I glanced at Melissa. "But I don't blame him for not letting MeeMee in on it . . ."

"Oh, hell, no! Not unless you want it all over DC by lunchtime . . ."

"I heard that!" Melissa said, still not looking at us.

Logan ignored her. "Looks like they planned this in advance." Lowering his voice, he cocked his head toward the other kids standing nearby. "Same for their folks. They work at ISC, too."

"Yeah, okay, I get that," I said. "But who ever thought Wilford would be assassinated and Shapar would take over?"

Logan gazed at me evenly. "Who said that the president was assassinated?"

"It's on the radio. The White House . . ."

Realizing what I was saying, I stopped myself. Logan slowly nodded. "There's more here than meets the eye," he murmured.

I was about to reply when Dad turned away from Logan's folks and started walking toward us. Jan followed him, and he paused to take Melissa by the arm. Logan excused himself as they approached my mobil; he knew a family meeting when he saw it coming.

"Here's where I'm going to have to leave you," Dad said. As usual, he got straight to the point, but even though my father wasn't the sentimental type I couldn't help but notice that his voice was choked. "You're in good hands, and when you get to where you're going, there's going to be people who will . . ."

"I don't understand." Melissa was both scared and impatient. "Where are you sending us?"

Clueless as always, she hadn't figured it out yet. "We're going to the space station," I told her before Dad could reply.

"No, Jamey," Dad said. "You're going to the Moon."

Now it was my turn to be surprised. No . . . surprised isn't the right word. Shocked? Stunned? I'm not sure there's even a word for what I felt at that instant.

When Dad told us that we were going to board a shuttle, I'd figured that it was one bound for Station America. Certainly it was big enough to take in six kids; more than three hundred people lived on the giant wheel in geosynchronous orbit 22,300 miles above Hawaii. And since it was visited almost every day by passenger shuttles, no one would notice one more scheduled arrival.

But . . . the Moon? I opened my mouth to say something, but the words refused to come out. I wasn't the only one who was speechless. Melissa had gone pale; she swayed on her feet, and for a second or two I thought she was going to faint. Jan wasn't surprised; she'd known all along what Dad and his friends were planning.

"I can't . . . I can't . . ." I finally managed to stammer.

"Yes, you can . . . and you will." Dad knelt down beside me, gently put his hand on my wrist. "There's no other place for you to go. The government has extradition treaties with just about any other country where we might send you, and they could easily pull you off Station America . . . and I have no doubt it'd be only a day or two before they found out that you were there. If I could send you guys all the way to Mars, I would . . ."

"The Mars colony is too small," Jan murmured. "Even if we had a launch window, it'd take months for us to get there."

"Right." Dad nodded. "Mars is impossible, and the space station is only a temporary solution. But Apollo is big enough for you to disappear into, and even if the government finds out you're there, it's under international control." A grim smile. "And believe me, I have friends there who'd sooner walk out an airlock than hand you over."

"But Mom . . ." I stopped myself before I could say the rest: *But Mom died there. She gave up her life to save mine, and I've been haunted by that my whole life. . . .*

"If Mom were still alive, she'd welcome you and your sisters with open arms." There were tears in the corners of his eyes; it was hard for me to see that, so I quickly looked away. I knew that he'd never remarried because Mom was the only woman he'd ever loved; the couple of girlfriends he'd had since her death had only reinforced his loyalty to her memory. "And the people up there you'll meet knew her, so . . ."

The terminal's back door opened and a man about my father's age stuck his head out. "We're ready," he announced. "You need to hurry . . . launch is scheduled for one hour from now."

I ignored him. "Why can't you go?"

"There's only six seats available. If we can get on another shuttle, we will. But until then . . . well, so long as they're searching for us, they're not going to looking for you." Dad glanced at Logan's folks and the parents of the two other kids. "We're getting out of here as soon as you lift off. With any luck, we'll be a thousand miles away by the time you reach orbit."

I rather doubted that—the shuttle would be in orbit only a few minutes after it left the island—but I let him get away with the exaggeration. He gave my shoulder a fond squeeze, the closest thing he dared to giving me a hug without hurting me. "I'll get in touch with you guys as soon as I can," he said as he stood up, speaking to Jan and Melissa as well as me. "And I'll bring you back home when . . ."

His voice trailed off. He didn't know when we'd be able to come home; he knew that, and so did we. Or at least Jan and I did; I wasn't sure if Melissa yet realized the full extent of our situation. But it wasn't going to be any time soon; of that, I was certain.

Dad gave Jan a brief hug; she was dry-eyed, but her mouth was trembling. Melissa was angry, and for a moment I thought she was going to throw a hissy fit and stalk away as she usually did when she didn't like something, but she relented and let Dad put his arms around her. Logan was saying farewell to his mom and dad; they seemed even more reluctant to let him go. As for the other kids . . . the boy was weeping within his mother's arms while his little sister remained stoical, calmly accepting a quick embrace from her father. Strange.

"Folks . . ." The guy in the doorway was becoming nervous. "I don't want to hurry you, but you need to . . ."

He suddenly stopped, and I saw that he was gazing past us. Turning my head, I spotted what he'd seen: the headlights of another car, turning off the road to enter the terminal parking lot. As it approached the rear of building, we saw that it was a black sedan with government plates.

"Oh, God, no," Jan whispered. "They can't have found us already."

"No," Dad said. "I don't think so . . ."

The sedan glided to a halt next to our van. The front doors opened and two men climbed out. Both wore dark business suits and straight black ties, and if it hadn't been night I'm sure that they would've been wearing sunglasses. The guy who got out on the passenger side waited beside the car while the driver approached our group. No one spoke, but I could practically hear everyone's hearts pounding with fear.

"Dr. Marguiles? Dr. Barlowe? Mr. Hernandez?" The driver looked like an average guy in his midthirties, but I had a sense that he could've killed any one of our fathers—or even all three at the same time—with his bare hands. "May I have a word with you, please?"

The three of them traded wary looks with each other, then they reluctantly walked over to him. The driver spoke to them in low tones that none of us could hear; my father and his friends listened, occasionally glancing back at us kids, then they spoke as well. The conversation lasted a few minutes, during which Melissa moved closer to me to kneel beside my mobil.

"You think these guys are here to stop us?" she asked.

"No." Logan came up behind us. "If this was a bust, they would've brought more people."

I had to agree. There were only two of them . . . or at least so I thought, until I saw Dr. Marguiles nod his head and my father reluctantly do the same. The driver turned toward his companion and made a small gesture; the other guy walked to the back of the sedan and opened the rear passenger door.

A girl about my age climbed out of the car. She wore black jeans and a dark grey pullover, and her ash-blonde hair was tucked up under a Washington Nationals ball cap. She had a small bag under her arm, and although she was trying hard to hide it, it wasn't hard to tell that she was just as confused and scared as I was.

She gave Logan, Melissa, and me a wary glance, then let her companion escort her over to where my father and his friends were huddled with the driver. Melissa glared at her. "You don't think she's trying to come along, too, do you?" she asked, not bothering to keep her voice down.

"If she is, she's out of luck." Logan nodded to the Hernandez kids, who were still hovering near their mother. "Counting those two and Jan, there's six of us . . . and my dad said there's only six seats on the shuttle."

The conversation came to an abrupt end. While the girl waited nearby, bookended by the two suits, my father and the other two men walked back toward their respective families. Mr. Hernandez looked angry; he said something in Spanish to his wife and children, and his son stared at him before bursting into tears again. Dr. Marguiles took his wife by the arm and gently led her over to where Logan was standing with Melissa and me. My father followed him, motioning for Jan to do the same. Jan stared at the girl for another moment or two, then reluctantly stepped over to join us.

"Her name is Hannah . . . Hannah Johnson," Dr. Marguiles said once we'd gathered together. "And . . . well, it's like this. She has to get on the shuttle."

"But there's no room," Ms. Marguiles said. "Didn't you tell them that?"

"They know there's only six seats. I've explained that to them already. But . . ."

"What Paul is trying to say is that she has to go to the Moon." Dad's face had become a mask; it was impossible to read the emotions behind it. "Jeanne, there's no time to explain, but . . ." He let out her breath. "It's absolutely imperative she gets on the shuttle. That's all there is to it."

Ms. Marguiles stared at him. "Even if one of our own children is left behind?"

My father nodded, and so did Dr. Marguiles. "Even if one of our kids stays here, yes," Dr. Marguiles said. "Tomas knows this, too," he added, looking over at the Hernandez family. "He's telling Rosita and the kids now."

Ms. Hernandez wasn't taking the news any better than Ms. Marguiles was. She addressed her husband in rapid-fire Spanish, angrily pointing at the girl who'd shown up out of nowhere. Hannah Johnson looked embarrassed; clutching her bag against her chest, she stared at the pavement, afraid to make eye contact with any of the kids who'd arrived before she did. Nor could I blame her; if our fathers had their way, one of the six of us would be bumped from the shuttle.

"So who's it going to be?" Ms. Marguiles's voice rose. "One of our children is going to stay here. We're going to have to pick which one, aren't we?"

My father slowly nodded . . . and as he did, his eyes shifted toward me.

Melissa looked at me, too. So did Logan, and even the Hernandez kids were gazing in my direction. Like it or not, they were right. Whoever Hannah Johnson was—she looked vaguely familiar, even though I was positive that I'd never met her before—someone had to give up a seat for her, and I was the one least likely to survive a magcat launch.

The others would get on the shuttle. I was to be left behind.

3.
LAUNCH

"I'll stay," Jan said.

For a second, I thought I hadn't heard her correctly. She had spoken so quietly, it was hard to hear her voice. Dad's eyes went wide as he turned to her.

"You can't . . ." he began.

"Yes, I can . . . and I have to." Jan looked straight at him. "If Jamey remains here, he'll be helpless . . . and so will you. You'd never abandon him, which means that he'd only slow you down."

"Then cut me loose," I said. "I can make it on my own."

"No, you can't." Jan nodded toward my mobil. "C'mon . . . how far do you think you'll get before someone picks you up? If they find you, then they can force Dad to turn himself in. And if that happens, this will all be for nothing."

My face felt as if it was burning. That was my sister: pragmatic even when it hurt. And boy, did it hurt. Seldom before had she, or anyone else in my family, made an issue of my having LBDS. They'd always worked around it, making allowances for the fact that I couldn't go anywhere without my mobil or at least a pair of crutches. This time, though, things were different. I'd be a ball and chain for my father as he was running for his life. And on my own, I wouldn't last a day.

Jan must have seen the pain in my eyes, because she knelt beside me. "Look, kiddo," she said, "you mean well, but I've got two good legs and you don't." A tight smile. "Besides, I've got a lot of friends. Time for me to call in a few markers."

"Jan, you don't have to . . ." my father began.

"I'm sorry, but we don't have time for this." The man at the terminal door was pointedly looking at his watch. "We should've started getting these kids ready five minutes ago." He held the door open a little wider. "Anyone who's getting on the shuttle, come now . . . or stay behind."

Logan turned to his folks; his father solemnly shook his hand and his mother gave him a quick hug, and neither of them dared to look at Jan or me. The Hernandez children were already going in; Eduardo was still mopping tears from his face—*what a crybaby!* I couldn't help thinking—while Nina remained almost eerily calm; she didn't even look back to wave farewell to their parents, but instead took her big brother's hand and led him into the terminal. Dad made up his mind; he gripped the mobil's rear handles and pushed it the rest of the way to the door, then bent down to detach my crutches from its side.

"You'll need to leave your mobil here," he said, unfolding the crutches and handing them to me. "Jan and I will take it with us and . . ."

"Sure, okay." Something that felt like a stone was stuck in my throat. I twisted around in my seat to look back at Jan. "I'm sorry, I . . ."

"Don't worry about it." She stepped forward to take my overnight bag from my hands, then helped me to my feet while Dad pushed the crutches under my arms. "We'll get in touch as soon as we can," she went on as she handed my bag to Melissa, who impatiently waited for me just inside the door. "Until then . . ."

"Break a leg," I muttered; an old joke between us. "Good luck."

"You, too." A quick kiss on the cheek, then she vanished.

It seemed as if my father wanted to say something else, but there was no time for long goodbyes. So he took my hand and grasped it as just as Logan's father had done with him, and I realized that no words were necessary, really. A final pat on the shoulder, and then he was gone.

He hadn't remembered that today was my sixteenth birthday. No one did, except Jan. There was a good reason why, but it stung nonetheless.

The last person through the door was Hannah Johnson. The two men who'd brought her to Wallops Island accompanied her all the way to the door; they seemed reluctant to leave her, but neither were there any overt displays of affection. They simply wished her good luck and she quietly thanked them, and then they both turned and headed back to their car.

Melissa was still glaring at Hannah as the door closed behind us. "Whoever you are," she hissed, "I hope you're worth it."

For once, MeeMee and I were in full agreement. "My sister gave up her seat for you," I added. "I hope you remember that."

Although she'd pulled her ball cap down low, it wasn't hard to tell that Hannah's face was red. The man who'd met us at the door saved her from making any sort of response. "All right, then," he said, "we're going to have to hurry now. Ms. Barlowe, Ms. Hernandez, Ms . . . um . . ."

"Johnson," she whispered.

"Right . . . Johnson." He pointed to a young woman standing a little further down the corridor we found ourselves in. "Please follow Ms. Cates. She'll take you to get you ready. Boys, you're coming with me."

Logan took my bag from Melissa, then accompanied me down the corridor, letting the others lead the way. The girls disappeared through a door marked PASSENGER PREP-F; a little farther down the hall was PASSENGER PREP-M, which is where Logan, Eduardo, and I went.

Our escort murmured something into his prong as he led us into the room, then he left us alone, shutting the door behind him. We'd barely had time to take in the hospital-style furnishings—gurneys, medicine cabinets, a counter with a computer terminal, some uncomfortable-looking chairs—when the door opened again and three doctors wearing lab smocks, surgical masks, and thin plastic gloves walked in.

For the next twenty minutes, I underwent the fastest physical I'd ever endured. I'll spare you the details except to say that it was painful and humiliating. The doctors were considerate enough to pull curtains around the gurneys the other guys and I sat on. This didn't give us very much privacy, since I could hear what was happening elsewhere in the room, but at least I didn't have to see it. And while Logan and I were used to having people seeing us without our clothes—joining a high school swim team isn't something you should do if you have body shyness—it was pretty obvious that Eduardo didn't like taking his clothes off even for a medical exam. He put up a stink that didn't stop until his doctor threatened to tell his little sister what a coward he was.

What is it with that kid? I thought. *Is he disturbed or something?*

The physician who examined me tried to be gentle, but he was in a hurry; every couple of minutes he'd glance at his watch, and then move just a little faster. One of the first things he did was to hand me a suppository, and once he was through giving me the jelly-finger treatment he asked me to insert it myself. The reason for this soon became clear; he'd barely finished taking a blood sample when my stomach began to cramp, and without a word the doctor handed my crutches back to me and hastily ushered me to a toilet where I was able to empty my guts. Dad hadn't given us a chance to eat breakfast before we left the house; now I knew why.

I had so many shots that my arms ached. But when the doctor opened my medicine box, he asked only a couple of perfunctory questions about the prescriptions and supplements I was taking before he closed it again and put it back in my bag. Apparently he already had my medical data in his pad; he didn't appear at all surprised to be dealing with a teenage kid who had LBDS.

It was obvious that he'd been expecting me. Dad must have sent him this info in advance. If that were true, though, then that meant my father must have anticipated that he might have to send his kids to the Moon long before he actually had to do so.

And if that was the case . . . did this mean he'd also expected President Wilford to be assassinated and Vice President Shapar to take his place?

I had no answer for that. But the very question itself made me nervous.

When the doctor was through, he left me alone for a few moments. I no longer heard Logan or Eduardo from the other side of the curtains, so I figured that they must have finished their own physicals. The doctor reappeared a minute later with an old-fashioned wheelchair and plastic-wrapped bundle containing a blue jumpsuit and a pair of cloth shoes. I'd never worn a single-piece outfit like this before; it fit snug but not too tight and had cargo pockets on its arms, chest, and thighs, with the ISC logo above the left chest pocket. The shoes were little more than athletic socks with plastic Velcro soles. He helped me into the jumpsuit but let me put on the shoes myself, then picked me up from the bed and carefully loaded me into the wheelchair. I'd been riding mobils for as long as I could remember, so an unpowered wheelchair was primitive beyond comparison.

I started to reach for my crutches, but the doctor placed my bag in my lap instead. "You won't need them," he said. "Not where you're going." And then he pushed aside the curtains and wheeled me out of the prep room.

The others were waiting for me in the corridor, each of them wearing identical jumpsuits and carrying their own bags. Hannah Johnson made her jumpsuit look good, and the Washington Nationals cap was a nice touch; I had to admit that, as much I was inclined to dislike her, she was easy on the eyes. On the other hand, Nina's outfit was a size too large, and she'd had to roll up the legs and sleeves for her to wear it at all. The doctor who'd examined me turned over to Melissa the job of pushing my wheelchair; he and the other doctors said goodbye and good luck, then disappeared through another door, once again leaving us in the care of the guy who'd met us at the door.

He took a quick head-count to make sure no one was missing, then without a word he turned to lead us to a security door at the end of corridor. His keycard opened it for us; an older man was standing on the other side of the door. One look at us, then he nodded and led us down another corridor to an elevator. It opened and we entered; the older man pushed the lowest button on the panel, and down we went.

As the elevator descended, Logan turned to me. "Was it fun for you, too?"

"Loads. Can't wait to do it again."

Melissa snickered and even Hannah managed a fleeting smile, but Nina's face remained without expression. Then Eduardo spoke up for the first time.

"I didn't have fun," he said. "It hurt."

At first, I thought he was being ironic. That, or just a bit dense. "Well, yeah . . ."

"I don't want to do that again," he went on, as earnestly as if we were discussing an important issue, then he looked at his little sister. "Will we have to do that again, Nina?"

"No, Eddie, we won't." Nina took his hand. "I promise."

He beamed at her. "Good. I like that."

Logan and I glanced at each other; neither of us said anything, but his left eyebrow raised a fraction of an inch. Eduardo Hernandez was intellectually disabled. He didn't show the physical signs of Down Syndrome, but it was clear to us that he had the mind of a child even younger than his sister. I was immediately ashamed of the unkind thoughts I'd had about him earlier.

The elevator stopped and we got out in what appeared to be a subway station. A glass-walled tram stood at the opening of a tunnel. The older man held up an ID to a uniformed guard standing within a nearby kiosk. The guard nodded and pushed a button on a control panel, and the tram's rear door slid open. The young guy who'd met us outside stepped back into the elevator without so much as a farewell; his friend ushered us into the tram, and once the others were seated on padded benches and my wheelchair was locked down, the door quietly shut and the tram began to move into the tunnel.

The trip took only a couple of minutes: a fast ride on an electromagnetic rail, with scarcely a bump along the way. When the tram reached the other end of the tunnel, we got out in what appeared to be an identical station. Another guard stood within another kiosk; she apparently knew that we were coming because she simply waved us through. We squeezed into an elevator a little smaller than the one at Operations and Checkout and let it take us up.

I don't know what I was expecting to see when its doors opened, but it wasn't anything I would've imagined. Before us lay an enormous hangar, and within it was the shuttle. Resting upon its launch sled, which in turn was mounted atop a long concrete and steel monorail, the spacecraft dominated the room. More than two hundred feet long, its down-swept wings and twin vertical stabilizers were positioned just past the three black exhaust bells of its scramjet engines. The twin doors of its cargo bay lay open beneath an *n*-shaped service tower, a stepladder leading from its upper platform down into the spacecraft.

I'd seen countless pictures of shuttles, of course, but I never thought I'd ever get so close to one. Melissa was pushing my wheelchair; I heard her gasp. Logan whistled beneath his breath. I didn't really notice how the others reacted, except that Eduardo—Eddie—yelped in childish delight, as if the shuttle was a toy some gargantuan kid had left for him.

"Wow!" he exclaimed, terror abruptly replaced by fascination. "What's that?"

"That's the magcat." I replied.

He gave me a quizzical look. "I don't see a cat."

I tried not to laugh, even though some of the ground crew did. "No, no . . . magcat is short for magnetic catapult." I pointed toward the open end of hangar, through which we could see the rail extending out toward the Sea Wall two and a half miles away, its beacons flashing against the reddish-orange first light of dawn coming over the ocean. "See, that's the launch rail. It's magnetized, and that thing carrying the shuttle," I gestured to the sled, "will shoot straight down it until it reaches the end. The sled will stop when it gets there, and that's when the shuttle will fire its main engines and lift off. Understand?"

"Uh-huh," Eddie mumbled, even though it was clear that he didn't. I glanced at Logan, and again he raised an eyebrow. Both of us knew this stuff cold, of course, but how do you explain superconductivity, opposing magnetic polarities, and 2-g acceleration to someone like Eddie? At least I'd managed to calm him down a little.

Men and women in overalls were waiting for us at the bottom of the service tower. One of them waved us over, and our guide quickly led us to the ladder. As we got closer to the shuttle, I spotted its name, stenciled to the forward fuselage just below the starboard cockpit windows: *Spirit of New York*. Someone came down the ladder from the platform and walked toward us. Almost as wide as he was tall, the muscles of his arms and legs bulging against his blue jumpsuit, he had red hair in a buzz cut and a face like a friendly bulldog.

"I'll take it from here, Gus," he said to our escort. The older man nodded and walked away as the man in the jumpsuit turned to us. "Hi, there," he said, forcing a grin that did little to hide his obvious discomfort. "I'm Captain Gordon Rogers, the LTV pilot."

"What's a LTV?" Eddie asked. The technicians laughed again, this time a bit more nastily, and he looked at his sister. "Did I say a dirty word?"

"No, you didn't." Nina took his hand again. "You need to be quiet now, Eddie, and listen."

Capt. Rogers didn't seem to mind. "LTV means Lunar Transfer Vehicle . . . it's what you'll be riding the rest of the way to the Moon after the *Spirit* drops us off in low orbit." He pointed to the service tower. "We'll use that to climb aboard. The shuttle pilots are already in the shuttle and set to go as soon as we're ready."

He paused to look us over, then his gaze settled on me. "You're Jamey Barlowe, right?"

I nodded and he smiled. "Okay, then . . . we're bringing you aboard first." Turning toward the ground crew, he stuck two fingers in his mouth and gave a shrill whistle. "Osama, Sally . . . give Mr. Barlowe a hand here, willya?"

If I thought I was going to leave Earth in any sort of dignified fashion, I was wrong. My wheelchair was left behind, of course—too much unnecessary mass that I wouldn't need in zero-g—but I could have climbed the service tower ladder by myself if I had my crutches. Instead, I had to put up with Osama lifting me out of the wheelchair and carrying me up the steps. He was big enough to make me feel like a baby in his arms. Sally followed us with my bag. She was nearly as big as her coworker, and when we reached the top platform, she squeezed past us to clamber down another ladder into the shuttle's cargo bay.

Nestled within the bay was the LTV, a cylindrical vehicle with narrow windows at the bow and along its sides and the nozzle of a liquid-fuel engine at the stern. Sally dropped my bag through the top-side dorsal hatch to another person waiting inside the vehicle, then reached up to carefully take me from Osama and then pass me down to the guy below her.

They were gentle about the whole business, but I'd rarely been more humiliated in my whole life. It didn't help that, when I happened to glance back at the others, I saw Hannah regarding me with pity. I always hated being thought of as the poor lil cripple boy, so I stared at her until she looked away.

The LTV interior wasn't much larger than my family van, with a small cockpit up front and six acceleration couches arranged on either side of a narrow passenger compartment. Correction: five seats and, in the very back beside a closed hatch, what appeared to be a refrigerator with a Dutch door open at the top half. The technician tucked my bag in a ceiling net above the oval portholes before turning to the fridge; he opened its door, revealing what appeared to be an acceleration couch surrounded by deflated plastic bags.

"Thanks, Dave. I'll take it from here." Capt. Rogers had come down the ladder behind us, and Dave grunted as he eased past him. The LTV pilot looked almost too big for his own craft; as he came toward me, he had to turn sideways to keep his broad shoulders from colliding with the forward seats.

"Jamey?" He loomed over me, making me feel like a little kid in the presence of a pro wrestler. "Pleased to meet you," he said, offering his hand. "You can call me Gordie."

"Hi . . . um, Gordie." Anticipating a big, manly handshake that would crush my fingers, I reluctantly took his hand, but his grasp was surprisingly gentle.

"Good deal. Now, then—" he patted the top of the fridge "—this is what we're going to use to get you safely into space. It's called a Linear Acceleration Restraint, but most people who've used it call it the cocoon. It's designed for people like yourself who were born on the Moon."

"Loonies, you mean."

"Uh-huh . . . so you've heard that before. Then you must be familiar with this, too."

I shook my head. I'd never seen a cocoon before; this was new to me. Gordie nodded and went on. "Anyway, every now and then loonies . . . um, people like you . . . come to Earth for a visit, and when they go back we use this particular LTV to get them there. In this thing, you won't be hurt when we take off. Understand?"

I nodded, and he reached down to carefully pick me up from where Dave had left me. "The seat and the cells all around you will fill up with a sort of gel," he explained as he placed me into the cocoon. "They'll cushion your body when we hit the high-g's during launch. Got it?"

"Sure." The seat was remarkably comfortable; I wouldn't have minded having it as an armchair back home. "But . . . when we take off, is it going to hurt?"

"Nope. Not a bit . . . and here's why." There was a small panel in the cocoon just above my head. Gordie opened it and withdrew a plastic face mask connected to a rubber hose. "You're going to wear this on the way up," he said, showing it to me. "It'll feed you oxygen mixed with anesthetic gas, the same stuff you get when you go to the dentist to have your wisdom teeth pulled. Just before we launch, I'm going to push a button in the cockpit that'll feed you the gas. In three seconds, you'll be out like a light." He snapped his fingers. "Next thing you know, you'll be in space."

I eyed the mask warily. "You're sure about this?"

"Done it a half-dozen times already." Gordie grinned at me. "Trust me, kid . . . you'll love it."

The others were beginning to come down the ladder; Melissa was first, her bag slung over her shoulders. I wasn't about to give Gordie a hard time while MeeMee was watching, so I nodded. "Make you a deal," Gordie said as he pulled the seat harness in place and attached it with a six-point buckle. "Sweat this out, and I'll show you how to fly this tin can. Okay?"

I had no interest in learning how to fly a spacecraft, but I gave him a thumbs-up that the pilot seemed to appreciate. He pulled the mask down over my lower face and adjusted its elastic strap, then closed the cocoon. It must have seemed as if I sitting in a refrigerator, because Melissa giggled when she saw me. Gordie gave her a wink, then he patted the top of the cocoon. "See you soon," he said before turning to make his way to the cockpit.

Logan took the seat in front of me, with Hannah across the aisle from him. He shoved his bag into the ceiling web next to Melissa's and mine, then paused to study me for a moment. "You look like a . . ."

"Shut up." My voice was muffled by the mask, but the look in my eyes must have told him that this was a bad time for a wisecrack.

Dave went down the aisle, helping the others pull their seat harnesses around themselves. In the cockpit, Gordie had seated himself at his console and had pulled on his headset. Dave had just buckled Eddie's when Gordie looked back at him. "Hustle," the pilot said. "They're moving up the countdown."

Dave raised his head. "What's going on?"

"Just hurry up and get out of here. We need to button down the hatch."

Melissa glanced at me; she didn't say anything, but something in Gordie's tone of voice bothered her. It worried me, too. I couldn't see anything through the porthole next to my seat except the inside of the cargo bay, but I could hear footsteps on the ladder rungs of the service tower.

Dave finished his work, then hastily climbed up the ladder. He pulled it up behind him and slammed the ceiling hatch shut; its lock-wheel turned, and a second later we heard him knock twice against the hull, signaling that it was tight. His shoes rang on the ladder rungs; a few seconds of silence, then what little light came through the windows was abruptly extinguished as the cargo bay doors lowered into place. A loud thump signaled that the LTV was sealed in.

Air began to hiss through the ceiling vents, pressurizing the passenger compartment. In the cockpit, Gordie bent over his console, murmuring into his headset mike as he scrambled to complete the prelaunch checklist.

"Gordie?" Logan raised his voice to call to him. "What's happening? Why are they moving up the countdown?"

At first, it didn't seem as if the pilot had heard him. He finished the checklist, then began to tighten his harness. "Don't want to scare you guys," he said, not looking back at us, "but Launch Control has informed us that federal marshals showed up just a few minutes ago. Apparently they're searching for you."

"Searching for us?" Melissa's hands gripped her seat. "Why would they be searching for us?"

"They're not after you." Hannah's voice was little more than a whisper. "They're after me."

"What?" Logan stared at her. "Who are you, anyway?"

Hannah didn't reply, but instead turned her face away from us. When I looked up front, I saw Nina staring at her. Once again, I had a sense that she was smarter than a little girl her age should be, and that she knew something about Hannah Johnson that the rest of us didn't.

I was about to say something—not that anyone would've heard me anyway—when the cocoon began to tighten around me. I gasped as its cells began to fill with gel. It felt as if I was being squeezed by dozens of small, cold pillows, soft yet unyielding, that locked my arms and legs in place. I could still breathe, but I couldn't move.

An instant later, a sudden thump ran through the LTV, followed by a prolonged vibration. "They're moving the shuttle onto the track," Gordie called back to us. "Even if the feds know you're here, they can't do anything about it. Not without scrubbing the launch, at least, and that would take a . . ."

Another abrupt jar. The vibration became more pronounced. "Aw, crap!" Gordie yelled. "We're going now!" He reached forward to his console. "Jamey! Count backward from a hundred!"

Something that smelled like peppermint entered my mask. "One hundred," I said.

The vibration became a sense of fast forward motion. Melissa yelled something obscene.

"Ninety-nine," I said. For some reason, now seemed like a good time to take a nap. Eddie was crying again, but I could barely hear him. I was falling into the cocoon, my body becoming heavier and heavier. "Ninety-eight . . ."

And that was it. I was unconscious by the time the shuttle reached the end of the launch rail.

4.
LOW ORBIT

It didn't feel as if I'd fallen asleep. I didn't dream, nor was there any real sense of the passage of time. My eyes closed for what seemed like only a moment or two, and when they opened again, it was to see Gordie bending over me.

"Jamey? Are you okay?"

"Umm . . . yeah, I guess." My mouth was parched and my ribs were sore, but otherwise I felt fine. "Did we take off?"

Beside me, Melissa made one of her *boy, are you an idiot* sighs. Gordie paid no attention to her as he reached down to remove the mask from my face. "Yeah, we got away," he said as he returned the mask to the compartment above my head. "Let's see if you can raise your hands. Can you do that for me?"

The cells that had cushioned my body were empty again, but there was still just enough pressure in them to hold down my arms. I lifted first my right hand, then my left; it took no effort at all to do so. "Good, good," Gordie said, smiling as he watched this. "Now let's see if you can stand up."

"But I don't have my . . ." I began, and then I noticed something that made me forget what I was about to say.

Logan was behind the pilot . . . but he was upside-down, his feet planted against the LTV's low ceiling. His hair was fluffed out in all directions, and there was a puffiness to his face that made him look as if he was sick.

I looked over at Melissa. She was still strapped into her seat, but her hair had also formed a halo around her head that no amount of mousse could have controlled. Her face was ashen and she clenched a plastic vomit bag between both hands. It wasn't hard to tell that she'd upchucked at least once already and was fighting hard to keep from doing so again.

Hannah had unbuckled her harness and had turned around to look back at me. Her baseball cap was holding her hair in place, and she gripped the back of Eddie's seat to keep from joining Logan on the ceiling. A small silver medallion on a matching chain floated a few inches from her neck. It looked like some sort of religious symbol, but that wasn't what attracted my attention to it. The way it lazily dangled in midair was what made me truly realize where we were.

We were in zero-g . . . microgravity, if you want to use the technical term, or free-fall, if you don't. I turned my eyes toward the porthole beside me, and saw something I never thought I'd ever see with my own eyes: a vast plain of tan and dark green, curved at its farthest edges of its horizon, a blue expanse just beneath it. An early morning sun cast shadows from filmy white clouds, highlighting hills, rivers, a silver-white sprawl that looked like it might be a coastal city.

I suddenly realized that I was looking down upon Texas and the Gulf of Mexico from a low-orbit altitude of about sixty or seventy miles. It was the most incredible—the most drop-dead *beautiful*—thing I'd ever seen in all my life.

"Yep. We're in space." Logan must have figured out what I was thinking, because he grinned at me. "C'mon, man . . . let's see if you can stand up."

"No, I don't . . . I mean, I can't . . ." I told myself that all I really wanted to do was stare out the window, but there was more to it than that. What he was asking me to do had always seemed impossible. Standing upright without the aid of a pair of crutches, a simple act that everyone else took for granted, had been beyond my ability for as long as I could remember. Everyone was watching me, and I didn't want to make a fool out of myself.

"Go ahead, Jamey," Gordie said. "I'd like to see you do that, too." He opened the lower part of the cocoon and began to unfasten my harness. Once the straps were floating free, he gently took hold of my wrists. "All right, on the count of three. One . . . two . . ."

"Don't rush me," I said. Gordie let go, but it was clear that neither he nor Logan were going to take no for an answer. They were using the Velcro soles of their sock-like stickshoes to attach themselves to the fabric strips on the deck and ceiling. Gordie stepped back as I carefully planted my shoes against the floor. I took a deep breath, then carefully pushed myself out of the cocoon.

No crutches. No braces. No helpful hands to steady me. For the first time in my life, I stood on my own two feet.

"Jamey, be careful." From behind me, Melissa's voice was a low whisper. I felt her hand brush against my back, as if she was reaching up to keep me from falling over. It wasn't often that she showed any sign of actually caring for me; every so often, I suspected that my sister might really be human, not an alien imposter. That alone made me want to take the next step . . . literally.

Holding my breath, I detached my right foot from the carpet, moved it forward a few inches, put it down again. Then I did the same with my left foot. And then again with my right foot. I was walking. Never mind the fact that I was in space; what was more incredible was the fact I'd just taken my first steps on my own, without having to rely on anything.

"Attaboy." Gordie unstuck his shoes from the floor and floated beside Logan, who'd turned himself right-side-up and had backed away to give me room. "You're doing great, just great."

"Yeah . . . I guess I am." I was tempted to yank my shoes off the floor and do a somersault, but Melissa was right; I needed to take it easy. Yet when I happened to glance at Hannah, I saw admiration in her eyes. No girl had ever looked at me that way before. Despite the fact that she was responsible for Jan having to remain behind, it made me feel like I was ten feet tall.

"Okay, then." Gordie let out his breath, looked back at Eddie and Nina. "And how are you two doing?"

Now that I was standing erect, I could see the Hernandez kids. Nina was just as pale as Melissa; she'd probably become sick, too, but she managed a solemn nod. On the other hand, her brother was as happy as a kid in a playground. "This is fun!" he yelped. "Can I fly, too?"

"No, no. Just stay where you are for now." Gordie motioned for him to remain seated. Eduardo looked disappointed, but he nodded. "All right, " the pilot went on, "now that Jamey's up and around, I'll let y'all know what's going on." Holding onto a handrail running along the ceiling, Gordie turned to face me again. "Since you missed it, I'll give you the details. We left Earth about an hour or so ago. I deliberately kept you under, though, until the *Spirit* reached orbit and jettisoned the LTV."

"Just as well that you slept through it." Logan remained where he was, back against the fuselage and feet dangling in the air. "We hit Mach 7 before we left the atmosphere. It was a rough ride for a few seconds."

"Sorry 'bout that." Gordie gave him an apologetic smile. "Should've warned you, I guess, but I didn't have time. We had to launch before the feds stopped us . . . and believe me, they tried. The acceleration might've squashed you a bit, but at least we were able to outrun the jets they sent after us."

"Jets?" Hannah's eyes went wide. "You mean . . . ?"

"Two Navy F-30s. I caught a glimpse of them on the video feed from the *Spirit*'s external camera. They couldn't have caught up with the shuttle, but they might've been able to splash us if they'd gotten close enough to lock on with air-to-air missiles. But the shuttle was travelling too fast, so . . ."

"Why were they trying to shoot us down?" I asked.

Gordie chose to ignore that question. "Point is, we made a clean getaway. And don't worry about the *Spirit*. Just before he jettisoned us, I heard the commander talking to Flight Control back in Wallops, telling him that they were having mechanical problems and that he was going to make an emergency landing at the ISC launch center in Spain. My guess is that he and the pilot will request political asylum as soon as they're on the ground so that they won't have to face the music back home."

I winced when I heard this. The shuttle crew had sacrificed their citizenship for our freedom; it would be awhile before they'd go home again, if ever. And they were lucky; no telling what might happen to the people on Wallops Island who'd aided and abetted in our escape. They would be detained and questioned, no doubt about it. Some of them might even land in prison. All just to make sure that six kids made their way to safety.

"What about you?" I asked.

Gordie shrugged. "I make the trip to Apollo about once a month. I've got plenty of friends there, so it's practically my second home."

"What else have you heard from Wallops?" Logan asked. "Did our parents get away?"

"I don't know. We're radio silent till we reach the Moon. No communications with anyone for the duration." Logan was about to say something, but the pilot shook his head. "Sorry, but that's all I can tell you."

Gordie pushed himself away from the ceiling so that his shoes attached themselves to the floor again. "Anyway, once we complete this orbit, we'll be in the proper position to fire the main engine and head for the Moon. It'll take about two and a half days to get there. A ferry will rendezvous with us in lunar orbit and carry us the rest of the way."

As he spoke, I gazed out the window again. We were directly above the Gulf now, the Texas panhandle visible to the north-northeast. It would be early morning down there, with only a few clouds in the sky.

"Until then," Gordie was saying, "make yourselves at home." He pointed to a hatch in the aft bulkhead behind Melissa and me. "There's a galley back there with plenty of food and water, and also the head."

"There's a head back there?" Eddie's voice rose in terror.

"No, no, no!" Too late, Gordie remembered that he was speaking to someone who might take him literally. "That's just what we call a bathroom. It's not a . . . y'know, a real head." Melissa snickered, and both Logan and I gave her a dirty look. "The seats can be folded down against the deck . . . sorry, Jamey, but your cocoon stays where it is . . . and I have hammocks that can be strung up for us to sleep in. In the meantime . . . well, I've got a couple of pads if you didn't bring your own. And if you get tired of reading or playing games, you can always look out the window."

I already was. While the others were talking, I caught sight of something that didn't look right: a small, bright point of light, rapidly rising from the curve horizon below us. At first I thought it might be a meteorite burning up in the atmosphere, except that it was headed in the wrong direction, toward space instead of away from it. Almost as if it was . . .

No, I thought. *That can't be a missile.*

"I need to go forward again, start laying in the coordinates for the next burn." Gordie glanced at Eddie. "A burn is when I fire the main engine," he quickly added, and Eddie nodded. "Unless there's any more questions . . ."

"Gordie?" I didn't look away from the window. "You might want to see this."

Gordie glanced my way, almost as if irritated that I'd interrupted him. Then he pulled himself over to the window next to mine. For a second or two he said nothing as he peered out. Then his mouth fell open in astonishment and he threw himself back from the window.

"Get in your seats and strap down!" he snapped. "Do it now!"

"Why?" Melissa stared at him. "What's . . . ?"

"Just do it!" Grabbing at the ceiling, Gordie launched himself toward the cockpit. "Coming through!" he yelled, pushing Nina and Eddie out of the way. "Make a hole!"

"It's a missile," I said. Gordie's reaction had confirmed my suspicions. "Someone down there has launched a rocket at us."

"Are you sure?" Logan gaped at me, then hauled himself over to the window Gordie had just vacated.

I glanced out my window again. Although the rising star was still far away, it was getting brighter, and its upward direction suggested that it was on a trajectory that would intercept us in less than a minute.

"Yes, I'm sure!" Gordie hastily turned himself so that he fell into the cockpit feet first; within seconds he was in the pilot's seat, snatching at the seat and shoulder straps and buckling them together. "That's an anti-satellite weapon. Probably air-launched by another F-30 sent up from Texas. They haven't given up on us yet. *Now get in your damn seats!*"

We scrambled to obey him, but none of us were prepared for this, so all we managed to do was get tangled in each other's arms and legs. I was trying to get MeeMee's feet out of my face when there was a hollow roar from the stern, and in the next instant an invisible hand shoved all of us toward the compartment's rear end. Gordie had fired the main engine; a second later, the entire LTV seemed to roll sideways, and I realized that he was firing the maneuvering thrusters as well.

He was trying to dodge the ASW. No time to get back in the cocoon; I grabbed the ceiling rung with both hands and hoped that our pilot knew what he was doing.

"C'mon, baby, c'mon." Logan floated above the seat row in front of me, clutching at the top of one of them as he stared out the nearest porthole. "Climb, climb, climb . . ."

"What's going on?" Melissa was trying to get into the seat beside my cocoon, but its straps were hopelessly snarled, and every effort she made to untangle them only made it worse. "Are we going to die? We're going to die, aren't we . . . ?"

"Shut up!" Gordie yelled. "Nobody's dying! Not if I can help it!"

His bravado might have been assuring, but it came too late. Eddie's earlier giddiness was forgotten as he let out a terrified scream. "I don't want to die! I don't want to die! I just wanna go home . . . !"

"It's all right. It's okay." Nina pushed her brother into one of the forward seats, then wrapped her small arms around him and held him tight. "We're going to be fine," she said quietly, and in that moment she seemed more like a mother than a little sister. "Hush, now. We're going to be okay . . ."

The only other person remaining calm—or at least not panicking, as MeeMee and Eddie were—was Hannah. She was crammed between a seatback and a bulkhead by Logan's legs, unable to strap herself down, but she didn't seem to care. Her eyes were shut, and she seemed to be saying something under her breath. Praying? Probably. Then her eyes opened, and she caught me looking at her. There was fear in her eyes, but something else as well: resignation to an inevitable fate.

She looked at me, and her mouth opened and her lips formed one silent word: *Sorry.*

I was still wondering why she'd say that—this wasn't her fault, was it?—when Logan yelled, "There it goes!"

Twisting my neck, I ducked my head to peer through the window again, just in time to see a brilliant, utterly soundless flash of light. The anti-satellite weapon had just detonated. How far away, I didn't know; all I could tell was that it exploded somewhere below and off to the port side of the LTV.

"It's a miss!" I shouted. "It didn't hit!"

A loud, sharp *bang!* that sounded like someone firing a pistol, and I knew at once that I was wrong.

* * *

A second later an alarm shrieked from the cockpit, followed by a loud curse from Gordie. "Blowout!" he shouted. "We've got a blowout!"

He didn't have to explain what he meant. The ASW had detonated close enough to throw debris our way, and the bang we'd heard was a fragment penetrating the LTV's outer hull and fuselage. The alarm was the decompression alert, signaling that the spacecraft was losing air.

"Oh my God!" Melissa's scream was even louder than the alarm. "Oh . . . my . . . God!"

"Shut up!" Logan shoved himself away from the porthole, began to look around. "Where's the hole? Where did it . . . ?"

"Look for it!" Gordie snapped. "It's gotta be around there somewhere." He switched off the alarm, but remained where he was in the cockpit. "You're going to have to find it and button it down! I've got my hands full!"

It wasn't until then that I realized the LTV had begun to tumble like a washing machine drum. True to Newton's third law, the fragment's impact had caused an equal and opposite reaction; with the escaping air pressure acting as a jet, the spacecraft was now rolling sideways. If Gordie didn't get our craft under control and fast, the LTV's orbit would decay and we'd commence a long, fatal plunge into Earth's upper atmosphere.

It was up to us to locate the source of the blowout. But even with the alarm shut off, it was almost impossible to tell where the hull had been breached. I couldn't hear a hissing sound, nor was there an obvious hole.

Eddie was in hysterics, and MeeMee wasn't helping much either. So when Hannah spoke up, her calm voice was almost lost in the din. "I think I found what did it," she said, and I looked around to see her holding up a small, jagged piece of metal about half the size of my little finger.

"Where did it come from?" I asked.

"I don't know. It bounced off here—" she pointed to the bulkhead above her head, on the starboard side of the compartment "—right after we heard the bang."

"That means it's gotta be around here somewhere . . ."

"Whatever you're going to do, guys, you better do it fast." Gordie wasn't shouting anymore, but his voice was still tense. "At this rate, we're going to lose our air in five minutes."

"You find the hole. I'll get the repair kit." Logan launched himself down the center aisle toward a bulkhead locker marked EMERGENCY. "Is this where it is, skipper?"

"You got it." Gordie took a second to glance over his shoulder. "Pull the handle up, then pull it down . . . that's how it opens. And don't call me skipper . . . I hate that."

I might have laughed if the situation hadn't been so serious. Instead, I was trying to figure out how to locate the breach. Hannah's finding the fragment helped a little—it meant the hole was closer to the rear of the spacecraft than the front—but it only gave me a general direction in which to look.

The hole could be anywhere. Worse than that, given the size of the fragment, it was probably no larger than the diameter of a pen. Easy to seal, but hard to find. And Gordie wasn't kidding when he said that we were quickly losing pressure; I swallowed, and felt my ears pop.

"Everyone, look around," I said, trying to stay calm. "Look for the hole." Melissa was still weeping, and I grabbed her shoulder and shook her hard. "You too. Stop crying and help me look."

"Oh, why don't you climb back in your little cocoon and shut up!" Her face was screwed up in terror, and tears leaked from the corners of her eyes. "At least you'll have air in there!"

She was wrong, of course; the cocoon wasn't airtight, and even if it was, I wouldn't have lived very much longer than anyone else. I was about to tell her this when I noticed something peculiar: in zero-g, her tears were forming tiny bubbles that drifted away from her face. Floating in midair, as if caught by . . .

An air current. The sort that would be caused by a hull breach.

"That's it!" I yelled, still staring at my sister. "That's how to find it!"

MeeMee glared at me. "What are you . . . ?"

Ignoring her, I pushed myself toward the aft bulkhead hatch marked GALLEY and yanked it open. The compartment on the other side of the hatch was no more than a cubbyhole, barely large enough for one person. It took only a second to find what I needed: a locker containing a couple of dozen half-liter bottles of water.

I snatched a water bottle from the galley and kicked myself back into the passenger compartment. By then, Logan had retrieved a plastic case from the emergency locker and had returned to the rear of the passenger compartment. "I got the seal kit," he said, then stared at me in bewilderment. "Hey, man, you picked a hell of a time to get a drink of . . ."

"Watch." I pried open the cap nozzle, pointed the bottle away from me, and squeezed. Water spurted from the nozzle and instantly coalesced into a thick, steady stream of bubbles, each perfectly spherical if not identical in size.

"What are you doing?" Melissa screeched like a cat who was about to get wet. "This is no time to be playing with . . . !"

"No! He's right!" Logan caught on; he grabbed a ceiling rail and pulled himself back from the water bubbles, making sure that he wasn't in their way. "Watch where they're going!"

The stream dispersed, becoming a cloud . . . and then the bubble cloud began to move, caught by air currents we couldn't feel but which nonetheless influenced the bubbles' direction. The LTV was no longer rolling—Gordie had regained control of the craft, at least for the moment—so there was no other force to act upon the bubbles.

The bubbles floated downward, slowly at first, then picking up speed as they moved toward the floor. As we watched, they began to form a spiral, much like a tiny waterspout, that jetted toward a spot in the aisle just past the edge of Logan's seat, across the aisle from where Hannah had been during the blowout. The airborne whirlpool disappeared through a tiny hole in the floor, the place where the fragment had punched through.

"That's it," I murmured. "There's where it is."

Logan opened the seal kit. Inside was a cylindrical object that faintly resembled a chalk gun and a set of flat, cellophane-wrapped patches of different sizes. I held the box while he quickly read the instructions printed on the inside of the lid, then he removed the gun and bent over to insert its pointed barrel into the hole. When he pulled the trigger, pink gunk that looked like chewing gum jetted into the hole. It filled the hole, stopping the remaining water bubbles—and the air—from escaping. The gunk hardened immediately; once it was solid, Logan selected a small patch about two inches in diameter. Tearing open its wrapper, he removed the cover from the adhesive backing and firmly pressed the patch against the sealed hole. The patch was made of some polymer as tough as the metal around it; it stuck to the hole, making it airtight.

"We're no longer losing pressure," Gordie called from the cockpit. "But let's be safe and check and see if there's not any more holes."

I moved through the cabin, squirting a little more water here and there. The bubbles lingered in midair, though, and didn't form any more waterspouts. "I think that's the only one," I said.

Gordie let out his breath as a long, relieved sigh. "That's as close as I ever want to get," he muttered, then he turned his head to look back at us. "Well done, guys . . . especially you two," he added, meaning Logan and me. "I don't know what I would've done without you."

I nodded, then looked over at Logan. He didn't smile as he packed the sealant gun back into the box. "Why did they fire that ASW at us?" he asked. "That's what I'd like to know."

"I've made the lunar trajectory burn," Gordie said, as if he hadn't heard him. "They're not going to be able to try that stunt again . . . we're out of range."

"I want to know the same thing." Melissa had calmed down again; so had Eddie, although he still clung to Nina for comfort. "Why did they try to shoot us down? Why are we so important that they'd want to kill us?"

For once, I had to agree with her. First the F-30s that had chased the shuttle after it took off from Wallops Island, then an anti-satellite weapon fired by another fighter. Seemed like someone was going to a lot of trouble just to stop a few kids from going to the Moon.

Gordie didn't reply for a moment or two. "I'm sure they've got a reason," he said at last, not looking back at us. "Anyway . . . we're safe, and that's what counts."

Logan and I traded a glance. Neither of us said anything, but I could tell we shared the same thought: something was going on that Gordie didn't want to talk about. I looked over at Hannah. She was smiling at me, her gratitude obvious. Then her expression darkened and she quickly looked away, as if trying to avoid answering the same question Gordie had refused to answer.

I remembered what she'd said to me, clearly yet silently: *Sorry.* As if she held herself to blame for the catastrophe Logan and I had only barely averted.

Hannah knew something, all right . . . but she didn't want to tell us what it was.

5.
FALLING TO THE MOON

The blowout rattled us, but good. It took awhile for everyone to get over our close escape. Once Gordie put us back on course, though, things calmed down a bit. Then we had to deal with a two-and-a-half-day ride to the Moon.

Imagine being stuck in a metal can about the size of a small bus with six other people just as bored and restless as you are. And that's just the half of it.

For one thing, there's problems with being weightless that you don't often hear about. Because gravity no longer draws your bodily fluids toward your feet, everything rises upward. So you're constantly congested, feeling as if you have a head cold that won't go away. You lose your sense of smell—which was probably for the better, since the head wasn't equipped with a shower stall and we had to clean ourselves as best we could with disinfectant tissues—and also your sense of taste, which was no loss either because our meals came from tubes or plastic wrappers. It was supposed to be beef, chicken, or seafood but only tasted like slightly different flavors of cardboard. Swallowing was difficult at first; it took a deliberate mental effort to choke down whatever was in my mouth. At least I was able to eat; Melissa and Nina were spacesick for the first day or so, and even Logan had moments when it looked as if he was about to barf. Eddie, though, had the appetite of a goat, and he claimed to love the food.

The head was . . . well, unpleasant. About the size of a small closet, it contained a toilet that consisted of a seat mounted above a hole equipped with a built-in pneumatic suction device. Once you've closed the accordion door, you use wall rungs to turn yourself around until you're in the right position, then strap yourself down with a seat belt. Taking a piss is easy; there's a tube with a unisex cup that you attach to yourself, and all you have to do is let go; the suction pulls your urine away from you and into the septic tank below the toilet.

The other part is a bit more tricky. In theory, the suction is also supposed to remove your feces, but sometimes it doesn't work that way; on occasion it . . . um, gets stuck. When that happens, there's a wall dispenser from which you pull a plastic glove. You put it on, reach down behind yourself, and finish the job the hard way. I'll spare you the details; they're pretty gross.

Strangely, the only one who didn't have any real problems was Eduardo. After Gordie instructed us how to use the head, Eddie alone got it right the first time and every time after that. Melissa had fits every time she had to use the head, though, and after one really bad accident she had to clean up the mess she'd made.

But we still managed to have fun. Once we folded down the couches, the amount of room doubled. Since we no longer had to worry about the couches or which side was up and which side was down, the LTV became our own little zero-g gym. We could do somersaults and cartwheels that had us spinning from one side of the cabin to the other. I'd never been able to take up diving when I was on the swim team—my bones were too fragile—but I would have won a dozen gold medals from the full-gainers I suddenly found myself able to do. Our first big workout had us bouncing off the walls, laughing like crazy even though we frequently collided with one another. Even Hannah joined the fun for a few minutes, until she sailed into the cockpit and nearly slammed into an instrument panel. After that Gordie lay down some ground rules: no more than two kids could play at a time, and the cockpit was strictly off-limits.

Most of the time, though, we lay in the hammocks Gordie helped us string across the cabin. We'd read or watch movies, but that got to be dull after awhile; I had some novels and vids stored in my pad, but the ones Gordie had aboard were mostly loaded with tech manuals or 20th-century comedies that none of us really liked. We'd sleep, even though it was almost pointless; in zero-g our bodies didn't require as much rest as they did on Earth, so our naps would last only a few hours.

So we spent a lot of time talking. Or at least Logan, Melissa, and I did. Conversations with Eddie were pleasant, and he was really nice once we got to know him better, but it was a little hard to have a meaningful chat with someone who had the mind of a second-grader. Nina was smart as hell, but she didn't seem to like us very much. Melissa was always on the verge of making fun of Eddie, and even after I told MeeMee to knock it off, Nina was constantly defensive of her brother.

As for Hannah . . . she remained a mystery, quiet, and reserved, only rarely smiling. She avoided both Melissa and Nina, and had as little to do with Logan or me as she could. Yet it seemed that, whenever I looked her way, our eyes would meet for a second and I'd find a warmth there which was both attractive and unsettling. She probably thought that I saved her life, and she may have been right. All I knew was that I wanted to dislike her . . . but how can you hate the first girl who's ever paid attention to you?

Nonetheless, she was keeping something bottled up inside. At one point, she went to the head and didn't come out for two hours; behind the door, we could hear her crying. She wouldn't tell us what was wrong, though, and no one could get through the wall she'd built up around her.

* * *

We were about halfway to the Moon when Gordie made good his promise about showing me how to fly an LTV. At first I was reluctant; after all, the promise had been made while he'd been trying to calm me down. Besides, I had no ambition to become a spacecraft pilot. But Gordie insisted, and I was bored, so while the others slept I went forward to the cockpit, where Gordie had me take his place in the pilot's seat while he hovered behind me.

The flight profile called for a mid-course correction, a routine procedure that has to be done two or three times between Earth and the Moon. In this instance, that entailed firing the reaction-control rockets and main engine in just the right order to keep us on the proper trajectory. "The autopilot can do this on its own," Gordie said, "but no self-respecting pilot lets a computer do a man's job."

Well . . . not exactly. The computer did most of the work, really. Once I was strapped in, Gordie had me take hold of the pistol-grip hand controller, then pointed to the two small screens directly in front of me. The screen on the left displayed a crosshatch with a tiny square in its middle and a tiny four-pointed diamond just to the right of it; the screen on the right displayed several vertical red and blue bars signifying the LTV's present speed, change of velocity (or delta-V), and rate of fuel consumption. All I had to do was use the hand controller to move the diamond into the middle of the square, and then squeeze the controller's trigger to ignite the main engine.

It seemed simple enough, but getting the diamond into position was harder than it appeared, particularly since it twitched with the slightest move I made. I chewed on my lower lip as I carefully slid the diamond into the square, trying not let it move too far away from the center of the screen. I finally managed to get it there, though, and squeezed the trigger the instant it was lined up. A soft rumble from behind us as the main engine fired, and for a second or two I felt myself being gently pushed back into my seat. I watched the left screen as the little red bar of the fuel gauge inched downward as the little blue bar of the delta-V indicator crept upward. When they met the hash-marks on the side of the screen, I released the trigger.

"And there we go." Gordie reached past me to snap a couple of toggle switches on the dashboard. "Locked and set. Nice work, kiddo. Couldn't have done better myself."

"Yeah, right." Although I was relieved that I hadn't put us on course for the Sun, I thought he was being patronizing.

"Don't believe me? Look for yourself." He pointed toward the window above the dashboard, which he'd told me to ignore while I was watching the screens.

I felt my breath catch in my throat. The last time I'd seen the Moon, it was on the right side of the window. Now it appeared to be almost directly before us. Not only that, but it was many times larger than I'd ever seen it before; it filled the window, sunlight casting dark shadows from its distinct mountains and craters. No longer a small orb in the sky, the Moon had become a vast world toward which our tiny craft was falling.

"You're almost home," Gordie murmured.

Despite the amazing beauty of what I saw, I looked away from the window. "That's not my home. I've never been there before."

"You were born there, weren't you?"

"Yeah, but . . ."

"Then you're a loony, true blue."

"Sorry, but you're wrong. I grew up in Maryland, not . . ." I nodded toward the window. "I know nothing about the Moon other than that's where I was born."

Gordie was quiet for a few moments. Thinking that he wanted his seat again, I unbuckled the harness and carefully pushed myself out of it. He took my place without a word, but as I was about to leave the cockpit he looked back at me. "How did that happen, anyway? I mean, being born on the Moon but winding up on Earth."

I'd been asked that question so many times that I'd come up with a pat reply: *just worked out that way, I guess.* But his interest seemed to be genuine, and considering what he'd done to help me escape the feds, I figured that he deserved an explanation. I grabbed hold of a bulkhead rung and turned toward him again.

"It's a long story . . ." I began.

"We got plenty of time." He glanced over his shoulder to make sure the others were still asleep, then lowered his voice. "Really. I'd like to hear it."

I hesitated, then went on. "I was born on the Moon, yeah, but it was kind of an accident. I was conceived on Earth, but my mother didn't know she was pregnant until she and Dad went to the Moon."

"Really?" Gordie raised an eyebrow. "She . . . um, forgive me for saying this, but she must not have been paying a lot of attention."

"Yeah, well . . . from what I've been told, I guess she was sort of an egghead, kind of like Dad. She'd already had Melissa and Jan, but they were still very little when Dad asked her to come along with him for a three-month stay on the Moon. Apollo was under construction then, and the ISC wanted him up there to help work out the details of the mining operations. And since Mom was a botanist, she could advise them on what sort of crops they'd need to grow for food and air. So they had friends look after my sisters while they went to the Moon, but it wasn't until they'd been there a few weeks that she discovered that she was pregnant."

"And she didn't go home?"

I shook my head. "By then she was well into her first trimester, and the doctors were unsure of how one-sixth gravity would affect my development. There'd been plenty of kids born on the Moon, but they'd never had a case like this before, where a woman is made pregnant on Earth but gives birth up there. The sonograms showed a normal fetus, but no one really knew how I'd turn out. So Mom and Dad talked it over, and in the end they decided that she'd stay on the Moon. If I had LBDS . . . which seemed pretty likely . . . she and I would remain in Apollo while Dad went home to pick up Jan and Melissa and sell the house."

"So your whole family was going to relocate to the Moon?"

"That was the plan, yeah." I nodded. "ISC offered Dad a permanent position as assistant general manager and Mom would've had a job in the life support division. They were still living in temporary quarters . . . one of the inflatable habs . . . but as soon as Apollo was finished, we would've moved into an apartment that had already been reserved for us. So they had everything figured out. And then . . ."

My voice trailed off, as it always did when I got to this part of the story. Which was why I usually avoided telling it. "Your mother was killed," Gordie said quietly.

"Yeah." I coughed to clear my throat. "I was about six weeks old when it happened. Mom and I were in the hab when some idiot outside who was messing around with a rover lost control of it. It crashed into the hab and broke the window of the room we were in. The inside doors started to shut, which is what I guess they're supposed to do when there's a blowout like that, and it happened so fast that Mom couldn't make it. But she had just enough time to throw me to someone who was standing just outside before the doors shut, and . . . well, that was it. She gave up her life to save mine."

"Damn." Gordie had a look on his face that I knew well: he didn't know what to say. "I'm sorry, Jamey. That's tough."

I had no memory of what had happened—hell, I didn't even know my mother—so all I could do was shrug. "Anyway, Dad hadn't yet gone back home to fetch my sisters, and after Mom died . . . well, that sort of took the wind out of the whole idea of moving my family to Apollo. By then it was clear that I had LBDS and that I'd never be able to walk on my own if I went to Earth, but Dad just didn't want to stay on the Moon. Fortunately, the doctors told him that I was healthy enough to survive the trip, so a couple of weeks later he took me . . . well, home."

"Uh-huh." Gordie was quiet for a few moments as he gazed out the cockpit window at the immense silver-grey sphere looming before us. "And you've never thought about coming back here? Until now, I mean?"

"No. Why would I?"

"Because you're a loony, that's why." A faint smile. "Maybe that's not how you think of yourself, but you should have seen the look on your face when you got up from your cocoon yesterday." He nodded toward the Moon. "That's your home, kiddo. Earth is just the place where you've been staying."

He was wrong, of course. I'd already pegged him as a hard-core space cadet, though, so I wasn't about to argue with him. "Whatever you say," I murmured. "I just know that Jan should have been aboard the shuttle when we took off. If it hadn't been for Hannah . . ."

"Leave her alone." Gordie's expression changed; a frown replaced the sympathetic smile. "There's a good reason for her to be here, and your sister did a very brave thing to give up her seat for her." He turned toward the console. "Don't let her sacrifice be for nothing."

I stared at him. "What are you . . . ?"

"Hey, look, I've got work to do." Gordie tapped his fingers against the keypad; diagrams and figures appeared on the right-hand screen. "Go grab a nap, okay?"

He clearly didn't want to talk anymore, so I left the cockpit and floated back into the passenger compartment. As I pulled myself toward my hammock, I moved past the other kids. Everyone else was still asleep, or at least so I thought until I passed Hannah. When I happened to look her way, I caught a glimpse of her face just in time to see her close her eyes.

She had been awake and listening to us.

* * *

The next day, we reached the Moon.

Just before the LTV began its primary approach, Gordie had us take down the hammocks and stow them away. We didn't unfold the seats, but instead held onto the ceiling rail. As he strapped himself into the cockpit seat, I positioned myself behind him so I could watch over his shoulder. I'd enjoyed my little taste of what it was like to fly a spacecraft, so it was interesting to watch a pro at work.

Gordie began by firing the reaction control rockets to make a 180 degree roll, turning the LTV end over end until it was traveling backward. That done, he fired the main engine in a succession of controlled bursts to gradually decelerate the craft, while at the same time coaxing the RCRs so that the LTV was on the correct trajectory for low-orbit insertion. Every time he did this, my body swung away from me as if I was a pendulum; my firm grip on the ceiling rail was all that kept me from sailing into the cockpit.

Gordie kept this up for about a half-hour or so until the LTV shed its velocity, then he rolled the craft again, bringing it back around until its bow once more pointed in the right direction. "Okay, you can let go now," he called back to us. "Take a look out the windows. You'll love it."

Logan and Eddie were on the port side, where the passenger windows faced away from the Moon. They immediately pushed themselves over to the starboard side, crowding in next to Melissa and Nina so that they could peer through the oval portholes as well. I barely noticed that Hannah had come up beside me until she grasped my shoulder. Maybe she'd only done this to steady herself, but I couldn't help but notice how close she was. I tried to ignore her—it wasn't easy, but I did my best—as we stared at what lay on the other side of the thick glass.

Until then, we'd seen the Moon only through the cockpit window, and then as a distant sphere that gradually became larger over the course of three long, boring days. Now, all of a sudden, it seemed as if it had become a vast, grey shield, so close that we could almost reach out and touch it.

We'd left Earth on the first night of a full moon. Three days later, the Sun still shined brightly upon the side of the Moon which always faced Earth, but the first thin shadows of the approaching two-week night were beginning to appear upon the mottled terrain slowly moving beneath us. The shadows cast in relief the lunar highlands, the dark grey lowlands of the maria, the dead volcanoes and impact craters scattered randomly across wastelands of rock and dust.

"Wow." Hannah's voice was an awestruck whisper. Her face was close to mine, and when I looked at her, I saw that her eyes were almost as wide as my own. "Just . . . wow."

"Yeah." My mouth was dry. "We're here. We're really here."

"Altitude 62.13 miles," Gordie said from the cockpit. "You should be able to see the Ptolemaeus crater coming up just about now. That's where Apollo is located."

A couple of seconds later, I spotted a cluster of tiny lights glimmering within a circular depression at the western edge of the highlands just south of the equator. The lights moved away too quickly for me to make out any details, but I knew I'd just had my first glimpse of our destination.

"Hey!" Melissa yelled from the other end of the passenger compartment. "We're going past it! Aren't we supposed to stay here until . . . y'know, someone picks us up?"

"We need to orbit the Moon first." Logan was hovering beside her. "Hohmann transfer orbit . . . right, Gordie?"

"Give the kid a star." Gordie sounded pleased with him. "Yeah, we have to swing around the far side and come back around before the ferry can rendezvous with us."

Apollo had already disappeared from sight; the LTV was moving across one of the darkened regions that people once thought were oceans before modern astronomers learned better. "Mare Nubium," Gordie said when I asked him which one this was. "The Sea of Clouds. That's where ISC has its regolith fields. If you look sharp, you might be able to see them from here."

Peering closer, I was able to make out a series of parallel strips running diagonally across the mare west of Ptolemaeus. Although obviously man-made, it was hard to believe that they were the principal source of Earth's energy reserves.

It took about an hour for the LTV to circle the Moon. We quietly gazed out the portholes as our craft's tiny shadow flitted across the vast expanse of Ocean Procellarum, the Ocean of Storms, until it reached cratered badlands east of the D'Alembert Mountains. Just beyond its peaks lay the point beyond which the lunar farside was invisible from Earth. We passed into night shortly after crossing the termination line, and suddenly the Moon was shrouded in darkness, save for a small cruciform of light in the middle of Mare Muscoviense that marked the location of the Lunar Radio Observatory. We had just crowded forward to peer over Gordie's shoulder and watch Earth rise over the limb of the Moon when the pilot clasped a hand to his headset.

"Pipe down," he murmured, then listened for a few moments before tapping his mike wand. "We copy, *Cernan*. LTV Six-Two on course for rendezvous and docking. See you in a few minutes. Over." Gordie reached forward to disengage the autopilot. "You kids need to go back now. We're on the beam for meeting up with our ferry, the *Eugene Cernan*."

"We don't need to raise the seats, do we?" I asked.

"No, not at all." Gordie grasped the hand controller. "Just hang tight and . . . um, stay out of the way when the Rangers come aboard."

The LTV was above Mare Undarum, the Sea of Waves, when the *Cernan* came into view. The ferry looked like little more than a toy at first, but it quickly grew in size, gaining detail as it came closer. Larger than the LTV, it had an octagonal lower hull from which four multijoined legs protruded around the bell-like nozzle of its nuclear main engine. Mounted atop the lower hull, two drum-shaped passenger modules rested lengthwise within their cradles; between them rose the turret of the command module, its bridge lined with windows. A flanged docking collar was affixed to its top like a weird beanie cap; radar dishes, oxygen tanks, and RCR pods stuck out at odd angles from every remaining space.

The *Cernan* slowly glided closer, its thrusters flaring now and then as its pilots corrected course. Through the bridge windows, I spotted two crewmen seated on either side of the cockpit, occasionally glancing up to see what we were doing. Gordie was just as busy as they were; constantly muttering into his headset, he guided the LTV in a delicate docking maneuver that brought its dorsal hatch into alignment with the ferry's docking collar. It seemed to take forever, but finally there was a jar and a thump as the collar's flanges grabbed hold of the LTV's dorsal hatch.

"Docking complete, *Cernan*." Gordie reached up to snap a row of toggle switches. "Putting all systems on standby, waiting for your entry."

One by one, the dashboard lights went out. Gordie re-engaged the autopilot, then unbuckled his harness and pulled himself out of the cockpit. Floating over to the ceiling hatch, he unlatched a recessed bar and cranked it up and down several times, pumping air into the collar. He waited until the light next to it changed from red to green, then banged his fist twice against the inside of the hatch. A minute passed, then two knocks answered him from the other side.

"Stand clear," he said as he reached up to turn the lockwheel counterclockwise. The hatch opened from the inside and Gordie peered through it. "Hey, look who's here . . . my favorite Ranger!"

"Hi, Gordie!" The voice that came down the hatch was young, enthusiastic, and female. "Long time, no see. Permission to board?"

"Of course . . . you have to ask?" Gordie pulled himself away from the hatch. "C'mon in. Meet my friends."

A couple of soft bumping sounds, then a girl came head-first through the tunnel formed by the two docked spacecraft. She wore what I'd later learn was called a skinsuit—a form-fitting pressure suit designed for short-term use in orbital conditions, and therefore not as heavy as lunar gear—which showed off a slender figure.

She wasn't wearing a helmet, so the first thing I noticed was her hair: a thin, blonde strip that ran from the top of her forehead back to the nape of her neck, with nothing but bare skin on either side. I'd seen mohawks before, but never on a girl. She was also tall; easily six feet, with maybe an inch or two to spare. At first I thought she was a full-grown woman, but when she turned toward us, I realized that she wasn't any older than Melissa, Logan, or me. And there was a small tattoo on her cheek: a crescent moon framed by a pair of angel's wings, identical to a mission patch sewn on the skinsuit's right shoulder.

Our eyes met, and I felt my heart skip a beat. Mohawk and tattoo notwithstanding, she was one of the prettiest girls I'd ever seen. She smiled back at me, amusement glittering in her pale green eyes.

"What's the matter?" she asked. "Never met a loony before?"

Before I could manage a reply, another voice came through the tunnel. "Clear hatch . . . I'm coming through."

The girl didn't respond, but instead grabbed hold of the ceiling rail and pulled herself further into the cabin. I tried to make room for her, but my legs drifted upward and got in her way. Her smile faded a little as she pushed me aside. "Guess not," she murmured, answering her own question.

"Allow me to introduce you." Gordie turned toward me and the others. "This is Nicole Doyle, Ranger Second Class, Lunar Search and Rescue." Nicole nodded as he pointed to each of his passengers in turn. "This is Jamey . . . that's his sister Melissa . . . over there are Eduardo and Nina, also brother and sister . . . and that's Logan . . . and this is Hannah."

Gordie was still naming us when another kid in a skinsuit came through the hatch. He was about the same age as Nicole and also about the same height; his dark hair was cut in an absurd bowl that lacked sideburns and had only a fuzzy fringe at the nape of his neck. He also had the winged moon symbol tattooed above his right eye. No welcoming smile, though. Instead, he regarded us as if he'd just come aboard the LTV and found it filled with rats.

"Great . . . just excellent." There was no pleasure in his voice as he turned to Gordie. "This is what you've brought us?"

"Billy . . ." Nicole glared at him.

"William Tate, Ranger Third Class . . ." Gordie began.

"*Second* Class." Billy gave Gordie a sour look. "Promoted last month."

"Oh, *really?* Finally managed to complete your walkabout, did you? Your second try, or your third?"

Billy's face went red, and Eddie laughed out loud even though he couldn't have possibly known what Gordie was talking about any more than I did. Billy's hostile glare told me that he'd just marked Eddie; I'd seen that sort of look before, usually from bullies.

"Glad to meet all of you." Nicole's smile returned; forced, perhaps, but nonetheless it could have thawed an ice cube. She looked at Gordie. "Are you ready?"

Gordie nodded, and I glanced at the hatch. "Are we going to need to put on suits?" I asked.

Yeah, it was a dumb question. I should have known better. Nicole only shook her head, but Billy wasn't nearly as forgiving. "You kidding?" he asked, his mouth curling into a sneer. "You'll never wear a suit . . . you're too retarded."

The cabin temperature seemed to drop ten degrees, the abrupt silence broken only by Nina's angry hiss. I didn't respond, but only because anything I might have said would have insulted Eddie. But just as Billy had marked me, I marked him.

That's one I owe you, pal, I thought.

Gordie coughed into his fist. "Anyway . . . let's get aboard the ferry before we lose our landing window. If you will follow me . . ."

Without another word, he reached into a ceiling net and retrieved his duffel bag, then pulled himself through the hatch. Billy followed him, but Nicole stayed behind to help the passengers. Although I was the closest to the hatch, I lingered in the LTV after I pulled down my bag, letting the others go first. I told myself that I was being courteous, but the truth of the matter was that I wanted to stay with Nicole. Melissa must have figured this out, because she smirked and rolled her eyes as she moved past me. Hannah gave me a sour look, but didn't say anything.

With Nicole bringing up the rear, I pushed myself through the docking collar into the ferry cockpit. Two pilots were seated at wraparound consoles on either side of a floor hatch. The pilot barely looked up at me as I came aboard. "Go on through," he said, waving me to the hatch. "Nicole, close up behind you."

"Aye, skipper." She turned to swing shut the LTV hatch. I pushed myself across the compartment until I was through the floor hatch. On the other side was a vertical access shaft, its walls lined with rungs, leading straight down the center of the turret. At the bottom were two horizontal hatches, one on either side of the shaft. Gordie was hovering in the hatchway of the one to the left, and I saw Billy's legs disappear through the hatch of one to the right.

"In here, Jamey," Gordie said, and I was only too happy to obey; I didn't want to have to ride down with Billy. I followed Gordie through the hatch and found myself in one of the ferry's two passenger modules. Its five fold-down seats were similar to the LTV's; not nearly as well-cushioned, but at least they were equipped with safety harnesses. They faced a pair of rectangular portholes. Nina and Eddie were already strapped in, their bags tucked into ceiling nets above their heads, when I took the seat next to them. Gordie put away his bag and mine, then waited at the hatch, and a minute later Nicole entered the module.

"Saved a place for you, kiddo." Gordie waved her to the seat on the other side of mine. "Did you button up the LTV?"

"Of course." Nicole pulled herself into the seat beside me and fastened its harness. "I also shut the LTV hatch, so don't worry about . . ."

Three bells rang from a ceiling speaker. Gordie had just enough time to strap himself down next to her before there was a sudden jolt. Eddie yelped in alarm and Nina hastily took his hand to comfort him. Through the portholes, I caught a glimpse of the LTV gliding away.

"You're leaving the LTV here?" I asked. "Aren't you afraid it's going to crash?"

"Nope." Gordie shook his head. "It's in a stable parking orbit . . . at least for the next nine months or so, which is about how long it'll take gravity to pull it down. But it won't be there that long. By then, it'll be refueled, restocked, and sent back to Earth with another load of passengers." He shrugged. "Maybe even you guys . . . although I'm not sure I'd count on it."

"You think it's that serious? I mean, what's going on back home?"

Nicole looked at me. "You haven't heard?"

"Heard what? We haven't received any messages since we left."

"My fault," Gordie said. "I was under instructions to maintain radio silence when we rendezvoused with the *Cernan*. We needed to keep ISC ground control from knowing exactly where we were and who was aboard."

"What's happening back there?" Nina asked.

"A lot." Nicole let out her breath. "President Shapar made a statement saying that President Wilford was murdered by a Chinese assassin who'd managed to sneak into the White House . . ."

"They're claiming the PSU is behind this?" Gordie asked.

"Uh-huh. She said the Secret Service shot and killed the assassin, but not before he got to the president. She also said that the Secret Service and FBI think he wasn't acting alone, and so she's ordered the military to take control of the Capitol and instructed federal marshals to apprehend anyone who may be involved."

Including my father, I thought, even though I knew that he didn't have anything to do with President Wilford's death. "What about his family?" Gordie asked. "His wife and daughter . . . did they say anything about them?"

Nicole was quiet for a moment. "They're in protective custody," she said at last. "The Secret Service has taken them to some undisclosed location where they'll be safe."

"That's a lie," Nina said.

I stared at her. Sure, she he was smarter than a girl her age ought to be, but how would she know that? Yet she seemed utterly positive in what she'd just said.

"How do you . . . ?" I began.

"Look at the Moon!" Eddie yelled. "We're falling!"

Through the portholes, the Moon had become a flat landscape slightly curved at its ends, its mountains, rills, and craters rushing toward us. "No, we're not," Nicole said, and a second later we heard the muted rumble of the ferry's main engine. "We're just on primary approach, that's all."

"We won't crash, Eddie." Nina clasped her brother's hand a little more tightly. "See? The rocket's firing. We'll be landing in just a little bit."

"Um . . . yeah, that's right. Nothing to worry about at all." Nicole glanced at me and silently mouthed a word: *slow?* It wasn't the word I would have used, but I nodded and she winced. "Sorry about Billy," she said quietly. "What he said, I mean. He can be a jerk sometimes."

Sometimes? So far as I could tell, being a jerk was a full-time job for him. "Hasn't changed since he made Second Class, I see," Gordie murmured, folding his arms across his chest. "I would've thought Luis would've straightened him out by now."

"Yeah, well . . ." Nicole shrugged. "Mr. Garcia's been working on him. I think that's why he sent Billy and me on this mission . . . to give us an assignment with some extra responsibility." Then she smiled at me. "You and your friends are in the hands of the Rangers." She pointed to the patch on her shoulder, and I noticed the inscription at the bottom. "'Failure is not an option' . . . that's our motto."

"The Rangers?"

"That's what they call Lunar Search and Rescue." Gordie said. "They do a lot more than just that, though. Sort of a team of all-purpose troubleshooters . . . including defense, if it ever becomes necessary."

"If you mean taking on Moon Dragon, that'll never happen." Nicole shook her head. "The PSU isn't bothering us and we aren't bothering them."

She sounded confident, but I wasn't so sure. If President Wilford had been assassinated by a Chinese agent, then it sounded to me like another war with the Pacific Socialist Union was inevitable. The China Sea War was before my time, but I'd learned in history class that it had ended only after the Third Treaty of Saigon brought an end to Taiwan's bid for independence and gave China permanent territorial control of the island. Relations between the PSU and the rest of the world had been frosty ever since, but at least neither side was back to sinking the other guy's ships. Reactionaries like Lina Shapar were aching for a rematch, though, and President Wilford's death might give them the excuse they wanted.

Another prolonged rumble from the main engine caused me to look out the windows again. The Moon was very close; the ferry was no longer gliding above its surface, but appeared to be in vertical descent. "We'll be down soon," Nicole said, then glanced at Nina and Eddie. "You might want to check your harnesses. The pilots usually give us a smooth ride, but the landing might be a little bumpy."

It didn't occur to me until then that, over the past few minutes, I'd been gradually feeling just a little heavier. Not nearly as much as I did on Earth, but nonetheless the weightlessness I'd experienced over the last three days was going away. When I experimentally moved my legs, though, I had no trouble bending my knees or wiggling my feet. Sure, this was only one-sixth Earth gravity, but still . . .

"You're not going to have any trouble walking." Gordie had noticed what I was doing. "No more than Nicole does, or Billy either."

"Why would he . . . ? Nicole began, and then she stopped to stare at me. "Oh, my God . . . are you the one? The one who was born here, I mean?"

I nodded. It didn't seem like such a big deal, yet Nicole was astonished. "Oh, man," she breathed. "We'd heard you might be coming up, but I didn't know . . ."

"Yup. That's him." Gordie's grin couldn't have been any wider. "Jamey Barlowe . . . the man, the myth, the legend."

My mouth fell open. "*Wha-a-a-a-t?*"

Anything else Gordie or Nicole might have said was forgotten in the next instant. The ferry's main engine fired, louder and longer than ever before, as a vibration passed through the spacecraft and caused the deck the tremble beneath my feet. Lunar gravity, distinct but not uncomfortable, pulled me into my seat. I gripped the armrests and watched through the windows as the rocky grey terrain rose up from below. A quick, hard jolt, and then the engine noise abruptly ceased.

We had landed on the Moon.

SECOND PHASE
CITY ON THE MOON

6.
APOLLO

If you go outside on a clear night toward the end of the month, you can see the Man in the Moon. He gapes at you with a wide-eyed expression that can be interpreted any number of ways—surprise, jollity, disbelief—and his mouth is open as if to laugh, scream, or simply say hello. And if you have a good pair of binoculars, you can look to the right side of his mouth and make out a small dimple on his pock-marked face. The mouth is Mare Nubrium, and the dimple is Ptolemaeus crater—pronounced "toll mouse," with a slight *ptt* sound at the beginning—the remnants of an extinct volcano partially filled by lava flows. In the upper right side of Ptolemaeus is a smaller crater, Ammonius, which was formed by an ancient meteor impact.

That's where Apollo was located.

When NASA sent the first men to the Moon, no one seriously thought they'd find anything other than rocks, rocks, and more rocks. For a while, that seemed to be the case; people thought the Moon was just a big ball of dust and stone, an interesting place to visit but where no one in their right mind would want to live. After the final Apollo expedition in 1972, nobody returned to the Moon for more than fifty years. What was the point of colonizing a dead world?

However, when geologists examined the samples of surface dust—or regolith, to use the technical term, since it's essentially powdered rock that doesn't contain the organic compounds that define soil—brought back by the Apollo astronauts, they discovered that the Moon wasn't as useless as first believed. The regolith contained ilmenite—a compound of iron, titanium, silicon, and oxygen—that could be extracted and used to build a self-sufficient lunar colony. Robotic probes sent in the early 21st century confirmed the presence of thorium and phosphorus; these rare-earth elements had become strategic resources in the 21st century, particularly since the countries in which they were most abundant tended to have dicey relations with the United States. And the discovery of subsurface ice in the south polar craters showed that the Moon had the resources to make inhabitation possible.

But the bonanza was helium-3.

An isotope that comes straight from the Sun itself as a byproduct of the fusion reactions that causes the stars to shine, He^3 is carried across space by the solar wind. Because most of it burns up in Earth's upper atmosphere before it can reach the ground, it's very rare on our world. There's no air on the Moon, though, so He^3 is relatively abundant there, particularly in the equatorial regions where it resides within the regolith as a thin layer.

On one hand, you need to process approximately 275,000 tons of regolith to extract about two pounds of He^3. On the other, even such a small amount makes it the perfect fuel for nuclear fusion. Once combined with deuterium and fed into a fusion reactor, two pounds of He^3 can generate 100 million kilowatt-hours of electricity while producing virtually no radioactive waste.

At first, few people took lunar helium-3 seriously. That changed when oil reserves began to run low at the same time as global energy consumption was increasing, and the effort of getting what little oil remained carried with it war, terrorism, and environmental destruction. The costs of mining He^3 and transporting it to Earth were considered prohibitively high until several countries, led by the United States and the European Union, combined their national space programs to establish a multinational public corporation, the International Space Consortium.

Apollo was the result. A city on the Moon, its main industry the mining and export of helium-3 and other materials, chartered by and belonging to the American, European, and Asian countries that contributed to its construction. The Pacific Socialist Union—China, the United Korean Republic, Vietnam, and Taiwan—followed suit with their own lunar mining colony, Moon Dragon, located in Mare Nectaris. The China Sea War prompted the PSU to go it alone; the United States and its allies still distrusted China, but so long as they stayed in their corner of the Moon, no one minded if they got their share of the goodies.

Lunar He^3 helped usher in a new era of global prosperity that brought an end to the years of turmoil that had defined the first decades of the century. But Vice President Shapar—it was still hard to think of her as *President* Shapar—and her cronies had their own agenda.

Which is why I found myself returning to the place where I was born.

* * *

From the north landing field, Apollo looked different than it did from space. It took a little while for the regolith kicked up by the ferry engines to settle, so all we saw through a grey, dusty mist was a vast wall so long that its curved sides disappeared below the visible horizon. About five and half miles in diameter, Ammonius was covered by a shallow dome that resembled an upended saucer; a narrow, band-like atrium stretched around its upper surface. Light gleamed from tiny windows set within the crater walls, the only obvious indication of its enormous size. The place was *huge*; even the small forest of antennas that stood near the dirt road leading to it were dwarfed.

My first sight of Ammonius was impressive enough to make me forget what Gordie had said to me just before the *Cernan* touched down. It wasn't enough, though, to make me overlook a small miracle. I unbuckled my seat harness, hesitated for a moment, then took a deep breath and . . . stood up.

No pain, and my legs didn't give way beneath me. Sure, I'd already done this aboard the LTV, but that was while wearing stick-shoes in zero-g; a quadriplegic could have performed the same feat.

But this was lunar gravity, one-sixth that of Earth's, and not only was I standing on my own, but . . .

I carefully took a step forward, then another. Yes. I was able to walk.

I didn't know whether to laugh, cry, or join the nearest basketball team. I settled for staring down at my feet and forgetting for a second or two that I was able to do this only because I was 240,000 miles from home. I was still giggling under my breath when Eddie asked, "What's so funny, Jamey?"

"Never mind." Gordie unfastened his harness and stood up to place a hand on my shoulder. "You okay? Not having any problems, are you?"

"No, I . . . whoops!" I'd turned around too quickly and tripped over my own feet; he caught me before I fell over. Sure, I was able to walk, but the coordination that comes with learning *how* to walk was something I'd have to work on. In any case, I wasn't ready to try out for the varsity team.

"Take it easy until you get used to it." Gordie made sure I was steady, then looked over at Eddie and Nina. "That goes for you two as well. Until we get some ankle weights, you're going to have to be careful. So look before you step."

Nina quietly nodded, but Eddie didn't understand. "Why?" he asked as he unsnapped his harness and stood up. "I can . . . *ow!*"

He'd gotten up a little too fast. His feet left the deck as if he'd jumped, and he banged the top of his head against the low ceiling. He winced and doubled over, and as Nicole darted forward to help, there was an unkind laugh from behind us.

"Yeah, dummy," said Billy, peering in through the hatch. "Watch where you're going."

Despite my own clumsiness, I angrily turned toward him. Nicole beat me to it. "Don't *ever* call him that again!" she hissed, her eyes narrow with anger as she put an arm protectively around Eddie's shoulders. "Never! Do you understand?"

Billy stopped grinning. He disappeared from the hatch. I caught a brief glimpse of Melissa; she'd been standing behind him and had heard the whole thing, and it was obvious that she was just as shocked as I was. Even she had learned not to make fun of Eddie.

Gordie slowly let out his breath. "Maybe everyone should just sit down and wait until the bus gets here," he murmured.

Good advice, but I wasn't ready to take it. Indeed, I didn't think I'd ever want to sit down again. Careful not to repeat Eddie's mistake, I stepped closer to the portholes. Figures approached the ferry; they wore moonsuits, and two of them dragged a thick hose from a caterpillar-treaded vehicle with a fuel tank at its rear. While they attached the hose to an intake valve on the ferry's lower hull, a third man slowly walked around the spacecraft, helmet visor lowered against the solar glare as he conducted a visual inspection.

I was still watching the ground crew when another vehicle came down the nearby road. Larger than the tanker, it resembled a subway car mounted atop six enormous, overinflated tires. It came to a halt nearby, then slowly began to move backward toward the ferry, with one of the ground crew raising his arms to guide the driver into position. The bus had an accordion-like docking hatch at its rear, and its car slowly elevated until that it was the same height as the *Cernan's* upper hull. A few moments later there was a muffled thump as the bus mated with the ferry.

"All right, then," Nicole said. "Everyone get their bags and follow me." She stepped over to the compartment hatch and looked through it. "Billy, why don't you go up top and see how the pilots are doing?"

Billy apparently didn't get the hint, because he started to argue with her. Nicole repeated the request, an edge in her voice this time, and a second later I heard Billy's boots clanging up the ladder to the cockpit. *Good riddance,* I thought as I pulled my bag down from the ceiling net. Billy Tate was someone I hoped I'd seldom see again.

Once the airlock was pressurized, Nicole opened the hatch and led us from the ferry, moving single-file through the short accordion tunnel and into the bus. It was about the same size as the LTV, with padded benches beneath thick-paned windows. A heavy-set guy sat up front in the driver's seat; when he turned around to look back at us, I saw that the name patch on his skinsuit read TOLLEY. Nicole waited until we were seated and had pushed our bags beneath the benches, then Tolley opened an overhead compartment and pulled out a plastic bag filled with what appeared to be thick, padded bracelets.

"Take two of these and fasten them around your ankles," he said, passing the bag to us. "They'll keep you from bouncing around when you walk."

It was hard to tell how much the anklets weighed; I guessed they were about twenty pounds each, although in lunar gravity they were only a fraction of that. I clamped one around each ankle, then experimented by standing up again and taking a couple of steps. It felt strange to have bracelets around my ankles, and when I noticed that Nicole didn't put on a pair, I wondered if I really needed them either. After all, it wasn't as if I'd spent a lifetime walking in Earth-normal gravity. I decided to err on the side of caution, though, or at least until I was sure that I wouldn't make a fool out of myself.

Once everyone had put on their ankle weights, Nicole asked Gordie to close the rear hatch. Once that was done, Tolley retracted the accordion, put the bus in gear, and moved forward, stopping for a minute to lower the bus to its normal position.

Logan was sitting beside me, with Melissa on my other side. "How did you like the ride down?" I asked them as we waited for the bus to start moving again.

"Great," Logan said, "except for Ace Starhunter."

I smiled, catching the allusion to the hero of the space adventure game he and I liked to play. "Yeah, I hear you," I said. "He's got some kind of attitude."

"If you're talking about Billy . . . really, he's not that bad." Nicole was seated across from us. "Once you get to know him, I mean."

"I hope I don't," Melissa muttered. That surprised me; I would have thought Billy Tate was her type: good-looking, arrogant, full of himself. Apparently he was too rotten even for her. "Please tell me we won't see much of him."

Nicole shook her head. "I can't promise that. There's only a dozen guys our age in the whole colony, and less than forty kids total. So you'll see everyone in school . . . and more often than that, depending on which Colony Service team you join." I started to ask what she meant by that when the bus started moving again. "I'll explain later," she said. "Me, or someone else. As a matter of fact . . ."

Nicole abruptly got up and walked to the front of the bus. She bent down to the driver and said something to him. Tolley nodded and Nicole returned to her seat. "We've got about an hour before we're supposed to meet the city manager, so I asked Ed to give us a quick drive around so we can get familiar with this place. Is that okay with you?"

I had no problems with that and neither did anyone else, so when the bus reached the end of the graded dirt road the driver turned to the right. I spotted an intersection sign: North Field Road was the way we'd just come, and now we were on Collins Avenue. To the left was a short road leading straight to the crater, but we didn't go that way but instead headed north.

As the bus trundled up the road, I saw what appeared to be a long row of giant, rectangular mirrors pointed toward Ammonius. They appeared to surround the crater as a ring; each mirror was independently mounted on swivels and elevated about ten feet above the ground, their polished sides pointed toward the top of the crater dome.

"Those are reflectors," Nicole said when I asked her what they were. "During the two-week day, they capture sunlight and point it toward the sun window." She pointed toward the circular window that surrounded the top of the dome. "There's another mirror that bounces the light down into the solarium on the crater floor. The mirrors are set to automatically move during a twenty-four-hour cycle, and that gives us sunrises and sunsets, just like on Earth."

"What about at night?" Logan asked. "That lasts two weeks, too."

"When we don't get any sun, the solarium is lit by florescent ceiling lamps. They operate on a twenty-four-hour cycle, too."

"That's stupid." Melissa was sitting beside Nicole; she gazed at the reflector ring with disbelief. "Why go to all that trouble? They could have just built the dome out of glass and let the sun shine straight in."

"The Moon doesn't have an atmosphere," Nicole said patiently. "That means there's nothing to protect us from cosmic radiation. You don't have to worry about that on Earth, but radiation overexposure can be deadly up here. So the dome is covered by several inches of regolith except for the windows. That shields us while the mirrors collect sunlight from outside. See?"

Melissa scowled and folded her arms across her chest. She didn't like to be made to feel like an idiot, but it served her right; Nicole was her age, but twice as smart and a Ranger as well. I hid my smile behind my hand. I had a feeling that my sister wasn't going to get away with goofing off at school here.

By then the bus had reached the end of Collins Avenue. Another signpost showed the way to Loop Road on the left and Krantz Avenue on the right. Just before the bus turned onto Loop Road, Nicole pointed out the long black rows of the solar farm and the adjacent dome of the fusion reactor, located just off Krantz Avenue. "Two weeks of the month, we get our power from the sun," she said. "The other two weeks, we get it from that little tokamok over there. We've also got hydrogen storage cells under the city to provide us with electricity if either one of those goes down. So energy is the least of our worries."

Loop Road led us back toward Ammonius. Across the road from the crater was a row of large hemispherical domes. A huge tandem rover, twice the length of our bus and with a open-top trailer riding on six balloon-like wheels, was parked near the closest of them. A chute had been lowered from its back end and two workers in moon-suits were using long-handled rakes to push regolith down the chute and through an open door in the dome wall.

"Here's the industrial park," Nicole said. "Each of those domes is a part of a refinery that processes the ore collected from the regolith fields and extracts helium-3, ilmenite, rare earths, even trace amounts of oxygen and hydrogen . . . everything we can possibly get." She gave us a significant look. "This is Apollo's cash cow. Without it, we wouldn't be here."

"And wouldn't Lina Shapar love to get her hands on that," Logan said softly. Hannah remained quiet, but she nodded in agreement.

"Why are the fields all the way out in Mare Nubium?" I asked. "That's a long way from here, isn't it?"

"About a hundred and sixty miles, yeah. On the other side of the crater walls. There's not quite so much helium-3 here in Ptolemaeus as there is in the mare, though, and we have to go through a lot of regolith to get even just a little He^3. But the main reason is that the harvesters kick up a lot of dust, and that's a major problem for us. Regolith may look soft, but it's really abrasive, and it causes a problem when it gets through the airlocks. So putting the mining operations at a distance from the colony helps us keep it under control."

Melissa eyed another truck as it slowly passed us on Loop Road. "So you have sent these things all the way out there just to get a load of dirt? That's . . ."

"The way things are done." Nicole gave her an annoyed look, and then smiled. "If you have any suggestions, you might take it up with the city manager when you see him. I'm sure he'd love to hear them."

Another patented MeeMee scowl, then Melissa turned her head away. Logan and I shared a grin but said nothing. Jan couldn't have done a better job of making my sister shut up.

The bus continued along Loop Road as it turned south, heading for Apollo's western side. We came upon two domed pits, each a fraction of the size of Ammonius. Near them was an open pit, the horizontal boom of a rotary excavator slowly moving within it. "Those are the agricultural domes," Nicole explained. "The farms, we call 'em. Most of our crops are raised there, and we're building a third one now."

"I thought you farmed in the crater, too," I said.

"Mainly grass and shade trees for oxygen production. We also raise some livestock for meat . . . goats and chickens, mainly. Apollo is almost entirely self-sufficient. Once Ag Dome 3 is finished, there won't be much we'll still have to import from Earth except for electronics, replacement machines . . . and, of course, people."

"I think you're well on your way to growing your own people, too," Gordie said, a sly smile upon his face. "You're a native, aren't you?"

"Uh-huh . . . I'm a loony, born and raised." Nicole hesitated. "But I'd like to visit Earth one day, if I can," she added wistfully.

Until then, it hadn't occurred to me that she might not have ever set foot on the world I called home. Glancing out the window, I saw Earth hovering above Ptolemaeus's southern rim, and wondered if it was as exotic to her as the Moon was to me.

The bus continuing moving east along Loop Road, passing the turn-off for Miner's Road, which Nicole told us led toward the gap the trucks passed through to reach Mare Nubium. A short distance later, we came upon the southern end of Collins Avenue, where the cargo landing field was located. After passing short roads leading to warehouses and depots, once again we found ourselves at the intersection of North Field Road, where we'd begun our tour of Apollo.

The driver turned left and the bus rolled toward Ammonius. It slowed down as it entered a ramp that had been excavated just beneath the crater wall. At the end of the ramp were a pair of large, tiger-striped doors. Tolley brought our vehicle to a halt and waited for the doors to open, then drove into a large room with a grated metal floor and a similar pair of doors at its opposite end. The outer doors closed behind us; the driver shut down the engine, folded his arms across his chest, and waited.

"Why are we stopping?" Eddie asked.

"This is a vehicle airlock," Nicole said. "Before it can be pressurized, we have to be decontaminated . . . ah, here it comes now."

Through the windows, we watched as massive rollers, much like those in automatic car washes on Earth but covered with hairy black bristles, descended from the ceiling. They silently moved across the top and sides of the bus, dislodging the moon dust that covered the vehicle. As they did, there was a dull roar from outside, like that of a giant vacuum cleaner.

"The scrubbers are magnetized," Gordie said, pointing to the rollers, "but they can't gather all the dust that's settled on the bus. So an exhaust system floods the chamber with nitrogen gas, which picks up the rest and sucks it away."

"We have to do this every time a vehicle enters Apollo," Nicole added. "Same for anyone who goes out on the surface in a pressure suit. There's smaller airlocks for individuals, but they operate on much the same principle."

For a minute or two, it was as if the bus was caught in the middle of a miniature cyclone; we couldn't see much through the windows except a swirling grey cloud. But the artificial dust storm quickly dissipated, and as it did, I heard a roaring sound that gradually increased in volume. Now that the bus was clean, the airlock was being pressurized.

When the pressurization cycle ended, the doors at the far end of the airlock opened. Tolley restarted the bus, and for the first time we could hear the rumble of its tires and the dull squeak of its chassis as it moved into an underground garage. Buses, rovers, and other vehicles I couldn't immediately identify were parked alongside one another, electrical power cables leading from them to recharger units in the walls. Our bus backed into an empty space between two other buses. The driver shut down the engine again, then stood up and turned to us.

"Okay, we're here," he said, the first time he'd spoken to us since we'd come aboard. "That'll be ten lunes, please."

"What are lunes?" I asked, pronouncing the same way he had, as *loons*.

"The local currency." Gordie stood up from his seat. "Don't mind Squid. He used to be a petty officer in the Navy before he moved here. Those guys are always cheap . . ."

"Hey!" Tolley gave him a mock scowl. "Watch the mouth, flyboy!"

Gordie ignored him as he headed for the rear hatch. "C'mon, grab your stuff."

I pulled my bag from beneath the seat and followed him to the hatch, the others falling in behind us. The hatch was opened from the outside by a guy wearing a dirty pair of overalls. As I climbed down the stepladder he'd pushed into place, my nose caught a strong, somewhat familiar odor.

I wasn't the only one who noticed. "I smell gunpowder," Nina said. "Did someone light a firecracker?"

"That's moondust." Gordie was waiting for us at the bottom of the ladder. "The scrubbers can't quite get all of it out of here, so don't touch anything. There's strict rules against bringing this stuff into the dome."

Indeed, the garage reeked like the aftermath of a Fourth of July fireworks show. Melissa made an icky face, and Eddie sneezed and rubbed his nose on his shirt sleeve, but I thought it was pretty neat. *The Moon smells like gunpowder*, I thought. *No one ever told me that!*

Once everyone disembarked from the bus, Nicole escorted us across to a nearby elevator. She waved a hand across a wall panel; its doors opened, and once we'd all crowded in, she pushed a button marked CR1.

"The city manager is supposed to be meeting us topside," she explained as the doors slid shut and the elevator began to ascend. An exhaust fan beneath the gridded floor activated, sucking away what little regolith had managed to adhere to the soles of our shoes.

"Good." Gordie nodded. "I'm going to need to talk to him about staying here awhile." His mouth narrowed into a tight smile. "I don't think I'm going to be welcome back home any time soon."

Nicole said nothing, but there was a sympathetic look in her eyes. I was still reflecting upon the fact that our pilot was one more person who'd made a sacrifice to get me to safety when the elevator came to a halt.

Its doors opened again, and we walked out into what appeared to be an ordinary airport security area. The wall sign read CUSTOMS. A guy in a blue uniform was seated at a desk and a woman in an identical uniform stood behind a nearby counter. Nicole told us to put our bags on the counter, and as the woman began to open them one at a time and sort through our belongings, we lined up at the desk.

Gordie reached into a pocket, pulled out a leather card holder, and flashed something at the customs official. He waved the pilot through without comment, then motioned to me. "Name?" he asked once I'd stepped up.

"Jamey Barlowe . . . James Y. Barlowe, I mean."

"Age?"

"Sixteen."

"Citizenship?"

"American . . . USA, I mean."

"Reason for visiting?"

"Umm . . ." I wasn't sure how to answer that. Before I could say anything, though, Nicole walked around to his side of the desk. Pulling a folded sheet of paper from her pocket, she placed it before him, then bent down to whisper something in his ear. The customs official listened without saying a word; a quick nod of understanding, then he looked at me and the others.

"You're all cleared through on special recognizance," he said. "Your guardians will be required to file immigration requests within the next forty-eight hours. Until then, you're free to go." He turned to his companion and shook his head; she stopped searching our bags and zipped them shut.

Grateful for the rescue, but mystified nonetheless, I picked up my bag and followed Gordie and Nicole through the doorway past the counter. "What was that all about?" I asked when we were out of earshot from the customs officers.

"The city manager's office is aware of your situation." Nicole held up the paper she'd shown the guy at the desk; I didn't have a chance to read it, but it had an official-looking seal and signature at the bottom. "Essentially, the six of you have been granted temporary visas until your immigration status is worked out."

"We're immigrants?" Logan asked.

Gordie nodded as Nicole led us down a short corridor to a pair of glass double-doors. "Yup . . . and so am I, or at least until I upgrade my residency permit from part-time to permanent."

I nodded, even though I didn't quite believe him. Officially, we might be immigrants, but all the same, I knew better. We were outcasts.

* * *

We reached the double doors. Nicole held one open for me, and when I walked through, I had my first good look at Apollo.

We stood on a veranda of a balcony on the lowest tier of the crater rim. The tier went all the way around the inside of the crater; two more tiers above it slanted upward toward the bottom of the dome, where sunlight shined brightly from the giant mirror at its apex. The tiers overlooked the crater solarium; over four miles in diameter, it was so vast that I could barely see its tiered walls on the opposite side.

I'd seen pictures of Apollo, of course. It was often described as one of the great wonders of the century. But holos are one thing, and seeing the place with my own eyes was quite another. The solarium resembled nothing less than an urban park at the bottom of an immense bowl. Groves of small shade trees—dwarf maple, sycamore, pine— were clustered around pebble paths, while benches and gazebos were arranged beside broad, fresh-cut lawns. Foot paths led between small cottage-like buildings scattered here and there; just below was what appeared to be a livestock pen, with goats grazing within a nearby meadow. People strolled along gravel walkways; I spotted someone on a bicycle pedal past a couple walking hand in hand beside a small pond. There were even birds in the trees; a robin landed to the veranda railing, gave me a quick once-over, then flitted away.

If I hadn't known that I was on the Moon, I would have sworn that I was back on Earth. Even Melissa, as jaded as she was, was impressed "Wow," she murmured. "I mean . . . y'know . . . wow."

"Yeah." Logan was also wide-eyed. "I've seen the vids, but . . ."

"Uh-huh." Gordie seemed to be enjoying our reactions. "It always gets me, too. No place quite like it."

I was still staring at the solarium when a handful of adults—two men and two women—came up a nearby stairway. The oldest of the four was a tall, dark-skinned man in his mid-fifties; he approached our group and stopped before Nicole and Gordie.

"Ms. Doyle, I take it that these are our guests?" he asked, and she nodded. "Good, very good," he said, then turned to Gordie. "And Captain Rogers . . . thank you for bringing them here. We're in your debt."

"I'll remember that, Loren," Gordie replied, and the other man's smile flickered a bit. "Let me introduce you to . . ."

"Allow me, please." The gentleman stepped closer to us. "I'm Loren Porter, Apollo's city manager. And these are—" he gestured to each of his companions "—Algis Lagler, our life support supervisor, Mary Rice, the chief of surgery at Apollo General Hospital, and Karl Ernsting, also on the staff of Apollo General. They'll be your legal guardians while you're with us."

The three of them smiled and murmured greetings. They appeared pleasant enough, but there was still an awkward moment; we kids were meeting our surrogate parents for the first time, and no one seemed to know exactly what to make of each other. I was still trying to figure out who was going with who when Mr. Lagler walked over to my sister and me.

"You're Melissa and Jamey?" A short, thick-set man with a trim goatee, he had a European accent that I'd later learn was Hungarian. "My wife and I are happy to be your guardians." A pause while Melissa and I took this in; we nodded, and he went on. "We know your father well, and your mother used to work in my department. Jamey, you've grown considerably since the last time I saw you."

"Umm . . ." I didn't quite know what to say to this. "I guess so, sir. Thank you."

Melissa was even more uncomfortable than I was, but for once she kept her mouth shut. From the corner of my eye, I saw Dr. Rice introducing herself to Eddie and Nina while Logan shook hands with Dr. Ernsting.

That left only Hannah. As always, she quietly hung back a little, silently observing as introductions were being made. Then Mr. Porter walked over to her. "Ms. Wilford?" he asked, extending his hand. "Pleased to meet you. My wife and I will be taking care of you while you're here."

"Thank you." Her voice was very quiet as she shook his hand. "I appreciate it."

"It'll be our honor." Mr. Porter's voice became sympathetic. "I was a great admirer of your father. I'm very sorry for your loss." He took her bag from her and gestured toward the nearby walkway. "If you'll follow me, please . . . there's some people you need to meet."

Hannah nodded again and moved to follow him. Just before she left, though, she glanced my way. Our eyes met for an instant and her face went red with embarrassment, as if she'd been caught telling a lie. Then she went away, leaving me staring at her.

"Did he call her Ms. Wilford?" Melissa was confused. "I thought her last name was Johnson."

I didn't have a chance to reply before Nina piped up. "You mean you didn't know?" she asked. I shook my head, and so did Melissa and Logan. Nina responded with an expansive sigh. "How dumb *are* you? That's Hannah Wilford . . . President Wilford's daughter."

7.
HANNAH SPEAKS

"**O**h my God," Melissa stammered. "Oh, my God . . . oh, my God . . . oh, my God . . ."

No one paid attention to her. We were watching Hannah and Mr. Porter as they walked away from us. When they disappeared through a door leading to a stairway, I looked at Nina.

"How did you know?" I asked.

"You didn't recognize her?" She gave me a patronizing smile. "I did. As soon as she got out of the car, I figured out who she was. I thought you did, too."

I could have explained to her that the last person I expected to see at Wallops Island was the daughter of the president of the United States, but I turned to Gordie instead. "Did you know?" I asked, and he reluctantly nodded. "Why didn't you tell us?"

"I didn't know myself until just before you showed up," he replied. "When the launch director told me that she'd be on the shuttle, he made me promise to keep my mouth shut. That way, if the feds had managed to stop the launch, the rest of you wouldn't have gotten in any trouble."

"We're already in trouble." Logan was glaring at him; I'd seldom seen him so angry. "We're all wanted by the feds. What difference does it make if one of us is the president's daughter?"

"Plenty." Dr. Ernsting had come over to join us. He was in his late twenties, with bushy brown hair and a pencil-thin mustache; we'd later learn that he was a psychologist, and with his German accent he couldn't have been more suitable for the role. "Sorry, Logan, but you have it wrong. The rest of you are just the children of federal fugitives . . ."

"Just?"

"Exactly, yes. The American officials don't want you as much as your parents. But Hannah is a fugitive herself. If anything, they want her even more than your folks. So, if you'd been caught and they'd found out that you knew who she was, then you could've been charged with aiding and abetting an attempted flight from the law."

I slowly nodded. It was the same reason that Dad had given for not telling Melissa and me where we were going until we reached Wallops Island; deniability was our best defense. And it explained a couple of other things, such as why F-30s had given chase to the *Spirit of New York* and tried to kill us with an ASW when that didn't work, and also why Gordie had observed radio silence during the two and a half days it had taken us to reach the Moon. The people who had arranged our getaway knew that the daughter of the late president was among us, and they'd done everything possible to protect her.

"But . . ." Melissa was still in shock. "Why didn't she tell us herself?"

Mr. Lagler shrugged. "Maybe she didn't want you treating her any differently than anyone else." He paused. "She just lost her father," he quietly added. "Perhaps she had other things on her mind."

Melissa didn't respond to that. I wondered if she regretted having treated Hannah so rudely. Something Dr. Ernsting said, though, spurred a question of my own. "Has anyone heard from our parents?"

The adults looked at one another, each reluctant to be the one to deliver bad news. "I'm very sorry," Dr. Rice said at last, and there was no missing the Scottish lilt of her voice, "but we've learned that they were among those who were arrested at Wallops Island just after you left."

Logan's mouth fell open, and even Nina appeared to be stunned. "They were caught?" she asked, and her guardian slowly nodded. "What's happened to them?"

"We . . . don't know," Dr. Rice said. "No official announcement has been made. What little information we have came from a source at Wallops just before the government severed all communications with the island." Kneeling down, she reached out for Nina. "My poor child. I'm sure your family will be all . . ."

Nina stepped back from her. Once again, the stoical mask had slipped down over her face, but I could see the fury in her eyes. She didn't want to be comforted by strangers. But Eddie burst into tears again, and his little sister took his hand before Dr. Rice could move toward him.

Something went cold inside of me. Dad had sacrificed his freedom to make sure that Melissa and I escaped, and Jan had done the same for Hannah. Now both of them were in the hands of the authorities. And if my father's fears about President Shapar were true, then Dad and Jan were in grave danger. It was possible that Melissa and I would never see them again.

"I'm going to get them." Logan's voice was a whisper only I heard. At first I thought he meant his parents, but then I looked at him and saw the barely restrained rage in his face. "That whole crew . . . Shapar and everyone around her. So help me, I'm going to get them."

You and me both, I silently added, although I didn't say so aloud.

"Yes, well . . ." Mr. Lagler cleared his throat with a discomfited cough. "You've come a long way. Perhaps you should get some rest and a good meal." He lay a hand upon my shoulder. "Come with me. I'll take you to my home."

The other grownups murmured in agreement, then they turned to collect their charges; Logan went away with Dr. Ernsting, and Nina reluctantly allowed Dr. Rice to herd Eddie and her toward the nearby stairs. Melissa didn't look very happy about following Mr. Lagler, but neither she nor I had much choice in matter. I didn't know if Apollo had an orphanage, but if there was one, I didn't want to wind up there.

"I'll be in touch," Gordie said to me just before we left him. "Maybe we can get in another flying lesson."

"Yeah. That would be great." I wasn't very enthusiastic about the offer; I was too wrung out from everything I'd just learned. Gordie forced a smile, then turned to walk off. Nicole favored me with a smile of her own that was a little more comforting, then she headed toward the customs entrance.

* * *

Mr. Lagler's apartment was located on the third tier of the crater wall. I'd later find out that Apollo's senior administrators rated the living quarters with the most space and the best views, so the Laglers' apartment was on the same level as Mr. Porter's, while Dr. Rice and Dr. Ernsting lived on the ground floor level near Apollo General. The sunlight within the crater was already beginning to dim by the time we climbed the stairs to get there; apparently the reflector mirrors were turning to provide Apollo with its artificial night. There were only a few elevators in Apollo, and most of them were used to connect the solarium with the sublevels beneath the crater, so we took stairs to get to his place. It felt odd to walk up stairs after a lifetime of using a mobil, but I managed to get the hang of it.

I didn't know what to expect from Mr. Lagler's apartment, so I was bound to be surprised in any case. His home was nowhere near the size of the house I'd left behind in Maryland: three rooms and a bath, with Mr. and Ms. Lagler in the master bedroom and Melissa and I sharing a slightly smaller second bedroom. Mr. Lagler informed us that, since their son was at college in Hungary, Melissa and I could use his room for the time being. It had only one bed, but a futon had been borrowed from a neighbor; I volunteered to use it and let my sister have the bed. MeeMee was hardly overjoyed by the prospect of sharing a room with her little brother and a bathroom with two strangers, but she had enough sense to keep her objections to herself.

The apartment was carved out of solid rock, with bamboo wall panels to cozy up the rooms a little. Indeed, it seemed as if everything was made out of bamboo: the beds, chairs, and tables, the cabinets and countertops of the small kitchenette in a dining nook of the living room, the doors, even the frames of the ceiling light fixtures. Bamboo was easily cultivated in the ag domes, while wood was expensive to import from Earth; no one cut down the trees in the crater park, since they were an important source of oxygen.

The highlight was a narrow window in the dining nook that faced the crater's outer wall. Looking through it, one could see the lunar landscape spread out below, with Earth high above the landing fields. But Mr. Lagler was particularly proud of his holo TV. Built into the ceiling, it had cost him nearly three months' salary to have it shipped up from Earth, but it was worth every lune if it let him watch European soccer games.

Ms. Lagler was a plump and pleasant lady who could have been anyone's favorite aunt. She fawned all over Melissa and me as soon as we came through the door, and already had a pot of lamb ragout simmering on the stove. Like most loonies, their diet was mainly vegetarian, but on special occasions the Laglers would spring for fresh meat from the colony's livestock pens. I wasn't crazy about lamb, but I was too polite to object. Besides, after three days of sucking on food pouches, I could have eaten horsemeat. Melissa wasn't picky, either; sitting across the dining table from her, I was almost embarrassed by the way she shoveled the food into her mouth.

Mr. and Mrs. Lagler didn't say much until after dinner, but once Melissa and I helped Mrs. Lagler clear the table, Mr. Lagler escorted us to the twin bamboo couches arranged in front of the holo. He and his wife didn't have many rules, he told us, but they expected us to obey the few they did. We were to help them keep the apartment neat and pick up after ourselves. We would abide by Apollo's water conservation laws, which meant no more than three showers a week for no longer than five minutes apiece; Melissa was horrified by that, until Mrs. Lagler explained to her that water was a finite resource which was constantly recycled. We would attend morning classes at Apollo High, and in the afternoons we were expected to do our time in Colony Service.

"What's that?" I asked. Nicole had mentioned it to me, but hadn't explained what it was.

"All residents above the age of twelve are expected to contribute at least twenty hours per week to community work," Mr. Lagler said. "No exceptions, not even visitors who expect to be here more than four weeks."

"We might not be here that long," Melissa said, confident that she'd found an exemption for herself.

Mr. Lagler gave her a forgiving smile. "Perhaps . . . but I wouldn't count on it. Besides, you'll find yourself getting bored if you don't do something once school is out, because that's what everyone else your age will be doing."

Melissa responded by folding her arms together and putting on her best MeeMee pout. "So what do we do in Colony Service?" I asked.

"Depends on what you volunteer for. You can do custodial duties like sweeping the walkways and emptying the recycling chutes. There's a lot of work in the farms and livestock pens, and the solarium maintenance crew is always looking for new people. If you'd prefer to work outside, you can get trained for dome inspection and repair." He paused. "You're both at least sixteen, aren't you?" he asked, and nodded when Melissa and I said we were. "Then you can join the Rangers . . . but that takes a major commitment, and the training can be pretty dangerous."

I liked the idea of seeing more of Nicole, but having to work with Billy Tate wasn't very appealing. Besides, I didn't think I was ready for a job that would have me risking life and limb. I shook my head, and Mr. Lagler shrugged. "As you will. But you'll need to sign up for something by the end of the week, or else you'll be assigned a job. Believe me, you don't want it to come to that . . . people who try to dodge CS usually get sent to the waste treatment center."

Melissa made a face, then yawned. "Yeah, well . . . thanks for the warning, but I'm tired. Do you think I can . . . ?"

"You're excused, yes. Go on to bed." Mr. Lagler made a show of half-rising from his seat, but Melissa didn't notice the courtly gesture as she stood up and shuffled away to the guest room. He watched her go, then looked at me. "Aren't you going to bed, too, Jamey?"

My eyes were feeling grainy, but I wasn't quite ready to sleep. "Could I sit up just a little longer? I want to . . ." I hesitated. "I'd like to ask you about something."

Mr. Lagler frowned. "Yes? What is it?"

I waited until I heard Melissa shut the door behind her. "On the way here . . . when I was on the ferry, I mean . . . Nicole told me something I'd never heard before. That I was famous, or something like that."

"Oh, really?" He raised an eyebrow. "And you didn't know this before now?" When I shook my head, he looked past me. "Imagine that, Elsa. The boy doesn't know."

Ms. Lagler had just finished cleaning up; she left the dining nook, wiping her hands on a rag. "Why would you be surprised? He was so young when it happened. He wouldn't remember . . ."

"Are you talking about my mother?" I asked, then quickly added, "Ma'am."

She smiled, appreciating the formality. "Of course," she said, settling down on the couch next to her husband. "Oh, Connie was such a beautiful woman. We were very fond of her, Algis and I. When she died . . ." The smile vanished and she shook her head. "Such a tragedy. Just terrible."

"You know how she died, do you not?" Mr. Lagler asked, taking his wife's hand. "And how you were saved . . . you know this, too, yes?" I nodded, and he went on. "That story has become well-known in the years since . . . how a mother, in her last seconds, gave up her own life in order to save her child. It's told to everyone who comes to the Moon as an example of the sort of courage it takes to live here, and what may be expected of all of us if we are to survive."

"I understand."

I thought I'd said the right thing, but Mr. Lagler shook his head. "No, I don't think you do. You're the child who was saved, and so you're part of the legend . . . but unless you find yourself in a similar situation, you cannot understand what a brave thing it is that your mother did. Not really."

"But it was an accident, right?" I asked, and he nodded. "Then how could I find myself in a similar situation if this was something that . . . ?"

"I don't know, but the day may come that you will. And when it does, you'll have to find for yourself whether you're worthy of your mother's . . ."

He was interrupted by a soft chime from the phone on the living room table. Mr. Lagler picked it up. "Hello?" he said, then listened for a moment. "Yes, they are, but his sister has gone to bed." Another pause. "Of course . . . yes, I will. Thank you for letting us know."

He put down the phone, looked at me again. "The town manager will be making a special address to Apollo in just a couple of minutes. His assistant called to tell me that it concerns you and your friends, and that you should watch." He reached over to pick up the holo's remote. "Maybe you should wake up your sister."

I thought about it for a second, then shook my head. "That might not be such a good idea, sir. She's pretty cranky when she has to get out of bed."

An understanding nod, then Mr. Lagler pointed the remote at the holo and thumbed a button. A miniature soccer field materialized before us, with doll-size players scrambling for control of the ball. Mr. Lagler touched another button and the field disappeared, replaced by a life-sized speaker's podium. The bamboo podium remained vacant for a few more seconds, then Loren Porter stepped out of thin air to walk behind it.

"My fellow colonists . . . thank you for taking the time to join me tonight." Although his voice came from a ceiling speaker, it sounded as if he was in the same room with us. *"I'm sorry to have to speak to you on such short notice, but a matter has occurred which may have significant impact on the future of Apollo."*

Mr. Porter glanced down at the podium, as if taking his cues from a screen we couldn't see. *"Earlier today, a transfer vehicle arrived in lunar orbit bearing passengers who left the ISC spaceport at Wallops Island three days ago. Those passengers are six children, their ages ranging from nine to seventeen. Most of them have parents who work for the ISC, and who decided to send their children to safety following the death of President Wilford."*

As he spoke, a small window opened to left side of him. Within it was a holo image of President Wilford: his official portrait, familiar to everyone.

"There is a reason why they did this," Mr. Porter continued. *"As many of you know, his former vice president, Lina Shapar, has proposed that the United States cede from the ISC and take control of helium-3 reserves here on the Moon. Such a unilateral action, of course, would be in direct violation of the United Nations Space Treaty, which has directed the international use of lunar resources for the last 130 years. It would also violate the accords that created the ISC itself, which state that helium-3 and other vital lunar materials are to be shared among the nations that belong to the ISC."*

Another window opened to Mr. Porter's right, this one displaying an official holo of President Shapar: blonde and beautiful, but somehow vaguely reptilian, with an unblinking gaze that I'd always found unsettling.

"Although Vice President Shapar's position was supported by many within her party," Mr. Porter went on, *"it was not supported by President Wilford, who was in favor of continued international control and sharing of lunar resources. This was not the first time since they came to the White House that the president and vice president were in disagreement. Vice President Shapar also spoke in favor of military confrontation with the Pacific Socialist Union, while President Wilford wanted to re-open negotiations with China and her allies."*

"Shapar was bucking for her boss's job," Mr. Lagler murmured. "That's why she worked against him . . . she had political ambitions of her own."

"Who is she, Algis?" Ms. Lagler asked. "You know I don't keep up with American politics."

Mr. Lagler folded his arms across his chest. "Lina Shapar used to be Miss America," he said quietly, "before she married a senator from her home state. She didn't have any political ambitions before then, but after they were married she began to be more outspoken. Most of what she said echoed her husband's conservative views, but she was more charismatic than he was, and the voters loved her. Then Senator Shapar was killed in a plane crash and the governor appointed Lina to fill out his term. She rose quickly within her party even though her politics became more radical than her husband's, and when George Wilford . . . who was a moderate . . . won the presidential nomination, he tried to appease his party's right wing by tapping her to be his running mate." He shrugged. "It's been obvious for awhile, though, that the two of them actually despised each other, or that Shapar wouldn't hesitate to take positions that undermined the president's agenda."

I only listened to this with half an ear. I was paying more attention to what Mr. Porter was saying. *"When it became obvious that Vice President Shapar was intent upon taking control of helium-3 reserves, a number of ISC officials signed a petition in protest of her position. This included the parents of the children who have come to the Moon. They did so with the support of their European and Asian colleagues, but not long after the petition was made public, they learned that the vice president had placed their names on a secret list of political enemies, and that she intended to persecute them if and when she became president."*

Mr. Porter paused to let his words sink in. *"This has occurred,"* he went on after a moment. *"As soon as George Wilford was pronounced dead and Lina Shapar was sworn in to take his place, her first act as president was to issue an executive order calling for the arrest of everyone she'd placed on that list. She did so on the grounds that they were involved in a Chinese-led conspiracy to assassinate the former president, and that these individuals posed a threat to the national security of the United States."*

The images of George Wilford and Lina Shapar vanished as Mr. Porter continued to speak. *"This has been the White House's position for* the last three days. *The parents of those children who've fled to Apollo have been arrested, and we have since learned that they will be charged with conspiring to kill President Wilford. . . ."*

"No," I whispered. "They're lying. Dad wouldn't do that."

"I know," Mr. Lagler said quietly, then held up a finger. "Just listen."

"However, we are now aware of something that people back on Earth don't know." Mr. Porter was staring straight at the camera. *"This information comes from another child who was put aboard that LTV before it left Earth."* Again, he paused for a moment. *"Please allow me to introduce you to Hannah Wilford, the daughter of the late President George Wilford."*

Mr. Porter moved away from the podium, but didn't vanish from sight. A couple of seconds went by, then Hannah appeared.

She looked better than she did the last time I'd seen her. She'd cleaned up a bit and combed her hair, and someone had given her a fresh change of clothes. Now I recognized her as being the First Daughter, but perhaps only because she'd been introduced as such. Until we'd arrived at Apollo, she'd been just another scared teenager on the run.

Hannah hesitated, as if unsure of herself. When she spoke, though, her voice was steady. *"I'm Hannah Wilford, and my father is President Wilford, and I'm here to tell you that Lina Shapar is lying. My father wasn't assassinated . . . he died of natural causes."*

She took a second to catch her breath, but it may have also been to emphasize what she'd just said. If so, it had the desired effect. Ms. Lagler gasped and raised her hand to her mouth, and Mr. Lagler bent a little closer. My father had hinted at this when we'd heard the news of President Wilford's death, but nonetheless I was surprised as they were.

"The truth of the matter is that my father was ill," Hannah continued. *"In fact, he'd been ill for quite some time. Only a handful of people knew that he was suffering from a heart condition . . . atrial fibrillation . . . that put him at increased risk for a stroke. He'd managed to keep this secret while he was running for office, and after he was elected the only people who were aware of his*

condition were my mother and me, his private physicians, the Secret Service, and the few persons in his administration who needed to know."

"That explains a lot," Mr. Lagler said, darting a glance at his wife. "Like why he refused to release his medical records."

"Why is that?"

"During the campaign, Wilford's opponent demanded that he release the results of his most recent medical exam. Wilford said that he'd be happy to do so, but only if the other candidate did, too. His opponent declined . . . it later turned out that he had health problems of his own . . . and so Wilford refused to divulge his medical records as well." A grim smile. "That must have been a lucky break for Wilford. It gave him an excuse to avoid admitting that he had a heart condition."

"My father had medicine that allowed him to live and work normally," Hannah was saying, *"but he had to make sure that he took it on time every day and that he avoided stressful situations. Both of these things became very hard to do, and on one occasion his doctors had to be rushed in for emergency treatment. But the public was not made aware of the fact that he wasn't well or that his condition was getting worse."*

Hannah paused again, this time to raise a hand and quickly wipe away a tear that threatened to reveal itself. When she continued speaking, her voice quavered, but just a little. *"Vice President Shapar was one of those people who knew my father was ill, and I suspect . . . I believe . . . that one of the reasons why she publicly opposed him on so many issues was that she wanted to increase the stress of his job as much as she could. But even if she didn't, she and her staff were preparing to seize control of the White House the moment he suffered a stroke. My father never trusted her . . . he told me so himself . . . but there was little he could do about this that wouldn't involve going public with his medical condition."*

Hannah took another deep breath; I could tell that she was struggling to remain calm. *"So, when my father had the stroke that killed him, Lina Shapar was ready to put the blame on the PCU and claim that an assassin was responsible. She and her people were also ready to issue orders calling for the arrest of anyone they believed would oppose their agenda. This includes the American ISC officials who signed the petition protesting their plans to lay claim to lunar helium-3. They believe that if the US can take possession of the helium-3 supply, then it will be able to control much of the world's energy."*

"They're right." Mr. Lagler's face was grim. "If America is able to do this, then . . ."

"Hush," Ms. Lagler murmured. "Listen."

"My mother was detained as soon as my father died, and I don't know what has become of her." Hannah's voice was shaking by then; Mr. Porter stepped closer to lay a comforting hand on her arm, but she barely seemed to notice him. *"Secret Service agents loyal to my father managed to get me out of the White House, and acting on instructions he'd secretly given them in advance, they got me to Wallops Island, where I boarded a shuttle along with the children of ISC officials who'd also learned of the plot."* She paused to wipe a tear from her face. *"One of those kids had to stay behind so that I'd be able to get away, and I . . . and I . . ."*

She was talking about Jan. No wonder she hadn't said much to me. She felt guilty about what had happened, even though it wasn't her fault. Hannah was openly weeping by then. When she couldn't go on, Mr. Porter gently pushed her away from the podium.

"Thank you, Ms. Wilford," he said. *"I'm sure I speak for everyone when I say that I appreciate your courage and along with that of your late father."*

Hannah nodded, then she turned and walked away from the podium. Mr. Porter waited until she'd vanished from sight, then he turned to look straight at the camera. *"This address is being simulcast to the global net on Earth,"* he said, *"and it's being seen in the US as well as other countries belonging to the ICU. So I will take the opportunity to read a public statement of my own."*

He gazed down at the podium again. *"A little more than an hour ago, following a private meeting with Ms. Wilford during which she explained the situation just as you've heard it, the Apollo town council convened in executive session during which we also conferred with senior ISC representatives both on*

Earth and here on the Moon. It is our decision that, until President Shapar and her administration offer a full public accounting for the circumstances of President Wilford's death, along with the arrest of American ISC officials and various other individuals, all shipments of helium-3 and other lunar resources to the United States will be suspended. This embargo will go into effect immediately and will continue until further notice."

Mr. Porter looked up at the camera. *"We hope that this crisis will be resolved soon, and to our satisfaction. Thank you for your attention, and good night."*

8.
STANDING IN PLACE

I went to bed shortly after that. I might have stayed up a little longer with Mr. and Ms. Lagler to discuss what Mr. Porter and Hannah had said, but exhaustion finally caught up with me, so I excused myself and went to my room. Melissa was sound asleep when I came in; she didn't stir while I got undressed and climbed into bed.

I was out cold almost as soon as my head touched the pillow. As I slept, events continued to unfold.

Mr. Porter's speech, along with Hannah's remarks, were transmitted back to Earth, where they were received by ground stations. Less than a minute after Mr. Porter started talking, though, the American netcasts were suddenly terminated; comp screens went blank and were replaced by error codes. The National Security Agency apparently had been ready to cut the lunar transmission before it reached US-based service providers. When pushed for an explanation, an NSA spokesman said that the transmission had been censored in the interest of national security, then punted the matter to the White House . . . which, in turn, offered no comment.

However, neither the NSA nor the White House were able to do anything about the rest of world. European and South American ground stations also received the transmission, and they immediately relayed it to overseas service providers. So everything said by Apollo's general manager and President Wilford's daughter was heard by hundreds of millions of people outside the United States, who called or emailed friends and associates in America to make them aware of what their government didn't want them to know. Within hours, mirror sites in the United States were echoing the speech from their European counterparts; the NSA did its best to shut them down, too, but the battle was already lost. By the end of the day, almost everyone in America had heard what Hannah said.

The White House went into damage control mode. The press secretary, Andreas Sullivan, claimed that the transmission was a hoax. Hannah Wilford's image had been computer-generated, he said, and to prove this the White House released footage of the First Daughter calmly reading a book at the undisclosed location where she and her mother had been taken for their own safety. This was debunked almost immediately, when a British news agency released an identical vid taken fifteen months earlier while the late president's family was on vacation in France.

Just as incendiary was Mr. Porter's announcement that Apollo would curtail helium-3 shipments to the United States until the Shapar administration provided candid explanations for President Wilford's death and the detainment of various officials. Press Secretary Sullivan was utterly livid when asked if it was true that the late president had been killed by a stroke instead of a Chinese assassin, but he couldn't provide a reason why Mr. Porter would lie about such a serious matter. He said that the He^3 embargo didn't matter very much because American nuclear fusion plants already had ample fuel reserves, and then stated that President Shapar was communicating with Ronald Voss, the ISC general director, in an effort to settle the dispute.

I was still in bed when Voss held his own press conference in Geneva. Speaking before a lightning storm of camera flashes, the general director said that President Shapar had threatened to withdraw the United States from the ISC unless shipments of helium-3 and other materials were immediately resumed, and that her administration would also consider taking other, as-yet unspecified actions against ISC countries unless Hannah Wilford was returned to Earth at once.

The White House dropped its line that Hannah's presence on the Moon was a fraud. Shortly after Voss spoke, Andreas Sullivan called another press conference, this time to claim that the First Daughter had been abducted by agents of the Pacific Socialist Coalition, which in turn were secretly conspiring with the ISC to shut off American access to vital lunar resources. No one believed him, and Sullivan left the room without answering the obvious questions shouted at him by the White House press corps.

No one knew it then, but that was the last time the Shapar administration would hold a press conference. It wouldn't be long before reporters were barred from the White House; after that, all presidential statements were either anonymous press releases or pre-recorded vids. The Shapar administration had been caught in a bald-faced lie; they wouldn't make the same mistake again if they could help it.

I didn't hear about any of this until after I got up. The Laglers knew how tired Melissa and I were, so they'd let us sleep in. It was late morning, Apollo time, when I finally pried open my eyes. MeeMee was still snoring softly when I put on a pair of shorts and a T-shirt. Clamping on my ankle bracelets so I wouldn't bounce around like I was on a trampoline, I slipped out of the room. Neither Mr. nor Ms. Lagler were around, but there was a plate of fresh muffins and a carafe of hot coffee on the dining nook table, along with a note asking us to make ourselves at home.

I wasn't ready for breakfast yet; the first thing I needed to do was take a shower. The bathroom was next to the Laglers' bedroom, and they'd laid out fresh towels for Melissa and me. Recalling Mr. Lagler's admonition against showers lasting more than five minutes, I kept my watch on, but that turned out to be unnecessary. The stall had a built-in timer and thermostat, and both were preset. Two minutes of lukewarm water at low pressure, just enough to get wet and soak my hair before the showerhead went dry. I soaped up and squirted some shampoo in my hair, then touched the button marked RINSE and received three minutes of hot water at high pressure which ended exactly thirty seconds after a warning chime. I didn't quite get all the shampoo out of my hair, but the stall wouldn't give me a second chance; I rinsed out remaining suds in the sink, using the five-second spurts of warm water the facet would allow me. Water conservation was apparently taken seriously on Apollo; I'd have to get used to taking showers in a hurry, and not every day.

I barely noticed. I was too busy enjoying being able to take a shower without having to prop myself up with a pair of support rails. Most of my life, I'd taken baths simply because they were less hassle. Now, for the first time, I could stand on my own two legs and watch water swim down the drain between my feet. Unless you've been stuck in a mobil for as long as you can remember, you'll never know just how happy this simple pleasure made me.

I came out of the bathroom to find that Melissa had just woken up. She was still half-asleep and her eyes barely open, but at least she'd remembered to put on her ankle weights. She scowled at me as she shuffled into the bathroom, slamming the door shut before I had a chance to tell her about the timer. She was in for a rude surprise; MeeMee loved a long, hot shower in the morning.

Figuring that she was on her own, I took the opportunity to get dressed; she and I would both have to make adjustments so long as we shared a room. In my bag were the jeans, sweatshirt, and moccasins I'd been wearing before changing into the ISC jumpsuit I'd been given on Wallops Island. Unfortunately, these were the only warm clothes I had; everything else I'd brought with me was more suitable for the beach than Apollo. I'd have to find something else to wear before long. But I laughed out loud when I discovered my trunks and swim fins in the bottom of the bag. Maybe I could use the fins as a wall decoration; they were probably the only pair on the Moon.

When I emerged from the bedroom, I found Mr. Lagler waiting for me. He'd used his lunch hour to come home and check on Melissa and me. We'd just said good morning to each other when there was an outraged shriek from the other side of the bathroom door, followed by an ear-blistering string of obscenities. I winced in embarrassment, but Mr. Lagler seemed to be more amused than offended.

"I take it your sister has discovered the shower," he said quietly.

"I tried to warn her, but . . ." I shrugged helplessly.

"It takes some getting used to." Getting up from the couch, Mr. Lagler walked into the dining nook. "Have you had breakfast yet? Don't waste the coffee . . . it's not scarce, but it is expensive."

"Thank you. I won't." Running a hand through my damp hair, I walked over to the dining nook and picked up the carafe. It was self-heating, so the coffee was still hot; I poured some in a mug and was about to ask for milk before realizing that this was an absurd request—the closest cow was nearly a quarter of a million miles away—and resigned myself to taking it black from now on.

Mr. Lagler put a muffin on a plate and handed it to me, then sat down at the nook table. "Have you seen the news yet?" he asked, then shook his head. "No, of course you haven't . . . you just got up."

"Sorry. Didn't mean to sleep late."

Shaking his head again, he pulled a pad from a shirt pocket. "You need to read this," he said as he ran a finger across its screen to open something he'd bookmarked. "Three or four news stories I've saved for you . . . mainly from British sites, since the American press appears to be either parroting the government line or avoiding it altogether." Another frustrated scream from the bathroom, and he pushed the pad across the table to me. "I'll knock on the door, see if she needs any help," he added as he got up. "Read."

I went through the stories Mr. Lagler had bookmarked, skimming them at first, then going back to read them more closely. I'd just gotten to Andreas Sullivan's stupid claim that Hannah had been abducted by the Chinese when a red light blinked in the pad's upper right margin, alerting me that a related news story had just appeared.

I tapped my finger against the light and a window opened on the screen: vid footage of a large mob of protesters running away from a dense white cloud billowing in their midst. The caption stated that this was a demonstration in Lafayette Park across the street from the White House; it had been broken up by Washington police and

National Guard soldiers, with at least twenty protestors taken into custody. The attached news story said that anti-government demonstrations—peaceful for the most part, but violent at a few—were spontaneously occurring in cities all over the country, with many also being squashed by local and federal authorities.

By then, Melissa had stomped her way back across the apartment, wrapped in damp towels and angry as a wet cat. I ignored her as she slammed the bedroom door and instead looked up at Mr. Lagler as he returned to the table. "This is because of what Hannah said last night, isn't it?"

"Yes, it is . . . although her speech was heard early yesterday afternoon in Washington. Apollo is on Greenwich Mean Time, so there's a five-hour difference in time zones." I glanced at the time stamp at the top of his pad, then took off my watch and reset it. "The White House must have been expecting something like this, because they were ready to shut down the feed to the ISPs. But they couldn't do anything about European sites, which is how it was leaked to the US."

I glanced again at the Lafayette Park demonstrators being dispersed by tear gas, and suddenly lost my appetite for the muffin in front of me. "So . . . what happens now? Are you going to send Hannah home? They'll probably want the rest of us, too."

Mr. Lagler shook his head. "I've spoken with Loren about that, and he's against it. So far as he and the town council are concerned, all six of you have sanctuary here for as long as you want. But it's not entirely up to him. Something as important as this had to go before the town. Apollo has a democratic government, and all major decisions are made with the consent of the residents."

"You're going to have a vote?"

"A town meeting is scheduled for this evening, at which time a formal resolution will be submitted." He paused. "Since you're not an Apollo citizen . . . not yet, at least . . . you won't be able to vote. So you don't have to be there . . . but it may help if people can see you and your friends."

I slowly nodded, understanding what he was telling me. If Hannah, the other kids, and I were going to remain on the Moon, the majority of Apollo's inhabitants would have to agree to let us stay. And that meant defying the president of the United States. Mr. Porter would have to make a case for us, but showing up for the town meeting would be in our own best interests, whether we wanted to be there or not. "I'll talk to the others and let them know what's happening. Can you tell me how to find them?"

"That reminds me." Mr. Lagler reached into his pocket, pulled out a pair of wristbands, and handed one to me. "You need to wear this at all times. The other is for your sister."

I took the wristband from him. A thick plastic bracelet, it contained a LCD, a miniature mike and speaker grille, and a green bar that I didn't recognize at once. "It's GPS-enabled," Mr. Lagler explained, "so we'll be able to find you at any time, even if you're out on the surface. And it's voice-activated, so all you need to do is say the name of the person you want to reach. It only works inside the crater and ag domes, though . . . you need to use a suit com when you're outside. But the most important thing is this . . ." He pointed to the green bar. "That's a radiation dosimeter. It should be green at all times. If it ever starts to turn black, it means you're in danger of exceeding the safe dose of REMS and you should get to a radiation shelter as soon as you can . . . the big one underground would be best."

"Thanks." I fastened it around my left wrist, next to my watch, then pushed back my chair. "So what should I do now?"

Mr. Lagler picked up my plate and cup. "There's little for you to do. We can't enroll you in school or Colony Service until we know for certain that you're staying, so . . ." He shrugged as he carried everything to the kitchenette. "Walk around a bit and get to know the place. Talk to the others and let them know about tonight's meeting. Other than that, I can't think of anything else."

It sounded like good advice. Knowing that it could take hours for Melissa to emerge from our room, I left the apartment before

Mr. Lagler did. Logan might not have a wristband yet, so I'd need to find him and speak with him about the town meeting. Nina, too, although I'd leave it up to her whether Eddie should be there or not; he might not understand what was going on, or be able to sit still and be quiet for the entire meeting. And as for Hannah . . .

Walking along the Tier-3 balcony, I was just thinking about her when an apartment door opened about a hundred yards away and who should appear but the First Daughter herself. It wasn't hard to recognize her from a distance; there couldn't be very many girls in Apollo who wore Washington Nationals ball caps. There was a slender, dark-skinned woman with her, whom I assumed to be Ms. Porter. As she shut the door behind them, Hannah happened to glance my way.

Both of us stopped dead in our tracks. For a moment or two, neither of us knew what to do, even though it was obvious that we'd spotted one another. Hannah tentatively raised a hand, and when I waved back she turned to Ms. Porter and said something to her. The city manager's wife looked at me, then gave Hannah a quiet nod. Hannah turned and started walking toward me.

I met her about halfway. "Hi. How're you doing?"

"Okay . . . you?"

"All right, I guess." I hesitated. "So . . . I saw you last night. On the holo, I mean."

Hannah's face colored. "You saw that?" she asked and I nodded. "Yeah, well . . . it was something I had to do, even though I didn't want to. Get in front of a camera, I mean."

"No, no, I understand. And I think you did fine. But . . ." Feeling a sudden flash of anger, I turned to lean forward against the balcony railing. "When were you going to tell us who you are?" I asked, not looking at her while trying to keep an even tone. "I mean, that you're really . . . ?"

"The president's daughter?" She rested her arms against the railing, clasping her hands together. "I was waiting for a chance."

"We were cooped up in a spacecraft for three days. You had plenty of chances then."

"I know that, Jamey . . . and you're right, maybe I should have."
Hannah sighed. "Try to look at it my way. My father had just died. I
still don't know what happened to my mother. I was pulled out of bed
in the middle of night by a couple of Secret Service agents who were
loyal to my dad and pushed into the back of a limo before the vice
president's people could get their hands on me. I didn't even know
where I was going until five minutes before I met you. Do you really
think I was going to jump up and down and say, 'Hey, guess what? I
live in the White House!'"

"No, but . . ." I floundered for a second or two, trying to figure
out what to say. "You could have trusted us."

"I *do* trust you." Unexpectedly, she laid a hand across my wrist.
"And if you want to know the truth, I like you."

Even if that hadn't come from the First Daughter, I would've
jumped out of my skin. How many girls do you think have said that
to me? You can start at zero and count backward.

"I . . . I . . . I . . ."

"You saved my life during the blowout. I never got a chance
to thank you for that, either. And even if you hadn't done that, I
would've been impressed just by the way you've learned to . . ."

Her voice trailed off and she looked away, embarrassed by what
she seemed to want to say. "Walk?" I asked quietly.

"Yeah, I guess that's what I mean." She looked at me again. "That
took a lot of courage."

I was still trying to come up with an answer when she glanced
at her watch. "Look, I've got to be somewhere just now, so . . . well,
don't be mad at me, okay? And next time we see each other, let's try
this again."

"All right, sure. . . ."

"Okay, then." She hesitated, then suddenly gave me a quick kiss
on the cheek. "See you later."

And then she was gone, which was probably just as well. It took
me a minute or two to learn how to breathe again.

* * *

The town meeting was held in the colony's largest room, the storm shelter beneath Apollo. This was the place where everyone was supposed to go when the colony received warning of solar flares. Every few years, storms erupt upon the Sun's photosphere, which cause massive geysers to shoot out into space. These flares release lethal amounts of radiation that can penetrate the crater's regolith shield.

The shelter was there to protect Apollo's inhabitants during these storms; behind its mooncrete walls were the colony's water tanks, which provided additional radiation protection. There were also reserve air tanks holding enough oxygen and nitrogen to keep everyone alive for up to thirty days. And since the bunker was designed to be large enough to hold a thousand people at a time, it provided enough space for residents to gather for events such as town meetings. There was even a big wall screen at the front of the room.

When Melissa and I arrived with Mr. and Ms. Lagler, I thought she and I would be hidden in the back of the room. We weren't full citizens, after all, but rather a couple of kids who'd shown up on the Moon like orphans abandoned on someone's doorstep. So I was surprised when someone met us at the door to usher us to the first row of folding chairs facing an elevated platform. Mr. Porter was seated in the middle of a long table set up on the platform, the five other council members on either side of him. He smiled when my sister and I were brought to seats directly in front of the table; clearly he wanted us to be seen by every person in the room.

Logan was already there, along with the Hernandez kids. I'd called him earlier that afternoon and told him that he needed to be at the meeting, and said the same thing to Nina once I got in touch with her. Eddie fidgeted in his seat; I could tell that he didn't want to be there, but Nina did her best to keep him calm. Shortly after I sat down, she pulled a pad out of her pocket, opened a children's maze game, and handed it to her brother. Eddie was instantly mesmerized, and we heard little from him for the rest of the meeting.

I glanced over my shoulder at the audience behind us. People were still coming in, but so far as I could tell from the scarcity of vacant chairs, it seemed as if nearly everyone in Apollo had decided to show up. I recognized almost no one, though. I caught a quick glimpse of Gordie as he made his way to a seat about halfway to the rear, and Nicole gave me a little smile and a wave from three rows back—I wanted to go over and say hello, but realized that this wasn't a good time to be seen flirting with a girl—but just about everyone else was a stranger.

It was not until Hannah came in that anyone paid attention to the six of us. An abrupt hush fell across the room as Ms. Porter escorted her in. Hannah wasn't wearing her cap tonight, and she proudly kept her head up as she walked down the center aisle. She was used to being the center of attention, I suppose, because she showed no sign of nervousness. Yet a low rumble of voices followed her, and although most people smiled as she walked past them, I noticed a few frowns as well. No doubt everyone had seen her speak the night before, and some probably thought she and the rest of us were nothing but trouble.

Hannah sat down beside me. She was able to do so because Melissa moved over one seat to make room for her. My sister was still mortified by the lousy way she'd treated her on the way to the Moon and was eager to make amends. Hannah barely paid attention to her, though; instead, she turned to me.

"Hi," she whispered. "Have I missed anything important?"

Other than your arrival? I thought. "No, not really," I whispered back. "They haven't started yet."

"Good." She hesitated, then bent a little closer. "Have you thought about what I said?"

That little kiss on the cheek had haunted me all afternoon; so had what she'd told me just before then. "Yeah . . . sure." I swallowed a lump, then looked her straight in the eye. "We're square, okay?"

"Sure, we're square." A quiet smile. "Hey, do you think maybe you'd like to get a snack after . . . ?"

She was interrupted by the sudden bang of a gavel. Mr. Porter was calling the meeting to order; the rest of our conversation would have to wait.

"I'd like to thank everyone for coming this evening," Mr. Porter began after the room had gone quiet, his voice carried by the prong in his ear. "I realize this is sudden, but the matters before us are too important to be held off until our scheduled monthly meeting. I'm sure most of you are already aware of the situation, but I'll begin by summarizing recent events . . ."

He gave a brief run-down of everything that had happened over the course of the last few days, beginning with President Wilford's death and continuing with the flight of my friends and I from Earth, ending with Hannah's testimony the night before and the town council's decision to suspend helium-3 shipments to the United States until President Shapar gave an honest account for her predecessor's death and the detention of ISC officials and others.

"Since then," Mr. Porter said, "the president's response has been unsatisfactory, to say the least. First, her spokesman claimed that Ms. Wilford is still in Washington—" some muted laughter at this "— followed by the allegation that she's been abducted by PSU agents working in collaboration with us." The laughter grew louder and more derisive, and Mr. Porter tried not to smile as he raised a hand for silence. "Less amusing is the White House's demand that we immediately send Ms. Wilford back to Earth. Although they haven't explicitly said so, we may assume that they'll want us to return the other children as well, since their parents are ISC officials who've been detained."

Once again, I felt a chill. Somewhere back on Earth, Dad and Jan were in federal custody, charged as criminals simply because my father had spoken out against Lina Shapar. Melissa made a hissing sound, and I looked around to see her face pinched in anger. My sister had finally realized the seriousness of our situation.

"If we refuse to do so," Mr. Porter continued, "President Shapar has threatened to retaliate against other ISC countries. They haven't yet said what actions they may take, but apparently they believe that our sponsor governments will pressure the ISC into forcing us to turn over the children."

He paused to let his words sink in, then went on. "The town council has acted on its own to impose an embargo, and in doing so we are acting within the provisions of the ISC charter, which allows us to forfeit production shipment to any member country that takes actions contrary to the interest of others. We also recommend that Apollo refuse the Shapar administration's demand to send back the children, However, the latter cannot be done without majority assent of Apollo's citizens. Therefore, as town manager, I'm entering a motion that these children—" he gestured toward the six of us "—be granted unconditional political asylum and allowed to remain here as Apollo citizens." He turned to another council member. "Ms. Fleming?"

A stern-looking woman with white hair stood up. "As moderator, I'm allowing one hour for debate before calling for a vote. Anyone who wishes to speak may now do so."

It took a few moments before anyone stood up, but I could hear townspeople quietly murmured to each other. Then someone near the back of the room raised a hand. He left it up while Ms. Fleming pointed a scanner in his direction; once she'd checked his identity by reading his wristband, she acknowledged him by saying his name. He got up and walked to a mike stand set up in the center aisle.

"Loren," he asked, "if we suspend helium-3 shipments to the US, isn't that going to take money from our pockets?"

"It will, at least for a while," Mr. Porter replied. "We estimate a ten to fifteen percent drop over a six-month period, if the embargo lasts that long. However, since we'll continue to provide He^3 and other lunar materials to the remaining ISC countries, we don't expect the shortfall to severely affect our profit margin over the long term."

Another resident raised a hand and approached the mike after the moderator pointed to her and said her name. "Have we received any word from Bill Sturges, the American ISC director, about the embargo?"

"Katherine, there's been no official communications from ISC's Washington headquarters since Lina Shapar took office," Mr. Porter said. "We're not sure what this means, but we suspect that all senior ISC officials in the US have been detained." The woman who asked the question stared at him as voices rumbled through the room. "However, Ronald Voss has assured us that he and the other European directors will stand behind whatever decision we make."

Another person stood up and started to speak immediately, but stopped when Ms. Fleming reminded him that he first had to be formally recognized. He apologized and waited to be identified and given permission to approach the mike. "Why does Lina . . . President Shapar, I mean . . . want us to send back Wilford's kid? Maybe she really does think we've kidnapped her."

Laughter and a few disgusted snorts greeted this question. Mr. Porter tapped his gavel, then let another council member answer the question. "If you'd seen last night's broadcast," he said, "you'd know that Ms. Wilford's testimony contradicts the White House allegation that President Wilford was assassinated by a PSU agent. No doubt the Shapar administration wants Ms. Wilford in their custody in order to prevent her from revealing the truth about her father's death. As for the second . . . you really don't think we're collaborating with Moon Dragon, do you?"

More laughter, and the guy who'd asked the question turned to shuffle back to his seat. Beside me, Hannah shook her head in disgust. "Can't believe anyone would think I've been kidnapped," she whispered.

I shrugged. "You never know. Some people don't . . ."

"Mr. City Manager!" an angry voice shouted from a few rows back. "Do you seriously think that Americans here should commit treason?"

Startled, I looked around to see who had yelled this. Not far from where Nicole was sitting, a heavy-set man with a shaved head stood up from his chair. Beside him sat Billy Tate; his arms were crossed, and there was an equally determined expression on his face.

Mr. Porter brought down his gavel again as Ms. Fleming glared at the man who'd spoken out of turn. "Mr. Hawthorne, " she said, "you may address the meeting at any time, but you must be recognized by . . ."

"Answer my question, Mr. City Manager! You're proposing that we commit an act of treason against the United States, aren't you? What right do you have to force any American here to . . . ?"

"Mr. Hawthorne, sit down!" Ms. Fleming's face turned red. "The floor has not recognized you!" She pointed to a hand that had been raised from the aisle just behind mine. "The chair recognizes Luis Garcia."

A short, muscular man with a salt-and-pepper mustache stood up and walked to the microphone. Mr. Hawthorne shut up, but he didn't sit down. "I'd like to address those last remarks, if I may," Mr. Garcia said once he reached the mike. Both Mr. Porter and Ms. Fleming nodded, and he turned toward Mr. Hawthorne. "Donald, with all due respect, no one here is suggesting that any American citizen here betray his own country. However, if you feel that strongly, I'm sure the town council would have no objection to you forfeiting your shares so that you and your nephew can take the next LTV back to Earth."

A few scattered chuckles from the audience. Donald Hawthorne scowled and appeared to chew his lower lip, but he didn't respond. Luis Garcia looked toward the rest of the room. "The actions undertaken and proposed by Loren Porter and the rest of the council are not directed against the United States or its people. Instead, they are directed against a president who has apparently assumed power through a *coup d'état*. This same president has also detained individuals . . . fellow Americans, in fact . . . who've spoken out against her administration's intent to unilaterally claim lunar resources protected by international law."

"Hear, hear!" someone in the back row yelled. It sounded like Gordie, but I couldn't be sure.

Garcia nodded in his general direction and went on. "As Apollo citizens, it's our right . . . and our responsibility . . . to preserve those same resources for the benefit of all humankind, not just the United States. . . ."

"You're going to be singing a different tune when the Marines land!" Hawthorne snapped.

Mr. Porter banged his gavel again. "Mr. Hawthorne, speak out of turn again, and I'll have the constables remove you from the room."

Hawthorne remained standing as Garcia turned toward him. "Donald, if Lina Shapar decides to send troops to the Moon, rest assured that my Rangers will be ready to meet them." He glanced at Billy as he said this, and Hawthorne's nephew looked down at the floor. "But resistance to injustice does not always mean having to take up arms and fight to the death. Sometimes it can simply mean standing in place . . . and refusing to move or be moved."

Applause erupted among the audience members and swept through the room. Donald Hawthorne sank back into his seat as Luis Garcia turned away from the mike. As he walked past Hannah's chair, though, he briefly laid a hand on her shoulder.

"Welcome to Apollo, Ms. Wilford," he said quietly. "Glad to have you with us."

Hannah gave him a grateful nod. She didn't say anything, but her eyes were rimmed with tears. Garcia caught me looking at him. A quick smile and a wink, and then he moved on. I had no idea who he was, but I was glad he was on my side.

After Mr. Porter tapped his gavel again, Ms. Fleming asked if anyone else cared to speak. She waited a minute, and when no one raised a hand, she told Mr. Porter that the town was ready to vote. The city manager read the proposition—that Hannah Wilford and her friends, my sister and I included, be granted political asylum and allowed to become Apollo citizens—and then called for a vote.

Looking over my shoulder, I watched as townspeople ran fingertips across the LCD screens of their wristbands. Apparently the measure had been transmitted to everyone; no show of hands, but rather a secret ballot. That must have been why Ms. Fleming checked the identities of everyone who wanted to speak; the council was making sure that any nonresidents who might have shown up for the meeting wouldn't be able to skew the vote. After a few minutes, Mr. Porter, Ms. Fleming, and another council member downloaded the ballot into their pads. The three of them studied the totals, checked the numbers they'd received against each other, and then Mr. Porter stood up to announce the results.

In favor: 732. Opposed: 209. Abstaining: 37. Absent: 22. The ayes had it; the motion passed.

And that was it. I was now a citizen of the Moon.

9.
LEARNING TO FLY

"Why walk when you can fly?" Nicole asked.

We were standing on the edge of a parapet overlooking Apollo. It was just below the bottom of the ceiling dome, about 300 feet above the crater floor, and we were about to jump off.

I tried not to look down, but couldn't help myself. The parapet jutted out from a guardrail-protected platform that circled the top of the crater and was normally used to inspect the dome. Just past its edge, the crater's interior walls sloped down toward Apollo's landscaped groves and meadows. The parapet didn't have a railing, so there was nothing to prevent a misstep that would cause me to make a long fall to the bottom.

Nothing, that is, except the paragliding suit I wore. It was a red, one-piece outfit, skin-tight and made of some elastic composite, with long, thin membranes that extended out from my arms and legs when I stretched them apart. The suit would let me glide upon thermal drafts rising from the solarium; wearing it, I would temporarily become an airborne hybrid of a human being and a flying rodent.

Yeah, right, I thought. *Just call me Batboy.* Paragliding was perfectly safe so long as I followed instructions. Or at least that's what I'd been told. "I'm not sure if I can do this," I murmured, stepping back from the precipice.

"Sure you can." Logan was up there with us. He stood on the other side of Nicole and wore a suit identical to ours except in color: his was dark blue, while Nicole's was teal-green. All three of us wore helmets and goggles; small packs containing parachutes were strapped to our backs. "The first step is the hardest. After that, all you have to do is keep from falling."

Not funny. I gave him a sour look and he grinned back at me. Logan had already done this before, with Nicole as his instructor. I'd watched from below, and when they'd landed I'd told them that I'd like to try this myself. Big mistake; they took me seriously. So for the next several days, I'd taken afterschool lessons in paragliding when I wasn't sweeping walkways and emptying trash containers. I wasn't bad at it, but up until then I'd only jumped off a low balcony on Tier 1 with a padded matt as my touchdown point. This time was the real deal. If I was going to earn my paragliding permit, I'd have to make a 91-meter jump. . . .

Who was I kidding? I wasn't really interested in paragliding. I was just jealous of the fact that Logan was spending more time with Nicole than I was. In fact, she was dangerously close to becoming his girlfriend. If I wanted her, then I'd have to show her that my best friend didn't have more guts than I did.

So there I was, about to do something crazy. Only a few weeks ago, my idea of risky behavior had been crossing the street in my mobil. And now . . .

"C'mon, Jamey." Logan was becoming impatient. "Jump already."

"Stop pushing him," Nicole said, then looked at me again. "If you don't feel like you're ready for this, then don't. . . ."

"Oh, the hell with it," I said, and then I jumped off the platform.

* * *

The morning after the town meeting, I began to settle in. Maybe I was rushing things a bit—after all, only a couple of days earlier I'd arrived on the Moon—but I didn't want to sit around and wait for someone to tell me what to do. Neither did Melissa, but that was to be expected. Her boredom threshold was even lower than mine; besides, I think she wanted to meet some boys. So Ms. Lagler took a day off from her job at the comptroller's office and escorted us to those places in Apollo we'd need to visit in order to fully become citizens in good standing.

First stop was City Hall, a warren of offices on Tier 1, where a clerk took fingerprints and retina images from Melissa and me and added them to information embedded in our wristbands. The wristbands were redundant—our fingers and eyes were all that we'd need for the scanners that unlocked doors throughout Apollo—but since they also contained our comlinks and dosimeters, we were told to wear them at all times anyway.

We were also registered to vote. The minimum voting age was sixteen, and as Apollo residents we were expected to cast our ballots in all elections and civil referendums. That was as much of a surprise to Melissa as it was to me; until then, no one had ever treated us as adults or respected our opinions in matters of public interest. I walked out of the clerk's office feeling just a little taller.

With the right to vote, though, came an obligation to help the community. Our next stop was the Colony Service office, where another clerk had us press our fingers against a scanner before downloading into our pads a long list of job openings. The list ranged all the way from cleaning toilets and sweeping floors to spacecraft maintenance and aeroponic farming: something for everyone, regardless of age, gender, or skills. As Mr. Lagler said, there was no getting around this; Colony Service was mandatory, no excuses accepted. Not that MeeMee didn't try, but the clerk only frowned at her when she tried to cite a list of ailments and allergies—most of them imaginary—which would prevent her from working twenty hours a week. We were told that we'd have a few days to pick something from the list, but if we didn't volunteer for a job by the end of the week, one would be chosen for us.

And finally, we dropped by Apollo High.

The school wasn't anything like my school in Burtonsville. Instead of a big, two-story building with three wings and a parking lot, we found ourselves at a three-room schoolhouse on Apollo's east side that somewhat resembled a Spanish hacienda. Classes were already over for the day—they began at 7 a.m. sharp and ended at 12 noon, five days a week—so only the principal and his secretary were present when Melissa and I came in.

As it turned out, Logan was there, too. He and Dr. Ernsting were in the principal's office when we arrived. The principal's name was Giovanni Speci, and he was one of the school's only two full-time employees; all the teachers were part-timers who did this as Colony Service. Apollo High had only twelve students, so we'd be in the same classes as the kids who were already there; our teachers would come and go through the morning, each taking turns to spend fifty-five minutes with us, until school let out at lunchtime, after which we were expected to report to our Colony Service jobs or, if we had any time left in the day, participate in sports.

At first, it sounded like Apollo High would be a piece of cake: shorter hours, smaller classes, and part-time teachers. Any notions that my new school would be easy, though, disappeared when Mr. Speci downloaded our textbooks into our pads. Trigonometry and calculus; German, Spanish, and Mandarin; third-level English, with an emphasis on grammar and composition; American and European literature; world history; biology, lunar geology, and physics, including a seminar in astronomy; ethics and philosophy. I had to dump all the texts already stored in my pad just to make room for the new material. Compared to Apollo High, my old school in Maryland was the cakewalk I'd been expecting here.

Melissa stared at her pad when she saw what it now contained. "How can you expect us to learn all this stuff?" she protested, her voice rising in horror. "We're in class only five hours a day!"

"Oh, you won't be getting it all at once," Mr. Speci said. "Some of this, like the language, literature, and science classes, will rotate every six weeks. But you'll need to spend at least a couple of hours a night on homework if you're going to stay on top of everything . . . if you have that much free time, that is."

Logan raised an eyebrow. "What do you mean?"

"The three of you are new here. That means you'll need remedial education in some areas." As he spoke, the principal turned to his secretary. "See if you can find someone who's available for the next three or four weeks to put them through Basic Lunar Skills." The young woman on the other side of the office quietly nodded as she typed something into her comp. "That's the course we give everyone who relocates here," Mr. Speci went on. "How to wear and operate EVA gear, how to react in an emergency, how to walk . . ."

"I already know how to walk, thank you," Melissa said testily.

"Really?" Mr. Speci pointed to her ankle weights. "Take those off, then walk to the coffee maker over there. If you can bring me a fresh cup without spilling it, then I'll believe you."

MeeMee glanced at the carafe on a table next to the secretary's desk. It was only eight feet away. "Sure, why not?" she said, then bent down to unfasten her weights. She was careful enough to stand up slowly, but the second step she took was a little too hasty. Suddenly, it was if she'd decided to leap headfirst toward the table. She went sprawling across the room, arms flailing for balance as she yelled something scatological, and probably would have careened into the opposite wall if Mr. Speci hadn't stood up to catch her.

"Nice try," he said dryly.

Melissa scowled at him. The last thing she liked was making a fool out of herself. I was laughing out loud, but I shouldn't have. As it turned out, I'd have plenty of chances of my own to look like a dunce.

* * *

For a second or two, I was certain that I'd just committed suicide.

I'd thrown myself far enough away from the platform that it was unlikely that I'd hit Apollo's upper tiers before I slammed into the crater floor far below. My arms and legs were stretched out as far as I could, forming the snow-angel shape that my paragliding instructor had drilled into me during practice sessions, and I was resisting the instinctive reflex to either curl into a cannon ball or flap my limbs in panic; either one of those would have resulted in a fatal plunge.

Nonetheless, I was falling. Not gliding. Not flying. Falling.

I opened my mouth and was just about to scream when it seemed as if an invisible hand reached up and, ever so gently, began to push against me. I was still falling, but not nearly as fast; air pressure exerted itself against the suit's thin membranes, acting as a force against lunar gravity.

I heard wind in my ears, felt it rush past my face. My velocity remained the same, but my trajectory was changing, becoming more horizontal than vertical. Just as it seemed as if I was about to clip the Tier 3 railing, my body shot forward and . . .

I was flying.

Not very well, perhaps, or very gracefully. I teetered back and forth, skittering this way and that as I fought for control. But it no longer seemed as if I was about to bury my face in a walkway I'd swept just a couple of hours earlier. Far below, I saw a couple of people look up from the park bench. One of them waved to me. I didn't wave back, but instead kept my arms and legs locked in position.

"Way to go!" Logan yelled.

I carefully looked to my left—my instructor had warned me that my head could act as a rudder and cause me to unintentionally change direction while in flight—and saw him coasting alongside me, only about fifteen feet away. He was grinning as he called out to me again. "Nice jump!"

"Thanks!" I yelled back.

"Jamey!" Nicole shouted, and I looked to my right to see that she'd settled into position on the other side of me. When she caught my eye, she gave me a thumbs-up with her left fist. I managed to respond the same way with my right hand and she grinned.

"Follow me!" she yelled. Then she pulled in her right arm and veered away from Logan and me, heading toward the crater wall.

I knew what she was doing, but I wasn't sure if I was ready for that yet. I didn't have much choice, though. Logan gave a rebel yell as he followed her. If I didn't want to be left behind, I'd have to do the same.

Cursing myself for letting jealousy get me into this, I pulled my right arm in ten degrees and followed them.

* * *

I didn't think I'd see Hannah at school. I mean, does anyone ever think they'll be sharing a classroom with the daughter of the president of the United States? Indeed, she later told me that Mr. Porter offered to find private tutors for her. But special treatment was the last thing she wanted; if every other teenager in the colony went to Apollo High, then that's where she'd go, too.

Eddie was almost our age, but he didn't go to Apollo High, nor did he attend Apollo Elementary on the other side of town. The colony didn't have a special-education school because . . . well, to be honest, because he was the only intellectually disabled kid on the Moon, and the youngsters at the elementary school probably wouldn't have been patient with a fourteen-year-old boy still learning to read picture books. So Dr. Rice found a couple of other doctors at the hospital who were willing to tutor Eddie on his own, and so I didn't see him or his sister Nina quite as often as I had before.

It's always tough to be the new kid in school. Everyone is a stranger, and since they already know each other, you can tell that they're trying to size you up as soon as you walk in. Melissa, Logan, Hannah, and I sat together in the back of the room on the first day, and I thought the twelve other kids in the room would sprain their necks staring back at us. Hannah wore her ball cap, but when it became obvious that this wasn't doing anything to conceal her identity—everyone already knew who she was—she took it off and stuck it under her desk, and I seldom saw her wear it again.

And she almost always sat beside me, even after the four of us who'd come from Earth stopped hanging together as a group. I was a little annoyed by this. I liked her well enough, sure, and had gotten over the fact that she'd taken Jan's place, but nonetheless it felt as if she was clinging to me. And as much as she was attracted to me, I was attracted to someone else . . . Nicole. I would've preferred to sit next to her, but Logan always found a way to beat me to the seat beside her. A couple of times, I managed to get there before Logan, yet while Nicole was cordial and polite, it soon became clear that she preferred my best friend to me . . . and whenever I'd glance over my shoulder, I'd find Hannah looking my way.

The only other kid in school I'd met before was Billy. Nicole had told me that there was a good side to him, but if there was, I couldn't find it. He was convinced that I had no business being on the Moon and never missed an opportunity to put me in my place. He hung me with a nickname, "Crip," because of the ankle bracelets I wore while learning to walk in lunar gravity, and continued to call me that even after I got rid of them.

Billy was hardly the swiftest kid in class, but my struggle to catch up was a constant source of amusement for him. He was always ready to make some remark at my expense, usually when I'd get the wrong answer about something everyone else in the room knew by heart, such as the exact circumference of the Moon or when the first American and Russian probes landed there. At first the others thought he was funny, but when it became apparent that he was being a bully for bullying's sake, a couple of people told him to shut up. He put a cork on it, but only reluctantly, and the contempt never left his eyes.

My first impression of Apollo High had been correct; it was much tougher than what I was used to. From seven to twelve, I was immersed in schoolwork so intense that I often had a headache by lunchtime. I'd been a pretty good student back home, usually scoring As and Bs on pop-quizzes and tests, but the rote-learning strategy that once served me well—memorize, regurgitate, forget—didn't work here. My new school wasn't interested in having us develop test-taking skills; our teachers wanted us to truly understand what we were being taught, not just spit out true-or-false answers. So we were expected to come to school prepared to discuss our assignments from the day before, and I soon found that, if I didn't spend enough time doing my homework, I'd be in danger of falling behind. And Apollo High had only two grades: pass or fail.

To make matters worse, one of my teachers was Mr. Lagler himself. Apparently he'd decided to keep secret from Melissa and me the fact that he'd be our language teacher. On the third hour of our first day, though, he sauntered into the room right after the five-minute break following physics class. At first, I thought it was a practical joke; so did Melissa, who laughed out loud when he told us to open our pads to chapter 2 of *Introduction to German*. But it wasn't a gag; our guardian was also one of our teachers, so there was no question of what we'd be doing after dinner from now on.

Melissa had it worse than Logan and I did. She'd never had classes with her little brother, and so she thought she'd been demoted. It took a while for her to realize that Apollo High didn't have grade-levels and that she'd graduate only when she completed the curriculum, whether she was eighteen or eighty. Back home, she'd spend her days passing notes to other girls, flirting with boys, sneaking naps in the back of the room, and getting her friends to let her peep over their shoulders during tests. None of that happened here. When it was 0700, everyone went to work, period; those five-minute breaks were used for stretching or visiting the restroom, and then our noses were back against the grindstone. And when there's only sixteen kids in the entire school, it's pretty easy to tell when someone is slacking off.

For the first week or so, I felt like I'd been tossed in the deep end with my arms and legs tied together. But just as I'd learned how to swim even though I was incapable of walking, I gradually learned how to cope with a workload far more demanding than what I'd had before. By the end of the second week, the headaches were over and I was too busy to really notice or care who sat beside me.

School occupied only the first part of my day, though. When the magic hour of 1200 rolled around and I'd close my pad, I had a choice of what to do with my time between lunch and dinner.

Back home, I would have usually gone down to the school gym, change out of my street clothes, then join Logan and the rest of the swim team in the pool, practicing for our next meet. Here, the very idea of a pool was absurd. Nicole, who'd been born and raised on the Moon, was appalled that anyone would waste water by swimming in it. "Do you know how many gallons of urine we have to recycle just to grow one tomato?" she once asked me, and I had to admit that I didn't. But there were other ways of having fun.

One of them was moonball. Apollo High had its own team, with Mr. Speci as the coach, which practiced on a court behind the school. Moonball was like a cross between soccer and volleyball. It was played on a fenced-in court with artificial turf and a big net slung halfway across. The ball was about as big as a volleyball, and two teams of five people each bounced it back and forth until someone missed. You couldn't use your hands, though; legs, feet, chest, and head were the only parts of your body that could touch the ball. But you could bounce the ball under the net as well as above it, and the surrounding chain-link fence could be used for ricochet shots.

In one-sixth gravity, you could do stuff that was impossible on Earth. One slick move was the flip-dunk: leap straight in the air, do a forward somersault, kick the ball with your feet, then make a two-point landing that would have you ready to intercept it when it came your way again. Another was striking the ball under the net so that it would come up beneath an unwary opponent's legs. Or simply jumping up and slamming the ball over the net so hard and fast that the other team's rear guard wouldn't be able to stop it before it hit the rear fence.

After watching a few games, I tried my hand at it. Or feet, rather. I gave up after a couple of games, though. I was in pretty good shape for someone who'd spent most of his life in a mobil, but I'd only recently learned how to walk without relying on a pair of crutches; my reflexes simply weren't up to a sport as hard and fast as moonball.

While Mr. Speci was willing to let me try out for the team, Billy was the captain, and he wasn't about to give me a break there either. "Go find a wheelchair, Crip!" he'd yell at me when I'd miss a shot and fall on my face. "You can't play this game!" Mr. Speci had a few words with him about this, but after awhile, I had to admit that Billy was right. Like it or not, a lifetime of sitting in a mobil wasn't good practice for moonball, and so I dropped out.

Rover racing was another sport. Apollo had a couple of teams, mainly comprised of adults but with a few kids as well, which customized lunar rovers for higher performance and raced them across Ptolemaeus. I wouldn't be able to join a team until after I learned how to wear a moonsuit, though, and it would be a while before I reached the point where anyone would let me enter an airlock on my own.

I was about to give up on doing anything after school besides sweeping walkways. By then, I had to volunteer for a Colony Service job, and since spacecraft maintenance was a bit beyond me, I had to settle for menial labor. Custodial work wasn't so bad, though; it gave me a chance to learn my way around Apollo, and it wasn't long before I knew where all the ramps, stairs, and elevators were located. It also let me see Eddie and Nina. Eddie had taken a job working in the solarium gardens, and although his little sister wasn't old enough to be required to do Colony Service, she often went along to help him. Eddie seemed to like what he was doing, and that eased my mind about him. At least he was having an easier time fitting in than I was.

Paragliding was even more risky than moonball, and I thought Logan was crazy to try it, but then I saw how he was using it to make time with Nicole, so . . .

* * *

The crater floor was ringed by a series of air vents, circular shafts that allowed warm air to rise from the atmosphere processing plant beneath Apollo. The vents were evenly positioned about a hundred yards apart from each other, and paragliders had learned how to use the updrafts to keep themselves aloft.

The trick was catching these thermals before you descended too far for them to be useful. Nicole and Logan had turned to head for the nearest vent, and I wasn't far behind them when they passed above its black slats. They abruptly rose, their descent braked by the rising air, then Logan made a deft maneuver by pulling in his arms for a second and going into a quick, shallow dive, then stretching out his wings again and using the added velocity to pass Nicole from underneath.

Nicole laughed out loud, obviously impressed. *Okay,* I thought, *two can play that game.*

A couple of seconds later, I passed above the shaft. A warm current of air passed across my body and I felt myself beginning to rise. I kept my arms and legs stretched out as far as I could and allowed the thermal to lift me until I was slightly higher than her and Logan.

And then I pulled in my arms and legs and dove toward them.

Almost immediately, I knew that I'd made a mistake. An experienced paraglider could safely pull a stunt like that, but I wasn't ready for aerobatics and I was too close to the ground. I threw my arms and legs apart again, but I'd already spilled too much air from the suit's membranes. The crater floor was rushing toward me . . . and worse, my friends were in the way.

"Watch out!" I yelled.

Nicole looked back in time to see me coming. She banked to the left, but Logan didn't react quickly enough. He was still flying straight ahead when I came down upon him from on high. For a second, it seemed as if we were about to collide. We didn't, but I came close enough to him that our hands brushed each other's as I swept past.

"Idiot!" Logan shouted, but I barely noticed. All thoughts of trying to score points with Nicole had vanished; my only concern was making it to the ground without breaking my neck. The next nearest vent was about two hundred feet away, but the heads-up display in the left lens of my goggles informed that this was also my present altitude. I'd never make it. Even at lower gravity, I was coming down too fast. . . .

"Use your chute!"

Nicole must have dived to catch up with me. When I looked to my right, she was beside me, only twenty feet away.

"Use your chute!" she yelled again. "Pull the cord!"

Our parachutes were intended to be used for landings, but they were also there for emergencies. *If you get in trouble,* my instructor had said, *don't try to be a hero. Pull the cord and make apologies later.*

Good advice. The rip cord extended through my right sleeve and into the palm of my right glove, its ring firmly attached to my middle finger. I yanked my arm straight up to pull the cord, and a giant claw reached down from the ceiling and grabbed me from behind. The chute had opened; seconds later, I was drifting toward the floor.

It was not a graceful landing. I came down in a goat pen. Anyone standing nearby would've seen my final descent, and I'm sure they were properly amused. I wasn't, and neither was the billy goat that decided I was a menace to society.

I was gathering my chute and trying to avoid being bitten or head-butted when a cart pulled up beside the pen. Mr. Porter was driving, and Hannah was in the front passenger seat. The city manager didn't look very happy with me, but before he could say anything, Hannah jumped out and ran over to the pen, hopping over the fence as if it wasn't there.

"Jamey!" she yelled. "Are you okay?"

Her eyes were wide and her face was pale, and if I hadn't been so angry with myself I might have noticed that she was genuinely concerned. "Yeah, yeah, I'm fine," I grumbled, then looked upward. Logan and Nicole were still airborne, but it looked as if they were headed for the designated touchdown point about a half-mile away. If I knew Logan, he'd have some fine words for me the next time I saw him. "Just great . . ."

"I was . . ." Hannah started to reach for me; maybe it was the look in my eyes when I yanked off my goggles that caused her to stop. "When I saw what was happening, I was worried about you."

Great. First moonball, and now this. My humiliation was complete. "Maybe I should stick to sweeping floors," I murmured as I opened the pen gate and carried my chute out of there. "Or chess. You can't get hurt playing chess . . . maybe."

Hannah was trying not to laugh, but her hands were over her mouth when Mr. Porter approached us. I was too embarrassed to wonder why he and Hannah would have come out to meet me when I landed. "I'm very sorry, sir," I said. "If there's been any damage, I'll . . ."

"There isn't. Least not as far as I can tell." There was a certain look on his face which stopped me short; all at once, I knew that this wasn't about my attempt at paragliding. "Jamey, something's happened. You need to come with us at once."

"What . . . ?"

Hannah answered me before he did. "There's been a message from your sister Jan."

10.
MESSAGES

I thought Mr. Porter was going to take us to City Hall. Instead, we went somewhere I hadn't been before: the Main Operations Center, located on the same underground level as the storm shelter.

Before Mr. Porter and Hannah retrieved me, they had dropped by the flying school to pick up the clothes I'd left in the locker room. I was glad that they had. I didn't want to go walking around in my paragliding outfit . . . and, to be honest, I wanted to avoid seeing Logan. No doubt he'd have a few things to say about the midair collision we'd nearly gotten ourselves into; the longer he had to cool down, the better.

I changed into the homespun trousers, shirt, and sneakers that had lately become my everyday wear. Apollo manufactured its own clothing from bamboo grown in Ag Dome 1; it was plain but durable, and cost less than clothes imported from Earth. Mr. Porter and Hannah were waiting for me outside; we entered a corridor leading into the crater wall and stepped into an elevator.

A couple of minutes later, Mr. Porter pressed a finger against a lockplate and let a retina scanner examine his left eye. The metal door in front of us clicked, and he pulled it open and led us inside. We found ourselves in the back of a large room with a floor that slanted downward to accommodate rows of control consoles facing an array of wall screens. The lighting was subdued, coming mostly from ostrich-neck lamps; men and women in ISC jumpsuits sat at the consoles, their voices a quiet, constant drone interspaced by the occasional electronic beep, burr, or buzz. The screens displayed split-screen images that changed every few minutes: trucks approaching the industrial park; harvesters moving across the regolith fields; a heavy-lift freighter being prepped for launch; a maintenance crew rappelling down the outside of Apollo's roof dome. It was the beginning of another two-week day, so the sunlight cast long shadows from everything it touched.

Gazing at the screens, once again I felt myself longing to go out on the surface. It had been nearly three weeks since I'd arrived at Apollo, but not once had I left the crater except for brief walks down the underground tunnel leading to Ag Dome 1, where Melissa had taken a Colony Service job helping out in the aeroponic farms. Although I had nearly finished Basic Lunar Skills, my instructor hadn't yet qualified me for moonwalking; I knew how to put on a moonsuit, but it would be still be a while before I'd be allowed to cycle through an airlock. I wasn't exactly cooped-up, but it still felt as if I was living in nothing more than an enormous greenhouse.

"Jamey?" Mr. Porter interrupted my train of thought. "This way, please."

Looking around, I saw that he and Hannah had stopped at the back of MainOps to wait for me. I hurried to catch up with them, using the fast shuffling gait I'd adopted after ditching my ankle bracelets; the trick to walking safely on the Moon was to never let your feet completely leave the ground.

Mr. Porter led us to a conference room just off to one side of the operations center. I was surprised to find Luis Garcia sitting at the long table that dominated the room. I'd seen Mr. Garcia from time to time since the town meeting, but had never had a chance to speak with him. Mr. Porter didn't bother to introduce us, though, and Mr. Garcia merely gave us a quiet nod. I wondered why he was there.

"I've sent someone to get your sister," Mr. Porter said to me once Hannah and I were seated, "but I want to show you something while we wait for her. The reason why I brought you here is that we'll have more privacy than in my office. So everything you see and hear in this room needs to stay here. Understood?"

I was suddenly nervous, but both Hannah and Mr. Garcia were watching me expectantly. "Yes, sir. I understand."

Mr. Porter nodded, then reached to a touchscreen imbedded in the table's polished surface. "As Hannah said, we've received a message from your sister Jan. Before I show that to you and Melissa, though, I want you to see another message, one which we received just yesterday." He glanced at Hannah. "You've seen this already, of course, but I think Jamey ought to take a look at it. Is that all right?"

"Umm . . . sure, okay." Hannah seemed reluctant, but she nodded anyway.

Mr. Porter tapped his fingers against the keypad and a wall screen at the end of the table lit up. Seated in an armchair was a middle-aged woman with short blonde hair. Although her posture was relaxed, she seemed nervous; it wasn't hard to notice the dark circles under her eyes. It took me a second to realize who she was: Cynthia Wilford, the former First Lady, Hannah's mother.

Mr. Porter touched another key and Ms. Wilford began to speak. *"Hello, Hannah . . . how are you?"* A brief smile that looked forced. *"I know it's been a long time, but I just wanted to get in touch with you again and let you know that everything is all right. . . ."*

From the corner of my eye, I saw Hannah intently watching the screen. She'd raised a hand to her mouth, so I couldn't quite make out her expression, but I could tell that she wasn't pleased.

"I'm okay here," Ms. Wilford went on. *"I'm being kept in protective custody until the FBI tracks down the rest of the people responsible for killing your father—"* a derisive snort from Hannah *"—but I'm very safe and comfortable."* Another tentative smile. *"I know how much you enjoy Camp David, honey-bunch. Sorry you can't be here. . . ."*

"Yeah, right," Hannah whispered.

"I miss you very much, dear, and I want to assure you that there's absolutely no reason why you should stay on the Moon. President Shapar has promised me that you'll be treated well if you come home. The same goes for your friends . . . their parents are fine, and they'll be detained only until the authorities complete their investigation. . . ."

My throat tightened when she said that. For a second, I was

inclined to believe her, if only because I wanted to. But then Hannah looked at me and shook her head.

"So, please, sugar plum . . . come home." Again, the tortured smile. *"I love you very much, and I want to see you again."*

Mr. Porter froze the image, then looked at Hannah. "Well?"

Hannah slowly let out her breath. "That was my mother, all right . . . but the only thing she said that I believe is that she loves me. Everything else is a lie."

I stared at her. "How do you know? She sounded . . ."

"I know what she sounded like. It's *what* she said that matters. She mentioned how much I love Camp David, but she knows I can't stand the place and that I hate going out there. I'm not even sure that's where she's being held." Hannah pointed toward the screen. "If you look closely at the background, the walls are plain . . . but just about every room in Camp David is wood-paneled, and even the chair she's sitting in doesn't look like the furniture there."

"So this could have been recorded just about anywhere," Mr. Garcia said, speaking up for the first time. "Is that what you're saying?"

"Uh-huh . . . and that's not all. She also called me 'honey-bunch' and 'sugar plum.'" Hannah's nose wrinkled in disgust. "When my father decided to run for president, I told him it would be okay with me so long as his first executive order would be to outlaw cute nicknames for girls. It became sort of an inside joke among my parents. So my mother would never call me anything like that. At least, not unless she was trying to tell me something without anyone catching on."

"Such as, 'don't believe what I'm saying'?"

"Yes, that's what I think she was doing. She was being coerced to tell me to come home, but she doesn't really want me to, so she threw in some stuff that she knew I'd recognize as being false and hoped that I'd catch on." A quick smile. "I guess they've given up the idea that I'm being held hostage by the Chinese."

Mr. Porter turned to me. "We received that yesterday on the standard frequency on which we usually get official US government communiqués. I've decided not to publicly release it, though, because I don't want people here thinking that it might be sincere. That's why I'm asking you not to talk about it outside this room."

"I understand," I said, "but why did you want me to . . . ?"

The door opened just then and a constable walked in, followed by Melissa. Her hair was pulled back under a bandana, and the damp, rolled-up sleeves of her overalls showed that she'd come straight from Ag Dome 2. Her impatient gaze flickered across Hannah and me before settling upon Mr. Porter.

"Well?" she demanded. "Where's the message from my sister?"

"We were just coming to that. Please take a seat." Mr. Porter blanked the wall screen before Melissa could see who was on it, then waved her to a chair next to Hannah and me. "I was telling your brother that there's . . . ah, a possibility . . . that the message we received about an hour ago might not be authentic, and we need to listen to it carefully to make sure that your sister is really saying what we think she's saying."

Melissa peered at him. "I don't get it. Are you saying that Jan didn't . . . ?"

"What he means is that Jan may not have sent this of her own free will," Hannah said. "You need to listen for anything that might sound wrong."

"Like, for instance, if she were to say, 'Wow, I'd really love a hamburger,' we'd know that's a lie because she's vegetarian," I added.

"Oh . . . okay," Melissa said, but I could tell that she was still a little confused. It might have helped if Mr. Porter had shown her the earlier message, but he was wise not to do so. Melissa was incapable of keeping secrets; back home, something whispered in her ear during homeroom would be all over school by lunch time.

"All right, then," Mr. Porter said. "If everyone is clear . . . ?" None of us had any more questions, so he tapped his fingers against the keypad again. Once more, the screen lit up . . .

And there was Jan.

Melissa gasped, and I nearly did the same. In just three weeks, her appearance had completely changed. She was thinner, as if she hadn't been eating often or well. Her hair was no longer either blonde or long; it had been died dark brown and cut to a shag. If I'd seen her on the sidewalk, I might have walked right past without recognizing her.

But that wasn't all. There was a haunted . . . no, a *hunted* . . . look in her eyes that I'd never seen before. Jan was a person who went through life with a smile; there was little that could get her down, no matter how bad things might be. That smile had vanished, and her expression was more serious than I ever seen it before.

She was seated in a metal folding chair. Behind her was a plain brick wall upon which an American flag had been draped. The lighting was bad and the picture was slightly blurred, as if someone had used a pad to record the message. Mr. Porter froze the image and turned to Melissa and me.

"Is that her?" he asked.

"Yeah, but . . ." I began.

"She looks like hell," Melissa finished. Maybe that's not the way I would've put it, but it got the point across.

"But you confirm that it's her, right?" Mr. Garcia asked. Both of us nodded, and he looked at Mr. Porter. "Go ahead, Loren."

Mr. Porter unfroze the image, and Jan began to speak:

"Melissa . . . Jamey . . . hi, it's me." A ghost of smile wavered on her lips. *"Just in case you don't recognize me, y'know."* She reached up to touch her hair. *"Obviously I've made a few changes lately. Had to do it so I wouldn't get caught. The feds have pictures of me all over the net, so . . . well, it's not something I like a lot, but so far it's helped keep me out of jail, so . . ."*

The smile vanished. *"Anyway, I've got to keep this short, so I'll get right to it. First, I'm safe. I managed to get away from the island when the federal marshals showed up. I don't want to say exactly how, just in case someone sees this who shouldn't, but . . . well, someone gave me a uniform and a badge so that it looked like I worked there, so when Dad and the others were arrested, the feds missed me. I've been on the run ever since.*

"Second . . . so far as we know, Dad is safe, too. But he's been arrested and charged with conspiring to kill President Wilford, so there's no way anyone's going to set him free. We think he and the others . . . Logan's parents, Mr. and Ms. Hernandez, a lot of other ISC people . . . are being held somewhere in upstate New York, but we're not sure. But at least they're alive, and hopefully unharmed. When I say 'we.' I mean . . ."

She paused to glance past us, as if listening to someone behind the camera. A couple of moments went by, then she went on. "Look, I have to be careful about how I say this, but . . . I've managed to hook up with some people. They really don't have a name for themselves other than the Resistance, but they're getting better organized with every day, and—" once again, the furtive smile "—they've got friends on the inside. Lina Shapar may be in the White House, but that speech Hannah Wilford made was seen by a lot of people in Washington, and they now know what really happened to her father." She shrugged. "I know you were upset when I gave up my seat on the shuttle for her, but I'm glad that I did it. If she hadn't gotten the word out, things here would be in even worse shape than they are now."

Hearing a quiet sob from beside me, I glanced at Hannah. She was holding a clenched fist before her face, and tears leaked from her eyes. She seemed to be having trouble looking at the screen. Then Melissa, who'd snarled at her when she'd taken Jan's place, reached out to take her hand, silently letting her know that all had been forgiven.

"Now here's the most important thing, the reason why I'm calling you in the first place." Jan leaned closer, staring straight at the camera. "Whatever you do . . . whatever anyone on the Moon does . . . you cannot give up. Not now, not tomorrow, not ever. Because the main thing Lina Shapar and her people want is power, absolute and total power . . . and the only way they'll get it is if they can gain control of the helium-3 pipeline. So long as Apollo remains free, though, they won't be able to do that. Sooner or later, the helium-3 supply will start to run low. When that happens, the Resistance will be able to make its move. But if Apollo folds . . ."

She stopped, shook her head. "I think you get the idea. So you need *to spread the word. Stay firm, don't give in . . . and be ready, because I think it's a pretty good bet that, sooner or later, Shapar will try to take control of the Moon, even if it means sending in military forces."*

Jan let out her breath, sat back in her chair. *"Okay, that's all for now. I'll try to get back in touch with you . . . well, whenever I can."* She struggled to smile. *"I love both of you. Stay well. Bye . . ."*

That was it. The message abruptly ended, as if someone had pushed a button.

No one spoke. For about a minute or so, we stared at the blank screen, each of us taking in what we'd just heard. Then Mr. Porter cleared his throat. "Was that really your sister?" he asked Melissa and me again.

"That was her," I said, and Melissa quietly nodded.

"Any hidden messages? Any double-meanings?"

Melissa raised an eyebrow, not understanding what he meant by that. "No, sir," I replied. "Not like . . ." I glanced at Hannah, and everyone but my sister caught my meaning.

"I didn't think so. If this had been some sort of trick, they wouldn't have changed her appearance." Mr. Porter let out his breath. "She's a brave young lady. No telling what she's been through."

"How did we get this message?" Mr. Garcia asked. "It couldn't have been sent via the usual channels."

"No, it wasn't. We received it earlier this afternoon as an unencrypted file attached to routine data sent from a ISC relay station in Morocco, and even they don't know exactly where it came from." Mr. Porter shook his head in admiration. "The Resistance must have bounced it from one pirate server to another to prevent anyone from tracking it back to its source, until someone hacked into the Morocco station and concealed their message in another transmission. However they pulled it off, though, they did their job well. The point of origin has been scrambled by privacy-protection software. Even the time stamps have been deleted to prevent anyone from knowing which time zone it came from."

"That indicates a certain amount of technical sophistication," said Mr. Garcia. "I'd be willing to bet they've established an underground network operating as individual cells and communicating with each other through pirate ISPs." He glanced at me. "Your sister probably belongs to one of those cells, and they asked her to pass along a message to us since you'd be able to confirm her as a legitimate source."

"I think she just wanted to let us know that she's okay," I said, trying not to bristle at the implication that Jan was being used by the Resistance.

"Oh, don't get me wrong. I'm sure she wanted to do that, too." Mr. Garcia favored me with a placating smile. "But that last part wasn't meant for just you and Melissa . . . it was intended to be heard by everyone on Apollo." The smile faded. "It was a warning, plain and simple. We can't back down even if it means that Shapar might come for us . . . and I have no doubt that she will."

Something clutched at my guts. I remembered what Billy's uncle had said during the town meeting: *You're going to be singing a different tune when the Marines land!* At the time, I thought Mr. Hawthorne was just blowing smoke, but if the Chief Ranger was taking this seriously . . .

"If that's so," Mr. Porter said, "then we need to prepare ourselves . . . beginning with letting everyone know what we've learned." He looked at Melissa and me. "Would the two of you mind if we put your sister's message on the colony newsnet? We'll edit out the personal stuff at the beginning, of course, but I think the rest of Apollo needs to hear what she has to say."

"Sure . . . no problem," I said, and Melissa murmured in agreement.

"Thank you." He drummed his fingers on the table for a moment. "I think the three of you can go now," he added. "Luis and I need to discuss some things in private."

"Certainly." Hannah pushed back her chair. "C'mon, Jamey . . . you can tell me about the jump you just made."

That was the last thing I wanted to talk about, but Mr. Garcia became interested. "Did you go paragliding today?" he asked as I stood up.

"Umm . . . yes, sir."

"First big jump?"

"Yes, sir." I felt my face grow warm.

"Well . . . you're still walking, so that's an achievement. You should try it again."

I didn't know quite what to say, so I nodded. Mr. Garcia gave me a wink, then turned to Mr. Porter. Whatever they wanted to discuss, it wouldn't be while there were kids in the room. So I followed Hannah from the room, with Melissa right behind us.

There was no one to take the three of us back the way we'd come, so I strolled slowly across the back of MainOps, gazing at the massive wall screens. I knew I'd eventually get a chance to leave the crater and walk on the Moon; after all, no one was keeping me a prisoner here.

Okay, so what then? I'd just be doing the same thing as the occasional tourist who paid big money to visit Apollo: put on a moonsuit, hop around, maybe take some pictures. And the rest of the time, I'd spend my days parasailing, sweeping floors, and going to school.

Meanwhile, Jan would be on the run, working for the Resistance while trying to find a way to rescue Dad. The enormity of what they were going up against was utterly terrifying: the entire United States government, with a power-crazy witch as president. No one had to tell me that the odds were against my sister and friends, or that they might lose their lives before it was all over.

What right did I have to be safe while she was in danger? How could I even consider having fun while my sister was fighting for my right to be free?

"Jamey . . . c'mon." Melissa stepped past me to tug at my arm. "We're not supposed to be here."

I started to follow her toward the door, then stopped. Once we left MainOps, the door would lock behind us; my fingerprints and retina scans wouldn't open it for us again. If I left, an opportunity would be lost. . . .

"Jamey . . . !" MeeMee's voice was an anxious whisper, but a few controllers were staring over their shoulders at us. "Let's go!"

Hannah stopped at the door. She turned to look back at me. "You're thinking about Jan, aren't you?" she asked quietly, and I nodded. "You want to do something for her, don't you?"

"Yeah . . . yeah, I do."

She nodded solemnly. "Then go do it."

Without another word, I pulled my arm from Melissa's grasp, then turned and walked back to the conference room. Mr. Porter and Mr. Garcia were huddled together at the other end of the table. Both looked up in surprise when I came back in.

"Yes, Jamey?" Mr. Porter asked, a little perturbed by my interruption. "What do you . . . ?"

"Mr. Garcia, about Lunar Search and Rescue . . . the Rangers, I mean." I swallowed. "It's also a defense force, isn't it? For the colony?"

Mr. Garcia slowly nodded. "That's one of our responsibilities, yes. Why do you ask?"

"I want to join . . . sir."

He said nothing, and neither did Mr. Porter. The two men regarded me with silent appraisal, as if trying to figure out whether I was serious or just acting out of childish impulse. I stood there and stared back at me, trying to ignore the trembling in my knees and the cold sweat seeping down my armpits.

"Search and Rescue isn't just another Colony Service job, Jamey," Mr. Garcia said after a few moments. "It's one of the most dangerous things we do here. If you join, it'll be hard work for you from here on out."

"I . . . I know that, sir."

"Have you finished Basic yet?"

"No, sir, but I'm nearly through the course."

Mr. Garcia said nothing, but I could tell that he was reluctant to take on someone who hadn't even stepped outside the dome. "This is Connie Barlowe's son," Mr. Porter said quietly. "Courage runs in their family, I think."

Mr. Garcia nodded but didn't look away from me. "I knew your mother," he said. "She died saving your life. Think you can live up that?"

"I don't know," I said truthfully. "If you'll give me a chance, I'll try."

Mr. Garcia didn't respond. He and Mr. Porter looked at each other again. Neither of them said anything, but Mr. Porter slowly nodded. The Chief Ranger let out his breath, then he turned to me once more.

"Sleep on it," he said. "If you still feel the same way tomorrow, come to my office at 1300 sharp and I'll sign you up for training."

"Thank you, sir," I said.

He shook his head. "Don't thank me yet. Not until you've done your walkabout." Then he waved me toward the door. "Now go. Get out of here before I change my mind."

THIRD PHASE
ONE SMALL STEP

11.
RANGER THIRD CLASS, PROVISIONAL

You know what's the worst thing about wearing a moonsuit?

It's not the weight. Although Ranger gear was a little less bulky than the standard-issue pressure suit I'd worn while earning EVA certification in Basic Lunar Skills, nevertheless it weighed 250 pounds. That was on Earth, though, where it had been made; on the Moon, it was only about 42 pounds . . . still more than I was used to wearing, but not so much that it felt as if I was going to collapse at any minute.

Nor is it the fact that you're breathing reprocessed air that tastes like it's being fed through an engine filter, or the subtle background hum of the internal electrical system. You get used to these things after a while. It's not even the hassle of putting the thing on. Since the suit is one piece except for the helmet, this involves shimmying feet-first through a small opening behind the hinged life-support pack, then wiggling around until your arms and legs are in the right place. Imagine doing a limbo dance while climbing into a hanging bag and you get the general idea.

Some people say that the biggest nuisance is not being able to scratch your nose through your helmet faceplate, but it wasn't long before I found a solution to that little problem; I'd ignore the itch and think about something else, and pretty soon it would go away. Mind over matter, that's all.

No. The worst thing about wearing a moonsuit is discovering that it can talk to you.

"Hello," my suit said to me the first time I put it on. *"My name is Arthur. Pleased to meet you."*

The voice that came through the padded earphones of my communications carrier—sometimes called a bonnet, although no one actually used that term—had a clipped British accent that sounded like it belonged to a London college professor.

I didn't realize at first that the suit was talking to me. Peering through the helmet's wraparound faceplate, I looked around Airlock 7's ready-room. Four Rangers—Nicole, Greg Thomas, Mr. Garcia, and my fellow "provo," Logan—were also getting into their moonsuits, aided by a number of suit technicians. None of them were paying much attention to what I was doing, though, and the person who'd spoken to me clearly wasn't the young woman who'd just latched my helmet in place.

"Excuse me?" I said, searching for the voice's phantom source.

"Not me," my suit tech replied, her voice muffled even though she stood directly in front of me. When I shook my head, she tapped a finger against her ear prong. "Turn on your comlink."

I reached for the row of recessed buttons in the suit's left wrist. It took me a second to remember which one activated the communications system. "I heard someone," I said once the suit tech and I could hear each other. "Some guy who says his name is Arthur."

"That's me," Arthur said.

I looked around again, still trying to figure who was speaking. The suit tech grinned; to my left, Nicole and Mr. Garcia shared her amusement. "No, no Arthur here," the technician replied, making an exaggerated effort to search the ready-room as well. "You sure you're not hallucinating?"

"No, I heard him." I was beginning to get annoyed. "Is this some kind of trick?"

"It's not a trick, I assure you." Arthur's voice was patient, endlessly forgiving. *"You put me on, and I decided it was time to introduce myself. May I ask your name, please?"*

"Jamey . . . Jamey Barlowe."

"Pleased to meet you, Jamey."

I was about to reply when Mr. Garcia's voice cut in. *"That's your suit's associate speaking to you, Jamey. Its personality subroutine is pro-*

grammed to emulate Sir Arthur C. Clarke, a science fiction author of the 20th century. I requested that this particular suit be assigned to you because Arthur is good with beginners."

Now I understood. My suit was much like my mobil back home; it contained a voice-activated comp that could respond to me much as a living person would, taking instructions given to it in plain English. Not a true artificial intelligence, but rather a clever facsimile. The EVA gear I'd worn during basic training and certification didn't have this feature, but that was because it was the simplified type used by tourists and other people who weren't professional moonwalkers. The moonsuits worn by Lunar Search and Rescue were much more sophisticated, though, so naturally they would have advanced comps.

"Glad to meet you, too, Arthur," I said, feeling rather self-conscious about the whole thing. In all the years I'd ridden my mobil, never once had I felt compelled to give it a name. "Umm . . . wait a minute. Mr. Garcia, what should I do now?"

A dry chuckle. *"Well, you could always ask him to tell you a story. 'The Nine Billion Names of God' is good. But if you'd like to get on with training, then I'd suggest that you ask him how to prepare to exit the airlock."*

"Oh . . . okay." The suit tech had already stepped around behind me. I felt the rear hatch slam shut, followed by a double-beep signaling that the life-support pack had automatically powered up. If I didn't do something about the air very soon, though, I'd start to suffocate. "Arthur, please begin pressurization."

"Certainly, Jamey." A faint hiss, then cool air entered the helmet. *"Incidentally, any time you'd like to have me tell you a story, please let me know. I have many I'm sure you'd enjoy."*

"Another time, thanks." The suit tech was watching to see what I'd do next, so I followed protocol. "Show me the checklist," I said, and a second later a translucent display appeared on the inside of the faceplate, showing all the suit's major functions.

As I began to run down the checklist, I couldn't help but look over at Logan and Nicole. One of the first rules of moonwalking is that the buddy system was always observed; no one goes outside without a partner. For this training exercise, Logan and I were partnered with two Rangers Second Class, with the Chief Ranger coming along as our instructor. Logan had asked Nicole if she'd buddy-up with him . . . and, of course, she'd immediately accepted. I didn't mind partnering with Greg. He was a good guy. But he wasn't Nicole.

Again, I wondered why Logan had decided to join Rangers at the same time I did. A few hours after I was shown Jan's message, it appeared on Apollo's newsnet. As Mr. Porter promised, it had been edited to leave out the personal stuff at the beginning. Nonetheless, it was strange to see my sister appear within the Laglers' holo tank, life-size and looking as if she'd been teleported to their living room. Logan was one of the many people who heard what Jan had to say . . . and the very next day, when I went down to Lunar Search and Rescue to formally volunteer, I was stunned to find him sitting in Mr. Garcia's office.

Logan told me later that he'd decided to join the Rangers after he'd heard Jan's message, and I didn't doubt that this was true. His reasons were the same as my own: if the fight was coming our way, neither of us wanted to be left out.

This was something Melissa didn't understand. *That's not why Dad sent us here!* she'd yelled at me when I told her of my intent to join the Rangers. *We're supposed to stay out of trouble, not get into it!* At least Logan didn't have to deal with a bratty big sister; I told mine that I was doing what I thought was right, and if she didn't like it she could jump out an airlock. Still, it was nice to know that she actually cared about what might happen to her little brother. Melissa wasn't MeeMee all the time, even if she sometimes came off that way.

Mr. and Ms. Lagler were a little reluctant—Ms. Lagler didn't like having me put myself in harm's way, and Mr. Lagler reminded me that I would still be responsible for my schoolwork—but they knew why I wanted to do this and gave their consent.

So did Dr. Ernsting when Logan came to him . . . but why hadn't he talked to me, too? That stung a bit. In the old days, we used to discuss important stuff like this. Logan was my best friend, but lately I'd begun to wonder if he still felt the same way about me. He'd been spending more time with Nicole than with me, and I eventually found out that, when the notion to join the Rangers first occurred to him, he'd called Nicole instead.

I tried to push all that from my mind. This was the fourth time I was going for a moonwalk, but only my first as Ranger trainee. Once Logan and I signed up for Lunar Search and Rescue, Mr. Garcia made sure that he and I were fast-tracked through Basic so that we could get our EVA certification as soon as possible. I'd never again touch a broom; from now on, my sole Colony Service obligation would be to be making it through Ranger training.

So now I was a Ranger Third Class, Provisional. The "provisional" meant that I could be washed out of Lunar Search and Rescue at any time. That was why Logan and I were called "provos." So far, I hadn't been thrown anything that I couldn't handle, but my first two weeks of training had mainly consisted of classroom work and demonstrations. Intense, yes, but nothing that could break me. Today was different. If I couldn't demonstrate that I knew how to handle a moonsuit, I might as well start hunting dust-bunnies again.

The checklist was easy. There were only a couple of minor glitches, and Arthur fixed both of them almost as soon as it—or rather, he—highlighted them on the heads-up display. I was ready to go at the same time as everyone else was. The suit techs gave each other the thumbs-up, and then Mr. Garcia came back on the comlink again.

"Okay, com check," he said. *"Barlowe."*

"Here," I said.

"Doyle."

"Here," Nicole said.

"Marguiles."

"Here," Logan said.

"Thomas."

"Here," Greg said.

"Very good. We're ready to go."

Mr. Garcia stepped forward from the rack, which had held his suit upright while he put it on, and gestured to the technician standing near the airlock's inner hatch. The tech pulled open the heavy door and the five of us trooped into a windowless compartment with a low ceiling and a tiger-striped hatch on the other side. The suit was easier to walk around in than I expected, but it still felt like I was wearing five layers of winter clothes.

The inner hatch slammed shut behind us, and then we stood in a circle and watched as an LED lamp in the ceiling went from green to orange to red, signaling that the air was being pumped out of the compartment. Our helmets hadn't polarized, so I could see everyone's faces. Logan was taking this very seriously—I'd seen that determined look before, when we were getting set for a 50-meter relay race with another swim team—but Nicole was all grins. When she glanced in my direction, I forced myself to smile back at her. Apparently I didn't convince her that I was confident enough to do this, because she shook her head within her helmet.

"Don't worry, Jamey," she said. *"This will be easy. Just like paragliding."*

I restrained a groan. My paragliding experience was something I would have preferred to forget. "Sure, okay . . ."

"Just don't run into me this time," Logan added, glaring at me in a meaningful way. Nicole laughed, but he wasn't kidding and I knew it. He still hadn't forgiven me for our near-collision a couple of weeks earlier. I'd tried apologizing, but he had accepted it with only a cold and distant nod.

What was wrong with him? I didn't know. And he wasn't letting me find out.

"I'm detecting a slight increase in heartbeat and respiration," Arthur said. *"You need to calm down, Jamey."*

I hoped the others hadn't heard this. When no one reacted, I realized that my suit's voice was for my ears alone. "Thanks, Arthur," I said, and took a few slow, deep breaths. "Better now?"

"You're doing fine. No reason to be nervous. I'll always be here to help you."

I knew Arthur was only a comp masquerading as a human being. Nevertheless, I found that reassuring.

The outer doors opened silently, revealing a long ramp leading up toward the surface. With Mr. Garcia in the lead, we slowly trudged up it, obeying the sign on the wall that read DO NOT JUMP. We came out of the crater's subsurface levels to find ourselves on Apollo's east side. On the right were vehicle ramps leading to the underground garage. Directly ahead, just past the reflector ring, was Collins Avenue, the landing fields visible a couple of miles away. I turned around to look behind me and saw the crater wall looming above us, its windows gleaming like rows of Christmas lights.

It was midnight in Ptolemaeus, which meant that the Moon presently lay between Earth and the Sun. However, although the Moon couldn't be seen from Earth, the same wasn't true for Earth as seen from the Moon. It was almost directly above us in the black sky, a white-flecked blue and green sphere that cast a wan glow across the dark grey basin and turned the distant mountains into lumps of melted lead. There wasn't enough earthlight to illuminate Apollo, so floodlights scattered around the crater's periphery had been switched on. Nonetheless, there were more shadows than light, and those shadows were dark enough to swallow us whole if we stepped into them.

Mr. Garcia led us past the reflector ring and across Collins Avenue until we came to a vacant patch of land between the north landing field and the solar farm. He stopped and turned to us.

"Okay, Rangers . . . go play."

For a moment, no one said anything. Then Logan spoke up. *"Pardon me, sir?"*

"I mean it. For the next twenty minutes or so, have fun. Hop around, play tag, build a sand castle, whatever you want to do. Especially you provos."

I was confused, too. We'd been told that this was going to be a training exercise. Instead, the Chief Ranger was treating us as if we were children being let out for recess. "Do we get grape juice and a nap when we're done?" I asked.

Mr. Garcia laughed. *"Sure, if you want. But right now, I want you and Logan to get used to wearing your suits, particularly in low-light conditions. If you're going to hurt yourselves doing something stupid, it might as well be here and now, when we can quickly pull you inside. So go have fun, and when we're done here, we'll separate into teams for the next exercise."*

That made sense, so Greg and I went off in one direction while Logan and Nicole went in another. We switched on our helmet lamps once we were far enough away from the crater that the nearest floodlight couldn't reach us, then Greg showed me a different way of walking when you're wearing a moonsuit and you're in a hurry. Bouncing from one foot to another is the most familiar gait, of course, but I soon learned that the bunny hop, as childish as it looks, let me cover a lot of ground pretty quickly; one good broad-jump could carry me as far as ten feet. But bunny hops could also throw me off-balance if I wasn't careful. I went sprawling face-first into the regolith when I got a little carried away with myself, and the bruises I earned were enough to teach me to watch my step.

Greg was a good moonwalk-buddy. Eighteen years old, he'd been living on the Moon for the past four years. He belonged to a clan, the Starhawks, an extended family of three intermarried couples and their kids; in effect, Greg had three fathers, three mothers, and five brothers and sisters, only one of whom was related to him by blood. Clans had come into existence shortly after Apollo was completed; while he showed me how to get back on my feet after taking a spill, Greg explained that group marriages made it easier for three families to raise children together, not to mention reduce the high divorce rate that had come from the feelings of loneliness and isolation that the early colonists had faced. There weren't many clans, though, and those like the Starhawks frequently had to deal with accusations of immorality, usually from earthside fundamentalist churches and politicians like Lina Shapar, who'd claimed that they were nothing more than an excuse for polygamy.

This was all very interesting, but as I listened to him and perfected my bunny hops, I kept looking around to see what Logan and Nicole were doing. I couldn't hear their voices, which indicated that they'd switched to a private channel, and at first I couldn't see them at all. Then, from the deep shadows about twenty yards away, I glimpsed intermittent flashes of their headlights, briefly revealing each other for a moment before they vanished again.

It took me a minute to figure out what they were doing. They were playing hide-and-seek, going dark while trying to find one another in the shadows. Logan and Nicole were having a great time together . . . and I wasn't invited.

I couldn't help but feel jealous, and was trying to cope with this when Mr. Garcia's voice suddenly cut in. *"Sorry to interrupt, but something has just come up."*

"What's happening, Chief?" Greg asked.

"We've got a medical emergency. Regolith Field Beta, out in Mare Nubium on the other side of Ptolemaeus. Harvester accident, man down."

Nicole's voice came online; she'd switched back to the main channel. *"Do you want us to return to the airlock?"*

"Negative. I'd like all four of you to come along. You and Greg are on duty, and Jamey and Logan might as well get a taste of what we do. So drop everything and head for the north landing field. We have a Pegasus waiting for us."

Logan and Nicole switched on their helmet lamps again, then they joined Mr. Garcia, Greg, and me as we bounded toward the nearby field. It was a good thing I'd practiced bunny hops, because everyone else was doing it; we reached the landing field in just a few minutes, where a Pegasus was already warming up its engines. Technically known as a Long Range Lunar Transport, the Pegasus was aptly named; it was a flying workhorse with a crew compartment up front, an engine cluster in the rear, and a strongback in between that could carry specialized service modules.

When we got to the field, the ground crew had just finished attaching an ambulance, a pressurized module with a red cross painted on its sides, to the strongback. Greg, Nicole, and Logan climbed into the ambulance, but there wasn't enough room for all of us, so Mr. Garcia led me up the ladder into the transport's cramped flight compartment. There were only seats for the pilot and copilot, though, so the chief and I had to stand in the rear and hold onto safety straps slung from the low ceiling.

The pilot watched us come aboard. I didn't recognize him at first, but as I grabbed hold a strap, I heard a familiar voice: *"Well, I'll be damned if it isn't Jamey Barlowe."*

"Gordie! What are you doing here?" I hadn't seen him in weeks. In fact, I'd been so busy that I had almost forgotten about him entirely.

"My new job, kid . . . flying this bucket." He grinned at me through his helmet faceplate. *"Better question is, what are you doing here? Don't tell me you've joined the Rangers!"*

"Yeah, I have. So has Logan . . . he's in the back."

"Really? Well, isn't that a kick in the . . ."

"I know the two of you are friends," Mr. Garcia interrupted, *"but we have an emergency call and really need to get going."*

"Right . . . sorry." Gordie turned back around to his console. *"If you'll shut the hatch, Jamey, we'll be off."* As I reached over to close the hatch, he looked at his copilot. *"Is the ambulance secure, Sam? Okay, let's light 'em up."*

A quick systems check, then Gordie grasped the throttle bars next to his seat and pushed them forward. The cockpit was unpressurized, so we couldn't hear the vertical thrusters when they fired; the deck shuddered against the soles of my boots, and I peered over Gordie's shoulder to see the landing field fall away. The Pegasus ascended to about 1,500 feet before he kicked in the main engines. I caught a glimpse of Apollo, its saucer-like roof illuminated by floodlights, then the transport peeled away on a west-by-southwest bearing.

The flight lasted only a half-hour, and I saw little of the terrain over which we passed, save for the Ptolemaeus crater wall when the Pegasus's searchlights briefly illuminated its mountainous western rim. Mr. Garcia was busy downloading information about the guy we were to rescue, and that gave Gordie and me a chance to catch up. As he'd expected, the FBI had issued a warrant for his arrest for his role in helping Hannah Wilford escape, so he didn't return to Earth. Instead, he'd settled in with "an old friend"—he didn't say so out-right, but I suspected that his friend was female—and found work as a Pegasus pilot. It wasn't as much fun as flying LTVs, but it was a steady job that enabled him to remain on the Moon until things got better back home.

"Not that that's going to happen any time soon," he added. *"I saw today that President Shapar's pals in Congress just killed an independent investigation of Wilford's death. Her party has majority control of the House and Senate, she can pretty much do whatever she wants."*

"There's still protests going on . . ." began Sam, his copilot. Sam turned out to be short for Samantha, and I suspected that she might also be the roommate Gordie had told me about.

"And they're busting protesters as fast as they can cart 'em off to jail. This new president of ours doesn't have much respect for the Constitution, babe, and it's only to get worse before . . ." He stopped himself as a light strobed on his navigation screen. *"Okay, here we are. Hang on back there, Jamey. It's gonna be a rough landing."*

He wasn't kidding. The Pegasus came down fast, with a touch-down hard enough to rattle my teeth and cause me to nearly lose my grip on the strap. But we were in a hurry, and Mr. Garcia ordered me to get the hatch open at once. The dust was still settling he and I clambered down the ladder. Nicole, Greg, and Logan had already climbed down from the ambulance; Nicole was carrying a large case with a red cross on its side.

Gordie had landed only a few dozen yards from the regolith harvester. It was a massive machine, nearly twelve feet high and sixty feet long, with a big scoop up front and a pair of funnels elevated above the rear. When in operation, the harvester would slowly roll across the terrain upon six wire-mesh wheels nearly as tall as I was, gathering regolith into its maw and feeding it through separators that would comb out the ore containing He³ and other vital materials; the stuff that couldn't be used was thrown out the back. Long, shallow furrows across the grey dust showed where the machine had already traveled; a bulldozer would move in front of it, pushing aside rocks and boulders big enough to jam the separators.

The harvester had come to a halt, and its searchlights revealed a couple of miners in moonsuits standing next to a third figure who lay face-down upon the ground. One of the workmen bounded over to us. *"He was standing on the upper platform when we ran through a small impact crater,"* the miner explained. *"The harvester lurched, and he fell off and hit the ground. He says he can't move his right leg and that he's having trouble breathing."*

"Okay, we'll take care of it." Mr. Garcia turned toward the four of us. *"Greg, Nicole, you'll assist me. Logan, Jamey, you can help, too. Fetch the stretcher from the ambulance."*

Logan and I bunny-hopped back to the ambulance, but when we climbed inside, we ran into a problem. Dozens of white plastic containers were strapped against the bulkheads. All field equipment was boxed this way to protect them from moondust, and it wasn't obvious which one held the stretcher. Logan was about to go back and ask for help when a notion occurred to me.

"Arthur, what does a stretcher case look like?" I asked.

"It looks like this, Jamey," my suit replied, and an image immediately appeared on the inside of my helmet: a long, flat container with a red cross on its front. *"Serial number EM-676,"* Arthur added.

I looked around and there it was, identical to the picture Arthur had shown me, right down to the serial number. "Thanks, Arthur," I said, then Logan and I unstrapped the case from its tie-downs.

"Nice trick," Logan murmured as we carried the case from ambulance. *"Maybe you'll impress her yet."*

"What are you talking about?" When I didn't get a response, I checked my heads-up display. Without my realizing it, Logan had switched to another channel. "Arthur, switch comlink to Three." I said. A sharp beep, and then I went on: "I don't know what you're talking about. I'm not trying to impress anyone."

"Sure you are. And she's already taken."

I suddenly realized that he was talking about Nicole. "I'm not trying to impress her," I said, which wasn't entirely true. "If that's what you think, then you're . . ."

"Later. We've got work to do."

Logan was right; just then, our top priority was assisting in a medical emergency. But later, yes, we'd have a little discussion about who was trying to impress who.

We couldn't open the suit of the man who'd fallen from the harvester, of course; that would have to wait until he'd been brought into the ambulance and it had been pressurized. But when Mr. Garcia accessed the miner's suit comp, its associate told the Chief that it appeared as if the worker had suffered a cracked rib along with a fractured femur in his right upper leg. That diagnosis wasn't necessarily accurate, since it was based on the suit's internal biofeedback systems, yet it gave us something to work with until we got the miner to the ambulance.

Nicole found a cartridge inside the case she'd carried from the ambulance and handed it to Mr. Garcia. As I watched, the Chief tapped a combination into the cartridge's keypad, then attached it to a valve in the miner's life support pack. A push of a button, and the cartridge released a sedative into an epidermal skin patch located within the miner's suit. The poor guy's groans and muttered obscenities soon became a relieved sigh. The pain was gone, at least until he reached Apollo General.

By then, Logan and I had opened the container we'd brought from the ambulance, pulled out the stretcher, and spread it out upon the ground. Once the miner's condition was stabilized, Mr. Garcia told the two of us to pick him up and place him on the stretcher. This wasn't as hard as I thought it would be; with his suit included, the miner weighed only about 75 pounds, easy enough for both of us to carry. And I knew a bit about putting people on stretchers. After all,

I'd spent my life being carried around by other people. So I knew how to be gentle and told Logan what to do, and the Chief seemed to be impressed by the fact that I had this sort of knowledge and experience.

Mr. Garcia, Nicole, and Greg walked alongside Logan and me as we hauled the injured man back to the ambulance. This time, it was Greg, the Chief, and I who got to ride in the back while Logan and Nicole shared the cockpit with Gordie and Sam. Mr. Garcia waited until the Pegasus had lifted off again before he pressurized the ambulance, then he opened the miner's faceplate so that we could talk to him.

Until then, I didn't know who we'd rescued. His helmet had been covered with regolith that hid his face. So it came as a surprise when I saw that the injured man was Donald Hawthorne, Billy Tate's uncle.

He recognized me, too. "Hey . . . you're Crip," he said, peering up at me. "You're the kid my nephew was telling me about."

"My name is Jamey Barlowe," I said evenly.

"Ranger Third Class Jamey Barlowe," Mr. Garcia added.

"Yeah, well . . . good luck with that." He said this as if he believed that my new job was only temporary. "So when are you going home?"

"Not any time soon."

"Uh-huh. Sorry to hear that. You . . . *ow!* Dammit, Luis, what are you doing!"

"Just checking you out, Donald." The Chief had twisted Mr. Hawthorne's broken leg ever so slightly . . . and perhaps a little more roughly than necessary. "I figured that if you're going to pull my Ranger's leg, I'd return the favor."

Mr. Hawthorne glared at him, but wisely shut up. All the same, when he look at me, the hostility in his eyes was obvious. He clearly blamed me for all of Apollo's current problems.

And I had little doubt that I'd be hearing the same from Billy as well.

12.
THE GRAVITY OF
THE SITUATION

My premonition was correct. I saw Billy shortly after my search and rescue team brought his uncle to Apollo General.

A bus was waiting for the Pegasus at the landing field. Its boarding ramp connected directly to the long-range transport, and since we'd removed Mr. Hawthorne's suit on the way back to Apollo, that allowed us to carry him aboard the bus without having to depressurize the Pegasus again. Dr. Rice met us in the garage along with a couple of ER medics, and they took Donald Hawthorne straight to the hospital.

In the meantime, Mr. Garcia escorted Logan, Nicole, Greg, and me back to Airlock 7 so we could get out of our suits. He congratulated Logan and me for a job well done. I didn't think our performance had been anything special, but I wasn't about to argue with him.

Nicole was proud of us, too, but it was Logan who got a hug as soon as we were out of our suits; I had to settle for a smile. Better than nothing, I suppose, but all the same it became obvious Nicole had picked him as a boyfriend. Maybe he should have been happy about this, but the look on his face told me that he hadn't forgotten our unfinished conversation. Instead of picking up where we'd left off, though, I went to Apollo General.

I told myself that I wanted to see how Mr. Hawthorne was doing, but the fact of the matter was that I was looking for an excuse to avoid Logan. A wall had come up between us, and there was no easy way to tear it down.

I was able to dodge my friend, but I wasn't so lucky with my nemesis. Someone had notified Billy that his uncle had been in an accident, because he was already at the hospital by the time I arrived.

He was sitting in the ER waiting room when I walked in; he silently watched as I went to the front desk and asked how Mr. Hawthorne was doing. The receptionist told me that he was in surgery, but that his condition was satisfactory and he was expected to make a full recovery, and that a doctor would soon come out to speak with us. Meaning Billy and me, since we seemed to be the only people who cared enough about Donald Hawthorne to come to the hospital.

Billy hadn't said very much to me after I joined the Rangers. Someone had apparently told Mr. Garcia that there was bad blood between us—probably Mr. Speci, who'd coached both of us during my attempt at moonball—because I'd noticed the Chief was doing his best to keep Billy and me separated. But even though I'd tried to keep clear of him during school, it was only inevitable that we'd eventually meet up.

I had a choice. Either I could make a long and detailed study of the potted ferns, or I could talk to him. So I walked over to where he was sitting.

"Hi. Mind if I join you?"

He shrugged. "Suit yourself."

There was a vacant seat beside him; he didn't seem to care if I took it. "Sorry about what happened to your uncle," I said as I sat down. "Glad to hear that he's going to be okay."

"Yeah, I guess." He was leaning forward, elbows on his knees, staring at the floor's patterned tiles. He didn't look at me, and seemed to be indifferent to my presence.

I looked around the room, saw no one else there. "Umm . . . don't you have an aunt, or someone else who . . . ?"

"My aunt moved back to Earth a couple of years ago after she got a divorce from my uncle. Haven't seen her since. I'll try to call her when I hear something from the doctor, but—" another shrug "—y'know, I think she'd care only if he died."

Wow, I thought, *that's cold.* I knew a little about Billy; he was born on the Moon, but his parents were divorced when he was a little kid and both had decided to return to Earth. Neither of them could take him with them, though, or otherwise he would've ended up in a mobil just like I had, so he'd remained in Apollo with his uncle and aunt. I wasn't aware that his aunt had left, too.

That made his uncle the only family he had on the Moon. Given the way Donald Hawthorne had carried on during the town meeting, it was no wonder that they didn't have many friends. However, when a half-dozen or so Americans loyal to President Shapar had left Apollo when the ISC embargo began, Mr. Hawthorne wasn't among them. I figured it was because he didn't want to give up a high-paying job as mining supervisor, but maybe it was because he would have had to leave his nephew alone.

I had taken a dislike to Billy the first moment we met, when he'd made fun of Eddie for being slow. But just then, I couldn't help but feel a little sorry for him . . . and wonder if he'd become a bully in response to his own insecurities.

I was trying to think of something to say when he beat me to it. "I suppose I ought to thank you now for saving Uncle Don," he said, still not looking at me.

"You don't have to. I didn't do much. Just put him on a stretcher, that's all."

"Yeah, sure, but . . ." He reluctantly stuck out his hand. "Thanks anyway."

That surprised me. I hesitated, then shook his hand. "No sweat. Just doing my job, that's all."

For the first time, he raised his eyes to meet mine. "You're serious, aren't you? About wanting to be a Ranger?"

"Sure, I'm serious. Why wouldn't I be?"

Billy didn't say anything for a second or two. He simply looked at me as if he was trying to make up his mind whether I was putting him on. "When I heard you were joining up, I thought you were just doing this to . . . I dunno. Try to be a big shot or something. I didn't think you could do it. Not after the way you screwed up at moonball."

My face became warm. "Moonball's a game. This is for real."

"I know how real it is . . . and I know you can screw up on an S & R mission even worse than you can playing moonball. But you didn't." He paused, then went on. "Look, if you think you can handle being a Ranger, then I've got your back. Understand?"

If a stray asteroid had crashed through the dome just then, I couldn't have been more shocked. "I understand, yeah. Thanks . . . I appreciate it."

He nodded, then a wry grin spread across his face. "Just don't screw up, or it's back to calling you 'Crip' again."

I was about to ask him if it was too much trouble if he'd simply call me Jamey when the treatment room door opened. I looked up, thinking I'd see Dr. Rice or another one of the doctors, and instead saw someone I hadn't expected: Hannah.

I had completely forgotten that she'd taken a Colony Service job at Apollo General. Although she was only a nurse's assistant, she wore doctor's scrubs, complete with a stethoscope around her neck. I was still staring at her when she walked over to us.

"Billy?" she asked. "Dr. Rice sent me out to talk to you. Your uncle is going to be fine. His right femur is broken and he has a couple of cracked ribs on his right side, but there was no damage to internal organs."

Billy took a deep breath, slowly let it out. "Good. Great."

"He'll probably have to walk with crutches or a cane for the next several weeks, and the doctor is barring him from EVA until he fully heals, but he'll be okay after that." Hannah looked at me. "By the way, the doctor also sends her compliments for the nice work you and your team did out there. She's impressed with the way you handled your first rescue mission."

"I didn't do . . ."

"That's just what I was telling Cri . . . Jamey," Billy said. "For a provo, he showed that he's got what it takes to be a Ranger."

I bit my tongue, remembering that only a few weeks ago Billy had been busting my chops for the way I played moonball. But Hannah's eyes were shining, and there was no mistaking the fact that she was proud of me . . . and maybe more.

"Can I see him now?" Billy asked.

"Umm . . . I think so, but let me check first, okay? Be right back." Hannah turned and went back into the treatment room. Billy waited until she was gone, then he turned to me.

"Want some advice?" he murmured. "You're not going to get anywhere with Nicole."

I blinked, wondering if my feelings for Nicole were so obvious that even the guy who'd been my enemy had noticed them. "But Hannah . . ." Looking away, he shook his head in disgust. "Man, you gotta be blind if you can't see she really likes you."

"We . . . we're just friends," I stammered. "I mean, she . . ."

The door swung open again; Hannah was returning to take Billy to see his Uncle Don. I shut up, but Billy had a sly grin on his face. "Don't pass up a good thing," he murmured, then he stood up to let her lead him away.

Hannah gave me one last glance before they disappeared through the door. There was a smile on her face. I wondered if Billy was right.

* * *

Even if I'd wanted to see more of Hannah, though, I didn't have much opportunity to do so. Matters back home soon took a turn for the worse, and they would affect everyone living on the Moon.

Demonstrations against President Shapar had become widespread over the past few weeks, occurring almost every day in one American city or another. Some may have been organized by the Resistance, but I suspect most were spontaneous. Not very many people believed the White House's story about President Wilford having been the victim of an assassination plot, and the administration's refusal to allow an independent investigation reeked of a cover-up. The demonstrations were usually broken up by police or National Guard, and scores of protesters being carried off to jail, yet the crackdown did little to prevent them from happening again.

In the meantime, the ISC embargo was beginning to have an effect. It doesn't take a lot of He^3 to fuel a fusion reactor, but its scarcity meant that American power plants usually maintained low stockpiles. As reserves began to run low, utilities suddenly realized that it wouldn't be long before they might not be able to provide electricity to all their customers. When government negotiators failed to reach a settlement with the ISC to end the embargo, President Shapar reacted by withdrawing the United States from the consortium. This decision may have pleased the reactionaries in her party who didn't trust "Eurosocialists," but it didn't do anything to solve the looming energy shortage. And since it was now late October, the prospect of a long winter made colder by rolling blackouts didn't do anything to boost her standing in public opinion polls.

The real crunch came in the last week of October when a White House insider came forward to state that President Wilford had died of natural causes: Dr. Owen Edwards, the late president's personal physician, who'd fled the country a few days after Wilford's death. Speaking at a press conference in Germany, Dr. Edwards confirmed Hannah's assertion that her father had suffered from a preexisting condition that had been kept secret from the public. To prove his claim, he released Wilford's private medical records, including a list of medications he'd prescribed to the late president. Other doctors quickly verified that the records were real and hadn't been falsified.

That was the smoking gun. Overnight, Lina Shapar's last shred of credibility vanished. It could no longer be denied that she'd lied to the American people about President Wilford's death. Her claim to the White House was still constitutionally legitimate, but the actions she'd taken—particularly the arrest of ISC officials and others—were a clear abuse of power. On Capitol Hill, key members of her party realized that they couldn't continue to support the president. Within days of the Edwards interview, forty-seven congressmen from all three parties—including her own—cosigned a formal motion calling for her impeachment.

But Lina Shapar wasn't about to go down without a fight. On Halloween night, she went live on the net to declare martial law.

The excuse she used for such an unprecedented action were the demonstrations and the coming energy crisis. Both posed a danger to civil order, she said, and so it was her responsibility to deploy military forces in order to keep the peace. The fact that the Constitution doesn't give the president the authority to impose martial law meant nothing to her. Within hours, trick-or-treaters were being swept indoors by their parents as federal troops moved to enforce the dusk-to-dawn national curfew ordered by the White House; by morning, the entire country was in lockdown, with arrest warrants being issued for known dissidents. Vice President H. P. O'Hanlon, the former New Hampshire senator who'd become Shapar's hatchet man on the Hill, officially dissolved the Senate, and when Speaker of the House Mildred Ferguson refused to do the same, she was detained by federal marshals and taken away from the Capitol in handcuffs.

On the Moon, we saw the president's speech on a netcast transmitted to Apollo. Until then, the problems back home seemed remote. Not that we didn't care what was happening, but 240,000 miles is a long distance; we weren't likely to have federal agents knocking on our doors any time soon. Yet one thing in the president's address was particularly ominous:

"The gravity of the situation demands that we take active measures to insure that all Americans continue to have sufficient electricity for their homes and businesses. Our country's access to vital lunar resources cannot be interrupted, and we must reclaim that which has been taken from us."

The next day at school, during a break between classes, a bunch of us kids discussed the speech. Mr. Lagler had just left, and Mr. Rupley's lit class was next. He was running late, though, so while some guys went outside to stretch their legs with a quick game of hackey-sack—which is amazing in one-sixth gravity, by the way—a few of us chatted about what we'd heard the night before.

"She's going to invade us." Billy leaned against the teacher's desk, arms folded across his chest. "She'll send in the Marines, and they'll take over."

"She wouldn't dare." Nicole shook her head. "The other ISC members wouldn't let her. They'd consider it an act of war."

"Really?" Billy raised an eyebrow. "Do you think Canada, India or Brazil would declare war on the US just because Shapar sent troops up here?"

"They might . . ."

"No, they won't," said Gabrielle Frontnauc. Along with Greg Thomas, she was the oldest kid in the room. "I hate to say it, but all my country really cares about is whether it receives its helium-3 shipments. So long as America makes a deal with France and the other ISC countries . . ."

"That's the whole point." As usual, Logan was sitting next to Nicole; I tried to ignore the fact that their hands were almost touching. "That's what this is all about. Shapar's not going to make a deal with anyone. She wants total control of the helium-3 pipeline, because she knows that if she gets it, the US will have a monopoly over most of the global energy supply."

"You're forgetting the PSU," Greg said. "Moon Dragon refines almost as much He^3 as Apollo does."

"Yeah, but it all goes to China, Korea, and Taiwan," Logan replied. "They're not going to share what they have with Europe or South America . . . and especially not with Japan."

"Why not?" Melissa asked. "I mean, they're on the same side of the world, aren't they?"

Gabrielle turned to stare at my sister. "Short of a major earth-quake, there is no way China will ever go to Japan's aid." There was just a touch of condescension in her voice. "The two of them have a long-standing distrust of one another. They've even gone to war a few times. We studied that last week in World History . . . remember?"

Melissa looked down at the floor. Even though she and I been on the Moon for almost nine weeks, MeeMee still hadn't gotten it through her head that Apollo High was a lot more serious than our school back home. She wasn't keeping up with her homework, was goofing off when she should be studying, and she'd sit in the back of the room and daydream when she needed to be paying attention. Occasionally she got away with it—MeeMee had always been good at conning teachers into believing that she was a better student than she really was—but at times like this her negligence became painfully obvious. I almost felt sorry for her, but not quite. If someone like Gabrielle, whose tongue was as sharp as her mind, wanted to come down on her, that was fine with me; I'd given up trying to change my sister's ways.

"Anyway," Melissa said, trying to save face, "I don't think they're going to attack us. Violence never solves anything."

The others regarded her with disbelief, and I wanted to crawl beneath my desk in embarrassment. Hannah was sitting across from me; she gave me a sympathetic smile and I refrained from rolling my eyes. Hannah knew that my sister could be a ditz at times.

"Actually, violence solves a lot of things," Logan said. "It's just messy, that's all."

Everyone laughed at this except Melissa. "I happen to be a pacifist," she replied, an arch tone in her voice.

"Oh, really?" Logan grinned at her. "You know what a cannibal calls a pacifist? Lunch."

That sparked even more laughter. My sister's face went red. "Oh, ha-ha-ha . . ."

"If you want to claim you're a pacifist," Logan went on, a little more seriously now, "that's your right. But if you were facing a hungry cannibal, I guarantee you'd forget all about being a pacifist and fight tooth and nail to stay alive."

Melissa scowled but didn't come back with anything. Maybe she couldn't. In any case, I decided to take the heat off her. "What do you think?" I asked Hannah. "You know Lina Shapar. What do you think she's going to do?"

Hannah winced, and I immediately regretted the question. She didn't like to discuss the fact that her late father had been president; all she wanted to do, really, was fit in with the other kids. She didn't duck the question, though. "Logan's right. She's a cannibal . . . I mean, totally ruthless. All she wants is power." She gave Melissa a sympathetic nod. "But you're right, too. There's other ways of staying out of the stew pot than killing the guy who's trying to eat you. You just have to figure out how."

The classroom door opened just then. We looked around, expecting to see Mr. Rupley, but instead Mr. Speci came in, followed by the guys who'd gone out to play. The principal stepped behind the desk and waited until everyone had returned to their seats before he spoke.

"I have an announcement to make," he began. "How many of you saw President Shapar's speech last night?" Almost everyone in the room raised their hands. "Good. Then you know what she said, especially the part about lunar resources. That means us . . . and it also means that we've got to be prepared for trouble if it comes our way."

He paused, letting his words sink in, then went on. "Several of you belong to the Rangers, even if you're still in training—" his gaze traveled to Logan and me "—while some have Colony Service jobs that are in vital areas of the community, like the hospital." He nodded to Hannah, who said nothing. "In any case, no matter what you do, each and every one of you have essential roles that are going to be important over the next . . . well, however long it is before this situation is resolved. And as important as your education is, right now you need to be spending more time at your tasks than you do here in the classroom."

Everyone glanced at one another, not quite believing what we were hearing. If Mr. Speci noticed, though, he paid no attention. "I've spent the morning discussing this with the school board and the city manager," he went on, "and we've decided that classes at both Apollo High and Apollo Elementary will be suspended until further notice."

I looked over at Hannah; she was just as surprised as I was. Melissa made a little squeal of delight that she quickly stifled when she realized that no one was sharing her joy. Everyone else was too stunned by what we'd just heard.

"So . . . well, I guess that's about it." Mr. Speci said. "Rangers, please report immediately to Search and Rescue to begin special training. Everyone else, you're to go to your jobs where you'll receive new assignments. We'll let you know when classes will be resumed."

He seemed to be at a loss for what to do next, so he simply turned and walked out of the room. For a second or two, no one said anything. Melissa jumped up from her seat and practically danced out the door, but the rest of us just stood up and shuffled away. School was out, but there was little reason to celebrate.

Everything had just changed, and not for the better.

* * *

Two hours later, the Rangers were assembled in Airlock 7, waiting for the outer door to open. For the first time since I'd joined them, all thirty-six members of Lunar Search and Rescue were in the same place at the same time, from Third Class provos like Logan and me all the way to the First Class pros. Mr. Garcia had called a full muster, but he hadn't yet told us why, only that we were expected to be in our suits and ready to moonwalk at 1200 sharp.

The airlock doors rolled open, and we tramped up the ramp into the lunar late-afternoon. Another long night was coming, and Earth was a silver crescent, shedding little light upon the shadows that had begun to stretch across the grey terrain. By then, I'd gone EVA plenty of times; it no longer felt strange to wear a moonsuit, and Arthur had become a friendly acquaintance, a kindly English gentleman ready to help me when necessary. A few of the First Class guys still treated me like I was a kid, but most had come to accept me as a fellow Ranger, albeit inexperienced. So I was with my crew, ready to take whatever was thrown at me.

We bounced and bunny-hopped out to the vacant field where Logan and I been doing most of our training over the past several weeks. A rover pulling a two-wheeled equipment cart was parked there. About twenty yards away, a row of discarded radiator panels had been erected on vertical stands. Someone had cut sheets of red insulation film into concentric circles and used epoxy goop to attach them to the panels; they looked like targets, and as it turned out, that's exactly what they were.

Once everyone was gathered in a semi-circle, Mr. Garcia stepped in front of us. *"Gentlemen, the day has come that I hoped never would,"* he began. *"Until now, our primary function has been to provide emergency services for Apollo. That's still our job, but we now have a new function . . . serving as the colony's first and last line of defense. Yet our motto remains the same. Let's hear it."*

"Failure is not an option," several people said. It came out as a ragged and half-hearted chorus that I barely heard through my communications carrier.

"Sorry, that's not good enough," the Chief Ranger said. *"Let me hear it again."*

"Failure is not an option!" This time I said it too, along with everyone else.

"I'm still not hearing you!"

"FAILURE IS NOT AN OPTION!" It became a determined, full-throated yell that made my ears ache.

"Outstanding . . . and never forget it." Mr. Garcia turned to a Ranger standing at the right end of the semicircle. *"Mikel, will you help me, please?"* Mikel Borakov, a First Class who'd been one of my instructors, skipped over to him. *"In order to accomplish this, we will need to show most of you how to do something that hasn't been included in regular Search and Rescue training . . . how to handle lunar-rated firearms. Mikel*

has had this sort of training, and so have I and a couple of others, but the majority of you haven't. In fact, I don't believe most of you have ever fired a gun in your lives."

He was right. My only previous experience with guns was playing combat games on my pad, and I was sure that didn't count. *"Most people here don't know this,"* Mr. Garcia continued, *"but Apollo has a small arsenal, provided to us by the United States in case our friends in the Pacific Socialist Union should ever decide to mount an attack upon us from Moon Dragon."* He paused, perhaps wondering if he should mention the ironic fact that we'd be using those same weapons to defend ourselves against our benefactors, then went on. *"Mikel, would you show them our guns, please?"*

Mikel went over to the trailer and opened its side panel. Stacked inside were dozens of long plastic containers, each with a red caution triangle stamped on its side. *"There are thirty-five HK L-11 carbines in this trailer,"* the Chief Ranger continued, *"along with three hundred rounds of ammunition. Fifteen more carbines are in storage, along with another nine thousand, seven hundred rounds of ammo. This, gentlemen and ladies, constitutes the entirety of our small-arms cache."*

Through my headset, I heard low whistles and disgusted murmurs. Someone cursed, and someone else told him to shut up. *"Obviously, we're a bit short of firearms,"* Mr. Garcia said, and a few bitter laughs came in response. *"However, we also have five shoulder-mounted grenade launchers and two hundred and fifty grenades, sixty short-range mortar rockets . . . and something else. Turn around and look behind you."*

We turned to see that something had moved up behind us while we weren't looking, an enormous vehicle which I first thought was a regolith hauler from the mines. As it came closer, though, I saw that it moved upon caterpillar treads instead of wheels, and upon its flat bed was a long gun mounted on a swivel turret. A driver sat within a transparent dome up front, and laser targeting apparatus stood atop a post beside the canopy.

"This is a . . ." Mr. Garcia began, and then suddenly yelled, *"Incoming!"*

I turned around so fast that I almost lost my balance. Even I struggled to keep from falling over, though, I spotted what he'd seen. Beyond Apollo, rising into the black sky above the Ptolemaeus's western ridge, was a small object that reflected the sunlight and left a reddish-orange trail behind it.

A missile, launched from the other side of the nearby mountains. It reached its apogee, then it turned downward and began to hurtle straight toward Apollo.

13.
GUNS AND
ST. CHRISTOPHER

For a second or two, no one moved. I think the other Rangers were just as surprised as I was, stunned motionless by the notion that an attack would come so soon from such an unexpected direction.

Then everyone snapped out of it. We began to run in all directions at once, bouncing or bunny-hopping away in a mad scramble to find cover in the open field. A couple of guys leaped behind the trailer, while a few others turned to flee back to the crater. Through my headset, I heard a cacophony of voices:

"Down, down . . . !"

"Hit the dirt!"

"Where the hell did that . . . ?"

"Rangers! Stand down!" The Chief's voice broke through the panic. *"Blitzgewehr . . . fire!"*

I happened to be looking at the tractor when he yelled, so I saw what happened next. The giant gun swiveled about on its turret, moving so fast that it almost seemed to blur. Then a narrow beam the color of a lightning bolt lanced from its barrel. The gun made no sound as it fired, and neither did the missile when it exploded a half-second later.

For a few moments, no one said anything. We all watched as the twisted, blackened pieces of metal that had once been the missile tumbled to the ground, disappearing from sight beyond the crater. I think the other Rangers had caught on to what had just happened; if they didn't, though, Mr. Garcia provided an explanation.

"Gentlemen, ladies . . . that was a demonstration," he said. *"The missile was one of ours. It didn't have a warhead, and it was launched from a site outside Ptolemaeus. Even if my little toy hadn't brought it down, it*

would have landed about a half-mile east of Apollo. You would have seen it fly overhead just before it crashed."

Mr. Garcia turned toward the gun. *"Now that you've been introduced . . . meet the* Blitzgewehr *PBW-1, a mobile artillery piece provided to us by our German partners. Its gun fires a neutral-charge particle beam at nearly the speed of light toward whatever its operator targets with his laser sight. Once its fire-control computer is activated, it can automatically track, lock onto, and fire upon several missiles at once. It can take out missiles launched at us from either the ground or the sky, and even defend us from low-orbit spacecraft. Any questions?"*

"Sir . . . ?" This from Mahmoud Chawla, a Ranger First Class who'd given me a couple of tips about getting into my suit with a minimum of hassle. *"I haven't seen this before, and I don't think anyone else has either. Are we missing something, or has this been kept secret until now?"*

"Yes, Mahmoud, it has. The Blitzgewehr *was transported here in sections several months ago and secretly assembled in a closed area of the garage. Very few people knew of its existence because we didn't want the PCU to think that we might use it to attack Moon Dragon . . . although we have little doubt that they have a PBW of their own. But the powers that be don't want to do anything that might provoke the Chinese, so nothing has been said about it."*

"Is this the only one?" Nicole asked.

"I hate to say it, Ms. Doyle, but, yes, it is. The Germans have a second Blitzgewehr—*incidentally, the name means 'lightning gun,' in case you're interested—on the drawing board, but they haven't yet had a chance to build it, let alone send it here. So we're going to have to make do with just this one. I think that'll be sufficient. Any other questions?"*

Mr. Garcia waited a moment. When no one spoke, he went on. *"All right, you've seen that the gun works fine. I wish I could say the same for the rest of you. Your response was pathetic. No, worse than pathetic . . . it was embarrassing. You were slow, and a couple of you—"* he turned toward the two men who'd tried to take cover behind the trailer *"—were borderline cowards. I realize that most of you have no combat training, but that's not an excuse. If Apollo is attacked, our friends and family will be counting on us to defend them . . . and since there's only three dozen of us, that means no one can run and hide when trouble comes."*

He paused, almost as if daring someone to disagree with him. No one did. Everyone knew what we'd done—or rather, what we hadn't done—during the phony missile attack. I was ashamed of myself, and I'm sure the others were, too.

"That's going to change," Mr. Garcia continued. *"From now on, being a Ranger is your first priority . . . you've been relieved of all other responsibilities. At 0800 each and every morning, we will meet here for drill, which will include special training in small arms and military tactics."* He turned toward me. *"Mr. Barlowe? You and Mr. Marguiles will continue your Third Class training, with Ms. Doyle and Mr. Tate as your instructors. In two weeks, I want both of you ready to take your walkabouts. No excuses . . . understand?"*

"Yes . . . yes, sir," I stuttered, and when Logan said that the same thing, I could tell that he was just as stunned as I was. It usually took months of training before a Ranger Third Class was ready for walkabout; Billy had to do it twice before he passed, and he'd been in Lunar Search and Rescue for over a year. It seemed impossible that Logan and I could be ready go solo by the beginning of the next lunar day. Yet the Chief wasn't giving us a choice. We would be ready; failure was not an option.

"Very good." Mr. Garcia pointed toward the trailer. *"All right, ladies and gentlemen . . . gather round Mikel here, and he'll show you how to use a gun."*

* * *

And that was the beginning of my career as a citizen soldier.

Officially, the Rangers were still a peacetime outfit; Lunar Search and Rescue was supposed to be doing just that, nothing more. Everyone knew better, though. We'd been drafted to fight a war that none of us wanted but which was being thrust upon us anyway: thirty-six men and women, charged with protecting Apollo from a foe which, only a few weeks ago, we would have considered to be our friend. If I still had any illusions that I was never going to have to go into combat, they evaporated as soon as I was given a gun.

At first glance, the HK-11 lunar carbine looked like an ordinary military assault weapon, save that it had only a rudimentary butt. The resemblance pretty much ended there. In fact, it operated on different principles entirely. A round ammo drum that jutted out from below its stock contained thirty rounds of what were called bullets, but which were actually 9mm hollow-point projectiles that were fired by a miniature electromagnetic catapult contained within the barrel. Sort of like having a little magcat of my own. This meant that the gun had virtually no recoil: no gunpowder, no kick. The butt was there only to brace and balance the weapon.

Although a sight was mounted above the barrel, it wasn't meant to be used visually. No one wearing a moonsuit would be able raise the gun high enough to gaze through a normal sight, let alone get a good fix on the target, because his helmet faceplate would get in the way. So the gun used a virtual gunsight instead. Once the carbine was interfaced with my suit computer, all I had to do was raise it to my chest and point it at the desired target, and a translucent red crosshairs would appear within my faceplate. When I moved the gun, the crosshairs would move as well, until I had a dead bead on whatever it was I wanted to shoot. I could select laser, ultraviolet, or infrared for the targeting medium.

Once I was ready to fire, I'd curl my index finger around the trigger and the gun would kick out a bullet. And if I kept pressure upon the trigger for longer than two seconds, the carbine would shift to full-auto mode and keep firing at a rate of thirty rounds per minute, until I either relaxed my finger or ran out of ammo.

In theory, the bullets could penetrate a moonsuit's polymer shell, although in actual practice that meant getting a direct hit at ten

feet or less. But helmet faceplates were vulnerable, as were the elastic
joints at a suit's shoulders, elbows, wrists, waist, hips, knees, and
ankles. We were told to aim for those joints; a head or stomach shot
would be instantly fatal, while an arm or leg shot would cripple or
immobilize an attacker.

Another target was a suit's life support pack. A direct hit at close
range could penetrate the oxygen-nitrogen tanks and cause the suit
to lose pressure. However, that would mean shooting someone in the
back, and I don't think any of us were bloodthirsty enough to do that.
As Mr. Garcia said, few of the Rangers had military experience, so it
was hard for most of us to even consider killing another human being.
Lunar Search and Rescue was supposed to save lives, not end them.
It was particularly difficult for Americans like myself to think that
we may have to soon go up against US Marines; their space infantry
would probably be the ones sent to the Moon, and I didn't like the
idea of shooting someone from my own country.

But Apollo had a couple of things in its favor. Earth lies at the
bottom of a deep gravity well, while the Moon is the bottom of a
shallow one. This means that any ship that leaves Earth has to climb
up an imaginary well before it reaches that place where gravity is no
longer an issue. Then it has to fire its engines to order to achieve lunar
trajectory, and again to brake for lunar orbital insertion or landing. So
a sneak attack was all but impossible; we'd be able to see an assault
force coming long before it arrived. The telescopes normally used for
astronomical research were aimed at Earth instead, and people were
assigned to maintaining a constant vigil.

The other advantage we had was that Ammonius was a natural
fortress. Its outer crater wall and dome was virtually impregnable to
everything except a missile attack, which the *Blitzgewehr* was supposed to repel, and once its windows were shuttered and airlocks
sealed, a strike force would have a very hard time gaining control of
the city.

So the inhabitants could hole up in the crater almost indefinitely;

it was the job of the Rangers to make sure that the Marines couldn't get through the airlocks. The fact that there were only thirty-six of us, though, didn't make that task any easier. We could only guess how large an attack force would be, although no one doubted that there would be less than three dozen Marines. No one had ever seriously believed that the Pacific Socialist Union would attack Apollo, and the idea that an ISC country would turn on us was ludicrous. So defense had never been a major priority until now.

Every morning, the Rangers suited up and went outside for combat training. It took several days for most of us to learn how to handle our weapons well enough to even be able to hit the targets set up on our make-shift rifle range. We didn't have a lot of reserve ammunition, though, so our practice sessions were kept short. The rest of the time, we were taught battlefield tactics: how to work as squads, how to mount an assault, how to retreat, how to keep from hitting each other in a firefight. All of which is hard enough to learn in any situation, but even more difficult when you're wearing a moonsuit.

Military training would end around noon, and then we'd return to the crater to replenish our life support packs and tend to the scrapes, cuts, and bruises we'd suffered the past few hours. A quick bite to eat, then it was back in the suits and out the airlock again. Most of the Rangers had been tasked to building temporary fortifications around Apollo—regolith berms, big mounds of moondust plowed into position around the crater and its environs—but Logan and I had our own job: learning everything we needed to know in order to become Second Class as soon as possible.

Here's just a few things I had to master. Celestial navigation, using visible stars and the current positions of Earth and the Sun to figure out where I was. Emergency medical procedures, both in and out of a suit. Repair techniques for all types of pressure suits. How to drive different kinds of rovers in all sorts of lunar terrain. Communication protocols. The proper use of emergency equipment ranging from portable solar cell arrays to life-support tents. How to recharge a life support pack's air tanks while in the field, and how to slow one's breathing in order to preserve air if extra tanks weren't available. What to do if your suit lost power. How to avoid hypothermia, hyperthermia, dehydration, radiation overexposure, blindness, and panic.

In short, how to stay alive on the Moon, as well as preventing someone else from dying. "Failure Is Not An Option" was the Ranger motto, but along with it was an unwritten corollary: the other guy's life is more important than your own. Given a choice between saving your skin and saving someone else's . . . well, there was no choice. If you had to die gasping for air so that another person could continue breathing for one minute longer, then that's what you'd have to do. If you don't like it, then don't become a Ranger.

I was beginning to wonder if I should have stuck to pushing a broom.

Billy was my instructor, just as Nicole was teaching Logan. The four of us went out together, but then we'd go our separate ways, each pair keeping within sight of the other but otherwise not having much contact. By then, I'd given up on Nicole; we were still friends, but it was obvious that she and Logan were steady. Probably just as well. I didn't have time for a girl, not with the pressure I was under to be ready for my walkabout in just a couple of weeks.

Logan and I had never had that little chat we'd promised each other. Perhaps we should have. Our rivalry over Nicole was over, but there was still some lingering resentment. We still got along well enough to work together, but we'd let things fester for too long. We'd pretty much stopped talking to one another, and it could no longer be said that we were best friends.

It may have been just as well that things worked out that way. After awhile, I noticed that Nicole wasn't pushing Logan very hard. When he screwed up during training, she often let him get away with it, showing him a shortcut that would allow him to get through that particular exercise with a minimum of effort. They didn't seem to be very serious about training; they would return to the airlock while Billy and I were still at work. It was clear that Nicole didn't want to knuckle down on her new boyfriend, and while she might be turning in satisfactory progress reports, I wondered how much he was actually learning.

On the other hand, Billy was relentless. No breaks or easy-way-outs, and any second chances he cared to give me were not to be wasted. If I did well, he'd say, "Not bad . . . let's see you do that again." But if I made a mistake, he'd snarl, "Stop messing around! Get it right or I'm bagging you!" It was an insulting and demeaning way to get through training, but I knew that if I wanted to keep Billy's respect, I'd have to earn it.

The long lunar night stretched on, and I seldom had a chance to do anything except train, eat, and sleep. But when the light of the rising sun touched the mountain peaks on the east side of Ptolemaeus, I received a brief message from Mr. Garcia: SOLO EVA EXCURSION SCHEDULED FOR 11.16.97. REPORT TO AIRLOCK 7 AT 0800 FOR SUIT-UP AND CHECK-OUT.

In other words, I'd completed my Third Class training. Tomorrow morning, I would take my walkabout.

That was a total surprise. Only yesterday, Billy had busted my chops over my failure at sealing a crack in a suit's lithium hydroxide canister. If you'd heard the way he scolded me, you would've thought that I was the most useless individual to ever set foot on the Moon. Figuring that there must have been a mistake, I went down to the ready-room, expecting another twelve hours of fun and games with Billy.

But he wasn't there. Logan was climbing into his moonsuit while Nicole patiently waited for him. He scowled at me when I walked in, but it was Nicole who spoke first. "Hey, Jamey, congratulations!" she said, raising the faceplate so that she could talk to me. "I hear you're going walkabout tomorrow."

"Yeah, sure, I guess so." I shook my head in confusion. "I got a memo from the Chief telling me that's what I'm supposed to do, but . . ."

"No one told you that you're through training, right?" She grinned. "No one ever does. That's the way we do it in the Rangers. Everyone passes, because . . ."

"'Failure is not a option.' Right." I looked over at Logan. "Hear that? I'm going walkabout tomorrow."

"Yeah . . . good for you." He didn't look at me, but instead concentrated on adjusting his wrist controls. "Have fun."

"When are you . . . ?" I began, then stopped myself. If he'd also received notification from Mr. Garcia that he was going walkabout, he would have told me. But he wasn't ready for that yet, and no one was going to send him out on his own until they were confident in his chances of success.

"Soon enough," Logan murmured. "Good luck."

"Thanks." I didn't know quite what to say. "I'm sure you'll . . ."

"What are you doing here?" Billy demanded.

I turned around to see him leaning against the ready-room door, holding a half-eaten sandwich he'd brought with him from the commissary. "Didn't you get the Chief's memo?" he asked, regarding me as if I was an unwelcome visitor. "You're doing your walkabout tomorrow. Get out of here."

"Huh?" I blinked, not quite understanding what he'd said. "You mean . . . ?"

"There's nothing more that I can show you." A wry smile. "Well, at least not for now. You're still a provo so far as I'm concerned. But—" an indifferent shrug "—if the Chief says you're ready, who am I to argue? Go home and get some rest. You'll need it."

There didn't seem to be anything else for me to say or do. I would have liked to talk to Logan, but not while Nicole and Billy were around. Besides, he didn't seem to be inclined to speak with me just then.

I'd jumped ahead of him. And he wasn't happy with me about that.

* * *

I left the airlock and headed back upstairs. For the first time in months, I was free to do whatever I wanted. No school, no Ranger training; I had a day all to myself. But by the time I got off the elevator, I was already bored.

I hadn't seen much of Melissa in the last couple of weeks, so I decided to head over to Ag Dome 2 and pay her a visit. Over dinner the other night, she'd told me about an experimental crop that was being cultivated in the aeroponics farm: chettuce, a hybrid form of lettuce that tasted a little like cheddar cheese. Meatless hamburgers and tacos were a favorite among loonies, but until now they'd had to do without cheese. There were no cows on the Moon to provide fresh milk, and who puts goat cheese on a taco? Chettuce was a bioengineered solution to this culinary problem. '

Perhaps Melissa could let me try some; I was curious to see if it was as disgusting as it sounded. To kill time, I decided to hike across the crater floor instead of taking a bicycle or cutting through the sublevels to the tunnels leading to the ag domes. It had been quite a while since I'd walked through the solarium; although it was late autumn back on Earth, in Apollo it was always summer. Warm sunlight streamed in through the circular window at the top of the dome. Wrens and robins chirped amid the branches of stunted shade trees, while bees and hummingbirds flitted around the cultivated flowerbeds. The solarium was a comfortable oasis, a miniature Earth surrounded by the harsh and airless desolation outside.

There weren't many people in the dome this time of day, so I had the paths all to myself. Or so I thought. I was about halfway across the solarium when someone called out to me. "Hi, Jamey! What are you doing here?"

I looked around, and there was Eddie Hernandez, squatting on his hands and knees beside a row of rose bushes. Sitting on a nearby bench was Nina, a school pad resting in her lap. Eddie raised his hand to wave to me. I waved back, then decided to walk over and say hello.

It had been nearly six weeks since I'd seen either him or his sister. Indeed, I'd nearly forgotten all about them.

"Hi, Eddie," I said. "Long time, no see. Hello, Nina."

"Yeah . . . long time, no see." Eddie wore grubby work overalls and a pair of gardening gloves, and he looked as happy as a kid making mudpies. Nina said nothing; she gave me the protective look she always had when she was with her brother, but I managed to get a smile out of her when I said her name. "How come you're here?" Eddie asked. "Aren't you supposed to be in school?"

"No school for me today . . . same as for you." I stopped to admire his roses. "I've been in Ranger training lately. I'm . . . well, I'm taking a day off, so . . ."

"You're a Ranger now?" Eddie's eyes widened. "Gosh, that's great, Jamey! You're a Ranger!"

I couldn't help but laugh. Eddie's admiration was unpretentious, almost bordering on hero worship. Even Nina seemed to be impressed, and I didn't think anything could get through that thick little shell of hers.

"Yeah, it's pretty good, I guess." I shrugged and changed the subject. "Those roses look really nice. Did you grow them yourself?"

"Uh-huh! They're mine! I planted them here . . . and here . . . and here." He pointed to the neat arrangement he'd made alongside the path, proud of his accomplishment, then his smile faded into a worried frown. "But they don't want me to do that anymore," he added. "They want to send me over to the ag domes to do aero . . . aero . . ."

"Aeroponics?"

He nodded. "Yeah . . . aeroponics. But I don't know how to do that, Jamey."

"Colony Service is transferring him to Ag Dome 2," Nina said quietly. "They say they're short-handed over there because they've lost one of the farmers to the Rangers. And since Eddie has been doing so well with this . . ."

I knew which Ranger she was talking about: Nick Gleason, a

Ranger Second Class whose main job was working as an aeroponics engineer. And I knew why Eddie might be nervous. Aeroponics involved growing crops in tanks without soil, with water and nutrients dispensed to them as a fine mist. It was a more delicate procedure than normal gardening; the soil in which Eddie had grown his roses was bioengineered from processed and fertilized regolith, which was suitable for grass, flowers, and small trees, but not food staples.

"I understand," I said. "They must think highly of you, Eddie, if they want you to do that instead." A smile flickered across his face, but he still seemed dubious. A new thought occurred to me. "Hey, look . . . I'm on my way over there now to see Melissa. She works there. I'll ask her if she can put you on her team. That way, you'll have someone you know who can teach you how it's done."

Eddie's face brightened again. "Melissa, your sister? Gosh, that would be great! I like your sister!" Nina seemed a bit reluctant—she remembered how rude MeeMee had been to her brother when they'd first met—but she nodded anyway.

"No problem," I said. "I'll . . ."

My wristband beeped just then, signaling an incoming call. "Excuse me," I said, then turned away from the Hernandez kids and raised my hand to my face. "Jamey Barlowe here."

"It's Hannah." Her voice came from the wristband's tiny speaker. "I just heard from Nicole that you're going on walkabout. Is that true?"

Nicole had told Hannah about that? That was a surprise, although it shouldn't have been; the two of them had become friends. "Yeah, it's true. Happens tomorrow."

"Oh . . . oh, wow." She sounded stunned. "Are you . . . I mean, are you okay with that? Do you think you're ready?"

"I guess so." I shrugged, forgetting that she couldn't see me. "I'll find out soon enough."

A long pause. For a second, I thought she'd cut the link. Then her voice returned. "I want to see you. Where are you right now?"

"In the solarium, talking to Eddie and Nina. Are you at the hospital?"

"*Yeah, but . . . look, stay there, okay? I'll locate you in the dome.*" She could use our wristbands to pinpoint my location in Apollo. "*Just stay where you are. I'm coming to you.*"

"Yeah . . . okay, sure. See you then."

Hannah clicked off. I had a hunch that she wanted to talk to me in private, so I said goodbye to Eddie and Nina, then strolled over to another bench about forty feet away and sat down to wait for her.

About fifteen minutes later, Hannah showed up on a bicycle. She hadn't changed out of her scrubs, but instead had pulled a cardigan sweater over them and left her stethoscope behind. She seemed to be struggling with her emotions when she saw me, her expression flickering between warmth and concern. She climbed off the bike and parked it beside the bench; before I could say anything, though, she spoke first.

"Look," Hannah said as she sat down next to me on the bench, "let me get this out before . . ." She stopped, took a deep breath. "What you're doing . . . what you're about to do . . . has me worried. I know it's something you have to do, but . . ."

"It's dangerous, sure." I shook my head. "The Chief wouldn't let me go unless he thought I was ready."

"I don't care what he thinks." She looked me straight in the eye. "Do *you* think you're ready?"

"Yeah, I do," I said, but perhaps I hesitated just a bit before I said that, because her face paled a bit. "No, really," I hastily added. "I can handle myself out there. I promise."

Hannah didn't respond, but her eyes never left mine. In that instant, I realized something that I suppose I'd known all along, but which I hadn't admitted to myself: Hannah really cared for me. All this time, while I had been chasing after Nicole, Hannah had been there, quietly waiting for me to give her as much attention as I'd been giving to another girl.

And with that realization, there came another: I liked her, too.

"Hannah . . ." My throat was dry, and it was hard to speak. "Look, maybe I should've . . . I dunno, spent more time with you, but . . ."

"Yeah, maybe you should have." An uncertain smile flickered on her lips. "When you get back, you can make up for that." She hesitated. "Is a date too much to ask for?"

This was the first time a girl had ever said that she wanted to go out with me. In fact, I didn't even think it usually happened that way. But I didn't care whose idea it was. "Sure. When I get back, we'll . . . I dunno, but I'll come up with something."

"Do that. It'll give you something to think about while you're . . ." Her voice trailed off, and the smile was again replaced by the worried frown. "Before you go, I want to give you something."

Unbuttoning the top of her sweater, she reached the front of her scrubs to produce a small medallion that hung around her neck upon a silver chain. I'd seen it before, floating around her neck when we'd been aboard the LTV that had brought us here. Ducking her head, she pulled the chain from around her neck, then she took my hand in hers and gently dropped the medallion into my palm.

"I want you to wear this when you go out tomorrow," she said. "For good luck."

The medallion was about the size of a quarter and was made of sterling silver. Now that it was in my hand, I could see it more clearly. Embossed upon it was a bearded man who had a walking stick in his hands and an infant riding upon his back. Around its rim was an inscription: ST. CHRISTOPHER PROTECT US.

"What is this?" I asked.

"It's a medal of St. Christopher's." Hannah leaned closer to me, her hair lightly brushing my shoulder as she traced the medallion's bas-relief image with her finger. "St. Christopher is the patron saint of travelers. Wearing this is . . . well, it can't hurt." The smile returned, a bit mystical this time. "Catholics have many patron saints, and we put a lot of faith in them."

This was not a good time to tell her that I'd never been to church, so I didn't. But still . . . "I don't know if I can take this. It looks like it's very valuable to you."

"It is." Again, her eyes met mine. "My mother gave this to me just before I was taken from the White House. She said I'd need it to get me safely to where I was going. It did . . . so now I'm passing it along to you, to get you back to me."

What could I say to that?

Nothing. I didn't even try. I just kissed her instead, and as I did, I felt her hand close my palm around the medallion and hold it tight so that I'd never let it go.

14.
WALKABOUT

Ahard thump as the Pegasus touched down, then Gordie's voice came through my headset: *"Okay, Jamey, we're here. Get moving."*

"Where am I?" I asked. I'd made the ride in a windowless cargo module, hanging onto a ceiling strap.

A regretful sigh. *"Sorry, kiddo, you know the rules. Can't tell you anything."*

All I knew was that the Pegasus had lifted off from Apollo's south landing field twenty-three minutes earlier. The deck had tilted beneath my feet a couple of times, an indication that Gordie had made at least two starboard turns. I didn't know if he'd done that out of necessity, though, or whether he'd simply flown in circles to throw off my sense of direction. I couldn't be sure of anything until I got out.

Letting go of the strap, I walked over to the hatch and cranked it open, then kneeled down to release the loading ramp. The regolith kicked up by the transport's VTOLs was still settling when I hopped down from the Pegasus. I didn't look around, but instead dragged the ramp into place before climbing back into the module to push aside the floor chocks securing the mule.

"Follow me," I said, and the robotic equipment carrier responded by doing just that, silently rolling along on its four wire wheels. I led the mule down the ramp and away from the Pegasus. When we were a safe distance from the transport, I turned around. "Clear."

"Affirmative." I could see Gordie seated in the cockpit, gazing back at me. *"You'll get your mission objective as soon as I'm gone, and I'll come to pick you up when you've completed it. Until then . . . well, you know what to do."*

"Uh-huh." I tried not to sound nervous, but I probably did anyway. "I'll see you then."

"And not before, I hope." He raised his left hand to give me a thumbs-up. *"Good luck, buddy."*

"Thanks, I . . ."

"Oh, yeah . . . and say hello to the Old Ranger when you get there."

I had no idea what he meant by that. Was the Chief going to be waiting for me? No one ever called Mr. Garcia the Old Ranger, though, so that didn't sound right. "What do you . . . ?"

A soft click told me that he'd switched off. I raised my hand to wave goodbye as the Pegasus lifted off again, ascending upon a cloud of fine grey dust until it reached 1,000 feet, where it made a port turn and headed back the way it had come . . . or at least so I presumed. Again, it was possible that Gordie was deliberately altering his course in order to hide the direction in which we'd travelled from Apollo.

I watched the Pegasus until it disappeared beyond a distant mountain range to my left, then I took a deep breath and forced myself to calm down. I was on my own. Until I reached my destination, no one would come to get me. Unless I ran into serious trouble, of course, or simply chickened out, in which case I could radio for help and a Pegasus would be sent to bring me home. If that happened, though, it would mean that I would have failed . . . and you know the Rangers motto. The only way I'd ever get a second chance would be after going through Third Class training again, and even then I'd have to beg Mr. Garcia for another walkabout.

I was alone on the Moon. Well, not quite. "Hey, Arthur," I said, "are you there?"

"Of course, Jamey. How may I help you?"

I didn't respond at once. Instead, I took a minute to look around. It appeared that Gordie had dropped me within a crater so large that I couldn't see its opposite side. Turning around, I saw steep, high walls looming above me; they curved away to both my left and right until they disappeared beyond the horizon. I was standing on top of a small hillock with two little impact craters, one to my left and one to my right. The ground gently sloped down toward a broad basin strewn with rocks and boulders. On the Moon, it's often difficult to accurately judge size and distance with the naked eye, so I had little idea how big the crater was or how far it was to the other side.

I was about to say something to Arthur when I heard a sharp, repetitive beep. An instant later, a tiny yellow arrowhead appeared upon my faceplate's heads-up display. Blinking in time with the beeps, it lay close to the horizon, pointing downward toward something on the other side of the crater.

"That is your mission objective, Jamey," Arthur said. *"It is an automatic beacon which you must reach in order to successfully complete this exercise."*

"How far away is it?" I asked.

"31.06 miles."

I hissed between my teeth. Damn, that was a long walk! Of course, I could dump everything off the mule and try to ride the whole way, but that would be dumb. The mule carried four air tanks to replenish the six-hour supply . . . make that five hours and nineteen minutes . . . I presently had in my suit, along with the water, food and tent I'd also need. So my legs were in for a workout.

"Where am I?" I asked.

"I can't tell you that," Arthur said, and I could have sworn there was an apologetic tone to his voice. *"You'll have to determine your approximate location for yourself before I can show you a map."*

Oh, hell. Someone must have reprogrammed Arthur to limit the amount of assistance he could give me; otherwise a translucent map would have immediately appeared within my visor.

"Silence the beacon, please," I asked, and the beeping stopped. At least I wouldn't have that to drive me crazy. "Now show me a compass."

"I cannot do that either. However, if you successfully tell me where you think you are, I can provide you with a map, compass, and direction finder."

So this was my first test: figuring out my position without the aid of either a map or digital direction finder. Of course, I had a set of rolled-up topographic maps among my equipment, but they wouldn't do me much good unless I knew my latitude and longitude. And Earth-type compasses are useless on the Moon because of its almost nonexistent magnetic field. Since Arthur was being uncooperative, I'd have to work out the problem from what I could see with my own two eyes.

All right, then . . . looking up at the sky, I noted Earth's apparent position from where I stood. On the lunar near side, Earth is always in the same place, depending on the observer's location; although it regularly changes phases, just as the Moon does when seen from Earth, it doesn't rise or set. Since Apollo was just seven degrees south of the equator, Earth perpetually remained almost directly overhead. Here, though, it was slightly closer to the horizon . . . about twelve to fifteen degrees below zenith, I estimated . . . which meant that I was still near the equator, but probably a hundred miles or more from Apollo.

Another helpful thing about celestial navigation from the lunar surface is that, because the Moon is rotation-locked with Earth, most of the major constellations are visible from or near the equator. So it was easy to find Draco, a small constellation midway between Ursa Major and Ursa Minor. Most of the time, Draco points toward the lunar North Pole, just as Polaris points toward the North Pole on Earth; the Moon's rotational wobble causes its pole star to periodically change, but for now Draco was the way to find the lunar true-north.

Once I had that direction, I determined the other points of the compass and compared them with Earth's position. That confirmed my belief that I was still south of the equator. I could have reached into the map case and pulled out one of the scrolls, but I didn't have to. I'd learned enough about lunar geography to make a good guess where I was.

"I'm on the west side of Alphonsus crater, Arthur. About . . . oh, 125 to 150 miles from Apollo. Is that right?"

"Yes, you are correct. Would you like to see a map and compass?"

I let out my breath in relief. "Yes, please."

A topo map of the Alphonsus region was superimposed upon my faceplate; a digital compass synched to Apollo's navigation satellites appeared in the top right corner. The direction finder pinpointed my present location as a tiny green triangle near Alphonsus's west side, and the beacon was a blue triangle near just past the crater's center. Studying the map, I noticed that the beacon was located just beyond Mt. Tobor, an isolated peak in the middle of the crater.

It looked as if I'd have to go around the mountain in order to reach the beacon. "Show me a direct line between my current location and the beacon, Arthur," I said, and he obligingly traced a red line between here and there. Sure enough, the line was 31.06 miles long, and appeared as if it would take me past Mt. Tobor.

Out of curiosity, I asked Arthur to trace another line to Apollo. It lay to the northeast, 155 miles away. Glancing in that direction, I had to smile; this was exactly the way the Pegasus had gone after it had dropped me off. Gordie had been trying to give me a hint. I suspected his comment about "saying hello to the Old Ranger" was another, but I hadn't the foggiest idea what he meant by that.

"Drop map and direction finder, display horizontal compass," I said. The map and direction finder disappeared, to be replaced by a horizontal bar that stretched across the middle of my faceplate. The bar was marked in degrees of longitude, with a red E and the beacon's yellow arrowhead silently glowing straight ahead.

So . . . I had just a little under thirty hours of air, and just a little more than thirty-one miles to cross before my supply ran out. If I set a pace of about two or three miles per hour, I could reach the beacon in about ten to fifteen hours, give or take an hour or so. But that was only if I didn't stop to rest, and I knew I couldn't do that. Sooner or later, I'd have to get some sleep.

"Is there anything else you want?" Arthur asked.

"Nope. Not a thing." I let out my breath, flexed my arms and legs a little bit. "Follow me," I said to the mule, and then I started walking.

* * *

The Lunar Search and Rescue exercise required for advancement from Third to Second class was technically called the Extravehicular Solo Lunar Excursion, but no one ever used that term. It got the name "walkabout" after something practiced by Australian aborigines; they'll sometimes leave their tribal communities and hike into the outback on their own, walking and walking, with no particular direction in mind. They do that to get away from people for a while, but it's also said that someone who goes walkabout eventually meets up with himself. The last part sounded a little too mystical for me; so far as I was concerned, it was just another way of saying that I was going to be do an awful lot of walking.

There's not much resemblance between the Australian desert and the surface of the Moon, appearances not withstanding: no brush, no water holes, and not a kangaroo in sight. And it wasn't as though I lacked either direction or destination. All I had to do was reach that beacon, then I could radio Apollo and wait for Gordie to retrieve me. Simple, really. Or so it seemed. But going solo was harder than I expected, and it wasn't long before I realized that this would be one of the toughest things I'd ever done.

For one thing, I made less time than I thought I would. The first couple of miles from the drop-off point took me down a slope that, while not treacherous, nonetheless prevented me from bunny-hopping. When I tried to do that, I lost my footing on the loose regolith and came close to falling head-first against a rock that would have shattered my helmet faceplate. That close-call sobered me up; from then on, I kept to a slower, more deliberate gait.

My pace was also restricted by the mule. Although it was solar-powered and could operate indefinitely, it travelled no more than a couple of miles an hour, and often had to roll around rocks that I easily stepped over. It wasn't long before I realized that I was in danger of leaving it behind. I couldn't afford to lose the stupid thing, so I frequently had to stop and wait for it to catch up with me. It gave me a chance to catch my breath and sip a little water from the tube inside my helmet, but it also nibbled away at my time-factor.

I thought I might be able to speed things up a bit once I reached the bottom of the slope and started making my way across the crater floor. Instead, I found that Alphonsus was a rougher place than Ptolemaeus. The ground was uneven, pocked with impact craters and strewn with boulders the size of cars. I could dodge most of this stuff, but the mule had to pick its way around them, and every so often it got stuck. When that happened, I'd have to go back, grab its tow-bar, and haul it out of a pit or over a rock. If the mule hadn't been carrying everything I needed to stay alive, I probably would have kicked it over on its side and left it there.

On Earth, when you're standing at ground level on flat terrain, your visible horizon is about three miles away. On the Moon, though, it's only about a mile and half. This meant that I couldn't see Mt. Tobor even though the map and direction finder told me that I was heading toward it. After awhile it felt as if, no matter how far I walked, I wasn't getting any closer to my destination. The mountain remained perpetually over the horizon; I knew it was there, but I couldn't see it.

So the going was much slower than I thought it would be. About eight miles after I left the drop-off point, a bell chimed and red light flashed on my heads-up display, signaling me that I needed to replenish my air supply. The way I'd originally estimated my consumption, I shouldn't have had to do that until I'd walked at least ten miles. I stopped, went back to the mule, and attached the feedline from one of the air tanks to the inlet port on the lower left side of my life support pack. It took only a few minutes to refill my pack; while I was at it, I also topped off the suit's drinking water tank.

I thought about discarding the empty air tank, but decided against it. We were supposed to be conscientious about littering the lunar terrain. Besides, now that the spare tank was empty, it wouldn't save that much weight for the mule to have to carry. Something occurred to me just then: I hadn't seen any other footprints. Tracks remain forever in the regolith; there's no wind or rain to erode them. That meant I was the first person to set foot on this part of the Moon. If other Third Class Rangers had made their walkabouts in Alphonsus, they hadn't traveled the same way I did.

Not only was I alone, but I was also in a place where no one had ever been. This realization was both awesome and terrifying. I looked up at Earth, and saw that it was nothing more than a thin silver crescent in the sky.

"Arthur," I asked, "what time is it in Maryland?"

"It is 11:47 PM, Jamey."

Almost midnight back home. Wherever Jan or Dad were, if they could see the Moon, they'd be looking up at me . . . but they'd have no idea where I was. If something went seriously wrong, if I had an accident so catastrophic that I didn't have time to either save myself or call for help, then I would die in this place and my sister and father would never know about it. Or at least not until someone at Apollo saw that I was overdue and a Ranger team came out to search for my body.

I tried to shrug it off as I kept walking, but the thought haunted me. What was I doing here? What was I trying to prove to myself?

—This is a hell of a time to ask that, said a little voice that sounded like mine.

"Okay, so maybe it is," I replied. "But I still want to know why."

"What do you want to know, Jamey?" Arthur asked.

"I didn't mean you, Arthur," I said. "I'm . . ."

—Talking to yourself? That's the first sign you're going crazy, isn't it?

"No, it isn't. People talk to themselves all the time." I concentrated on putting one foot in front of another.

—Sure they do. But let's not change the subject. Why are you doing this? Are you trying to impress someone? Nicole, maybe?

"No. Nicole is going with Logan now. And it's not Hannah, either."

—Really? Maybe you're right. You really haven't been paying much attention to her, have you? But she likes you a lot. I mean, she's kissed you a couple of times, and that St. Christopher's medal you're wearing under your suit . . . that means something, doesn't it?

"I know what it means. And, yeah, I really should spend more time with her. But that's not why I'm doing this."

—So what's the point? I mean, look at you. You're walking on the Moon. A couple of months ago, you couldn't even get to the bathroom without crutches. Jan and Dad would be impressed, sure . . . but they have no idea what you're doing, so why are you putting yourself through all this? If you'll just give up . . .

"I'm not giving up!"

—Suit yourself. Maybe they'll carve that on your tombstone.

My stomach was beginning to rumble; it had been quite a while since I'd had anything to eat. I'd learned during training that, if you're expecting to spend more than a few hours in a moonsuit, you shouldn't have any solid food. Not unless you want to take a dump in your suit and are willing to live with the consequences; peeing was easier, though, because the urine went into the suit's wastewater recycling loop and was used as coolant.

So my last meal had been the bowl of tomato soup Ms. Lagler had given me for breakfast. The voice in my head was hunger talking. But I couldn't feed myself until I made camp, and I had miles to go before I could afford to do that.

—Call out for a pizza. Or better yet, call Gordie and ask him to pick you up. In an hour, you can be having tacos with chettuce . . .

"Shut up and leave me alone."

"Jamey, who are you talking to?" Arthur asked.

"No one," I said, and kept walking.

* * *

The terrain got rougher the farther east I traveled, but at least it remained level. I kept the nagging voice out of my head by asking

Arthur to tell me a story. In his memory were the collected short stories of his namesake; he recited "Rescue Party" and followed it with "The Sentinel." Both were obviously written long before people actually went into space, so there were a number of anachronisms, but they were still pretty good, and they kept me from talking to myself.

I'd almost exhausted my first tank of air by the time I called it quits for the day. By then, I was in sight of Mt. Tobor. The massive butte thrust up from Alphonsus like the snout of a buried dragon, casting its shadow across a pair of deep rills that lay between me and the mountain. I'd already walked fifteen and a half miles, and was too tired to take on the rills, so I decided to make camp and get some sleep.

The tent was a small, inflatable A-frame that could be pressurized from within. It was used by the Rangers for rescue operations in case someone needed to camp out until help arrived. I removed it from the mule, spread it out on the ground, then attached its nitrogen cylinder and turned on the pump to inflate it. While that was going on, I refilled my suit air from the second tank, then unpacked the meal kit and another water bottle. Once the tent was set up, I switched off the pump, then got down on my hands and knees and climbed inside.

The tent was airtight, its silver outer skin reflecting the harsh and constant sunlight. Once it was sealed, I switched on its internal air supply and thermal control system. It took a few minutes for the tent to pressurize and become warm enough to be habitable; I made sure that the carbon-dioxide filtration system worked, then switched off my suit air and opened the faceplate. The tent was lit by a small light-patch in the ceiling; there wasn't enough room for me to climb out of my suit, but at least I was able to brace my back against an inflatable pillow that had been generously provided. It didn't matter that I'd have to sleep in my suit; I was too tired to care.

Dinner came from a pair of self-heating pouches. One was supposed to be beef stew and the other banana cream pie, but those were rather misleading descriptions; they both tasted like kindergarten paste. Again, I didn't care; I sucked the pouches dry and promised myself a pizza when I got back to Apollo. The tent's air supply was good for six hours. That would give me enough time to sleep. I asked Arthur to wake me in five and a half hours, then I lay back against the pillow and closed my eyes.

I don't remember what I dreamed about, but the last image I retained had something to do with Hannah asking me if she could borrow my swim fins so that she could go moonwalking. Then Arthur was telling me to get up and playing Beethoven's "Moonlight Sonata" to ease me awake. I had enough time for a breakfast pouch—allegedly oatmeal with apples and cinnamon; whoever made these things was a bad liar—before the tent's air ran out. I closed my faceplate and reactivated my life support pack, depressurized the tent and unsealed it, then crawled out into the burning sunlight.

Once I broke camp and loaded the mule again, I had a decision to make. According to both my heads-up display and the plastic map I pulled from the mule, the rill that lay directly ahead of me was too long to go around, at least not without adding another four or five miles to my trek. However, if I took a slight detour to the south, I'd come upon a small, level ridge that separated the rill from its nearby companion. Once I crossed the ridge, all I'd have to do was head northeast until I was resumed the eastbound course that would take me past Mt. Tobor. The detour would add another mile or two to the distance I needed to travel, and thus cut into my remaining air supply, but it would keep from having to go through the rill.

There was also a third option: go straight through the rill. It was a deep crevice, like a dry riverbed back on Earth. When I got closer, I saw that the other side was only about 300 yards away. So the shortest distance was definitely a straight line. But its walls were both steep and deep, and there was a possibility that, if I went down there, I might have a hard time getting out. And I also had to consider the mule; would it get trapped down there, therefore depriving me of my cargo carrier?

Studying the problem, I walked a few dozen feet south, and suddenly came upon something I'd given up hope of seeing: signs that someone had been there before me.

A pair of footprints approached the rill from the southwest, followed by wheel tracks identical to those left by my mule. No doubt they'd been left by another Third Class Ranger who had made his walkabout through Alphonsus.

I followed the tracks, and sure enough, they went down into the rill. So whoever had been here before me had decided not to make the detour. But did that person get out again? The rill's opposite side was too far away for me to discern any footprints, but the fact that I couldn't see any didn't give me any comfort.

I thought about it for a minute or so, and decided to play it safe. I took the detour instead.

The ridge was an easy traverse. I walked between the two rills with no problem at all. But by the time I reached the place where I would have emerged from the northern rill if I had descended into it, my suit was alerting me that it was time to replenish my air supply again. I recharged the suit from the third tank; only one more was left. The detour had cost me air, all right . . . but I didn't find any more tracks on the other side of the rill. Unless my predecessor had found a rocket down there, he must have gotten stuck.

Billy never told me why he'd failed his first attempt to make a walkabout. He refused to talk about it. I had a feeling I'd learned the reason why.

Now I had a different problem. Past the rills, the terrain sloped upwards, forming a steep grade that surrounded Mt. Tobor on all sides. There was no way around that; I'd have to climb. So I began the long, hard trudge up the mountain's lower slopes, relying on the direction finder to show me the way.

One small step. Then another. And then another. The slope rose before me as a steep wall made of loose regolith and gravel; every time I'd plant a booted foot in front of me, it seemed as if it would slide back to where it had been a moment before. Before long I was using my hands to pull myself upward. Sweat flowed down my forehead and dripped into my eyes.

—Having fun yet? the annoying little voice said to me.

"Loads," I replied behind gasps. "Shut up and . . . let me work."

"Who are you talking to?" Arthur asked.

"Same guy . . . I was . . . before."

—Sure you are. And you still haven't answered my question. Why are you putting yourself through all this?

"Because . . . I need to . . . I need to . . . help my family."

—Dad and Jan? They're almost a quarter of a million miles away. How is this going to help them?

"If I . . . if I become a Ranger . . ." My right foot skidded on loose regolith and I fell to my knees again. I cursed under my breath, then pulled myself to my feet. "I can . . . I can protect Apollo. That's what . . . Jan wants me to do."

—Yeah, okay. That's why you decided to join, sure. But isn't there something more? Like trying to live up to your mother's memory? She's remembered as a hero. What does that make you?

He was right. That was a big part of why I'd decided to join the Rangers; I just hadn't admitted it to myself until now. "All right," I mumbled, "you got me there. Now . . . shut the hell up and let me . . ."

—That's all I wanted to know. Oh, but just one more thing. What happened to your mule?

I stopped to look back. The mule had fallen behind . . . way behind. Sixty feet or more. As I watched, I saw that its wheels were spinning uselessly as it tried to make the ascent. It wasn't designed for mountain climbing, and it was clear that it wouldn't be able to keep up with me.

Again, I had no choice. I went back downhill and unlashed the remaining air tank and water bottles from its cargo bed, then used the cords to strap them against my back. Their combined weight was negligible, but they were cumbersome all the same. The mule carried nothing else I'd need; if I didn't make it to the beacon before my air ran out, the tent wouldn't do me any good. I'd have to call Apollo and tell them to send Gordie.

I was damned if I was going to let that happen. So I kept climbing.

It seemed as if it took hours for me to struggle the rest of the way up the slope, but it really wasn't that long. All of a sudden, I found myself at the top of the rise. Mt. Tobor was at my back; before me lay the eastern side of Alphonsus.

I celebrated by drinking a mouthful of water, then I checked the direction finder again. The beacon's yellow arrowhead was pointing at something on the crater floor; for the first time, I could see my destination with my own two eyes. About three miles away, something reflected the sunlight.

The mountain's eastern slope was shorter and less steep than the western side; I made it to the bottom in less than an hour. Once I was there, though, I had to stop to replenish my life support pack again. That was it for the air reserves, and I was down to one last water bottle. If there were any more nasty surprises in those last two miles, I was sunk.

There weren't. No longer having to worry about the mule, but still carrying the empty tank and bottle, I bounced the rest of the way to my destination. I didn't have to rely on the direction finder or the beacon; the reflection was sufficient to guide me there. And the closer I came, the more obvious it became that I was approaching something man-made.

At the end of my journey, I came upon a pile of wreckage. A long time ago, an object had crashed into the surface of the Moon, sending pieces of twisted metal in all directions. The heap at the center of the debris field was surrounded by footprints and tire tracks; I definitely wasn't the first person to visit this place. And, indeed, as I walked closer, I came upon something that had been left behind.

Beneath the tripod holding the radio beacon I'd been following for the last two days was a burnished aluminum plaque. It was engraved with the image of a space probe that looked a little like a witch's hat that had sprouted wings, and below it was written:

RANGER 9
UNITED STATES OF AMERICA
NATIONAL AERONAUTICS AND SPACE ADMINISTRATION
MARCH 24, 1965
FOURTH SPACECRAFT TO REACH THE MOON

Aha. Now I knew the real reason why Lunar Search and Rescue were called the Rangers. No one had ever told me that. It was a secret that was reserved only for those who'd made the long, lonely walk to reach this place.

"Hello, Old Ranger," I said. "Nice to meet you."

Then I got on the radio, called Apollo, and asked Gordie to come pick me up at the beacon.

15.
A LIGHT IN THE SKY

Gordie picked me up about forty-five minutes later. He had been on standby for the last couple of days, waiting for my call and hoping that it wouldn't come too soon. When his Pegasus touched down a hundred yards from Ranger 9, I saw that a personnel module was now attached to the strongback. I climbed in and discovered that it already had a passenger.

Mr. Garcia was sitting on one of benches, wearing a skinsuit. He stood up as I came aboard. *"Hello, Jamey,"* he said. *"Or perhaps I should say, Ranger Second Class Barlowe."*

I don't know which was the bigger surprise: the fact that he was there, or what he had just said. "Pardon me?"

"Is there something wrong with your comlink?" A smile appeared behind his faceplate. *"You heard me right. You've successfully completed your walkabout, which means that you've earned the rank."* He stuck out his hand. *"Congratulations, son. I'm proud of you."*

"Thank you, sir." Not knowing what else to do, I shook his hand. "Umm . . . I don't know if it makes any difference, but I had to leave my mule behind."

"Don't worry about it. Half the time, that's what happens." He stepped past me to close the module hatch. *"We're more concerned about getting you back than your equipment. We'll send someone out later to retrieve it. Isn't that right, Captain Rogers?"*

"Whatever you say, Chief." I couldn't see Gordie; he spoke to us from the cockpit. *"Whenever you're ready, I'll take off. There's some ration bars back there, Jamey, but I wouldn't eat 'em if I were you. You've got a party to go to."*

"Party?" I managed to take a seat just before the Pegasus lifted off again. "Oh, no, no . . . man, I'm too tired."

"Sorry . . . Ranger tradition." Mr. Garcia laughed. *"And failure to show up for your walkabout party is not an option."*

He was right. I didn't have a choice. A bus carried Mr. Garcia and me from the south landing field to Apollo, dropping us off at Airlock 7. The Chief told me I'd have to go through the suit scrubber on my own, and for good reason; my moonsuit was so caked with dust, it took twice as long as usual for it to get clean. But when the scrubbers finally shut down and the airlock pressurized, the inner hatch opened . . .

And thirty-four Rangers gathered in the ready-room began to applaud.

I didn't know what to do. I simply stared at them, my mouth sagging open. The applause lasted for several seconds, then from the other side of the room, Billy spoke up.

"Now isn't that just the saddest excuse for a Ranger you've ever seen?" he said.

Everyone in the room cracked up—except for me; I was still speechless—and then a half dozen guys rushed forward to help me out of my suit. I hadn't shaved in two days and stank to high heaven, but that hardly mattered to the people who practically carried me from the ready room upstairs to the Ranger barracks. In the lounge was the first decent meal I had eaten in almost three days. I was shocked to find a T-bone steak among the potatoes and asparagus, and later learned that it had come from the small stock of frozen beef imported from Earth and saved for special occasions. Hunger quickly trumped incredulity, and I wolfed it down while the party went on around me.

Mr. Garcia showed up a few minutes after I sat down at the table. He said a few words of praise about my performance, then left to take care of business elsewhere. No sooner had he left when Mikel Borakov took a seat next to me. Reaching into a trouser pocket, he pulled out a battered aluminum flask, twisted open the cap, and placed it in front of me.

"Drink up," he said. "It's on the house."

My nose caught the scent of vodka. "Umm . . . thanks, but I'm not old enough." Which was true enough, but the fact of the matter was that I'd never liked the taste of hard liquor; I was just trying to get out of it without seeming rude.

"You sure?" I heard Nicole say. "You may need it for what's coming next."

I turned to look at her. She was standing behind me, Logan at her side. There was a broad grin across her face and even Logan was smiling a little. "What are you . . . ?"

"Time for you to get one of these." Nicole reached up to tap the moon-and-angel wings Ranger tattoo on her cheek. "Right here," she added, then bent over to give me a kiss in the exact same place.

Logan didn't seem to appreciate that very much, but it wasn't long before I stopped caring whether or not he did. Vodka I could turn down, but I couldn't refuse the tattoo. Before I knew it, I was lying across the table, with Mikel holding my head steady while a skin artist used her stylus and dyes to etch the Ranger seal below my left eye.

Nicole was right; the vodka might have helped. On the other hand, I was so tired that it didn't make much difference. The party was still going when Gordie and someone else helped me upstairs to the Laglers' apartment. I managed to shake hands with Mr. Lagler and get hugs from Ms. Lagler and Melissa—my sister shocked me by even crying a little; perhaps all those times she'd told me to drop dead weren't meant to be taken seriously—before exhaustion finally did me in. I fell into bed still wearing my clothes and was asleep within seconds.

* * *

I slept solidly for the next ten hours. When I finally woke up, the apartment was empty; everyone had gone off to work. Ms. Lagler had left me a couple of fresh-baked muffins and a pot of coffee. After I had breakfast, I showered, shaved, and put on fresh clothes. Then, feeling a lot less grubby, I went to see Hannah.

The conversations I'd had with myself while walking across Alphonsus had convinced me that I needed to get serious about paying to attention to her. So I called her and asked if we could get together and . . . well, do something fun, just the two of us.

We agreed to meet at the same place where we'd last seen each other, the park bench in the atrium. I got there first, and before I sat down, I muted my wristband. I was supposed to report to duty later on that day, but until then I didn't want any interruptions. For once, I wanted to be alone with her. Or at least as alone as we could be in a public place. Here and there, other loonies were strolling through the atrium gardens; I hoped they'd mind their own business.

Hannah showed up a few minutes later. She wasn't on a bike this time, nor was she wearing scrubs. She'd put on a long hemp skirt and matching top, and when I saw her walking toward me, I wondered why I'd ignored her for so long. In that moment, she was the most beautiful girl I'd ever seen.

I stood up, but before I could say anything, she threw her arms around me. Neither of us spoke for a few seconds. We simply held one another, sharing relief in the fact that I'd come back alive and unharmed. Then she lifted her face for me to give her a kiss, but when I started to do so, her eyes suddenly widened.

"Oh, my God!" she exclaimed. "What have you done to yourself?"

"What? I don't . . ."

"Your face! What *is* that?"

"Oh, yeah," I mumbled, touching the new tattoo. I'd almost forgotten it was there. "It wasn't my idea. Just something Rangers do after they've made their walkabout. Sort of a ritual, I guess."

Hannah scowled. "I don't care if it's a ritual . . . I think it's ugly! Can't you get it erased? Or at least have it in a different place?"

It hadn't occurred to me until then that I didn't necessarily need to have the tattoo on my cheek. I'd seen other Rangers display them on their biceps or chests. The location had been Nicole's idea, but I wasn't about to tell Hannah that. "If you want, I'll have it removed and redone on my arm. Would that be all right?"

"Well . . . okay." She smiled. "You've got a nice face, Jamey. I don't want to have to look at that when I do this."

She kissed me, and although this was the third time she'd done so, by far it was the best. Neither of us cared if anyone saw us. It was a while before either of us came up for air.

Eventually we did, though. We sat down on the bench and I told her all about the walkabout, starting when Gordie dropped me in Alphonsus and ending when he picked me up at the Ranger 9 crash site. The only thing I left out were the long chats I'd had with myself; this was something she didn't have to know. Hannah listened to my story, interrupting only a few times to ask questions, and when I was done, she slowly nodded.

"So you got through it," she said, "and now you're back, safe and sound." She hesitated. "I'm proud of you, you know I am. But . . ."

She stopped. "But what?" I asked.

Hannah looked away from me, her gaze traveling to the roses Eddie had planted nearby. "It means you're going to be putting yourself in harm's way again. Maybe sooner than you think."

Something in the way she said that sent a chill through me. Before I could ask, she leaned a little closer. "Maybe I shouldn't tell anyone about this," Hannah said quietly, "but I've heard Mr. Porter talking to town council members about what's happening back home. Looks like Lina Shapar is getting set for an invasion. They believe it could happen any day now."

"What makes them think that?"

"For one thing, the government has stepped up the propaganda. The newsnets back home have been carrying a lot of stories the last few days about how terrible things are here. How Americans on Apollo have become second-class citizens and are being forced to work without pay. How we're on the verge of starvation. How the ISC intends to use the embargo to topple the United States . . ."

"That's crap! None of it is true!"

"Of course it isn't. But look at history. When a country is seriously gearing up for war, one of the first things they do is concoct stories about the enemy so that the public will believe that theirs is a just cause. Mr. Porter persuaded the local net not to rebroadcast the stories. He's afraid of what might happen to morale if people here saw what was being said about them. But that's not all."

"What else?"

"They've received reports of increased activity on Matagorda Island. A number of shuttles are being prepped for lift-off, and it looks like troops are being mobilized." She paused. "It's hard to know what's going on. Our sources . . . the Resistance, I mean . . . can't get close enough to see exactly what's happening. But . . ."

"Jamey! Hey, Jamey!"

I looked around to see Logan jogging down a path toward us. I closed my eyes and mentally swore a curse against him, and Hannah sighed in an annoyed way. *Bad timing, pal,* I thought, and he must have realized the same thing himself, because when he saw Hannah and me sitting together, he'd stopped in his tracks.

"Oh," he muttered, his face going red. "Sorry, man. I didn't . . . y'know . . ."

"S'okay," I said, even though I could have strangled him. "What's going on?"

"You didn't answer your wristband, so the Chief sent me to find you." Logan quickly walked over to us. "We're being called up. The Rangers, I mean."

"Called up?"

"Uh-huh. Priority One. Everyone's supposed to report to the barracks for a emergency briefing, right now."

As he said this, Hannah's wristband chimed. She glanced at the readout, then looked at me. "The hospital's calling me in, too," she said quietly. "It's starting."

I didn't have to ask what she meant. We both knew that it was the very thing we'd just been discussing. I gave her a quick kiss, then she rushed off to Apollo General while I followed Logan toward the nearest elevator. We'd only walked a dozen yards when he glanced over his shoulder at where Hannah and I had been sitting.

"So . . . are you two a pair now?" he asked, his voice almost a whisper.

"Yeah . . . yeah, I guess we are."

"Good." Despite our hurry, he stopped and turned to me. "Look, man, I know things have been kinda . . . y'know, difficult . . . between us because of what's been going on with Nicole and me, but . . ."

His voice trailed off, but I knew what he meant. "Forget it," I said. "I guess both of us got who we deserve."

"Since you put it that way . . ." Logan stuck out his hand. "Friends again?"

"Sure." I was glad that he was willing to put all that behind us; I'd missed not being able to talk to him. So I shook his hand. "Friends again."

"Good. Now let's get going before the Chief fries us for being late."

* * *

When we arrived at the barracks, we found a note on the door, telling us that the meeting was going to be held in the civic auditorium. A couple of other Rangers were heading over there, so Logan and I fell in with them. The auditorium was located just off the solarium, a large hall that had been cut within the crater wall and normally used for plays or lectures. I wondered why Mr. Garcia was holding the meeting there instead of at the barracks, but it wasn't until we arrived that I saw why.

Lunar Search and Rescue wasn't the only organization to show up. The town council was there, too, as were representatives from the various major departments: Main Operations, Life Support,

Maintenance, Agriculture, and so forth. Logan and I had just found seats in the second row along with the other Rangers when several members of the hospital staff arrived. A few steps behind Dr. Rice was Hannah; she and I spotted each other, and she gave me a little wave, but neither of us made a move to sit together. This wasn't the time to be boyfriend and girlfriend.

Mr. Garcia was seated at a table on the stage along with Mr. Porter. The city manager waited until everyone was seated, then he stood up and walked to the podium. "Thank you for coming," he began, his voice carried by the ceiling speakers. "I apologize for the short notice, but a situation has come up that can't wait for an official town meeting. I'm counting on the various department heads to report everything discussed here to their staffs, so that they can work together in making preparations."

Murmurs passed through the auditorium. About seventy people were in there, and from what I overheard it seemed as if everyone already knew something of what was going on. Mr. Porter raised a hand for silence, then went on.

"As you know, President Shapar has made public statements hinting that the United States may resort to using military force against Apollo in order to break the embargo. Over the past several weeks, we've responded by preparing for a possible invasion. We've retrained our Lunar Search and Rescue personnel to act as a defense force, asked the staff at Apollo General to initiate emergency procedures to be used in the event of an attack, and requested other departments to develop ways and means of coping with damage that might come from a military assault. I don't think I'm speaking only for myself when I tell you that I was hoping none of this would be necessary, and that the current crisis would resolve itself without violence."

He took a deep breath. "Unfortunately, it appears that we were right to take precautions. Reliable sources on Earth have informed us that, over the past couple of days, there's been a surge of activity at the US military spaceport on Matagorda Island. Our sources haven't been able to determine the extent of those preparations, other than to say that it appears that military personnel have been transported to the island and that magcat shuttles have been prepared for liftoff."

Mr. Porter pressed a button on the podium keypad, and the wall behind him became an enormous screen. Displayed upon it was a shot of Earth as seen from the Moon; it was in third-quarter phase, with the sunlight terminator falling across the Gulf of Mexico. To the right was a bright spot of light, a star more brilliant than those around it.

"Early this morning at 0800 Greenwich Meridian Time, 0300 Eastern Standard, two shuttles lifted off from Matagorda, about a half-hour apart. Shortly after that they rendezvoused at Station America, where the freighter *Charles Duke* has been docked since the embargo began." Mr. Porter pointed to the screen. "This picture was taken about two hours ago by our observatory telescope. It shows the *Duke*'s nuclear main engine being fired. Consequent footage shows that the engine hasn't been shut down, and that the freighter itself is on course for lunar rendezvous and orbital insertion."

Again, murmurs passed through the room. Everyone there knew the *Charles Duke*. It was one of three heavy-lift lunar freighters built to transport cargo to the Moon and haul He^3 and other lunar materials back to Earth. If its gas-core nuclear engine was under constant thrust, the *Duke* could make it to the Moon in a fraction of the time it took for an LTV to make the same journey.

Before anyone could ask the obvious question, Mr. Porter answered it. "We estimate that the *Duke* will arrive in approximately twenty hours, including time for braking and orbital insertion. Mr. Garcia will now take over the briefing. Luis . . . ?"

The Chief stood up and approached the podium, with Mr. Porter stepping aside to make room for him. "What the *Duke* will do once it gets here is anyone's guess, but I think we can safely assume that it's not coming to bring us chocolates and roses." A few chuckles, but most of the people in the room weren't in the mood for a joke, and

Mr. Garcia wasn't smiling either. "Chances are that it's carrying two or more landing craft which will descend to the lunar surface. So, we can count on a direct attack upon Apollo . . . and chances are also that they know we're ready for them."

He touched the keypad, and the light in the sky was replaced by topo maps of the Moon's two hemispheres. "Because of that, it's possible that they may try to pull an end-run around our defenses, and attack what they may consider to be our Achilles heel . . . Cabeus Station, our lunar ice mine at the South Pole."

Mr. Porter pointed to the map of the lunar nearside, and a small yellow circle appeared above a small crater an inch or so from the very bottom of the map. "They may believe that if they seize Cabeus, they can take control of most of our water supply, which would then cut short any prolonged siege of Apollo . . . and they would be right. Cabeus is our weakness. We can hole up in here almost indefinitely, but if we run out of water, surrender will be inevitable. So Cabeus Station must be protected as well as Apollo."

He looked at the Rangers. "I want to send a team of twelve Rangers to the South Pole while the rest of us stay here to defend Apollo. Gentlemen, ladies . . . do I have any volunteers?"

I didn't think twice. I held up my hand. Logan didn't hesitate, either; his hand went up at the same time as mine did. Nicole was seated in the row in front of us. She glanced over her shoulder, saw what Logan and I were doing, and then her hand rose as well. Nine more hands were raised—Mikel, Greg, Mahmoud, several others I didn't know quite so well—until the Chief had his dozen volunteers.

"Thank you." Mr. Garcia nodded in satisfaction. "Once this briefing is over, I want this group to report at once to the Airlock 7 ready-room for suit-up. You'll depart for Cabeus Station within two hours."

I was ready to go that minute, but had to wait while Mr. Porter returned to the podium to cover other items on the agenda. Mining operations were to be immediately suspended, with the regolith harvesters relocated to the nearby mountains and camouflaged with tarps to prevent them from being bombed. Airlocks would be sealed, and only Rangers and a few support personnel would be allowed to leave the crater. Colonists were to be evacuated to the storm shelter if and when Apollo came under attack. The shelter was already stocked with food and water, and the Apollo General staff were asked to set up emergency medical facilities down there. Once he'd covered everything on the list, the city manager asked if there were any questions.

From the back of the room, Donald Hawthorne raised his hand. Mr. Porter seemed reluctant to acknowledge him, but he did so anyway. Mr. Hawthorne was still using a cane to get around, and his face expressed irritation as he used it to push himself to his feet.

"Loren," he said as he stood up, "considering the danger we're in, shouldn't we at least think about the obvious solution . . . immediate surrender?"

Angry mutters and whispers rose from the audience. Although Mr. Garcia glared at the mining operations director, Mr. Porter remained stoical. "We've thought about that, Donald," he replied. "In fact, the council discussed that at some length. And the answer is no. We will not surrender. President Shapar is engaged in unilateral actions that are in clear violation of international treaty, and . . ."

"Then you can count me out!" Mr. Hawthorne snapped. "I refuse to be a traitor to my country!"

"No one here is a traitor!" someone yelled. "We're defending ourselves!"

Mr. Hawthorne ignored him. Without another word, he turned to stalk out of the room, leaning heavily upon his cane. Quite a few people hissed and booed, and when I glanced over at Billy Tate, I saw that, even though his expression remained stoical, his face had gone red. I couldn't help but feel sorry for him; his uncle had just made an ass of himself.

Mr. Porter waited until the auditorium door slammed shut behind Mr. Hawthorne before he spoke again. "Are there any other questions or comments?" he asked. No one raised a hand. "Very well, then. If everyone knows what they need to do, then the meeting is adjourned."

Everyone stood up to leave. I wanted to head over to Billy and talk to him, but he shoved everyone aside and hurried from the room. "Leave him alone," Logan murmured as we watched him go. "Not his fault that he's got a jerk for an uncle."

Not long ago, I'd decided Billy was a jerk himself. I'd since learned that Nicole was right: he could be a pretty good guy when he wanted to be. Maybe his bad side came from his uncle. Still, the fact that he hadn't volunteered for the mission made me wonder where his loyalties lay. Was he staying here to defend his home . . . or did he agree with his uncle?

I didn't know, but I had more important matters to deal with just then. Mr. Garcia had just come down from the stage, and the other Rangers who'd volunteered for the mission were gathering around him. I didn't think he was planning to lead the mission, but it looked as if he was about to give us some last-minute orders. I started to head over there when I felt a soft hand on my shoulder. Looking around, I saw that Hannah had come up behind me.

"Hey, you," she said. "You planning to run off without saying goodbye?"

Damn. I was about to do that, wasn't I? "Y'know what's a drag?" I asked, trying to change the subject. "Before Logan found us, I was about to ask if you . . . well, wanted to go out with me. Like, to get a pizza, or see a vid, or . . ."

"Jamey Barlowe . . . is that the date you promised me?" A sly smile appeared on her face.

I'd forgotten about that. Obviously she hadn't. "Well . . . um, yeah, but if you don't want to . . ."

The smile vanished, "What makes you think I don't?"

I guessed I'd confused her a little. Maybe I was bit confused myself. I was trying to figure out how to answer that when something else occurred to me. "Oh, yeah," I said, "and there's another thing."

I reached into my pocket, pulled out the medallion she'd given me a few days earlier. "Here . . . you can have this back."

Hannah looked down at the medallion. "I think you should hold onto it a little while longer," she said. "You need it more than I do."

"Maybe, but . . ." I hesitated, not knowing how to say what was on my mind. "It belongs to you, and . . . well, y'know, it'll be safer with you, I think."

My mind was on the mission, not her. I was going to a dangerous place where there was a very real possibility than I might lose my life. If that happened, I didn't want my body brought back to Apollo with her St. Christopher's medallion still around my neck. I wanted to spare her that . . . but I didn't realize that she might not see things the same way I did.

Hannah stared at me for several seconds. Behind us, I heard Logan calling for me. I paid no attention to him. Hannah's mouth trembled, and behind the tears that crept into the corners of her eyes I saw a hint of anger.

"You really don't get it, do you?" she said, her voice almost a whisper. "I didn't give that to you because I think it's a good luck charm. I gave that to you because . . . because . . ."

I glanced past her. The briefing was already underway; Mr. Garcia's back was turned to me, but several other Rangers were looking my way. I was supposed to be with them, receiving final instructions from the Chief, not fooling around with my girlfriend.

"Because what?" I said, more impatiently than I should have.

Hannah's mouth fell open; now the anger was obvious. "If you haven't figured it out by now, then you probably never will," she snapped, her voice no longer subdued. "God, I'm so tired of chasing you . . ."

"Hannah . . ." From the corner of my eye, I could see several people staring at us. "C'mon. I didn't . . . I mean, I don't . . ."

"I think I figured out what you don't want." Before I could stop her, she snatched the medallion from my hand. "Good luck," she finished, and then she turned and dashed out of the auditorium.

INVADERS FROM EARTH

16.
TO THE SOUTH POLE

In the early years of the 21st century, NASA sent its Lunar Crater Observation and Sensing Satellite to the Moon to confirm the presence of subsurface ice deposits at the South Pole. Upon reaching the Moon, LCROSS released its spent second-stage booster and sent it crashing down into Cabeus Crater. The probe's cameras and spectroscopes caught the plume of debris raised by the rocket's impact; when scientists back on Earth analyzed the images, they discovered that as much as 8.5 percent of the regolith was comprised of ice, possibly the remnants of an ancient comet collision. Since the crater floor lay in perpetual darkness, this ice had never melted.

That meant Cabeus was an oasis, a large source of water—nearly a billion gallons, it was eventually learned—in a place where H_2O was hard to come by. The Chinese would later discover another ice deposit about a hundred miles to the east in Scott Crater, but by then the ISC was making plans to exploit the Cabeus ice field as a primary source of drinking water for future lunar colonists.

Cabeus Station had been manned for only as long as it took to build a semiautomatic mining facility at the bottom of the crater; it was much too remote for anyone to live there for long, and helium-3 deposits were sparse in the polar regions. Instead, robots teleoperated by controllers in Apollo prowled the crater floor, using diamond-head drills to sink narrow shafts into the ground wherever their spectroscopes detected ice crystals. The robots extracted the ice-laden regolith and carried it back to the station's main facility, where a fusion furnace melted the ice and processors distilled pure water from the heavy metals within the sediment. The water would then be stored in tanks to await pickup by a Pegasus.

Sure, the loonies could extract H_2O from the regolith mined closer to the colony, but not nearly in the same amounts as from Cabeus. Moon Dragon had its own lunar ice mine at Scott, and they were welcome to it. So long as both the ISC and the PSU exercised water conservation at their separate colonies, there was enough ice to keep everyone happy for years to come. No one had ever seriously thought that Cabeus Station would need to be defended . . . until now.

From the passenger compartment windows of the Pegasus, I could see the terrain over which we flying. The lunar South Pole was a wilderness of dust and stone, its ragged mountains and deep craters shrouded by an endless twilight. The landscape was nothing like the basalt oceans of the equator. This was one of the Moon's most treacherous regions, harsh and unyielding, where Earth barely peeped above the horizon and the Sun was almost a stranger.

Once again, Gordie was flying the Pegasus I was in. No surprise; I didn't think he would have wanted to sit this one out. After liftoff from Apollo, he headed due south from Ptolemaeus on a high-altitude trajectory. He could have gone suborbital and cut the travel time in half, but this was the way long-range transports flew when they carried water tanks back and forth from Cabeus Station. With luck, anyone aboard the *Duke* who might be watching for unusual activity on the Moon might mistake our Pegasus for a routine resupply mission.

Because we didn't want our adversaries to determine our defense strategy, my team was observing strict radio silence: no contact with Apollo unless absolutely necessary. But the silence wasn't restricted to satellite communications. It was quiet in the Pegasus, too. Twelve men and women sat across from each other in the personnel module, and I don't think any of us spoke more than a few words during the three and a half hours it took to travel 1,300 miles. We'd pressurized the module and opened our helmets, yet no one was in the mood for conversation.

Let's be honest: we were scared.

I was learning that fear can be a good thing. It keeps you alert and wary, ready for whatever may come your way. But it can also immobilize you, make you afraid to do whatever needs to be done in order to stay alive. If Mr. Garcia had been with us, he might have given us a good pep talk, or at least told us to relax until we got to where we were going. He'd put Mikel in charge of our team, though, and he was handling the job with typical Russian stoicism. That pretty much left each of us alone with our thoughts.

Mine were about Hannah. She'd been scared, too . . . for me. And like an idiot, I'd said the wrong things, even given back a good-luck charm that she'd clearly wanted me to keep. I shouldn't have been so fatalistic. I should have kept the medallion and told her not to worry, I'd return soon. What I'd done instead was practically tell her that I didn't think I was coming back. That was even worse than giving her the impression that I no longer wanted to take her out on a date. To a girl who was still getting over losing her father and didn't know where her mother was, this was . . . well, I could have handled it better.

So I stared out the window beside me and watched the shadows grow longer upon the battered moonscape, and tried not to think too hard about what we were about to get ourselves into. And around the same time that it seemed as if I could no longer see anything except the highest mountain peaks, the transport's bow tilted forward and I felt the VTOL engines surge to life beneath the deck plates.

"Coming in for landing," Gordie said, his voice a muted murmur within my helmet. *"We'll be on the ground in five minutes. Close your helmets, I'm beginning depressurization."*

"Roger that," Mikel said from the other end of the module. "You heard him, guys. We're going on comlink now. Channel Three."

I reached up to shut my faceplate. "Pressurize suit, please, Arthur," I said once my helmet was airtight. "Switch comlink to the emergency freak."

"Yes, Jamey." A second later I heard the thin hiss of air entering my suit. *"You'll pardon me for saying so, but I'm registering a seven percent increase in your cardiac rate. You need to calm down a little."*

I started taking long, slow breaths. That usually helped settle my nerves, but this time it didn't. Across the aisle, I could see Logan doing the same thing. We looked at each other, and he managed a wry grin. By then, everyone had switched their comlinks to the seldom-used UHF channel reserved to Lunar Search and Rescue for emergency transmissions. With luck, enemy forces wouldn't figure out that we were on this particular frequency. I could hear scattered comments from the others, which meant that they'd be able to hear what Logan and I said, too.

"*So,*" Logan asked, "*who do you think is going to the state championship this year?*"

I couldn't help myself; I laughed out loud. "Burtonsville, of course. You should know that. We . . ."

"*What the hell are you two talking about?*" Nicole was seated next to Logan. She'd just closed her helmet, and she stared at us from the other side of her faceplate.

"*Just swim team stuff,*" Logan said, as if this was still something that mattered to us. I hadn't thought about it in months. "*Jamey's got more school spirit than I do. Our team hasn't been the state champs in years.*"

"Yeah, maybe so," I replied, "but that doesn't mean we can't . . ."

"*Okay, knock it off, you two,*" Greg said. "*We've got more important things to worry about.*"

He was right, of course. All the same, it helped me remember, if only for a few seconds, where Logan and I had come from. We grinned at each other, sharing a private joke only the two of us understood. Of course our swim team never went to the state championships. It was a well-known fact that Burtonsville High had the worst team in Maryland. But it never stopped us from trying . . . and I was glad that Logan and I were able to talk about that kind of stuff again.

There was a mild jolt as the Pegasus touched down. The transport had barely settled upon its landing gear when Mikel stood up. "*Let's go, Rangers!*" he snapped as he cranked open the main hatch. "*Grab your gear and move out!*"

I pulled out my gun from where I'd stashed it beneath my seat, then followed Logan and Nicole as they joined the line of Rangers exiting the Pegasus. We tramped down the ramp and stood within the glow of the spacecraft's floodlights. I asked Arthur to switch on my helmet lamp, then paused to look around.

Cabeus was smaller than Ptolemaeus, about sixty-one miles in diameter, but much deeper, surrounded by sheer walls two and half miles high. At this latitude, the crater's depth was significant; sunlight never reached its floor, so its power supply came entirely from a fusion tokamok near the dome-shaped distillation facility. The rest of the station was a collection of modules and sheds, visible only by the wan illumination of red and blue beacons set up around its perimeter.

Nothing moved. We were the only people here.

"Okay, look sharp." Mikel bunny-hopped away from the Pegasus until he stopped to face the rest of the squad. *"We've got only a little while before the Marines show up, and we need to be ready and in position when they arrive. Is everyone locked and loaded?"*

I checked my carbine, making sure that its ammo drum was firmly attached. "Yes, sir," I replied, joining the chorus from those around me.

"Good. Excellent." Mikel pointed to the mule that had followed us from the Pegasus. *"There's more ammo over there. Everyone take two spare drums and carry them with you. It's also carrying spare air tanks, which will be distributed once the fire teams have taken their positions. Now, we need to . . . Rogers, what do you think you're doing?"*

Turning around, I looked back at the Pegasus. Gordie had opened the cockpit hatch and was climbing down from the transport, his copilot right behind him. *"Coming to join you guys, that's what,"* he said.

"Like hell you are!" Mikel sounded angry. *"Get back in that thing and . . ."*

"And do what? Be a couple of sitting ducks?" Gordie bounded toward us. *"Sam and I talked it over, and we want to be in on this. Fourteen is better than twelve, don't you think?"*

He had a point. If he and Sam remained in the Pegasus, they'd be nothing more than targets if the Marines decided to take out the transport. And if there was a firefight, we could use all the help we could get. But neither of them were wearing Ranger moonsuits; instead they wore standard-issue skinsuits that offered zero protection in a combat situation.

"*Sorry, but no,*" Mikel said. "*I want you to take the Pegasus over to the other side of the crater, turn off the lights, and await further orders. I don't want to give the Marines an easy target, and we're going to need to keep the transport safe until we're ready to pull out.*"

Gordie grumbled something under his breath that I didn't quite catch, but he didn't argue with the squad leader. Mikel turned to the rest of us. "*All right, then . . . here's the plan,*" he said, then bent down to scratch a diagram in the grey dust at his feet. "*I want six fire teams, two people each, spread out in a semicircle around the station. We'll keep the station at our backs, and count on the crater wall to provide protection at our rear.*"

"*What if they come at us from that direction?*" Logan asked.

"*They won't.*" Mikel pointed toward the distillation facility and the crater wall looming above it. "*They'll most likely land here, where we're standing, and advance on the station from this direction. The top of the wall is too far away to give them much advantage . . . and if they do decide to use it, we can redeploy our teams to cover the rear.*"

"*We hope.*" This from Toji Kanaku, another Ranger First Class.

Mikel ignored him. "*We'll use the station as our base of operations,*" he went on. "*We'll eat, sleep, and recharge our packs in there. Between now and then, I want to build up our defenses. That means finding whatever we can use . . . robots, empty tanks, anything we can get our hands on . . . and placing them so that they can provide protection for us. We'll send the mule around to distribute the spare air tanks once we've established our firing positions.*"

"*We're going to try to ambush them?*" Nicole asked.

"*No. We're going to make it as hard as possible for them to know where we are or how many people we have. If they believe we got them outnumbered,*" *maybe they'll think twice about trying to take the station. With luck, we may even be able to talk them down."*

That sounded a little too much like wishful thinking. I didn't say so, but instead asked a question. "What if we're outnumbered and they get us boxed in? What then?"

"If that happens, we'll fall back to the operations center. There's an airlock on the west side. If I call for retreat, go there as fast as you can. We can hole up inside and wait them out. . . ."

"Or they can wait us out," Gordie murmured.

"We have approximately fifteen hours to get ready," Mikel continued, *"so use your time wisely. Nap and eat in shifts when you're in the station. At 0700, fourteen hours from now, I want everyone in their suits and on the firing line. Once everyone is in position, switch off your helmet lamps and observe radio silence unless it's absolutely necessary. Any questions?"*

"Just one," Gordie said. *"Do you seriously believe US Marines will back down from a fight just because we bluff them into thinking they're outnumbered?"*

This time, Mikel didn't ignore him. *"I don't . . . but I'm under orders to avoid a fight if at all possible."* He paused. *"Look, I realize that the Americans among you aren't eager to engage our own people. But you have to remember that you're defending this place from an enemy that would use it to force Apollo to surrender. We can't let that happen. So I'm going to try to reason with them, if and when they land here, but I'm going to do that with my finger on the trigger, and I expect everyone here to back me up. Can you do that for me?"*

Everyone murmured in the affirmative. *"All right, then,"* Mikel said. *"Let's get to work."*

* * *

The next thirteen hours were among the busiest of my life. Cabeus Station was never meant to be a fortress, but we did our best to turn it into one.

The first thing we did was enter its seldom-visited operations center, a pair of pressurized modules adjacent to the furnace dome, and shut down all the mining equipment except for the robots, which we reverted to local control. The robots were huge, flat-bed tractors with barrel-shaped horizontal drills mounted on one end and cylindrical collection tanks at the other; there were six in all, scattered across the crater floor. One of the Rangers had been to Cabeus before and knew how to operate them, so Mikel put him in charge of moving the 'bots until they were repositioned in a semicircular ring around the dome.

The robots were big enough for two people to easily hide behind, but they were only part of the barrier we set up. There were also several empty tanks stacked nearby, insulated cylinders with a 200 gallon capacity each. We rolled them into place between the robots, then added stuff we found in a storage shed—replacement bulkhead panels, spare rolls of electrical cable, an old airlock hatch that had been discarded—and lugged them over to the fortifications. By the time we were through, we'd built a makeshift stockade that, while not solid, would provide some measure of protection.

Greg pointed out that we might be able to use the crater's perpetual night to our advantage, so Mikel had him enter the operations center and shut down the beacons. Once this was done, the crater was plunged into darkness. Our carbines were equipped with ultraviolet night-vision rangefinders and our helmet faceplates could be filtered to see the same, so we'd be able to make out one another in the dark; nonetheless, we'd have to be careful not to accidentally target each other during a firefight.

The operations module was small, but at least it had its own airlock and ready-room, and adjacent to them was a bunkhouse with a few collapsible cots and a small galley. It was meant to be used by the maintenance crews that periodically visited the station; there wasn't enough room for all of us at once, but we were able to visit it four at a time. I took the second shift, once I was done shoving water tanks into place. It was a relief to climb out of my suit for a few hours and get a bite to eat, but I can't say that I slept well. I stared at the ceiling for a long time, and it felt as if I'd just closed for a few minutes when another Ranger shook me awake and told me that it was his turn to nap. I chugged a cup of coffee, visited the toilet, then climbed back into my suit.

Gordie and Sam stayed at the station for as long as they could, working alongside the Rangers, but twelve hours after we arrived at Cabeus, they reluctantly climbed back into the Pegasus and lifted off. I watched the transport as it rose from the landing pad, its formation lights the sole source of illumination within the crater. It ascended to about 500 feet, then turned south and headed for the other side of the crater. I knew Gordie didn't want to leave; if he could have, he would've rigged the Pegasus with mortar rockets and provided air support. But the transports were never meant to be gunships, and his craft would've been an easy target for any Marine with an RPG and a good eye.

After that, there was nothing left to do but take our positions.

I was partnered with Greg, and we'd put ourselves behind a mining robot. Mikel and Toji hid behind a water tank about fifty feet away to our left; Logan and Nicole were concealed behind another robot about forty feet to our right. There was an extra oxygen tank on the ground between Greg and me, along with four ammo drums. The other six Rangers were in pairs to either side of us. When I switched on my night-vision, I could make out the others as vague, green-hued silhouettes, featureless and ghostly.

Mikel had us sound off, answering verbally and raising our hands when he called each of our names, so that we'd all know where everyone was. Then we went radio silent, continuing to monitor all channels but using Channel Three only if necessary. That may have been the most tense time of all: standing in the pitch darkness, barely able to see anything at all, not hearing much except the hiss of respirators, watching the starlit sky above Cabeus and wondering when . . . and even if . . . the Marines would land.

We waited. And waited. And waited.

And just as I was beginning to seriously wonder whether the Chief had made a serious mistake by sending us down here, that was when they came.

I happened to be looking up at the sky when I spotted a bright point of light moving among the stars. At first I thought it was a satellite, until I realized that it was going in the wrong direction, from north to south, away from the equator.

I reached over to Greg, prodded his elbow. Within the dim backglow of his helmet visor, I could see his face; he nodded, yes, he'd seen it, too. We watched as the light disappeared beyond the south crater wall, only to reappear a few seconds later, brighter this time and lower to the ground. As it came closer, the light quickly assumed shape, becoming a tiny, comet-like flare that waxed and waned. Engine exhaust. A spacecraft coming in for a landing.

The vessel slowed as it approached us, RCRs winking every now and then, until it was hovering a couple of thousand feet above the crater. Then it slowly began to descend. It was blacked-out save for its cockpit lights and exhaust flare, but it soon became apparent that it was a ferry much like the one that had rendezvoused with the LTV that had brought me from Earth. Although I couldn't see it clearly, it didn't look quite the same; instead of passenger modules, it appeared to be carrying six upright cylinders, mounted in a ring around its control turret.

The ferry didn't use the landing pad. It came down about a mile away from the station, closer to the crater's center. We couldn't hear anything, of course, but we knew that it had landed when its exhaust flare abruptly vanished, a sign that the pilot had cut its main engine.

All we could see was the distant glow of its cockpit lights, then those disappeared as well.

Mikel's voice came over the comlink: *"Stand by."*

That was all he said, and it was an unnecessary order. Everyone had seen the ferry land, and I had little doubt that the others had figured out the same thing that I had. The pilot had put his craft down at that distance to give his passengers a chance to disembark before being fired upon. This could only mean one thing: they were expecting the station to be defended.

The Marines had landed. And they were looking for trouble.

"Ready carbine, Arthur," I said, keeping my voice low. I didn't need to whisper; it just seemed right. "Activate UV targeting system."

"Yes, Jamey." A green bar appeared across the top of the faceplate; it was marked twenty at its left margin, the number of rounds I had in reserve. I raised my carbine and pointed it the direction of the freighter, and the translucent red crosshairs of the virtual gunsight appeared in the center of my faceplate.

The night-vision didn't show me anything except an indistinct black object approximately a mile away, a few tiny dots moving around it. As I watched, though, the dots began to move toward us . . . and then they began to hop, leaping up into the air and coming down again a few dozen yards closer than they'd been before, like fleas travelling across a black dog's fur.

What was this? I could bunny-hop, too, of course, but never so high or so far. As the fleas came closer, I saw that there were only six. We had them outnumbered by two-to-one . . . yet there was something in the way that they moved that made me shiver.

Within minutes, the six figures crossed the distance between the freighter and the station. As they crossed the landing pad, we got our first good look at our enemy. When I saw what they were wearing, I suddenly realized that numerical superiority didn't matter.

They were wearing Cyclops suits.

Any kid who'd ever played a war game on his pad knew what they were: powered armor for space combat, a military spin-off of the EVA gear originally designed for the International Jupiter Expedition. The suits were over seven feet tall and resembled eggs that had sprouted arms and legs; no helmets or faceplates, but instead a smooth, round carapace with a periscope jutting from the top hatch. Each Cyclops had its own rocket-pack, enabling the soldier who wore—or rather, drove—the suit to jump as much as a hundred feet in lunar gravity. Even their weapons were different: shoulder-mounted carbines, looking like fat sausages, positioned on a swivel beside the periscope.

I fought a sudden urge to pee in my suit. Perhaps we should have expected that the Marines would be wearing powered armor, but we didn't, and that was our mistake. This was the enemy, and he'd come to kick our ass.

The Cyclops team came to a halt just past the landing pad: six giants, facing a barricade hastily built by a handful of pygmies. They didn't come any closer, though. A few seconds went by, then I heard an unfamiliar voice in my headphones:

"Cabeus Station, do you copy? Over." A pause, just long enough for me to glance at my heads-up display and see that the speaker was using Channel One. *"Cabeus Station, this is Liberty Force One. Respond at once. Over."*

Mikel came over the comlink. *"Liberty Force One, this is Apollo Lunar Search and Rescue. You're intruding on a facility operated and protected by the International Space Coalition. Please return to your craft at once."*

Another pause, then the voice returned. *"Apollo SAR, we're here to take possession of this station in the name of the United States of America. Surrender immediately."*

A short beep, then Mikel spoke to us on Channel Three: *"I'm going to try to negotiate."* He switched back to Channel One: *"I'm sorry, but we don't recognize the authority of the United States to take control of this station. I should also warn you that you're greatly outnumbered. Any attempt to take this facility by force would be a grave error. Again, return to your craft and once and leave."* He paused, then added, *"This is your final warning."*

For a few moments, there was no response. I slowly raised my carbine, braced it against the robot's upper platform, and took aim upon the nearest Cyclops. As the red crosshairs was painted on the center of the suit, I noticed that it was stenciled with a cartoon figure of a penguin wearing a top-hat and carrying a walking stick. But no American flag. Odd . . .

"Okay, I understand." When the Cyclops team leader spoke again, his tone a little less formal. *"Look, maybe we ought to talk this over before anyone gets hurt. Would you be willing to discuss this?"*

"Yes, I believe that can be done," Mikel said.

I may have been wearing a moonsuit, but that didn't stop me from smelling a rat. "Don't trust him, Mikel," I blurted out. "He's up to something."

"Stand down, Ranger. If they want to talk, then it's in our best interest to do so." Mikel hesitated. *"Look sharp. I'm going out there."* Then he switched back to Channel One: *"Coming out to speak with you, Liberty One."*

"Sure. Ready when you are." The Cyclops leader sounded positively avuncular.

Don't do it, I thought, but Mikel was already emerging from cover. Gun pointed at the ground, he stepped out from behind the water tank where he and Toji had hidden.

Walking slowly, careful not to seem menacing, he approached the row of Cyclops soldiers waiting for him.

He was about halfway there when the one in the middle shot him.

17.
THE BATTLE OF
CABEUS STATION

There was no gunshot, no muzzle flash. I heard a thin, ragged crack through the comlink as the Cyclops's machine gun shattered Mikel's faceplate. Tiny shards of glass sprayed outward from his helmet, carried by the abrupt decompression of his moonsuit. Mikel collapsed, hitting the ground face-first, raising a small cloud of dust. They had never intended to negotiate.

For a heartbeat, no one moved. Then Greg screamed *"Fire!"* and all hell broke loose.

My gun was already trained on the Cyclops nearest me. I aimed at the stupid penguin in the middle of his chest and curled the index finger of my right hand, but my target was no longer there. Penguin had fired his rocket pack; his leap carried him up and away before my bullets could reach him.

"Arthur!" I yelled. "Track and lock onto target!"

"Which one, Jamey?" As always, Arthur's voice was calm and unruffled.

Looking up, I saw Penguin a dozen feet or so above the ground, just starting to come down again. I jerked my carbine toward him. "That one!"

I fixed my red crosshairs fixed upon Penguin, but they had barely flashed to indicate that I had a lock-on when the Cyclops suddenly changed position. Penguin had used his rockets again to get out from under my sights before I had a chance to fire. He came down about forty feet away, then lunged to the left when I tried to track him.

"Damn it!" Greg shouted. *"They've got countermeasures!"*

I didn't have time to ask what he meant by that. Penguin had evaded me, but when I started to step out from behind the mining robot, a bullet clipped the platform fender, forcing me back under cover. The shot had come from another Cyclops; I caught a glimpse of a happy-looking raven on its chest as I ducked behind the 'bot again.

"Fire at will!" Mahmoud cried, sounding like he was on the verge of panic. *"Fire at will! Pick someone and . . . ah!"*

I couldn't tell whether or not he'd been hit, nor did I really care. Just then, I had problems of my own. Penguin was coming at Greg and me, bouncing from one foot to another, dodging left and right as he closed the distance between us. My crosshairs were useless; every time I had him in my sights, he'd dance away, almost as if he knew . . .

Right. Of course he did. I suddenly realized what Greg meant. The Cyclops suits were equipped with electronic countermeasures which would detect a lock-on by our carbines' targeting systems. All Penguin had to do was move when he heard the warning and my bullets would never find him.

"Arthur! Disengage targeting system! Go to manual!"

"Jamey, are you sure you . . . ?"

"Yes! Do it!"

The crosshairs vanished; I was now on manual fire control, dependent on nothing more than my own two eyes. Penguin was less than ten yards away. He stopped moving, and the sausage-like machine gun on his shoulder swiveled toward me. By then, though, I'd raised my gun and was using a small knob at the end of its barrel as an improvised sight. When Penguin didn't jump away again, I curled my forefinger around the trigger and kept it there.

Penguin staggered backward beneath my salvo. I couldn't tell whether my bullets had fully penetrated his thick armor, but I must have hit something vital because his gun suddenly tilted upward. All I knew was that he couldn't run from me, nor could he retaliate. Screaming in rage, I kept firing, and suddenly a white jet of mist spewed from the center of his top hatch. Penguin didn't fall, but his arms went limp at his sides as he sagged upon his thick legs. Even if the man inside the armor wasn't dead, it didn't look as if he was going to give me any more trouble.

"Got one!" I shouted, then I looked around to see that Greg was no longer beside me. He was crouched at the other end of the robot, firing at Raven as he tried to come at us from around the 'bot. "Greg! Switch off your . . . !"

"*I know! I know!*" His gun swept back and forth as he sought to get a lock on his target. "*Get this guy off me!*"

The Cyclops team had broken formation. Raven was the nearest, now that Penguin was down, and he was using his rockets to dodge Greg's bullets. I pointed my carbine at him and squeezed the trigger, but I got off only a couple of shots before my weapon abruptly went dead.

"*You are out of ammunition, Jamey,*" Arthur said.

Until then, I hadn't realized that I used up an entire ammo drum taking down Penguin. Swearing, I bolted for the spare drums. They lay on the ground beside the robot's treads, but I'd barely bent over to grab one when something slammed into my back.

For a horrifying second, I thought I'd been struck by a bullet. Then a piece of the robot's high-gain antenna fell next to me, and I realized what had happened. Raven had hit the 'bot by mistake, clipping off its antenna. That meant that Raven was trying to get me, too. Sure enough, when I tried to reach for the ammo drum, bullets pocked the grey dust beside the drum, forcing me to yank back my hand.

"Can't help you, Greg!" I shouted, kneeling beside the robot to use it a shield. "You've gotta . . . !"

"*Aw, damn it!*" he snarled, and then he bolted out from behind the 'bot. "*Somebody cover me!*"

From where I was crouched, I couldn't tell what was happening to him. But I could see everything else that was going on. The Cyclops team were coming at us from all sides, the five remaining soldiers doing their best to break through the barricades. Logan and Nicole were fighting back to back, each covering the other's rear, while Toji tried to keep the water tank between him and a Cyclops emblazoned with a bald eagle. Farther away, other Rangers fired, ran, ducked, or did whatever else they could to stay alive.

The battle was fought in almost total silence. No gunfire, no ricochets, no explosions. The only thing I heard where the voices of my friends. For a second or two, I had a sense of being disconnected from reality; the helmet faceplate between me and everything else made it seem as if I was simply watching a vid with its volume turned down low.

"Jamey! Where the hell are you?"

Greg's voice snapped me out of it. I reached again for the ammo drum and this time was able to grab it. I ejected the spent drum, slapped the new one into place, and charged out from behind the robot.

Raven saw me coming. His shoulder gun swiveled in my direction, but I fired before he did. My aim wasn't good, but my shots distracted him from Greg and forced him to jump away. Greg and I concentrated our fire on him, and although the Cyclops was in midair, one of us managed to hit his rocket pack. A lucky shot. Liquid oxygen spewed from its fuel tank as a crystalline shower that froze instantly. Raven fell to the ground; something must have gone seriously wrong with his armor, because its hatch sprang open and a figure in a skin-suit began to scramble out.

Two Cyclops down. I didn't have time to savor our victory, though. Four more Cyclops were still active. I glanced at Greg. "Are you okay?"

"Fine. Thanks for . . ."

"Logan!"

That was Nicole. I turned about just in time to see Logan fall backward from the robot the two of them were using for cover. Eagle had broken off his attack on Toji and was now hovering about ten feet above the 'bot. Logan lay on his side, left hand groping at his suit's chest plate. Through my headset, I could make out his voice: *"Nicole . . . I . . . I . . ."*

"Hold on!" Ignoring the Cyclops leader, Nicole rushed toward him. Eagle wasn't about to give her a chance to tend to a wounded comrade. Settling to the ground behind Nicole, the Cyclops stamped toward her and Logan, his gun pivoting about to lock on them.

"Nicole!" I yelled as I bolted toward them. "Get out of . . . !"

All of a sudden, Eagle seemed to forget about my friends. He stopped and turned around, and in that instant, a white shaft beam of light lanced down from above, capturing him in its glare. Eagle's machine gun turned toward its source, but before the Cyclops could fire, it seemed as if a windstorm came out of nowhere to sweep a cloud of regolith upon him.

"Eat my dust!" Gordie yelled.

As Eagle staggered back, I glanced up to see the Pegasus descending upon Cabeus Station. The transport might be unarmed, but Gordie was far from helpless; he was using the VTOLs to whip up a dust storm. Blinded by the swirling regolith, his periscope and targeting systems disabled, Eagle lurched away from Logan and Nicole.

"Take him out!" Gordie shouted.

Greg and I raced toward Eagle, but before we could get to him, another Cyclops turned its carbine upon us. I heard Greg cry out, but I didn't stop running until I reached the 'bot. Putting it between me and the second Cyclops, I crouched and aimed at Eagle. But my gun alone wasn't enough to drop him; my bullets bounced off his armor, and all they did was let him know that he was under attack.

Eagle turned toward me, and I barely had time to duck back behind the robot before his machine gun chipped paint from its side. I swore and scrambled backward, and in that second realized that the scene had become dark again.

Gordie was no longer covering me. The Pegasus had moved to another part of the battle, providing air support for the other Rangers. That meant I was exposed, though . . . and with Mikel dead, both Logan and Greg down, and Toji nowhere to be seen, that left only Nicole and me to defend ourselves against two Cyclops.

"Die, you bastard!" Nicole screamed, and I looked around to see that she'd returned to her feet. Logan lay still upon the ground and she stood above him to opened fire upon Eagle. *"Die! Die!"*

Eagle turned toward her. Now was my chance. I leaped out from behind the robot, took aim at the Cyclops's vulnerable point, the rocket pack on his back. This time, I didn't miss; my bullets ruptured its fuel tank and Eagle fell back from Nicole, arms flailing about.

Eagle was down, or at least no longer a threat. I was about to rush forward to help Logan when there was a bright flash to my left. The explosion pitched me off my feet; I sailed several yards, came down hard on my right side. There was a violent pain as my arm twisted in an awkward direction, and I yelped as warning lights flashed on my heads-up display.

"Jamey, you've lost your carbine," Arthur said, still irritatingly calm.

He was right. I no longer had my gun. Where it had fallen, I didn't know. But it wasn't in my hands anymore.

Hissing between my teeth, I rolled over to try to get up. I knew what had happened. In the heat of the moment, I'd forgotten the Cyclops that had attacked Greg and me.

He stood only a dozen feet away, looming above me like an avenging golem. His first shot had missed me and hit the robot instead, causing a fuel cell to explode. But now that I was on the ground, unarmed and helpless, he had a clear shot.

He marched closer, his machine gun tilting toward me. He wanted point-blank range to finish me off. As he approached, I made out the emblem on his chest: a goose, cross-eyed and with a long red tongue hanging out of its bill. *What kind of a jerk would put that on his suit?* I wondered, even as I realized that this would probably be the last thing I'd ever see.

"Jamey!" Nicole yelled. *"Duck!"*

"Duck?" In my last moment of life, I was giddy with fear. "Who cares about Duck? It's Goose who's going to . . . ."

And then Goose exploded.

One moment, he was there. The next, he was a ball of fire, a thing that silently detonated where he once stood. I managed to put my head down and cover my faceplate with my left arm before twisted pieces of Cyclops armor rained down around me. Something hit the top of my helmet, stunning me for a moment; when I looked up again, I saw that it was a severed arm, frozen blood turning black at the twisted edges of an armored sleeve.

I stared at the arm in disbelief, but I didn't have time to wonder what had just happened to its former owner because a new voice came through my headphones: *"American military forces, cease fire and surrender!"*

What the hell? Crawling to my hands and knees, I looked around to see the bright beams of helmet lamps. Figures in moonsuits were advancing toward us from just beyond the landing pad. It was hard to tell just then how many there were, but there seemed to be a dozen or more.

A sudden flash of light from their midst, then something shot overhead. I barely recognized it as a mortar rocket before it exploded several hundred feet away. Another Cyclops had met Goose's fate.

"This is your last warning! Surrender at once or be annihilated!"

It seemed as if everything went still. But not silent; I could hear Nicole saying Logan's name over and over, her voice harsh and choked with tears. I clambered to my feet and started toward them, then realized that I might draw fire from our rescuers, whoever they were. But I couldn't leave her and Logan alone, so I paused to switch on my helmet lamp, hoping that its light would distinguish me from a Cyclops, and bounced over to their side.

Logan lay where he'd fallen. As soon I got near, I saw where a bullet had punched through his moonsuit. Nicole was crouched over him, her hands on his shoulders. She was trying to shake him awake, but when the beam from my helmet touched his face, I saw that his eyes were closed and his mouth was sagging open.

Bending down beside her, I shoved Nicole aside and ran a diagnostic cord to Logan's suit. "Download biofeedback, Arthur!" I snapped, and a moment later Logan's suit was linked to mine, his vital signs appearing upon my heads-up display.

It took a second for me to realize the significance of all those flat red lines. I was still staring at them in disbelief when a voice came through my headphones.

"Who's in charge here? Who is your commanding officer?"

I didn't look up. "I dunno . . . someone, I guess."

"Is that person dead?" I dully recognized the voice as being the same one which had demanded the Cyclops team's surrender.

Unwilling to answer that question, I raised my eyes. A figure in a moonsuit that looked a bit different than mine stood a few feet away, a heavy-looking rifle cradled in his hands. Until then, I'd somehow assumed that our rescuers were other Rangers, so it took a moment for me to recognize the emblem on the front of his suit—a red star against a green background—for what it was.

The flag of the Pacific Socialist Union.

"Who are you?" I asked.

"Colonel Thahn Kim, commander of the People's Lunar Defense Force." A not-unkind face regarded me with sympathy from behind a faceplate. *"Was that a friend of yours?"*

I started to reply, but something got stuck in my throat and I had to fight to keep from throwing up. So I just nodded, even though it was unlikely that Col. Thahn would see the movement of my head. Yet apparently he did, because he lowered his gun and lay a hand upon my shoulder.

"I'm sorry. If we had arrived sooner, we may have been able to save him." He hesitated. *"Would you tell me your names, please?"*

For a moment or two, I was tempted to tell him to . . . well, I don't know what I wanted him to do, just that I didn't care to answer any questions from him. But we were in a combat situation, and this was the man who'd just saved my life. I needed to put my grief on hold and deal with matters at hand.

"Jamey Barlowe, Ranger Second Class." I looked over at Nicole. "This is Nicole Doyle, also Ranger Second Class." Nicole didn't respond; she barely seemed to notice either of us. "You . . . you're from Moon Dragon, aren't you?"

A dumb question with an obvious answer, but Thahn didn't seem to care. *"Yes, but we didn't come from there. When it became apparent that the Americans were sending a military force to the Moon, my team was dispatched to Scott Crater to protect our ice mining facility. And when we saw that they were invading your station instead, I decided to . . . shall we say, intervene? Just in case there was need for us to back up your own defense force."*

Col. Thahn spoke English very well, with hardly any accent; perhaps he'd been educated in the United States before the PSU cut its ties with the west. Although I was exhausted to my very bones, I stood up to face him. "I'm glad you did. I . . ." I took a deep breath. "You saved my life. Hers, too. Thank you."

"You're welcome, Ranger Barlowe. As I said, I'm sorry that we didn't arrive earlier." He pointed in the direction of the landing pad, and for the first time I noticed the squat form of a long-range transport that faintly resembled a Pegasus. It had touched down not far from the ferry that had brought the Cyclops team; I figured that it must have landed while I wasn't looking. *"Now, again . . . who is your commanding officer?"*

I let out my breath. "Mikel Borakov . . . but he's dead. They shot him when he went out to negotiate a cease-fire. The second-in-command was Greg Thomas, but . . ." I shook my head. "I don't know what happened to him. He was with me, but he . . . he . . ."

"I see. Just a moment please." He stopped talking to me, but I could see his lips moving. Apparently he'd switched to another channel and was speaking with someone else from his team. A few seconds went by, then his voice returned. *"My men have located another survivor, Mahmoud Chawla. Is he superior to you in rank?"*

"Yes, he is." It took a moment for what Thahn just said to sink in. "Another survivor? How . . . how many are there?"

"Counting him, Ranger Doyle, and yourself . . . only six. And two of them are wounded." Col. Thahn paused again to ask another question in his own language. *"That doesn't include the pilot and copilot of your transport,"* he added after a moment. *"It's amazing that they survived as well. What they did was very brave, but very foolhardy."*

I wasn't even thinking about Gordie and Sam. What the colonel had just told me caused my legs to go weak. Half of my Ranger team was dead. Greg was probably gone, and I had little doubt that Toji was, too. And Logan, my best friend . . .

"We've captured three members of the force that attacked you," Thahn went on. *"Including their leader."*

He gestured behind me, and I turned to see another PSU soldier standing guard over a figure in a skinsuit who lay face-down on the ground, arms spread out before him. His Cyclops suit rested nearby, its hatch open; when I saw it, I realized that the man on the ground was Eagle. The guy who'd murdered Mikel in cold blood, and probably killed Logan, too.

"My people have ordered the others to climb out of their suits as well," Thahn said. *"If you wish, you can be present while I interrogate them."*

"Yes," I said, "I'd like that very much."

* * *

Three PSU soldiers escorted the prisoners into the station, where they stood watch over the remaining members of Liberty One. The hab modules were too small for everyone to crowd inside, so once Gordie landed the Pegasus at the station again, the two wounded Rangers were carried into the transport; once it was pressurized, they received medical treatment from another survivor.

While this was going on, Mahmoud, Nicole, and I went about the grim business of recovering our dead. As I suspected, Greg had been killed; his suit had been punctured by a bullet and he'd decompressed before he could seal the hole. Toji hadn't made it, either. They were among the bodies we dragged over to the Pegasus and laid out in a row. There was no choice but to leave them in their suits; their corpses would have been mutilated by the airless cold, and we wanted to bring them back to Apollo.

Nicole said nothing while we performed that awful duty. She remained quiet the entire time. Yet when it was done and Mahmoud turned to go into the station, she chose to remain with Logan's body. I lay a hand on her shoulder and she responded with a nod, but her eyes never left Logan.

I was numb. It felt as if, only a few minutes ago, he and I had been talking about our home town swim team. Now he lay before me, and all I could see of him was his face, tinted by the glass of his helmet faceplate. His death was unreal, an abstract fact that I hadn't quite absorbed. My best friend was dead? No, that wasn't true. This was just some guy in a moonsuit. Logan was somewhere else. Any minute now, he'd be back . . .

"Jamey?" Mahmoud's voice was low. *"Do you want to come with me? To interrogate the prisoners?"*

"Yeah . . . sure." There was little I could say or do for Nicole. There wasn't even much I could do for myself. So I left her with Logan and followed Mahmoud to the airlock.

The three Cyclops soldiers were seated in a row on the ready-room floor. Their helmets had been removed, but they still wore their skinsuits. The PSU soldiers standing above them had taken turns removing their moonsuits; when Mahmoud and I cycled through, we found them standing guard over the prisoners, each with a rifle aimed at their heads. The Cyclops team was quiet when we came in, but Col. Thahn had already begun their interrogation, and it was obvious that they were scared.

Thahn was younger than I thought he'd be. Although he was probably only in his midtwenties, he had the no-nonsense look of a military professional. I was glad that I was his friend, at least until he proved otherwise. Two of the Liberty One guys were about the same age as Thahn, while the one in the middle was in his early fifties, heavy-set and with a handle-bar mustache. They all had cold, predatory eyes. I was in the company of killers.

Thahn pointed to the two younger men. "Those are Raven and Sparrow, and this one—" he meant the man in the middle, "is Eagle, their leader. They won't give us their names, only their team designations."

"Figures," I said. "Marines are tough guys. They won't talk."

Eagle said nothing, but his lips compressed into a contemptuous sneer. "You're mistaken, Mr. Barlowe," Thahn said. "They're not Marines. In fact, I don't believe they belong to any American armed service." He paused. "And they will talk."

"Not Marines?" Mahmoud was startled. "How do you . . . ?"

"There is no American military insignia on their armor," Thahn said. I nodded, remembering that I had noticed the same thing when the Cyclops team approached the station. "In fact, there's no identification of any sort. When my team accessed Eagle's suit computer, we discovered that its memory was scrubbed just before he was captured. We're still checking the other suits, but I imagine we'll find that they did likewise." He regarded Eagle with merciless eyes. "You're trying to cover your tracks, but I assure you that it won't work."

"So if they aren't Marines," I asked, "then who are they?"

"That's what we will find out." Thahn's gaze never moved from Eagle. "Speak. Tell us who you work for . . . now."

Eagle stared back at him. "Go to hell."

Thahn looked at one of his men and quietly nodded. The soldier walked forward, grabbed Sparrow by his arm, and roughly yanked him to his feet. "Take him to the airlock," Thahn said, "and throw him out."

Sparrow squawked, tried to pull away. The PSU soldier slammed the butt of his rifle into his stomach, and when he doubled over, grabbed his suit's neck ring and began to drag him across the room.

I don't know whether Thahn was bluffing or not; either way, he was very persuasive. Eagle let out his breath and closed his eyes in resignation. "Okay . . . stop," he murmured. "I'll tell you whatever you want to know."

"Wise decision." Thahn nodded again to his soldier, and Sparrow was thrown back against the wall beside Eagle and Raven. "Where are you from? Who sent you here?"

"Ball North IU."

"Ball North?" Thahn shook his head. "I've never heard of this."

"I have." Mahmoud's eyes were wide with astonishment. "Independent military contractors. They'll hire out to anyone who will pay them. Covert missions, black ops . . . the sort of stuff governments want to get done, but don't necessarily want to do themselves."

"What does IU mean?" I asked.

"'Independent Underwriters' . . . or 'International Undertakers,' if you believe what's been written about them." Mahmoud let out his breath. "Really nasty outfit. There's no job too dirty, if the money is right."

"Mercenaries." Thahn's tone was icy. "Where did you get your equipment? Cyclops armor is too sophisticated for such as you."

Eagle went silent, but Raven spoke up. "From the same people who hired us . . . the US government." He glanced warily at the airlock; he was obviously afraid that he'd go through it without a helmet if he didn't confess. "They supplied us with the suits, trained us how to use them, provided us with transportation."

"And your mission?"

"Take this station, kill everyone who got in our way." Raven looked down at the floor. "We were told not to leave anyone alive."

I felt a chill colder than the crater outside. Just then, I wanted to pitch all three of these guys out the airlock. "Why did the American government hire you?" Thahn asked. "Why didn't they simply send their own troops instead?"

"I don't know," Eagle said. "Maybe they couldn't get the Marines to attack a base where they knew there would be American civilians.

Or maybe they just wanted deniability." He shrugged. "No one told us . . . not me or my men, at least . . . and I didn't ask."

"How many more of your people were sent here?"

Eagle stared at him. "You don't know?" When Thahn didn't answer, he glanced at Raven and Sparrow, then shook his head. "Sorry, pal. I don't rat out my comrades."

Thahn was quiet for a few moments. I thought he was going to give his men the order to blow out Eagle, Sparrow, and Raven, but instead he turned to Mahmoud. "Have you been in communication with Apollo since you've been here?"

"No. We've been observing strict radio silence, so . . ." Mahmoud stopped. His face went pale, and without another word he bolted from the ready-room, nearly colliding with the colonel in his haste to reach the adjacent control room.

"I don't understand," I said. "If there are others like them here, then why haven't they attacked us?"

Once again, a cold smile appeared on Eagle's face. It vanished when he met Thahn's gaze; he quickly looked away, but the colonel was no longer paying attention to them. "The attack on this station may have been only one part of their operation," Thahn said to me. "They may have had another objective as well."

"Another objective?" I stared back at him. "What other objective could they . . . ?"

My voice trailed off. Thahn didn't reply, nor did he need to. The answer was obvious.

Eagle's words were still sinking in when Mahmoud reappeared in the control room door. "Get your gear, Jamey," he said as he headed for the airlock. "We're pulling out right now."

I stared at him. "Is it Apollo? Did you get in touch with them?"

"I just tried . . . and there was no answer."

18.
ULTIMATUM

As soon as I saw Apollo, I knew a lot of people had died there.

"Oh, my God." Nicole was sitting beside me in the Pegasus. She had been quiet during most of the flight from Cabeus; at one point I'd put my arm around her and let her cry against my shoulder. Now she was staring past me out the porthole beside us, and both of us stunned by what lay below.

At first glimpse it seemed as if Apollo was undamaged. As the Pegasus flew in low over Ptolemaeus, it became evident that this was only an illusion. Something had ripped through the northwest side of Apollo's crater dome, leaving a long, jagged tear that extended from the crater wall almost halfway to the sun window. An explosion, no doubt caused by a missile. Yet it couldn't have been a direct hit; otherwise Apollo would have been obliterated. So where did they come from . . . ?

Then I looked away from the dome and felt my heart stop. Where Ag Dome 2 once lay, there was only a big, black hole surrounded by debris. The blast had badly damaged the dome, but it had completely destroyed one of the colony's farms.

The one where Melissa worked.

"Put it down, Gordie." My mouth was dry. "Put it down and let me get out."

"Can't do that, Jamey." His voice came to my headset from the cockpit. *"I've been instructed to land near the industrial park. The landing fields aren't safe, and . . ."*

"I mean it, man. Put it down *now!*" I was already reaching beneath the seat for my helmet. "I need to get to Ag Dome 2. My sister was there. She . . ."

"Jamey . . . stop." Nicole's voice was quiet but insistent. "You know he can't let you get out on your own. We'd have to depressurize the whole module."

She was right. After the Pegasus lifted off from Cabeus, Gordie had repressurized the passenger module so that we could remove the injured Rangers from their suits and tend to their wounds. They lay upon stretchers on the module floor; a blood bag was suspended above one of them, and the other guy was so heavily bandaged that he could barely move. Getting them back into their moonsuits was out of the question; we would have to wait until a bus came to pick us up, so that we could carry them straight to Apollo General.

Once again, my gaze involuntarily turned toward the tarp-covered forms that lay in the back of the module. Logan, Mikel, Greg, Toji, the two other Rangers who'd perished at Cabeus . . . they were all back there, silent fellow travelers. Gordie had wanted to leave the bodies at Cabeus, if only temporarily, saying that we didn't have time to load them into the Pegasus. Nicole wouldn't have it, though; we'd take our fallen comrades back to Apollo, not leave them with the Ball North mercenaries who'd killed them. Colonel Thahn had volunteered to take custody of Eagle, Sparrow, and Raven until someone at Apollo figured out what to do about them; it didn't seem right to leave behind six dead Rangers, too.

"Yeah . . . okay, sure." Tearing my gaze away from the bodies, I looked over at Mahmoud. "Anything more from MainOps?"

Mahmoud was huddled over the shortwave transceiver, its headset clasped against his ear. "Only what Gordie just said," he replied, shaking his head. "The landing fields aren't safe, so we're to land east of the park and wait for a bus to pick us up."

I nodded. The shortwave had become our sole link with Apollo, and even then we hadn't been able to use it until we were within a few hundred miles of Ptolemaeus. Under interrogation, Eagle had reluctantly told us that Ball North's strategy had included taking out the ISC lunar communications satellite, thus severing Apollo's long-range radio link with anyone who might be at Cabeus. This would happen just before Liberty Two, Ball North's second Cyclops team, attacked Apollo, which was timed to be simultaneous with the assault on Cabeus Station.

Fortunately, we still had the emergency transceiver as a backup. Whoever was handling communication at the Main Operations Center wasn't telling us very much, though. They were probably worried that our transmissions were being monitored. If so, that could only mean one thing: there were enemy forces on the ground, and they were still capable of doing us harm.

The Pegasus banked left as Gordie made a port turn. Through the window, I saw Apollo pass beneath us, and noticed that sun window had gone dark. Apparently the reflector ring had been knocked out, leaving the solarium—whatever remained of it—in darkness. Then there was a rumble as the VTOLs kicked in, and a vibration passed through the hull as the transport made its final approach.

We had a rough landing. Gordie came in fast, and the Pegasus slammed down on its landing gear so hard that Hans Geller, the unhurt Ranger tending to the wounded, swore at him through the comlink. The ceiling lights flickered and went dark, replaced a second later by the amber glow of the emergency lamps. A moment later, the steady hiss of the air vents suddenly ceased as well.

"Killing all power until the bus gets here," Gordie said. *"Don't want to give their mortars something to lock onto."* Then there was a click as the comlink went silent; he wasn't taking chances with the radio either.

Gazing through the windows, I could see the clustered domes of the industrial park. Its floodlights had been turned off, and nothing moved near it. On the other side of the Pegasus, Apollo loomed as a vast, dark wall, its outer windows blacked out. Over the past few months, I'd become accustomed to the constant bustle of men and machines around the crater. Now it was as if I was looking at a dead city, lifeless and abandoned, populated only by ghosts.

I was just beginning to get spooked when I spotted a bus

approaching us from Loop Road. Bouncing upon its tandem wheels, it came toward us faster than I'd ever seen a lunar ground vehicle move before. Just behind it was an open-top rover, with two Rangers carrying carbines hunched behind the driver. Once the two vehicles were within ten yard of the Pegasus, the bus fishtailed around until its rear was pointed toward the transport. As it began to back toward us, the rover came to a halt. The Rangers jumped out of the back and trotted alongside the bus, carbines raised and ready to fire.

A hard jolt as the bus connected with the Pegasus's port side, and barely ten seconds later the hatch sprang open. The last person I'd expected to see was Mr. Garcia, yet that was who was standing on the other side. The Chief wore a skinsuit, its helmet faceplate open, and he was in no mood for small talk.

"C'mon, c'mon . . . move it!" he snapped. "Hustle!"

Nicole and I didn't bother to pick up our helmets or carbines. Instead, each of us took one end of a stretcher and carried a wounded Ranger aboard the bus, with Mahmoud and Hans bringing out the second stretcher. Once the wounded were aboard, the Chief told Nicole and me to go back and fetch our helmets and guns. She and I grabbed our gear as fast as we could; as soon as we returned, Mr. Garcia slammed the hatch behind us.

"Get us out of here!" he yelled to the driver. "Go west on Loop Road. That'll keep the crater between us and the snipers."

The driver was Ed Tolley, the guy who'd picked me when I first landed on the Moon. He put the bus in gear, and we barely had time to take our seats before it sped away from the Pegasus, bouncing across rocks and craters as it made a beeline for the road. I was about to tell him to stop and wait for Gordie and Sam, but then I glanced through a window and saw them climbing into the back of a rover along with the Rangers.

"We're going to have to take the long way back," the Chief explained. "The bad guys have taken up positions in the hills east of town so they can take potshots at anything coming out of the garage.

We managed to catch them by surprise when we left, but now that they know we're here, I doubt we'll be so lucky going back." He pointed to our helmets. "Put 'em on. If we draw fire, you'll need to close your helmets if the bus collects a bullet."

I picked up my helmet and shoved my head into it. "What about them?" I asked, looking at the two wounded Rangers. We'd left their moonsuits aboard the Pegasus.

"They're just going to have to take their chances." Mr. Garcia caught the look on Nicole's face and shook his head. "Sorry, but that's just the way it is. We can't stop to . . ."

"I know that, sir," she said. "But we also left behind the . . . the people we lost, I mean. They're still in the transport."

"I'm aware of that, and I'm sorry to have to leave them there, but there's nothing we can do for them just now. Bringing them aboard would have cost us time, and the snipers might have drawn a bead on this bus if it had remained there any longer." He gave her hand a brief squeeze. "When this is over, I'll send someone out back here to get them . . . I promise."

"All right," she said, staring him straight in the eye. "So long as you pick me."

"Fair enough." The Chief turned to Mahmoud. "All right, Mr. Chawla . . . let's hear your report. What happened down there, and why did you return?"

As quickly as he could, Mahmoud told him about the battle at Cabeus. He skipped a few details for the sake of brevity, but the gist of it was there. The Chief listened carefully, asking questions every now and then but otherwise remaining quiet. When Mahmoud got to the part of the story where PSU soldiers from Moon Dragon came to our rescue, the chief's eyebrows lifted in surprise. Then Mahmoud told him that the enemy wasn't the US Marines but rather Ball North mercenaries, and Mr. Garcia stared at him in disbelief.

"I'll be damned. I would've never thought she'd stoop that low." He sighed and shook his head. "That colonel . . . Thahn, did you say his name was? . . . was probably right. President Shapar probably gave the order to send private soldiers. That way, her administration would have plausible deniability if there were civilian casualties and put the blame on . . . well, who knows?"

"Yes, sir," Mahmoud said, "but Colonel Thahn also raised another possibility . . . that Ball North was hired because the Marines refused to take on this particular mission."

"Marines refusing a direct order from their commander in chief?" The Chief gave him a skeptical look. "I rather doubt that . . . but if it's true, then Shapar could be in serious trouble." A grim smile. "We can only hope that your friend is right."

By then, the bus had made the turn on Loop Road that brought us within sight of the remains of Ag Dome 2. I stared at the blackened hole that had once been the farm; on the other side of the bus, the others were gazing at the massive rip in the lower part of Apollo's dome.

"What happened?" I asked.

"The first wave of the attack came from space," Mr. Garcia said. "The *Duke* was outfitted with a missile launcher. Just before it landed, it fired six missiles at us. Fortunately, none of them were nuclear-tipped . . . I guess Lina Shapar wants Apollo intact, more or less . . . and when we saw them coming, we had just enough time to sound the evacuation alarm."

"But didn't the *Blitzgewehr* . . . ?"

"The *Blitzgewehr* managed to take out four of the missiles before they hit. But it couldn't track all six at once, so two got through. The fifth missile destroyed the *Blitzgewehr*, and the sixth destroyed Ag Dome 2." The Chief pointed to the remains of the ag dome. "When it hit the farm, some of the debris ripped through the solarium ceiling. We were lucky, though. Almost everyone made it to the shelter, so there were few casualties. But we still lost some people . . ."

"Sir . . . what about my sister Melissa?" I tried not to stammer, but wasn't very successful. "She . . . she worked in Ag Dome 2. Was she . . . I mean, did she . . . ?"

"She managed to get out. Your sister is safe and sound. But . . ." Mr. Garcia hesitated. "We lost one of our friends. I'm sorry."

I stared at him. "Who?"

"Eddie Hernandez," he said quietly. "He was in the farm when the missile hit."

* * *

The bus had barely reached the Depot Road entrance ramp when it came under sniper fire. There was a loud tap against the vehicle roof as the vehicle turned onto the ramp; I didn't recognize the sound for what it was, the ricochet of a bullet, but Mr. Garcia did. He yelled for Tolley to step on it, and he responded by flooring the accelerator and sending the bus down the ramp at breakneck speed.

I glanced through the rear windows to see that the two escort Rangers had jumped off the rover. Crouched beside the ramp, they raised their carbines and returned fire, covering our escape. Gordie and Sam were still in the back of the rover, and it looked as if Gordie was trying to find a gun of his own when both vehicles hurtled into the garage. Its doors were already open, and they shut as soon as the Rangers ran down the ramp behind us. Nonetheless, no one breathed easily until the dust scrubbers kicked in.

A med team was waiting for us in the garage. As soon as the bus came to a halt, Mr. Garcia opened the hatch and let them aboard. I half-expected Hannah to be among the medics who carried away the stretchers, but she wasn't. Which was probably just as well; I'd lost too many friends today, and wasn't quite ready to see her again.

"Get out of your suits and leave them here," Mr. Garcia said as Nicole, Mahmoud, Hans and I climbed out. "We'll have someone carry them back to the Ranger ready-room. I want the four of you to go straight to the shelter. Find your families, get a bite to eat, grab a nap. You'll be back on duty soon enough, and I want you rested by then."

I couldn't even think of doing anything except finding my sister, but I nodded and followed the others from the garage. Since the solarium had been sealed off, the elevators were no longer operating; we went up a short flight of stairs, then through a pressure door leading to one of the mooncrete corridors that honeycombed Apollo's underground levels. The corridors were crowded with loonies; it seemed as if everyone had urgent business of one sort or another, and none of them paid much attention to four exhausted, battle-weary Rangers making their way to the storm shelter.

The shelter was packed. What had once been an immense room seemed to have shrunk, now that nearly a thousand people were living there. The floor was lined with plastic cushions arranged in uneven rows, with translucent curtains hung from the low ceiling to provide a modicum of privacy. Some people lay upon their makeshift beds, reading or trying to sleep; others sat with their backs against the walls or simply wandered about as if looking for somewhere to go, something to do. Families clustered together, while individuals had found friends or coworkers to keep them company. The air was thick with the stench of too many people bunched together, and hundreds of voices speaking at once produced a cacophony that was almost deafening.

It took a while for me to find Melissa. It wasn't until I happened to run into Ms. Lagler, who was ladling out soup in a breadline, that I knew where to look: a remote corner of the shelter, where she and Mr. Lagler had pitched camp along with the Rices. When she told me that, I knew that I'd find Nina there, too.

I made my way through the crowd until I located them. I'd never seen my sister like this before. Sitting in the corner, legs drawn up against her chest, she held Nina in her arms. As I came closer, Melissa looked up and spotted me. For a second or two, she stared at me in shock, then she hastily pushed Nina aside, scrambled to her feet, and rushed toward me.

"Jamey!" she shouted, sailing into me so hard that she almost knocked the wind from my lungs. "Oh, thank God, you're alive!"

"Yeah . . . yeah, you too." I held her tight. "Are you okay? Did you . . . ?"

"I'm all right, I'm fine, I . . ." And then she broke down, and all I could was hold her and let the tears come. In that moment, I'd somehow become the older sibling. At least it felt that way; I was giving her comfort, not the other way around.

I waited until she stopped sobbing, then I led her back over to the cushions she and Nina were now calling home and sat down with them. Nina was as stoical as always, but I could tell that her brother's death had hit her hard. It didn't look as if either of them had slept at all since the attack: there were dark circles under their swollen eyes and their faces were wet with tears. They'd probably been crying for hours, and both were scared to death.

It took a bit of prodding, but I finally managed to pry from them what happened. Eddie and Melissa had been working in Ag Dome 2—and, as always, Nina was there, too, to shepherd her brother— when the attack came. They'd been through numerous evacuation drills, of course, so when the alarm sounded, they immediately dropped what they were doing and headed straight for the underground tunnel leading from the farm to Ammonius.

"We were almost there when Nina fell . . ." Melissa said.

"I tripped," Nina said, correcting her. "Someone left a wheelbarrow in the aisle, and I fell over it."

"Uh-huh, yeah. And it wouldn't have been so bad except . . ." Melissa shook her head. "There were so many people, and everyone was trying to get to the tunnel at once. So when Nina went down, I couldn't see her at all. I could hear her yelling, but . . ."

"There were people stepping on me, pushing me down." Nina stared at the floor. "I couldn't get up. They were trampling me."

"I was in the tunnel entrance, but I couldn't get back to her. Everyone was pushing against me, and they wouldn't get out of my way. And someone was shouting, 'Hurry, hurry, the door's about to close . . .'"

"Eddie was behind me." Nina spoke calmly as if she was describing something she'd seen in a vid. "He picked me up and tried to run forward, but there were too many people in the way." She raised her hands above her head. "So he . . . he just threw me . . ."

"I couldn't believe what he did!" Melissa's eyes were wide; even in the retelling, she was plainly astonished. "Maybe it's because . . . I dunno, maybe because she just weighs less here, but . . . Eddie just pitched her like she was a football or something, right over everyone's heads, and I reached up and caught her, and then we fell back into the tunnel, and then . . ."

"The doors shut." Nina was still staring at the floor. "We were the last people to make it into the tunnel before the doors slammed down. And a couple of seconds later . . ."

"There was a huge boom from the other side and . . . and that was it. The missile hit, blew the whole place up." Melissa slowly let out her breath. "Eddie was still in the farm, along with everyone else who didn't get out in time. But he saved Nina, just like when you . . ."

"I know," I whispered. It was if a pit had opened in my stomach. Eddie saved Nina's life very much the same way our mother saved mine when I was an infant; the similarity couldn't have been more obvious.

"I . . . I . . . I . . ." Melissa shook her head. "Oh, God . . . Jamey, I'd made so much fun of him, and then he . . . then he goes and does something like this, and I . . ."

The tears came again, and this time some of them were my own. I told them about Logan and how he'd died, and then the three of us huddled together, arms around each other, sharing our misery with each other.

I felt a hand upon my shoulder, and I looked up to find Hannah standing behind me. I don't know how long she'd been there, but it didn't matter; she already knew what happened to Eddie, and she'd just learned about Logan, too. In any case, words were unnecessary, our parting argument forgotten. I stood up and took her in my arms, and we were that way for a long time until Melissa joined the circle, and then Nina, too.

Six kids had left Earth. Now we were down to four. All I could do was hope that we wouldn't lose anyone else.

* * *

I wasn't very hungry, but Hannah insisted that I eat something, so I let her take me back to the communal breadline that had been set up in the middle of the shelter, where we each received a bowl of vegetable soup. Several rows of folding chairs had been set up nearby as a dining space, and while we had lunch—or was it dinner? I wasn't sure—I told her everything that had happened since the last time we'd seen other. It wasn't until I was done, though, that I recalled the way she and I had parted company.

"So . . ." I looked down at the paper soup bowl in my hands. "Sorry about how our first date is turning out," I murmured, not sure what to say next.

"Sure know how to show a girl a good time, don't you?" She said this with such a straight face that I thought she was serious. But then she forced a smile. "Don't worry about it. I'm sure you'll come up with something better next time."

"You want there to be a next time?" I asked. "I mean, the last time we talked . . . y'know, I think I said something stupid . . ."

"Maybe you did. Or maybe I just took it the wrong way. I don't know, and I don't care. I'm just . . ." Hannah closed her eyes, shook her head. "I'm just glad you're still alive, that's all."

"Yeah. So am I." I didn't mean it to come out that way, and for a second we stared at each other in awkward confusion. Then both of us started laughing, and that was it. Apologies given and accepted.

We might have hung around with each other for a while longer, but Hannah had to get back to the emergency clinic set up on the other side of the shelter, and I desperately needed sleep. So we promised each other a real date once everything went back to normal—I wasn't sure they would, but there was no harm in pretending—and then I returned to where I'd left Melissa and Nina. My sister had found a spare cushion for me while I was gone; I unrolled it beside hers, lay down, shut my eyes, and did my best to sleep despite the constant noise around me.

I thought I was going to sleep through the night, but that didn't happen. I was awakened by a hand gently shaking me. "Jamey . . . Jamey, get up," a voice said quietly. "There's something you need to see."

I woke up to find Mr. Lagler kneeling beside me. "What's going on?" I asked. "Are we being attacked?"

"No, nothing like that." The ceiling lights had been dimmed, so I could barely see his face. "We've received a netcast transmission from Earth. Loren Porter is putting it up on the big screen."

Rubbing my eyes, I sat up to look around. I wasn't the only one being awakened. All around me, others were being prodded out of sleep by their families and friends. "What's so important that . . . ?"

"It's from the White House. I don't know what it's about either, but Loren says that it concerns us."

I didn't like the sound of that, so I clambered to my feet. The ceiling lights were being turned up; there were groans and muffled curses as the room became brighter. At the far end of the shelter, the immense wall screen had been lit. Wondering what this was all about, I started making my way toward it, doing my best to step around others who were still getting up.

I was about halfway across the room when I found Hannah. She looked as if she hadn't slept at all, and I didn't have to ask why; she had probably been spending her entire time in the infirmary, taking care of those who'd been hurt by the missile attack.

"Do you know what's going on?" I asked.

She shook her head. "No . . . but I don't think it's going to be good news." She slipped her hand in mine. "C'mon. I want to get closer."

We continued to make our way toward the screen. By then,

almost everyone in the shelter was awake. Nicole caught up with us; she hadn't slept much either, but at least she'd calmed down. I spotted others I knew—Gordie and Sam, Gabrielle, Billy and his uncle Don—and they seemed to be just as bewildered as everyone else.

We'd just reached the front of the room when the screen lit. Mr. Porter appeared on it, a giant peering down upon the loonies gathered in the shelter. *"Good evening,"* he said, his voice coming from the ceiling speakers. *"I apologize for having awakened those of you who were asleep, but this is too important to wait until morning. Just a short time ago, a government netcast was transmitted to Apollo. This netcast was carried throughout the United States and was probably seen in most other countries as well, and apparently originated in the White House. I could tell you what it's about, but perhaps it's best that you see it for yourselves."* He paused. *"Here is the President of the United States. . . ."*

He disappeared, and the screen went blank for a couple of seconds. Then President Shapar appeared. She was dressed in a dark blue business suit, a flag pin on her right lapel, and she stood at a podium with the presidential seal on its front. The background was a featureless wall, but I didn't think anything of this until Hannah hissed under her breath.

"That's not good," she whispered to me. "Whenever my father addressed the nation, it was either from the Oval Office or the Treaty Room." She nodded toward the screen. "She's doing this from a bunker under the White House, next to the Situation Room."

Lina Shapar began to speak.

"My fellow Americans, I'm speaking to you regarding a matter of national importance. As you are no doubt aware, during the past three months our country has been faced with an embargo of vital lunar resources that was imposed upon us by the International Space Consortium, an organization of which the United States was a charter member. This action was clearly taken by the other ISC countries in an attempt to take control of the helium-3 necessary for the continued operation of America's nuclear fusion plants. . . ."

Angry murmurs from around the room. Again, Lina Shapar was twisting facts, trying to make it seem as if the United States was the hapless victim of an international conspiracy. *"Our response has been to demand an end to the embargo and to withdraw from the ISC,"* the president continued. *"Our efforts to reach a diplomatic solution to this crisis have been ignored. In the meantime, our country's energy reserves have begun to run low. As a result, we have had little choice but to use military force to break the embargo.*

"Earlier today, special forces units from the United States Marine Corps landed on the Moon, where they mounted a two-prong attack on Apollo, the ISC mining facility at Ptolemaeus Crater, and also on Cabeus Station, its support facility located at the lunar South Pole. The effort to take control of Apollo is still underway, and we expect positive results. However, the unit which attempted to take control of Cabeus Station was attacked by a superior force already in place there. I regret to say that this unit was defeated, with its members either killed or taken prisoner.

"Since then, we have learned that the enemy force at Cabeus Station included soldiers from the Pacific Socialist Union. Through their actions, it is now clear that the PSU is rendering aid and assistance to the ISC embargo. Our government sees this as a dangerous provocation by the PSU, with their actions at Cabeus Station as tantamount to an act of war."

As President Shapar spoke, the camera gradually moved in, her image slowly expanding until the podium vanished and her face filled the screen. I'd always been unnerved by the way she stared at the camera without blinking. Now it was worse. I realized that I was looking into the eyes of a fanatic.

"The United States will not tolerate these efforts to undermine our national security. Therefore, as President of the United States, I am issuing an ultimatum to both the PSU and its allies in the ISC. Complete and total control of Apollo must be given to the United States. Any refusal to do so will be considered a signal of hostile intentions, and will result in a declaration of war on the Pacific Socialist Union.

"Good night, and may God bless America."

19.
SIEGE

I barely heard the president's last words. Everything she'd said before then caused the sheltered to erupt. All around me, people were yelling; every face I saw was contorted in shock, anger, or horror. I was still staring at the wallscreen when Hannah nudged my arm and said something to me. I couldn't hear her, so I shook my head; she put her mouth closer to my ear.

"You're getting a call," she repeated, speaking louder this time.

I glanced at my wristband. Its beep couldn't be heard above the noise, but a light was blinking next to its speaker. I raised my wrist to my face. "Jamey here."

"Jamey, this is Loren Porter. I need to see you immediately. Come to MainOps at once."

"Yes, sir. I'm on my way." I switched off, then looked at Hannah. "I've got to . . ."

"Hold on." Hannah had just received a call as well. She listened to her wristband, made a brief response much like my own, then took my hand again. "He wants me, too. Let's go."

Leaving Nicole behind, we began to pick our way through the crowd. It wasn't easy. Everyone seemed to be shouting at once; I spotted a couple of men in an argument so intense that a third guy had to step between them before fists started flying. Others were crying; we passed a woman who'd gone down on her knees to wrap her arms around her children. And some were just staring into space, their mind's eyes seeing a terrifying fate they were helpless to prevent.

No one paid attention to Hannah and me, and we finally managed to get out of the shelter. It was a quick walk down the corridor to the Main Operations Center; we were obviously expected, because Mr.

Garcia was waiting for us outside. "C'mon, guys," he said, opening the door for us. "We've got a job for you."

Hannah and I traded an uncertain look as we followed the Chief through the door. MainOps wasn't as calm as it had been the first time I was there. Controllers were barking orders at each other as they stared at their comps or the images on the wallscreens. A quick glance at the screens caused me to stop dead. Figures in moonsuits, each of them carrying a carbine, were advancing toward the cameras. One look at them, and I knew they weren't Rangers.

"Are we under attack?" Hannah had also stopped to gaze at the screens.

"Not right now. At least we don't think so." Mr. Garcia pointed a map projection of Apollo; from the hills to the east, one small group of red dots were moving toward Loop Road, while another group appeared to be heading toward Krantz Road. "It looks as if they're getting into position. They're preparing for another attack, but it probably won't happen quite yet."

I glanced at the door we'd just come through. "I need to get down to the ready-room to suit up for . . ."

"No, you don't." Laying a hand on my shoulder, Mr. Garcia gently but urgently pushed me toward the nearby conference room. "We have a much more important task for you. And your friend Ms. Wilford can help."

Mr. Porter was waiting for us in the conference room. So were two men setting up a portable vid camera and its recording equipment. The city manager walked over to us. "Jamey, thanks for coming so quickly. I don't have to ask if you saw President Shapar's speech, do I?" I shook my head. "Good. Then you know she's lying, right? About what happened at Cabeus, that is."

"No sir . . . I mean, yes sir." The anger felt by others in the shelter was beginning to rise in me as well. "That wasn't the way I saw it. They . . ."

"Good. But don't tell me about it. Not just yet, at least." Mr.

Porter pointed toward the camera. "I want you to do something for me . . . for all of us. I want you to stand over there, in front of the camera, and give your side of the story. Don't exaggerate, don't make it sound any better or worse than it was . . . just do what the president didn't do, and tell the truth."

It was if someone had just thrown a bucket of ice water in my face. "I . . . I don't . . . why . . . why do you want me to . . . ?"

"First, you were there. Anything I might say would be only second-hand information, so it would better if it came from an eye-witness. Second, you're an American. Mahmoud is from India and Nicole is a loony, and the others are either wounded or from other countries. You're a US citizen, though, and that matters. And third—" he grinned "—you're a good-looking kid, and in that department, I'd pit you against Lina Shapar any day of the week."

I'd never thought of myself in that way before, but from the corner of my eye I saw Hannah smile in agreement. Mr. Porter turned to her. "You've done this before, so I want you to coach him . . . not in what to say, but how to say it. Do you think you can do that?"

"Sure." Hannah studied me for a moment. "He's kind of a mess, though. Maybe we should clean him up a little first."

"No." Mr. Garcia regarded me critically. "Less than ten hours ago he was on a battlefield. I want him to look the way he does now . . . like he just came from Cabeus Station."

I still wore the same clothes that had been under my moonsuit for the past two days, and I'm sure I must have smelled something awful. "Shouldn't I rehearse this?" I asked. "Maybe write it down so I don't forget . . . ?"

"No time for that," Mr. Porter said. "I want to transmit this to Earth as soon as possible. The US government will probably block our signal, but they can't prevent it from being picked up elsewhere and put out on the net. But we've got to act fast, before Shapar can get any mileage from her speech." He grinned again. "We've got her right where we want her . . . caught in the middle of a big, fat lie."

"Uh-huh." Mr. Garcia nodded. "She doesn't know it, but she may have just made the biggest mistake of her life." Looking at me again, he raised an eyebrow. "Here's your chance, kid. Do this right, and you can stick it to the president of the United States."

I didn't say anything, but instead looked at Hannah again. There was a cunning smile on her face as she slowly nodded. We both had personal reasons to make Lina Shapar suffer; our opportunity to do so had just arrived.

"All right," I said, "let's do this."

So I stood in front of the camera while Hannah took her place directly behind the guy operating it; he bent low so that I could see her face. She told me to ignore the lens and look straight at her instead, and to speak as if I was talking only to her and no one else. While the sound technician took a few minutes to adjust the levels, Mr. Garcia quietly excused himself from the room, leaving Mr. Porter behind. When the technicians were ready, I took a deep breath, counted to three, and then began.

"My name is Jamey Barlowe," I said, "and I'm from Burtonsville, Maryland. I'm a Ranger Second Class, ISC Lunar Search and Rescue, and I was at Cabeus Station when it was attacked . . ."

I went on to describe everything that happened, starting with the arrival of the Cyclops unit and continuing through the battle that followed. I was careful to mention that the Cyclops leader fired the first shot, and that he killed the Ranger who'd gone out to negotiate a peaceful ceasefire. I explained that my team was rescued by PSU soldiers who'd come to our aid, and until then we were unaware that they were present. When I said this, Mr. Porter made a rolling gesture with his hands—*tell us more*—and I added that the Pacific Socialist Union had nothing to do with the helium-3 embargo. Then I revealed what the Cyclops leader had told us after he and the other surviving members of his unit were taken prisoner: that they weren't Marines, but rather private mercenaries who'd been hired to do the dirty work.

I stopped, uncertain what to say next. It suddenly occurred to me that this vid would soon be seen by millions of people; the realization made me self-conscious, and I started to look down at the floor. Hannah whispered my name and I looked up again to see her pointing two fingers at her eyes. *Talk to me!* she mouthed. Behind her, Mr. Porter was rolling his hands again, more urgently this time.

I hesitated, then went on. "So . . . anyway, it's like this. President Shapar is lying. She isn't telling the truth when she says that the PSU is behind all this or that Marines were sent to the Moon. She wasn't there, but I was."

Again I paused, although not as long as I did before. "My best friend was killed in that battle, and all he was trying to do was to protect Apollo's water supply. Another friend of mine died when Ball North fired missiles at Apollo from orbit, and he was just trying to save his sister. A lot of other people up here have died, too, just because President Shapar wants . . . well, I'm not sure what she wants, but she's not going to get it. Because we're going to hold onto to what's ours, and we're not going to let go."

I stopped, not knowing what to say next. "Cut," Mr. Porter said, running his forefinger across his throat. "That's fine, Jamey. You did well."

"Really?" I didn't believe him. "I thought I sounded stupid."

Hannah practically danced out from behind the camera. Before I could do anything, she swept me into her arms and planted a kiss on my lips. "No, you didn't," she said when she let me come up for air. "You were perfect."

"I was?"

She nodded, her eyes shining. "Trust me. Lina Shapar is going to die when she sees this."

"Yeah, well . . . maybe. If we don't die first."

"No one is going to die." Mr. Porter leaned against the conference table, arms confidently folded across his chest. "Trust me. They've done their worst. Now all we have to do is sit back and wait for it to end."

$$* \quad * \quad *$$

He was right . . . almost.

The same time while I was making the vid, Ball North's Liberty Two team launched another attack on Apollo. I watched the assault from MainOps, and although I still wanted to put on my suit and get into the fight, my help wasn't necessary. There were twenty men in Liberty Two; unlike Liberty One, though, they didn't have Cyclops armor. The *Duke* wasn't big enough to carry that many powered suits, so they were forced to rely upon moonsuits not much different from our own, and their guns were also HK-11 lunar carbines. So the odds were more evenly matched than they were at Cabeus Station.

Liberty Two's intent was to take control of the solar farm and fusion reactor on Krantz Road. So they'd divided into two squads: one to cover Apollo's airlocks and keep anyone from coming out, and the other to attack the power stations. If they'd been successful, they might have shut down our power supply and forced us to surrender. What they'd neglected, though, was the fact that Apollo had dozens of auxiliary airlocks, and they simply didn't have enough men to cover them all.

The Chief knew this, of course, so when he figured out what Liberty Two meant to do, he instructed the Rangers to exit through Airlock 29, at the northeast side of the crater across Loop Road from the industrial park, and take positions on Krantz Road near the solar farm. The Ball North goons never had a chance. As soon as they tried to take the power stations, the Rangers opened fire from behind the regolith berms we'd spent weeks building for this very purpose.

Liberty Two lost three men almost immediately, and two more when the squad sent to cover the airlocks came in as reinforcements. The fifteen survivors were forced to retreat to the freighter. The Rangers didn't lose a single person. Some of our guys wanted to go after them, but Mr. Garcia ordered them to return to the crater.

"That was their best shot," the Chief said to me as we watched the battle come to an end, "and they blew it." He nodded to the left-center wallscreen; it displayed a distant image of mercenaries bounding toward the distant hills. "I give them . . . oh, three days, maybe four . . . before they give up and leave."

I gave him a sharp look. "How do you figure that?"

A wry smile. "They're using the *Duke* as their staging base. It probably has only enough air and water for a hundred hours, tops. Meanwhile, we have enough air and water in reserve to keep everyone in here alive for three weeks." He shrugged. "Like I said, all we have to do is hunker down for a while, and we'll outlast them."

"Standing in place, you mean."

He raised an eyebrow, surprised that I'd remember what he'd said months ago at the town meeting. "Something like that, yes."

It wasn't quite that easy, though.

We couldn't ration air, but we did have to carefully monitor our water consumption. Bathing was out of the question—besides, the only showers were located in the crater apartments, which were inaccessible until the dome was repaired—and everyone was limited to one quart a day for drinking water. Disinfectant towels were issued to everyone, and they helped a bit when it came to personal hygiene, but it wasn't long before all of us began to stink.

Food was likewise in short supply. We'd already stockpiled plenty of vegetables from the farms, and there were crates of ration bars as well, but with about a thousand mouths to feed every day, we could've quickly eaten our way through the pantry. So, the community breadline shut down right after breakfast and didn't open again until dinnertime, and even then we were often hungry again within a few hours. No one starved, though, and I actually learned to like chettuce.

For entertainment, we had vids. Someone had the foresight to stash a small collection of disks in the shelter; after dinner each evening, the ceiling lights would dim, the wallscreen would light up, and we'd all sit down to watch something together. Much of what we saw was fairly recent, but there were also a few 20th-century classics: *The Wizard of Oz*, *The Big Sleep*, the Star Wars movies. Some people managed to grab their pads before they fled underground, so they had books to read and games to play; after awhile, a lending-library system came into being, with pads being shared and swapped much like everything else we had.

Indeed, the shelter was filled with a spirit of a comradeship as its inhabitants figured out they'd need to rely on each other to get through. To my surprise, no one exemplified this spirit better than Melissa. Something happened to my sister when she saw how Eddie sacrificed his life to save Nina's. Almost overnight, MeeMee vanished, to be replaced by someone who was no longer vain and selfish. Never once did I hear her complain about the lack of privacy, not being able to bathe, or having to wear the same clothes day after day. She spent a lot of time with Nina, comforting her as best she could, and she also helped Ms. Lagler in the breadline, doling out soup and sandwiches with a smile on her face. For the first time, I became proud of my sister.

Nonetheless, we were living under siege conditions. Just outside was a small yet well-armed force, and although they couldn't get to us, that didn't mean that they had given up trying. Every day, I put on my moonsuit, picked up my gun, and went on patrol with five other Rangers, making sure that our airlocks remained sealed and that the enemy hadn't found another way in. Nothing happened while I was outside, but there was the occasional skirmish when another patrol would come under attack and would have to return fire.

Only once were we seriously threatened . . . yet that incident was probably the worst of all.

The third night of the siege, I was about to go on duty when the patrol that was already out there came under attack near the North Field Road entrance ramp. A Ball North squad opened fire on them from behind a rover they'd stolen from the depot, and the Rangers took refuge behind the reflector ring supports and returned fire. I was still getting into my moonsuit when I heard another report over my headset: the mercs were giving up the attack, and instead were piling into the rover and taking off again.

This was weird. There didn't seem to be any point behind the attack. After all, the garage doors were shut tight; there was no way the bad guys could have gotten through. But one of the Rangers who'd fought off the attackers noticed that the assault team consisted of only a half-dozen mercenaries, and that made someone in MainOps wonder where the rest of the goons were.

So MainOps quickly scanned the periphery, checking all the external cameras one at a time . . . and sure enough, they picked up thermal images of nine other mercenaries trying to hide within the shadows of large boulders near Apollo's southern end. They weren't moving, but instead seemed to be waiting for something.

I was about to close my suit when Mr. Garcia's voice came over my headset: *"Barlowe, Tate . . . head down to the south airlocks and check them from the inside. I want to make sure they're secure."*

"Copy," I said, and looked over at Billy. "Suit or no suit?"

Billy was about to climb into his moonsuit. He thought about it a moment, then grabbed the bar above his head. "No suits," he replied, doing a chin-up while withdrawing his legs from his outfit. "We can move faster that way."

My thoughts exactly. Moonsuits would be unnecessary if we were going to remain within Apollo's underground levels, and wearing them would only slow us down. So, I had a tech come by to help me out of my suit, then I picked up my carbine and joined Billy at the ready-room door. We took a few seconds to grab a couple of headsets from a locker and do a quick radio check with MainOps, then we set out for the south end.

Once we were past the shelter, we entered the point in Apollo's subsurface labyrinth where the corridors had been blacked out to preserve power during the siege. I found a couple of flashlights in an emergency locker, though, and once we switched them on, we were able to locate the stenciled wall signs pointing the way to Airlocks 1 through 4. Unfortunately, we didn't also find one of the electric carts used by maintenance crews to move through the base; apparently they had been parked somewhere else. We would have to make our way on foot. I was glad we'd left our moonsuits behind; they would have been cumbersome in the narrow corridors.

Billy and I said little to each other as we headed for the south end. It had been a long time since we'd been foes, but we hadn't really become friends either. I owed him for getting me through Ranger training, but I hadn't forgotten the way he'd treated me and the other outcasts—particularly Eddie—when we'd first arrived on the Moon. Nor had Billy ever apologized for the things he'd said and done back then; he stopped acting a jerk, but that didn't mean he wasn't still one. So, while I was willing to work with him in the Rangers, I hadn't yet figured out whether I could trust him.

The air became colder as we moved away from the inhabited areas of the underground, and every now and then we'd come to a pair of pressure doors which had been shut. One of us would quickly check the adjacent wall gauge to make sure that there was pressure on the other side, then we'd use our wristbands to unlock the doors. We did this six times before we reached the corridor leading to Airlocks 1 through 4, and when the final pair of doors quietly slid back into the walls, we immediately realized that we were no longer alone.

Until then, the only illumination we'd seen had been wall gauge readouts or the beams of our flashlights. When the doors parted, Billy and I saw something new: about fifty feet down the corridor, a glowing rectangle seemed to hover in midair. As soon as I saw it, I knew what it was: the window of an inner door leading to an airlock ready-room.

Someone was in there, all right.

Billy and I glanced at each other. Neither of us spoke, but instead we raised our guns and switched off our lights. Then we crept down the corridor, passing Airlock 4 as we carefully approached Airlock 3.

Upon reaching the airlock, we discovered that the inner door was shut. I inched closer to the window, ducked down low, then slowly raised my head to peer through the window. The ready room was vacant, but the door leading to the airlock was half-open. I checked the wall gauge next to me; neither room had been depressurized. Or at least not yet; a quick glance at the suit racks, and I saw that one of the moonsuits was missing.

I looked at Billy and nodded. He nodded back, then grasped the door handle with his free hand. The door came open, but not without a faint creak of hinges that, in the silence of the darkened corridor, sounded as loud as a rusted cogwheel. I winced and Billy swore under his breath, and we both froze, but nothing moved on the other side of the airlock inner door.

We waited another moment or two, then slowly stepped into the ready-room, walking on tiptoes with our carbines raised to firing position. Step by careful step, we made our way to the airlock. We'd almost reached the inner door when we heard a quiet voice from the other side:

"Mole Man to Beta Team . . . Beta Team, this is Mole Man . . . standing by for insertion . . . do you copy? Over."

"Aw, dammit!" Billy snarled, so loudly that he could just as well have used a bullhorn. Before I could stop him, he slammed the door the rest of the way open and barged straight into the airlock, pointing his carbine at the figure standing near the outer door.

"Uncle Don," he yelled, "what the hell are you doing?"

Caught by surprise, Donald Hawthorne turned around so fast that he almost tripped over his own feet. He wore the missing moon-suit, although he hadn't closed his helmet faceplate, and in his left hand was a small unit that could have only been an encrypted short-wave transceiver. He stood within hand's reach of the airlock control panel, and propped against the wall was the cane he was still using to get around.

"Billy." Hawthorne stared at his nephew, his eyes wide with . . . I wasn't sure what. Astonishment? Fear? Maybe just a bit of shame? "What are you . . . ?"

"You know damn well why I'm here." Billy's voice was taut with anger. He didn't even notice that I'd come up beside him, my own gun raised as well. "And it's pretty obvious why you're here, too."

"No, Billy." Hawthorne slowly shook his head. "This isn't what it looks like. I'm just . . ."

"Checking the airlock to make sure it's shut?" I couldn't help myself; I was almost as mad as Billy. "There's a Ball North squad waiting just outside. Tell me you didn't know that."

Hawthorne gave me a mean look, but didn't bother with any more denials. He knew that we knew why he was there. And although he could have punched the EMER. EVAC. button which would have jettisoned the outer doors and instantly voided the airlock, I knew he wouldn't. Doing so would have killed me, but also his nephew as well. He was wearing a moonsuit; we weren't.

Instead, he turned his gaze toward Billy.

"You know what to do." His voice was low and menacing. "Put this little twit down."

Hearing this, it felt as if every nerve in my body had suddenly turned to ice. My gun was pointed at Mr. Hawthorne and so was Billy's . . . but I'd seen Billy play moonball, and I knew how quick he could be. In an instant, he could turn his gun on me and blow my head clean off my neck. And sure enough, his eyes twitched in my direction, as if calculating the distance between the two of us.

I'll never know what thoughts ran through his mind in that moment. But in those seconds that seemed much longer, he came to a decision that probably haunted him for the rest of his life.

"Jamey," he said, so quietly that I barely heard him, "call MainOps and tell the Chief we've found someone down here trying to open the door."

Mr. Hawthorne stared at him. "Billy, don't do this . . ."

"Shut up." Billy's gun remained leveled at his uncle. "Just back away from the airlock and drop the radio."

Donald Hawthorne didn't respond. He regarded his nephew with eyes that seemed to burn. When I was sure that Billy wasn't going to obey his uncle, I raised my hand to my headset. "MainOps, this is Ranger Barlowe," I said. "We've . . . we've got a situation in Airlock 3. Please send a backup team. Over."

The Chief's voice came over: *"Copy that, Jamey. What's going on down there?"*

I couldn't bring myself to explain. "Just hurry up and send someone." I left the mike open, though, so that he could hear what I was saying. "Mr. Hawthorne, drop the radio and get away from the hatch."

The radio fell from Mr. Hawthorne's hand. It broke apart as it hit the mooncrete floor, but he didn't seem to notice. "Billy," he said, raising his hands unnecessarily, "I cannot believe that you'd ever stoop to treason."

"I'm not a traitor," Billy replied. "I'm a Ranger."

20.
ACTS OF TREASON
AND LOYALTY

Billy and I held Mr. Hawthorne at gunpoint until two Rangers in moonsuits arrived at Airlock 2. Accompanying them were Mr. Garcia and—much to my surprise—Mr. Porter. By then, Billy's uncle was a broken man, his anger replaced by humiliation, unable to look his nephew in the eye. I had no sympathy for Mr. Hawthorne, yet I couldn't help but feel sorry for Billy. Of all the people to catch his uncle, it was sadly ironic that he'd have to be the one.

In hindsight, it wasn't surprising that Mr. Hawthorne had done this. He'd always been opposed to both the embargo and the refusal to surrender Apollo, claiming that it was treason against the United States. When Mr. Porter questioned him, he confessed that he'd swiped the transceiver from the mining crew; once he'd used it to get in touch with Ball North, they coordinated a sneak attack in hopes of taking control of Apollo.

Mr. Porter and Mr. Garcia stepped away from us and spoke quietly for a couple of minutes. Then they came back to Mr. Hawthorne and gave him a choice: he could leave Apollo right then and there, or he could stay and face everyone whom he'd betrayed. Donald Hawthorne quickly made up his mind. Borrowing my headset, he contacted his pals waiting outside and told them that he was coming out alone. Then Mr. Garcia got on the line and told the Ball North strike leader that they were opening the airlock, but that several Rangers would be standing just inside and that they'd shoot anyone they happened to see.

The goons got the message. No shots were fired when Airlock 2 was opened. Mr. Hawthorne left Apollo without a final word to anyone, not even Billy. The last we saw of him, he was hobbling on his cane back to the *Duke* with the Ball North team.

I tried to talk to Billy, but he didn't want to discuss the matter. He walked back to the shelter in silence.

That was Ball North's last attempt to take over Apollo. For the next six hours, nothing moved outside the city. No more mercenaries came our way. Then, suddenly and with no further communication, the *Duke* lifted off from beyond the hills east of the colony. MainOps tracked the freighter as it ascended to low orbit; it swung once around the Moon, then its main engine fired and it headed back to Earth.

Just like that, the siege came to end.

* * *

It was unbelievable how long and loud everyone in the shelter cheered when Mr. Porter announced that the enemy was gone. All around me, people hugged each other, danced, yelled and screamed in delight. Of course, it was always possible that the White House might dispatch another strike force to the Moon, one better equipped and more determined than Ball North. For the time being, though, victory was ours, and it tasted sweet.

Yet our triumph wasn't complete, or without cost. Fifteen people had died during the invasion, including those who'd been killed defending Cabeus Station. The crater dome was still damaged, so most of Apollo was uninhabitable until it could be repaired; until then, we'd have to continue living like rats in a cellar. And there had been no further contact from anyone on Earth. The loss of the communications satellite had severed our broadband links, and there hadn't been any further transmissions since President Shapar's ultimatum. We didn't even know for certain whether anyone had picked up the speech I'd made; the only response was silence.

So we did the only things we could do. We recovered our dead and temporarily entombed them in an underground storage area, with Mr. Porter leading a memorial service in their honor. We took care of those who'd been injured; most were on the way to recovery, and a few had already left the infirmary. And then we rolled up our sleeves, put on our moonsuits, and began the long, back-breaking business of rebuilding Apollo.

I was among those who entered the solarium for the first time since the attack, and it was awful to see what had happened. It was as if a tornado had ripped across the crater floor. The sudden decompression had torn apart the entire solarium, tearing up grass, gardens, and trees, then flash-freezing everything that hadn't been blown through the hole in the western side. Most of the livestock had been evacuated to the shelter, but a few didn't make it, and none of the songbirds had survived; their bodies lay everywhere. Most of the apartments in the crater wall were undamaged, since emergency pressure doors had come down when the blowout occurred, but the schools were in ruins, along with most of the other free-standing structures on the crater floor.

I didn't visit Ag Dome 2. I just didn't have the heart to go looking for Eddie's body. But Melissa surprised me by volunteering for that duty. She felt like she owed it to him. When she got back, she held Nina in her arms and cried for a long time.

I saw Hannah only occasionally. Both of us were too busy to do anything else besides have lunch now and then. Besides, privacy was scarce, and we'd become all too aware of the fact that curious eyes turned our way whenever the two of us were together. Perhaps it was only inevitable that, even if the invasion hadn't been forced everyone into the shelter, people would've learned that the former First Daughter had a new boyfriend. Neither of us were comfortable with the attention being paid to us, but there was nothing we could do about it.

At least, so I thought.

Four days after the *Duke* lifted off, that evening's vid was an obscure movie from the late 20th century called *Moon Zero Two*. The Apollo High kids decided to get together to watch it. Now that the crisis was over, we had a little more time to see each other again, and we wanted to get away from the adults for a little while.

So we claimed a spot over to one side of the room where we could rest our backs against the wall. As a bonus, there was also a support column that would hide us from most of the room. We dragged our sleeping cushions over there and put them close together, and cold-shouldered anyone older than eighteen who tried to sit with us. It had been weeks since the last time we all had been in the same place at the same time; the adults seemed to figure out that we wanted to be left alone, and so they gave us our space.

Hannah and I sat together near the edge of the group. We carefully maintained a couple of inches of distance between us until the lights went down, just in case anyone happened to look our way, but even before the opening credits were over I'd put my arm around her and she'd curled up against me. Nicole favored us with a sly smile and a wink, Melissa stared at me until I glared at her and she turned away, and after that everyone decided to ignore us.

The movie was terrible. Trying to show what life out here would be like and managing to get everything wrong, now and then it was unintentionally funny, but most of the time it was just a bore. As it dragged on, though, Hannah gradually drew closer to me, until her head was on my shoulder and her arm was draped across my knee. All I had to do was turn my head a little and her face would be against mine, her mouth only an inch or two away. It wasn't long before even that distance ceased to exist.

In the middle of the scene where the space cowboys start brawling in the space saloon, Hannah suddenly pulled herself away from me and rose to her feet. For a moment I thought I'd done something wrong, but then she reached down and took my hand. She didn't say anything, nor did she need to. I got up and let her lead me from the room. Glancing back, I saw Melissa watching us go. My sister didn't say anything, yet there was a knowing smile upon her face.

There was a large storage closet just down the corridor that Apollo General had turned into a temporary surgical room. It had all the necessary medical equipment, but just then the most important thing in there was the operating table. It was narrow and not very soft, yet it was just large enough for two people. The ceiling lights went off again almost as soon we shut the door, leaving only the red and blue glow of diodes.

From nearby, we could hear the sounds of the movie, the occasional burst of laughter from the audience. Otherwise, we were alone. I started to sit on the table, but then Hannah pushed me all the way down upon its thin mattress. A second later she was on top of me, straddling my hips, her hair falling down around my face. My hands found her body in the darkness, and it was warm, tense, and eager. Her lips were soft against mine, and it wasn't long before we were fumbling at each other's clothes.

She'd just opened my shirt and I was starting to remove hers when there was an sudden uproar from the shelter, as if everyone in there was shouting at once. Both of us stopped for a second to listen, then we decided that nothing could be happening over there that was more important than what was happening in here. Yet Hannah was about to oblige me by pulling her shirt over her head when the door banged open.

"Jamey!" Melissa stood in the doorway, silhouetted against the light streaming in from the corridor. "You gotta . . . !" Seeing what she'd just interrupted, she stopped. "Oh . . . sorry," she mumbled. "I didn't know . . . I mean . . ."

"What do you want?" If there was ever a time that I wanted to murder my sister, this was it. Hannah hastily pushed herself off me, yanking her shirt back down. "You better have a . . ."

"There's a transmission coming in!" she snapped. "It's from the White House . . . and it's not President Shapar!"

Hannah and I stared at each other for a second. An instant later, we were off the table, straightening our clothes as fast as we could as we ran down back the corridor, Melissa right behind us.

Everyone in the shelter was on their feet, yet a silence had fallen across the room. The only thing we heard was the voice of the woman on the wall screen. It took me a moment to recognize her: Mildred Ferguson, the Speaker of the House of Representatives, last seen in handcuffs as federal marshals escorted her down the front steps of the Capitol. Now she was standing behind a podium upon which was the symbol of the President of the United States.

Hannah, Melissa, and I came in after she'd begun speaking, so the first thing I heard was: *". . . inform you that, at 5:45 PM Eastern Standard Time today, officials from the Department of Justice, under armed escort by members of the Virginia National Guard and the Federal Bureau of Investigation, accompanied me to the White House, where we confronted President Shapar in the Oval Office. There she was informed that the United States Supreme Court, by a majority decision of six-to-three, had ruled that there were sufficient grounds for immediate removal from office for both her and Vice President O'Hanlon, pending federal investigation of charges that her administration has acted against the interests of the people of the United States . . ."*

Hannah's hand clenched mine so painfully that my knuckles hurt. I barely noticed. My attention was fully upon the woman on the screen.

"President Shapar refused to voluntarily surrender office, so she was taken into custody by FBI agents. Vice President O'Hanlon was arrested ten minutes later when a car containing him and his aides was pulled over by District of Columbia police while it was attempting to leave the city. By then, I was administered the oath of office by Chief Justice Marco Gonzales and sworn in as President Pro Tem, a duty I will serve while an impeachment trial is . . ."

I didn't hear the rest. Everyone around me was yelling too loud. All except Hannah, who let out her breath and closed her eyes.

"It's over," she murmured, almost too quietly to be heard. "It's all over."

* * *

In the end, it wasn't guns that brought down Lina Shapar, but words. Hannah's, the ones of the Resistance and the International Space

Consortium, even mine . . . but most of all her own. It wasn't until everything was over and done that we got the whole story, but what essentially happened was this:

When my firsthand account of what really happened at Cabeus Station was transmitted back to Earth, the Shapar administration made sure that it was blocked from American newsnets. As before, though, the transmission was also received in Europe and South America, and the Resistance made sure that it was fed to pirate servers in the United States that the government hadn't been able to shut down. So within hours of Shapar's speech, my rebuttal was seen by hundreds of millions of people across the world.

Public support for Lina Shapar had been steadily eroding ever since Hannah revealed the fact that her father had died of natural causes, not from an assassin's bullet. The declaration of martial law, the detainment of dissidents, the shutdown of the legislative branch, the US withdrawal from the ISC . . . all of these actions had led even the most passive citizen to become worried about what the president was doing. In the meantime, the Resistance wisely adopted a nonviolent approach; no bombings or other acts of sabotage that would have been considered terrorism, and therefore could have thrown public support behind the Shapar administration. Instead, they opted for peaceful demonstrations, even when the usual result was mass arrests, along with the dissemination of uncensored information about what Shapar and her cronies were doing.

When it came out that it wasn't American special forces who'd attacked Apollo and Cabeus, but private mercenaries instead, the public wasn't the only ones who were surprised. Throughout the crisis, the military had remained loyal to President Shapar in keeping with its mandate to follow any orders issued by the commander in chief. Nonetheless, the Pentagon had refused to send Marines to the Moon, the joint chiefs telling the president that it wasn't defense policy to attack American civilians when they did something the White House didn't like. So they were already aware that President

Shapar was lying when she told the nation that Marines had been dispatched to the Moon, and they were still trying to swallow this when they learned that the Shapar administration had attempted to get around them by hiring Ball North IU instead.

The fact that Lina Shapar was using the Cabeus Station battle as a pretext for declaring war on the PSU was a threat no one could ignore. So the chairman of the joint chiefs quietly got in touch with his counterpart in People's Army of the Pacific Socialist Union, using diplomatic back-channels that even the president didn't know about, and asked him if my account was true. The Chinese general who knew about these things confirmed my side of the story.

Further confirmation came a few days later, when the surviving Ball North forces returned to Station America following their retreat from Apollo. They were immediately taken into custody by real Marines, and once they were questioned by military intelligence officers, a classified report was sent to the Pentagon. When the joint chiefs received this information, they secretly convened to discuss the matter, whereupon they decided that the commander in chief had gone out of control. Like it or not, President Shapar had to be removed from office before she declared war on the PSU.

At the direct command of the Pentagon, a company of Virginia National Guard soldiers was sent to the former resort hotel in the Blue Ridge Mountains where the Speaker of the House and other government dissidents were being held in custody. Once they'd set Mildred Ferguson free, she immediately got in touch with the nine justices of Supreme Court; they convened in emergency session and, in private, determined that there was sufficient evidence for the removal both the president and vice president from office, pending investigation of the claim that President Shapar's actions were illegitimate and constituted a threat to the people of the United States.

The speaker of the House then returned to Washington and, escorted by National Guard soldiers, FBI agents, and Justice Department officials, went straight to the White House. The justice officials ordered the Secret Service detail to stand down, then the Speaker went to the Oval Office, where Lina Shapar was found seated behind the presidential desk, wondering why her phone had suddenly gone dead.

She refused to surrender, of course, but her fate was no longer hers to decide. Five minutes later, she was led from the White and taken to the same Maryland military base from which she'd summoned troops the day she'd taken power. Someone must have told Vice President O'Hanlon that the jig was up, because a few minutes later Capitol Hill police pulled over his limo on Independence Avenue just before it crossed the Potomac.

As her first act of office, President Pro Tem Ferguson issued an executive order calling for an end to martial law; all federal troops were to stand down, and all political prisoners were to be set free at once. No shots were fired; the insurrection was peaceful. By midnight, the crisis had come to an end.

At least, that's the way it was back on Earth. Where I was, things were a bit different.

* * *

I'd just dropped another armload of dead branches into a wheelbarrow when my wristband beeped. Brushing wood chips from my hands, I pulled off my work gloves and raised it to my face. "Jamey here."

"The ferry just touched down at North Field," said the voice of a friend who worked in MainOps as a traffic controller. *"Passengers will be here in about twenty minutes."*

"Thanks, Stu." I'd asked him to let know me when the ferry arrived. It was supposed to rendezvous with an LTV from Earth scheduled to reach the Moon that day, and I wanted to meet the passengers when they showed up. No sense in sitting around until then, though. There was no shortage of work to be done, and Colony Service was now a full-time job for everyone.

Shoving my gloves in my back pocket, I turned around. Hannah was kneeling on the ground, pulling up dead flowers from a nearby garden. They may have been ones that Eddie had planted; it made me sad to see that, but now that the dome had been repaired and the crater's atmosphere restored, the next step in bringing the solarium back to life was gathering and composting all the plants killed by the blowout. I told myself that Eddie probably would've been happy to do the job again; these gardens had been his pride and joy.

Hannah glanced up as I walked over to her. "Ferry's here," I said. "Want to come with me to meet them?"

"Umm . . . I dunno." There was a hesitant look in her eyes. "I'm not sure if that's such a good idea. I mean, they might not be so happy to see me."

"Yeah . . . maybe you're right." I squatted beside her. "It's not like you haven't met them before, but now that we're going together . . ."

"That's what I mean. I . . ." She shook her head. "Maybe you ought to do this on your own. It might be . . . y'know . . . awkward."

The last thing I wanted to do was make her uncomfortable. "Okay, sure. Maybe later?" She nodded, giving me a quick smile. I kissed her on the forehead, then I stood up and headed for the bike that I'd parked nearby. If I hurried, I'd have time to run up to the Laglers' place, change into some clean clothes, and get to Customs before the ferry passengers showed up.

Melissa was already at the apartment. I'd asked Stu to call her, too, and she'd left her job in Ag Dome 1 as soon as the call came in. I hastily pulled on a clean shirt and a fresh pair of trousers, and Mr. Lagler showed up just as we were getting ready to leave. There was no reason to ask why he wanted to come with us; he knew who was on the ferry.

The three of us went back downstairs, where a small crowd had already gathered on the balcony outside Customs to await the incoming passengers. Mr. Porter was among them; I gave him a brief wave, which he returned with a smile and a nod, then Mr. Lagler excused himself and went over to speak with them. I made small talk with a couple of people, and it wasn't long before the Customs exit door opened and the first of the newly arrived passengers came through.

Dad was the third person to walk through the door. Jan was the fourth.

Melissa and I had spoken to both of them a couple of times already, after the lunar comsat was replaced during the month that had gone by since Lina Shapar was forced from office. Nonetheless, their physical changes since the morning they'd put Melissa and me on the magcat were startling. My father had put on weight during the time he'd been held prisoner in upstate New York; too much starch in his food and virtually no exercise had done a number on him. Although Jan had washed the brown dye from her hair and was starting to let it grow long again, she was still scrawny from being on the run with her Resistance cell. Both of them had haunted eyes; although they'd been reunited shortly after Dad was freed, I don't think an hour had gone by when they weren't worried about each other, or Melissa and me.

The first thing they noticed was that I was standing upright, without crutches or leg braces to hold me up. They'd never seen me do that before, not in my entire life. Jan's mouth fell open in astonishment, and I don't think Dad even recognized me at first. They were still getting over their disbelief when I walked over to Jan and, without any effort at all, wrapped my arms around her.

"Hi, sis," I said. "Good to see you again."

Jan's duffel bag fell to the floor. She slowly let out her breath, then her body shook within my arms. She was sobbing with relief, but that wasn't what I noticed. Until then, I'd always looked up at her from the seat of a mobil. Now, all of a sudden, I discovered that she and I were the same height.

Dad had also dropped his bag to hug Melissa, and it seemed to me that he was surprised to find that she was letting him do so, without any trace of self-conscious embarrassment. Melissa had made some changes, too, since she'd been away; he was going to be pleasantly surprised to find how different she'd become.

But then he looked at me again, and an eyebrow went up in disapproval. "So . . . who said you could get a tattoo?"

I felt my face go red. "Didn't you see it when you called me?"

"The phone picture wasn't clear. I thought it was just a smudge on your face."

"I think it's cute." Jan smiled as she reached up to touch the wings-and-crescent moon Rangers symbol on my right cheek. "Does your girlfriend like it? Hannah, I mean."

"She wants me to have it moved to . . ." Then I stopped. "Hey, who told you she's my girlfriend?"

I'd deliberately refrained from mentioning Hannah when I'd spoken to both of them on the phone. I didn't know how they would feel about the fact that I was having a relationship with the girl for whom Jan had given up seat on the shuttle. After all, she'd made that sacrifice so that President Wilford's daughter could escape her father's enemies, not so that her little brother would have a steady girl when he got to the Moon. Hannah had felt the same way, too, so the revelation that they already knew about her was something of an embarrassment.

"Your friend told us," Dad said, then he nodded to someone standing beside me. "Didn't you, Captain Rogers?"

I looked around to see Gordie's broad grin. "Y'know how it is," he said. "Three days from Earth to here . . . you got a lot of time to talk about stuff."

I'd all but forgotten that Gordie had gotten back his old job as an LTV pilot, and that his first round trip would include transporting my father and older sister to Apollo. Maybe it was because, when he'd left two weeks ago, his outbound cargo had included the caskets containing Logan and Eddie's bodies. Nina had gone with him, too, and Melissa and I had spent a lot of time preparing her for that sad ordeal.

It had been painful for all of us, and during the last couple weeks, I tried to put it out of my mind.

"You told them . . ." I began, and Gordie's grin disappeared when he saw the expression on my face.

"Don't worry about it." Jan gave me another smile. "It's okay. I mean . . . y'know, it's nice to know my little brother has good taste in women."

Dad didn't appear to be quite so amused. Perhaps the knowledge that his son was going steady with a president's daughter was just as much of a shock as discovering that he was no longer an invalid. And the tattoo didn't help, either. He was about to say something when Mr. Lagler walked up to us.

"Algis . . . good to see you again." Gently disengaging himself from Melissa, Dad offered his hand to him. "Thanks for taking care of my kids."

"The pleasure's been all mine, Stan. Same goes for my wife." Mr. Lagler took my father's hands in both of his. "We're just relieved that you and your daughter are safe again. It was a terrible thing, what you've been through."

"Yes, well . . ." Dad's voice trailed off as he looked down at the balcony tiles. I'd already noticed that he didn't like talking about his incarceration. He hadn't been tortured, but apparently the interrogations he'd gone through had been pretty grueling. He was probably mending wounds of his own, and it would take time for them to heal. "So long as Jamey and MeeMee . . ."

"Melissa," my sister said quietly. "I'd rather not be called that anymore . . . please."

Dad and Jan both stared at her. "Please" had never been a word in Melissa's vocabulary. Jan shot me an inquisitive look and I slowly nodded. If they were shocked by the fact that I was walking, then they were going to love the changes that Melissa had gone through. Before either of them could respond, though, Mr. Porter came over to join us.

"Dr. Barlowe?" he asked. "I don't know if you remember me . . . Loren Porter, Apollo city manager."

"Of course, Loren." Dad shook hands with him. "Thank you, too, for . . ."

"Not a problem. Having them here has been a pleasure." Mr. Porter laid a hand on my shoulder. "And Jamey here has been . . . well, I'm sure you've already heard about what he's done for us."

"So I've heard." Dad nodded toward Gordie. "Captain Rogers told us everything."

Gordie gave me a quick wink. I could've kicked him just then, and had to remind myself that I needed to be on my best behavior. "Very well, then," Mr. Lagler said. "In that case, perhaps you and your daughter could join us for lunch a little later. After you've found your rooms in the hotel, of course."

Melissa and I gave each other a sidelong glance. This was something neither of us had expected. "I'd be happy to," Dad said as he bent over to pick up his bag. "If you'll tell me where to go, we'll . . ."

"I'll get it, Dad." Melissa reached for his bag before he could get to it, slung it over her shoulder. "It's this way. . . ."

Jan stared at her as Melissa walked off with Dad's duffel bag. "When did that happen?" she whispered to me.

"There's been a lot of changes lately," I murmured. And I wasn't looking forward to telling them about the biggest one.

* * *

Lunch was rather meager: red beans and rice, seasoned just well enough to hide the fact that it came from the supply of freeze-dried food that was what the loonies were eating until we were once again able to grow enough vegetables to feed everyone. I was embarrassed that this was all we had to offer, but Dad and Jan didn't seem to mind. They'd been living on space rations for the past three days, so anything that didn't come from a plastic bag tasted just fine to them.

I sat quietly at the end of the table, listening to the technical discussion between Mr. Lagler, Mr. Porter, and my father. One of the reasons why Dad had come to the Moon was to advise Apollo's recovery efforts. The ISC wanted to send a senior administrator who'd been there when the city was being built, and since my father had personal motives for making the trip, he was the logical choice; he'd brought Jan simply because she wanted to see Melissa and me. So I picked at my food while they talked about various life-support issues, including the cost of rebuilding Ag Dome 2, and waited for the conversation to change to an inevitable topic.

"So . . ." Mr. Porter wiped his mouth on a napkin and dropped it next to his plate. "I imagine that, when you're done here, you'll be taking Jamey and Melissa with you."

"Of course." My father gave him a querulous look, as if he'd just stated the obvious. "I appreciate the hospitality you've shown them, but I think it's time for them to go home." He glanced across the table at Melissa. "Isn't that right, Mee . . . I mean, Melissa."

"Uh-huh. That's right." She tried not to look eager, but everyone knew better. Perhaps her experiences had made her a better person, but the fact of the matter was that she'd never fit in well here.

"I thought so." Dad smiled at her, then looked at me. "What about it? Ready to go home?"

"No, I'm not." I took a deep breath. "I want to stay."

For a moment or two, Dad simply stared at me. The smile faded from his face. "Come again?" he said at last, as if he hadn't heard me correctly.

"I don't want to go back," I said. "I'm sorry, but . . . I really want to remain here. On the Moon."

No one said anything for a second or two. Jan was sitting beside me; from the corner of my eye, I saw her lift a hand to her mouth, something she did when she didn't want anyone to see her expression. "Jamey . . ." Dad stopped, shook his head. "Son, you can't stay here. You need to come home now."

"Why? There's nothing there for me . . . besides you and my sisters, I mean." I'd been rehearsing this moment in my mind for almost a month; the time had come for me to make my case. "Look at this," I went on, pushing back my chair to stand up from the table. "Look at what I'm doing. I'm standing on my own two feet. Back on Earth, I'd just be stuck in a mobil again. . . ."

"It doesn't have to be that way. You can always go swimming. . . ."

"Swimming?" I almost laughed out loud. "Dad, I've walked thirty-one miles across Alphonsus. I've flown across this crater in a paragliding suit. I've learned to play moonball." *Not well*, I silently added, but I didn't mention that. "I'm a Ranger. How can—" I pointed to the open door of my bedroom, where the swim-fins mounted above my bed were visible, "*that* compare to anything I've done here?"

Dad laid a finger against his lips, the way he did when he was listening. Jan didn't say anything, but she was watching me intently. "Go on," my father said quietly.

"Dad . . . Jan . . . Melissa . . ." I let out my breath. "This is home. The Moon is where I was born. Earth is just the place where I grew up."

Dad winced. "Was it really that bad?"

"No, it wasn't. I didn't mean it to sound that way. It's just that . . . here, I'm no longer a cripple who has to be helped around all the time." I looked at Jan. "I know why you didn't go away to school. You stayed behind to take care of me. But you don't have to do that anymore. I can get by on my own now . . . or at least I will, if I remain here."

Jan didn't respond, but there were tears in the corners of her eyes. A wan smile and a nod told me that she understood what I'd said. I turned back to Dad and went on. "I know it's a lot to ask, but . . . please, I'm begging you. Let me stay."

Mr. Lagler cleared his throat. "If I may say something . . . ?" My father nodded. "Stan, I haven't talked about this with Jamey, but I think he's right. In the short time he's been here, he's made a place for himself. My wife and I would be willing to keep him for awhile longer, or at least until our son returns from college."

"That isn't necessary, Algis," Mr. Porter said. "We have another boy . . . another young man, I should say . . . who's now on his own. Another Ranger, in fact . . ."

"Billy Tate," I said.

"Uh-huh." Mr. Porter smiled at me. "He needs a roommate, now that his uncle has . . . um, decided to leave us . . . and I think we could find an apartment that the two of you could share. With proper adult supervision, of course."

I'd never thought that I'd be willing to share space with Billy, but the days when he was my nemesis were long over. "Sure, I could do that."

Mr. Porter nodded, then looked at Dad again. "I'm not trying to break up your family, but . . . well, Jamey is one of us now. A loony. He's earned his right to stay . . . if you'll let him."

My father didn't say anything for a long time, but instead regarded me with thoughtful eyes as he absently ran his finger back and forth across his lips. Beneath the table, I felt Jan touch my leg. When I glanced at her, she smiled and nodded, giving me her silent approval. So did Melissa. I think she was happy to get rid of her kid brother anyway. Some things never change.

"Three conditions," Dad said after a few moments. He raised a finger. "One . . . you stay out of trouble. No more getting into wars without permission."

All of us laughed at that. "Done," I said. "I'll call home first before my next firefight."

"Which brings me to my second condition." He raised another finger. 'Two . . . you call home at least once a week, every week, and let us know how you're doing. And let us visit you whenever we can."

"Sure." That was an easy stipulation. I didn't want to divorce myself from my family. I just didn't want to live with them anymore.

"And three . . ." He grinned. "You get rid of that ugly tattoo."

* * *

The days pass slowly on the Moon, and night comes with the gradual lengthening of shadows. You can't see this when you're in the dome, where the reflector ring and sun window impose an artificial sunrise and sunset upon the solarium, but out on the surface, time passes at a different rate. You have to step out an airlock to really see this.

A few days after my father agreed to let me stay on the Moon, he and Jan were ready to go home—their home—again. Melissa was going with them, of course . . . and so was someone else.

A few hours before the ferry left, Hannah and I went out on the surface. She'd gone moonwalking before, but never with me. The sun was beginning to set upon the distant mountains, and this would be our last chance to see it together.

We left through Airlock 10 and walked out past the reflector ring until we crossed Collins Avenue. The blasted remains of the *Blitzgewehr* lay a short distance away, but we tried not to look at them. They were a reminder of a war we'd fought, and although we'd won, it had been at the cost of the lives of our friends.

Holding hands is almost meaningless while you're wearing a spacesuit, because you can't feel the other person's warmth. Kissing is impossible, even absurd to think about. But we could switch to a private frequency, so that the things we had to say to each other wouldn't be overheard by anyone else.

"Do you have to go?" This wasn't the first time I'd asked that question. Maybe I was just hoping for a different answer.

"'Fraid so," she said. *"I've been here too long already. My mother needs to have me come home . . . and besides, when Lina Shapar's criminal trial starts up, they're going to want to have me as a material witness. So, yeah . . . I gotta go."*

I nodded within my helmet. Since we were facing the sun, its faceplate had automatically polarized. So Hannah couldn't see my expression, and I couldn't see hers. But the tone of her voice told me that she was just as unhappy about this as I was.

"Do you think you'll ever come back?" I asked.

This was something I hadn't asked her until now. There was a long silence, and I caught myself holding my breath as I waited for her to answer.

"You bet I will," she said at last.

That was good enough for me. The kiss would have to wait until we got back inside. For now, though, we stood together upon grey sands, our shadows stretching out behind us as we watched the sun go down behind the mountains of the Moon.

ACKNOWLEDGMENTS

Apollo's Outcasts is a work of fiction, but quite a bit of it is based on solid science . . . or at least solid speculation. While some of the technology here is my own invention, much of it was derived from books or papers written by established experts in the astronautics field. I've tried to take as few liberties as possible, and any factual errors or misconceptions are my own.

Apollo is loosely based upon a design for an advanced lunar habitat that was presented at the second Lunar Development Conference in July 2000, hosted by the Space Frontier Foundation. Details can be found in "Conceptual Design of a Crater Lunar Base" by Alice Eichold, published in *Return to the Moon II: Proceedings of the 2000 Lunar Development Conference* (Space Front Press, 2000).

Further information about large-scale lunar colonies, including the prospects for helium-3 mining, came from "Final Report on System Architecture for a Self-Sustaining Lunar Colony," a study written in 2000 by Dr. Douglas O'Handley of Orbitec for NASA's Institute for Advanced Concepts and the Universities Space Research Association.

Other major sources of information about lunar colonization and mining included *The Moon: Resources, Future Development and Settlement* (Second Edition) by David Shrunk, Burton Sharpe, Bonnie Cooper, and Madhu Thangavelu (Springer-Praxis, 2008); *Lunar Bases and Space Activities of the 21st Century* edited by W. W. Mendell (Lunar and Planetary Institute, 1985); *The Lunar Base Handbook* by Peter Eckart (McGraw-Hill, 1999); *Return to the Moon* edited Rick N. Tumlinson with Erin R. Medlicott (Apogee 2005); and *Entering Space: Creating a Spacefaring Civilization* by Robert Zubrin (Tarcher/Putnam, 1999).

The Wallops Island spaceport, including its magcat, or magnetic catapult, is based on a concept study, "Spaceport Visioning" created in 2002 by the architectural consulting firm ZHA for NASA and the Florida Spaceport Authority.

Several news stories contributed to my understanding of the prospects for lunar ice at the Moon's south pole: "Tons of Water Ice Found at the Moon's South Pole" by Tariq Malik (Space.com, March 1, 2010); "Moon Crater Contains Usable Water, NASA Says" by Kenneth Chang (*New York Times*, October 21, 2010); and "Is Mining Rare Minerals on the Moon Vital to National Security?" by Leonard David (Space.com, October 4, 2010).

Details about the Moon's geography, particularly Ptolemaeus and Alphonsus craters, came from *Atlas of the Moon* by Antonin Rukl, edited by Dr. T. W. Rackham (Kalmbach Books, 1990) and recent NASA lunar maps located online by Google Moon™. Further information about Cabeus Crater came from its entry on Wikipedia®.

I'm grateful to my friends Rob Caswell and Dr. Horace "Ace" Marchant, who read the book while it was being written and offered invaluable insights and suggestions. Rob also took my pencil sketch of Apollo and transformed it into the layout that appears as this book's frontispiece. Dr. Gregory Benford, Dr. James Benford, and Emily Cambias read the final draft and offered feedback of their own.

I also wish to thank my agent, Martha Millard, whose encouragement for this project went above and beyond the call of duty; my editor, Lou Anders; and my copy editor, Gabrielle Harbowy.

As always, my greatest appreciation goes to my wife, Linda.

Whately, Massachusetts
August 2010–December 2011

ABOUT THE AUTHOR

ALLEN STEELE was a journalist before turning to his first love, science fiction. Since then he has published seventeen previous novels and nearly one hundred short stories. His work has received numerous awards, including three Hugos, and has been translated worldwide. A lifelong space enthusiast, he has testified before Congress in hearings regarding space exploration, has flown the NASA space-shuttle simulator, and serves as an advisor for the Space Frontier Foundation. Steele lives in Massachusetts with his wife and dogs. Visit him online at www.allensteele.com and at www .facebook.com/Allensteelesfwriter.